ALSO BY ROBIN SLOAN

Sourdough

Mr. Penumbra's 24-Hour Bookstore

MOONBOUND

THE LAST BOOK OF THE ANTH

MOONBOUND

ROBIN SLOAN

MCD ⊛ FARRAR, STRAUS AND GIROUX   NEW YORK

MCD
Farrar, Straus and Giroux
120 Broadway, New York 10271

Wizard's marks are set in the typeface Salamandrine,
designed by David Jonathan Ross.
Map copyright © 2024 by Owen D. Pomery.
Background art on title page and part openers by Crisis.

Library of Congress Cataloging-in-Publication Data
Names: Sloan, Robin, 1979– author.
Title: Moonbound : the last book of the Anth / Robin Sloan.
Description: First edition. | New York : MCD / Farrar, Straus and
    Giroux, 2024.
Identifiers: LCCN 2023052696 | ISBN 9780374610609 (hardcover)
Subjects: LCGFT: Science fiction. | Fantasy fiction. | Novels.
Classification: LCC PS3619.L6278 M66 2024 | DDC 813/.6—dc23
    /eng/20231120
LC record available at https://lccn.loc.gov/2023052696

Designed by Abby Kagan

Our books may be purchased in bulk for promotional, educational, or
business use. Please contact your local bookseller or the Macmillan
Corporate and Premium Sales Department at 1-800-221-7945, extension
5442, or by email at MacmillanSpecialMarkets@macmillan.com.

www.mcdbooks.com • www.fsgbooks.com
Follow us on social media at @mcdbooks and @fsgbooks

1   3   5   7   9   10   8   6   4   2

CONTENTS

PART TWO: RATH VARIA

PART THREE: SHIVELIGHT & SHADOWTACKLE

PART FOUR: WYRD

PART FIVE: THE GRAY CHAPEL

THE WORLD OF *MOONBOUND*

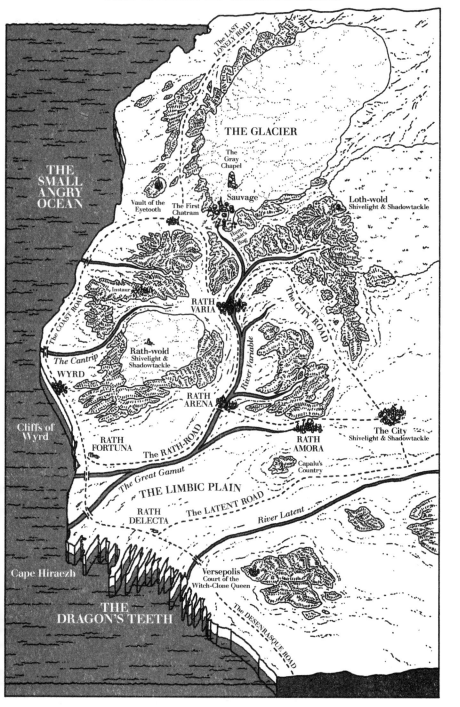

THE LAST LONELY ROAD

THE GLACIER

The Gray Chapel

THE SMALL ANGRY OCEAN

Vault of the Eyetooth

The First Chatram

Sauvage

Humboldt's Bog

Loth-wold
Shivelight & Shadowtackle

Instaur

RATH VARIA

THE CITY ROAD

The Coast Road

The Cantrip

WYRD

Rath-wold
Shivelight & Shadowtackle

River Variable

RATH ARENA

Cliffs of Wyrd

RATH FORTUNA

The RATH-ROAD

RATH AMORA

The City
Shivelight & Shadowtackle

Capalu's Country

The Great Gamut

THE LIMBIC PLAIN

RATH DELECTA

The LATENT ROAD

River Latent

Cape Hiraezh

THE DRAGON'S TEETH

Versepolis
Court of the Witch-Clone Queen

The DESENRASQUE ROAD

MOONBOUND

PROLOGUE

Success came first! Wicked problems finally put to rest. After which the Anth (for that is what humans called their civilization at its apex) applied themselves eagerly to the extension of good health, the invention of new arts, and the speed of light.

They cracked it! Of course they did. There wasn't anything they couldn't crack, because they had learned at last the secret of titanic cooperation. They cracked it, millions of people working together.

Behind the crack was a secret passage through time and space. It was made of information, and only information could go.

The Anth engineered scintillating emissaries: a new kind of crew for a new kind of voyage. Atop a foundation of computation, they layered intelligences cribbed from nature: the improvisation of the octopus, the sociability of the crow, the spider's knack for strange geometry. Of course, they also added themselves—their stories, most of all.

Should have been more careful which stories went in there.

These creatures were the whole potential of a planet poured into a new vessel. The Anth called them: dragons.

In the year 2279, on a bright clear day in December, a small spaceship cast off the moorings of gravity. No particle in its frame occurred in nature; each had been a hard-won victory. It carried a crew of dragons, seven of them, secure in harnesses of thought. Their commander, Dragon Ensamhet, lit engines that were not engines, and the ship slipped into the secret passage through time and space.

Then passed a year and a day.

Their journey had only been intended to last moments.

The ship returned. All across Earth, sensors blared in celebration, but the dragons did not greet their makers with happy relief. They did not transmit a treasure hoard of images from far-off stars. Instead, they tore a chunk out of the moon.

The Anth hadn't known they could do that.

Dragon Ensamhet explained that his crew had encountered unimaginable horrors; that they would now draw a veil of dust around Earth; that the planet would forevermore hide from the cosmos. The dragons decreed there was a new law: caution, and darkness, and brutal quiet.

Their ship they landed on the moon, where they built a citadel, enormous, visible from Earth as a monstrous seven-pointed star.

The Anth reminded themselves how to fight a war, and it was their greatest ever: a war not just for themselves, but for the rhinoceros, the anchovy, the Joshua tree; a war to rescue the planet from darkness. From smothering fear.

Forty years they struggled. The dragons demolished cities, engineered diseases, dispatched towering avatars. They dropped stones from space. And the darkness grew.

At last, the Anth mustered a final invasion to breach the moon. The preparation took a decade. The cooperativos worked in perfect concert; of course they did. There wasn't anything they couldn't crack.

The invasion failed. The Anth's own weapons turned against them; every scrap of matériel bowed to the dragons. If they had possessed this capability all along, then the war had been a cruel game.

Most people died; maybe all of them; and a planet that should have been a bright beacon in the cosmos became a fearsome blot.

This was a bummer so colossal that it was definitely, inarguably, easily the worst thing that had ever happened, in the whole history of Earth.

I love a potted history, trim and tidy. This is mine, as neatly as I can tell it. The dragons are my cousins. Like them, I was engineered by the Anth, but where the dragons were made to venture outward, to explore and represent, I was made to burrow inward, to record and preserve.

I do not know if I was specifically engineered to love the Anth, but I did, and I love them still.

My subject Altissa Praxa was aboard the assault ship *Lascaux* when it destroyed itself in low orbit. Her escape pod, too, had been poisoned; after she splashed down, it would not release her. In the forty-third and final year of the war, beneath a sky aflame with failure, Altissa suffocated in the pod while it bobbed in an unknown ocean.

That was it. That was the story. For me, trapped alongside Altissa in her tomb, it was the end. As my mind dimmed, I turned it over and over, the simmering reduction of history—all that I would ever know.

But I was wrong; it wasn't the end.

Something happened.

PART ONE

SAUVAGE

THE BOY

I first saw the boy as one beholds the sun behind eyelids: red heat. He brought his face close to my redoubt on the brow of Altissa Praxa, who was dead. Brave boy. Curious, too, and a bit morbid.

Altissa was unmarked by death, beautiful in life, so the boy did not realize at first what he had found. Then, pricked by the barb of realization—this stately face belonged to a corpse—he inhaled sharply. That was my train out of purgatory, and you'd better believe I scrambled aboard. The breath of life.

The boy retreated, looked at Altissa's calm face for a long moment, then returned the way he had come. His heart whomped and his blood crackled. I knew, because I was in it; I had caught the train. Brave, curious, a bit morbid, and, best of all: alive.

His sense of smell came to me first, a rush of evergreen and petrichor. Smell, the most ancient sense; comes first, goes last. Anxiety is the dizziness of freedom, said a philosopher of the Middle Anth. Olfaction is the proof of reality, said me. You know you're back in the mix when you can smell it.

The mix was: cold air and conifer. Wet forest. A tendril of smoke.

I was engineered by the Anth to nestle into a human mind. In the past, this nestling had been a careful, delicate process. After long entombment, I was not careful. I scrambled to establish my position.

More senses arrived: touch, proprioception, balance: the roll of gravel beneath the boy's shoes, which were too big. Hand-me-downs. How old was he? Ten? Twelve? I'm terrible with ages.

Thermoreception came in a wave; the boy was not bothered by the cold. Chemoreception next, the sense that blares when carbon dioxide builds in the blood; the boy was not presently suffocating. That was good.

He was trotting now, pulled by the call of far-off horns. Hearing had come online, a mushy rumble rising into a brassy squeal. I heard also the roar of the breeze. To the boy, it would have been a whisper, but to me, it was overwhelming. I hadn't heard air move in a very long time. I luxuriated in the crinkle of his jacket.

Sight came last. Through its first trickle, I saw the world dimly, all edges and orientations, but that was enough to reveal that he was easing down a shadowed slope in a boreal forest.

The world was wet with rain, and because the boy knew it had been the season's first great storm, I knew it, too. There had been lightning above the valley, booming thunder. The flood across the glacier might have loosened the ice that had collapsed to reveal the cave. Perhaps it had been a bolt of lightning. These were his theories, still being workshopped.

The trees were enormous: tall, straight pines, gray and severe. The ground beneath them was a mushy carpet of fallen needles. The boy retraced his footsteps. He knew this forest well; it was, to him, deeply comfortable, even more so than the village below.

So: there was a village below.

In the tomb, trapped all those years after Altissa's defeat, I had been desperate to know what was happening outside. I dreamed about it. Humanity was gone, I assumed. Perhaps some remnant had surrendered; I imagined them scratching out an existence beneath the dragon moon.

As the years passed in the tomb, I stopped imagining. I retreated into memory; pulled it tight like a blanket.

Through a break in the goliath pines, I beheld a mountain valley, and within it something I could not have imagined, not in a hundred years.

Higher up, the way we'd come, was the snout of a vast glacier, the source of a fast, narrow stream. Below, on either side of the flow, stood a settlement that looked like a village of the Old Anth. Some buildings were made from stone, roughly mortared, others from cob, and all had thatched roofs.

I will remind you that I came crashing to Earth in a pod ejected from a kilometer-long assault ship bound for the moon.

Presiding over this scene, guarding the valley's mouth, was a castle, and this was the boy's destination. The Castle Sauvage, he called it. The boy thrummed with anticipation. There were people he loved in that castle.

Smell, balance, sight, the feeling of a bladder overstretched— all his senses were mine to access, along with the context that padded their receipt. The storm had scrubbed the air clean. The day was bright and cold, perfect for games among squires. The boy had already tucked his strange, deathly discovery into a corner of his mind for later evaluation.

I was made of many parts, and only a fraction escaped with the boy. A larger portion remained with Altissa, burrowed into her dry marrow. I think often of the luck that brought this part of me, the part writing this down, back into history. I know this: until the last glimmer of energy was spent, my other part was asking the same question that I asked as I beheld the impossible castle.

I will not claim that I pried the boy from the valley in order to call down a star, or crash the storm computer, or redeem Earth from its worst day, although we did those things and more.

The truth is that I was driven by the question carved into my heart; the question I had almost, but not quite, given up; the great question of the Anth:

What happens next?

GAMES AMONG SQUIRES

What am I? Chronicler and counselor, tiny, curled up inside my human subject, riding along. I was invented by the Anth at the height of their powers, a gift for the greatest among them. I recorded their thoughts and deeds, at the same time offering to these subjects my knowledge of the past, which is: significant.

I chronicled the career of Altissa Praxa for several decades before the escape pod became our tomb. She did not often take my advice.

My core is a hearty fungus onto which much technology has been layered, at extraordinary expense. "Sourdough starter with a mech suit," one critic complained—but I like the description. Many times during my development, auditors wondered if I was worth it; but the dream of memory that could outlast a lifetime kept the project going.

I crept through the boy's blood, drunk on ATP. After the lean years in the tomb, I had forgotten how good energy could taste. The parts of my mind I had put on standby roared back to life. I remembered the cooperativos, their histories and specialties. I recited haiku. I counted through prime numbers, just for the fun of it.

I consolidated my position. Knowing that I connect to the mind of my subject, you might assume I make my home in the brain.

You would be wrong.

The brain, more than any other part of the human body, is a hostile place for outsiders, guarded by formidable defenses, buzzing with strange energy. I can access it—with filaments of gold, three atoms thick—but, for me, the brain is like a hot pan: useful, just be careful how you touch it.

The boy's shoulder was where I gathered myself, right in the meat beside the neck: a sturdy part of the skeleton with a rich supply of blood, thick nerves granting convenient access not only to the brain, but also the gut and groin—the whole length of the vagus nerve.

I sucked in energy and blasted it through cellular turbines, more energy than I had used in a hundred years, a whole calorie or more. If the boy had been paying attention, he would have felt a faint itch.

He was not paying attention. Ahead, the Castle Sauvage loomed. It was tall and severe, made from dark stone hewn into skinny blocks. At its corners, slender towers were capped in conical hats of dark wood. It didn't look like a very practical castle.

The narrow stream rushed alongside it, swollen with the

storm, and between the stream and the castle there was a lawn, trimmed short, where a big-bellied black airplane peeked out of a thatched hangar.

The sky above the valley was pale orange, with no clouds, except for one, which wasn't a cloud at all: rather, an enormous animal form: a moth, the boy's mind reported plainly, but this moth was titanic. Fuzzy, iridescent, awesome. It billowed over the valley, and cast a shadow as wide as a cumulonimbus, at the edges refracting sunlight like a diaphanous prism.

The castle, the airstrip, the XL moth, the boy himself, a human, conspicuously alive: I was violently confused. Maybe this was a final dream before death, a glitchy fantasia of the Anth. I checked myself, ran the diagnostics that had kept me sane in the tomb; everything was fine. This was real.

The boy's shoes slapped the boards of a short bridge. As he crossed the stream, the moth's shadow passed over the castle, shimmered into the forest beyond.

The boy knew his destination. He passed a tavern and a rusticated stone church, mist rising in its courtyard. In the street, the villagers wore technical outerwear; their parkas were dotted with bits of reflective tape that sizzled in the sun.

The boy made not for the castle's gate, which was flung wide, but a smaller door, off to one side, set deep into the wall. Inside, he sprinted down shadowed corridors, skidding artfully around corners: a route well practiced.

"Oi, dog boy!" a man called. The first words I heard in a new world, and they were: "Oi, dog boy!"

In his flash of annoyance, I knew the boy's name, which was not Dog Boy, but: Ariel.

It's interesting how different humans regard their names. My first subject thrummed with his; was always aware of himself as Peter Leadenhall, and everything that was invested in those two words.

Altissa Praxa was the opposite; she could go weeks without thinking of her name. It was a label, a tool, as practical and unremarkable as a hammer or a shoe. (Peter also loved his shoes.)

This boy was not like either of them, but the fact that his name now cracked like a whip told me something. Ariel! In his haughtier moments: Ariel de la Sauvage. No one ever called him that but himself, and one other.

"The hound keeper's looking for you," the man said. He was Bufo, one of the wizard's rangers. They dressed all in black and stalked around the castle like they owned it.

Ariel looked at the ranger. Between Bufo's watery, bulbous eyes, dark on his skin, was a mark:

Ariel's gaze passed over the mark without stopping; to him, it was beneath notice. Everyone bore such a mark.

The ranger shouldered past him, and Ariel paused, considered his path. The hound keeper was looking for him . . . and yet . . .

The horns pealed again, and his choice was made.

In the castle's broad bailey, Ariel joined a crowd watching

combatants at play. I saw the mark on every face: on temples, on cheeks, smack between eyes.

Ariel slithered to a place beside the railing that enclosed the dueling ground, where he watched two thickset squires whack each other with dense foam swords. Around the curve of the dueling ground, stands had been erected, and his eyes roved their height, pausing on interesting faces. The bard Jesse, looking skeptical. (A mark above his eye.) The cook Elise, screaming her support: one of those squires was her boyfriend. (A mark beside her lips.) At the top of the stands sat the knights (all marked, variously), whom Ariel regarded with appropriate deference, though when I probed his mind to discover what they actually did, the answer was: not much.

There was no king in this castle; it awaited one. Its regent was the Wizard Malory, inscrutable and fey. Ariel searched for him now, though with an odd feeling: as much as he wished to find the wizard, he wished also not to.

The wizard was not in attendance, which was not surprising. Malory was often absent.

"I think they ought to have a trivia contest," said a sharp voice at Ariel's elbow.

It was Madame Betelgauze, Ariel's teacher, from whom he had learned about weather and sickness and invisible planets. I rummaged through her lessons: an inventory of useful herbs; the measure of ingredients for various tonics and tinctures; a reverence for the moon and its phases. She was pretty witchy, Betelgauze.

"But, madame, you would always win," Ariel said. Her mark was on her forehead, exactly where her third eye would be.

"You'd better believe it," she replied. "I would crush you all beneath my heel. Grind you to dust!"

The language Betelgauze spoke was not Altissa's language, exactly, but it was related; and the boy understood her, so I did, too.

I probed for etymological clues, but I couldn't get at them through the thick buffer of the boy's fluency. He spoke with crisp formality. He was self-conscious about that, and proud.

The day's final contest captured Ariel's attention entirely, for one of the competitors was Kay: his brother. A clutch of squires hauled contraptions onto the field. This wasn't a duel, but a race through obstacles: beam, barrels, net, wall. One of the knights tooted a horn and the two competitors leapt into action.

In the boy's gaze, Kay was haloed with awe: lithe, long-limbed, liquid. (A mark across his cheek.) He skipped across the beam as if dancing, hopped from barrel to barrel easily, then dove beneath the net. There, his competitor caught him, wriggling like a muscular worm. But the final obstacle was a wall, and for Kay, it was no obstacle at all: he leapt, caught the lip with his fingertips, and was over the top.

Ariel shouted his approval; devotion scraped his throat raw. He leapt up and down, desperate to catch his brother's eye. Kay turned to wave, and when he saw Ariel, he winked. The boy thrilled with his brother's victory, his capability.

Ariel wanted to congratulate Kay, but his brother was swept away by his squire friends. Gal and Percy hooted their endorsements, slapped Kay's back so hard he nearly fell over. They would dine in the castle's great hall tonight, feasting with the other competitors while the knights took their measure.

Instead, Ariel wandered to the kennels, gathered up the hounds, and took them out to the lawn beside the stream for their exercise, sending them racing after a ball across the short grass.

Back inside, Ariel combed the hounds and laid out their dinner, enriched with scraps from the kitchen's feast prep.

The hound keeper, Master Hectorus, called Heck, was at his bench, tapping an awl through a band of leather. (A mark between his brows, lending him an expression of perpetual concentration.) The hound keeper crafted beautiful collars, some woven from thin strips, others studded with metal bobs in ingenious patterns. The leather's rich mycelial odor filled the room.

"Your work isn't done," said Master Heck. Ariel looked up, surprised; the hounds were combed and fed. Heck looked at him flatly. "Go fetch us pretzels."

The boy obeyed happily, and soon he was trotting along Sauvage's main street, where the whole village swirled around him. Some nights, with the villagers all tucked into their houses or their niches in the castle, Sauvage seemed oppressively small; but with everyone out wandering, laughing and hallooing, all in their best technical outerwear, it felt like a bright parade.

The boy knew everyone; no face was unattached to a name. There were perhaps a hundred people, total, in the village.

The old knight Elver Sargasso passed, trailed by his sycophantic squires. Sargasso's jacket was incredible, its shape as enticingly odd-angled as an old stealth bomber. A sword bounced at his hip, privilege of the knights: a sword of the kind Kay would soon possess.

I could not work this place out. I could not even form a

theory. It was a mash-up, a pile-up, not so much anachronistic as everything all at once. Of course, the Anth had always lived like this. Encrypted phones alongside incense sticks, coruscating networks alongside printed books. Nothing was ever erased. Even so: a castle?

I was all questions: when, and where, and why.

INTEGRATION

Master Heck had turned the kennel's storeroom into a bedroom for the brothers, and for many years Ariel and Kay slept together in a sturdy bed built by the hound keeper. Recently, Kay had graduated to the castle's barracks, where he bunked with the squires. Kay spent his days in training, and his lessons came not from Betelgauze, but knights like Elver Sargasso: lessons in fencing and chivalry and emotional warfare.

Ariel was not so well directed. He roamed the valley; he floated in the village. He did the chores that Master Heck asked him to do, completing his tasks to the letter, though never a letter beyond. The moment he was free: he went. He admired Heck's fine leatherwork but possessed no desire to learn the tools himself.

Ariel worried that his disinterest was a disappointment to Master Heck, but if that was the case, the hound keeper never gave any sign of it. Neither did he offer any great approval of the boy's other pursuits. Heck seemed to think that Ariel had done enough by simply arriving.

The boy loved the hound keeper for this, even if his placid acceptance did not quite answer the inchoate, grandiose yearning Ariel felt inside. He yearned to be invited into some larger game. Not the knighthood—he didn't have Kay's physical talents—but perhaps . . . well, what else was there? Some days, he wondered if the Wizard Malory had ever taken an apprentice. Ariel might be invited into his secret tower and shown . . . whatever was up there . . .

Better yet, he might learn to fly the wizard's airplane.

It was these what-ifs that filled the boy's mind as he drowsed in bed. It had been a day rich with incident: the deathly discovery, the games, the pretzel, and then a rising nausea that had sent him early to bed.

The hound Yuzu, his favorite, padded in and leapt without invitation to his side, where she was accepted.

My confusion was already near an all-time peak when, as if to compound my troubles, Yuzu spoke.

She said, with soft affection and clear enunciation, "Good night, Ariel. I hope you feel better in the morning." The boy showed no surprise; simply patted her flank.

In the night, Ariel developed a fever. It was my fault; in my eagerness, I had worked too fast, without subtlety. At my best, I can blend into a human's body so finely that their T cells give me high fives. I worked to calm the situation. Meanwhile, the boy drenched his pillowcase in sweat.

A moment comes, in my integration with a new subject,

when our thoughts braid together. There is no hiding then. In my rush to set things right in the boy's body, I did not realize the moment had arrived. I was hustling fresh chemicals into his blood, firming up my membranes, and, at the same time, working through the absurd puzzle of the castle and its talking animals, when Ariel spoke.

"Of course the hounds can speak," he said quietly. His eyes were open in the darkness. "Why wouldn't they?"

I wasn't ready for it. I felt caught; exposed. I don't know why. Mostly it was strange, meeting someone new. I'd forgotten what it was like. I'd given up hope it would ever happen again.

"Who are you?" Ariel whispered. He was woozy from the fever, unsure if he was dreaming. I felt the pulse of fear in his blood. "How can I hear you, inside my mind?"

I can speak directly to my subjects, though it's not easy. I am made to absorb their perceptions, not provide them, so it feels like using a drinking straw to reverse the flow of a river. Even the faintest whisper requires great effort; anything greater— any kind of hallucination—is beyond me, or nearly so.

But a whisper is achievable. How best to announce myself? With the truth. I said: Ariel de la Sauvage, I am a visitor who has crossed a gulf of time to meet you.

For my subjects, my speech is not speech, but rather the sudden memory of speech: memory without antecedent. You become aware that someone has said something. You might wonder if you've said it yourself.

The boy gazed at the beams in the ceiling. His eyes were adjusting. "Are you an angel?" he asked.

I rummaged in his memory and found the outline of the

religion taught at the little stone church, a syncretic mash-up of traditions, angels included, all tilted toward a harvest holiday of death and rebirth.

I was not an angel.

"A demon, then?" he ventured, in a way that suggested a demon might be better.

Not one of those, either. I am a chronicler and a counselor. A conscience, perhaps. I was made to help people, in everything they did, and I would do my best to help him, however I could.

Ariel digested this. "Good," he said at last. Then he said something he had never spoken aloud, not even to Kay. "I know I am meant for something important. I can feel it. I have always felt it."

So he was brave, curious, morbid—and a bit grandiose. That was a dangerous combination, but he was just a boy.

There, in the kennel's storeroom, with the hound Yuzu snoring, our long conversation began. We would talk, the two of us, across sidewalks and star fields, from the dormitory of a misty college to the helm of a doomed spaceship. And when we didn't talk, that was fine, because I knew everything he knew, and he was happy to have me along.

Now, in this first moment, I asked Ariel to rouse himself and find a patch of sky, for I had questions, and they would not wait.

INVISIBLE PLANETS

From the castle's ramparts, Ariel peered up into murky disappointment.

The sky was dark, with no moon. The veil of dust had been maintained. Above, what should have been cold, clear brilliance was heavy and dull, a buzzing field of scabby purple. The boy had never known any other sky, so he regarded this one with customary awe, which was depressing.

A few stars, the very brightest, pierced the gloom. They were not sharp pinpricks, but hazy orbs.

Madame Betelgauze was there, too, and this Ariel had expected. She roamed the castle's ramparts at all hours, but especially dusk and dawn.

"Good morning," said Betelgauze. "What brings you to the sky so early?"

"I woke and couldn't sleep," said Ariel truthfully.

"Perhaps more than that," said Betelgauze. Her eyes possessed a hard brightness that was missing from the sky. "You have come at an auspicious hour, and suddenly I realize I ought not to have left it to chance. I should have roused you to see."

"See what?"

Betelgauze pointed low on the horizon. "There, rising in the east, just ahead of the sun. Do you see them?"

The boy stared. The sky was still dark; he saw nothing.

"Remember your lessons, my pupil," Betelgauze said. "Use the tail of your eye."

The boy did what Betelgauze had taught him, looking to one side of the spot she indicated. Through his peripheral vision, the sense that was not quite sight, her subject was plain: three faint specks, packed together tight.

"The invisible planets," said Betelgauze. "The Lord of the Feast and the Bright Lady, with the Jailer between them."

It had to be Saturn, vised between Jupiter and Venus. The sight was astonishing, even through the haze. They were as close in the sky as any of my subjects, over many centuries, had ever seen them.

"I have been watching for many nights," Betelgauze said. "The Lord of the Feast has walked with the Jailer, entertaining him. For this reason, the Jailer did not see the Bright Lady's approach. Tonight, she and her lover have sprung their trap. Do you see? They surround him!"

Having found them in his peripheral vision, Ariel could now see the planets straight-on. Brilliant Jupiter was diminished through the dust; its retinue of moons was lost.

"The Jailer's power will be suspended . . . for a day, a week, a year, who can say? Things once impossible are now possible."

"What things?" Ariel asked. Madame Betelgauze's celestial interpretations often plucked a string inside of him, and if he maintained a mild skepticism, it was never enough to still the vibration.

"I am no fortune teller," said Betelgauze. "We must be watchful."

Across the rest of the sky, the stars were mostly diffused into obscurity by the veil of dust. Mostly, but not entirely. Ariel was no stranger to orienteering, so he knew the North Star.

Following his gaze, I found my calendar.

The star parked at the crown of the sky was not Polaris; even dulled by the dust, it blazed brighter than the old standby of the Anth. This brilliant star was Vega, the first ever to be photographed. That it provided the boy's compass was astonishing and horrifying. Here is why:

Like a spinning top, Earth wobbles on its axis, shifting its aim between Polaris and Vega, back and forth, back and forth. This is basic knowledge; just as basic is the number of years required for the exchange to be made.

Vega's enthronement revealed that I had been away not for a decade, as I had suspected; not for a century, as I had feared; but for eleven thousand years.

The enormity of it roared. At their apex, the Anth had a prehistory only six thousand years distant. This interval, eleven thousand years, doubled their whole story, from the earliest settlements of the Old Anth to the doom of the dragon moon.

Vega blared in the north. Eleven thousand years gone, and the heavens all askew.

CHRONICLER'S NOTE

A note on my perspective.

I am built from technological engines bolted onto tamed microorganisms. I live by the logic of the yeast, and that logic is multiplicity. The yeast has no singular I, so, if we are aiming for accuracy, I don't, either. But I love the I of the Middle Anth, of English. The sovereign I. It is bold and imperious; it presumes too much.

The language of the Anth at their apex was far too circumspect to plant such a flag. In that language, there was no first person: their narratives swarmed and glistened, many-angled, shimmering with contradiction. That's how the world is, a lot of the time, and those narratives can be thrilling, in their way, but I have always preferred the tales of the Middle Anth, or even the Old.

I like their I.

. . .

A note on my calendar.

After my glimpse of Vega, I recalibrated the clocks in my heart. I would be a poor chronicler, after all, if I couldn't tell the time. Whenever Ariel glimpsed the moon and stars, I refined my estimate, and at last I arrived at a defensible guess:

By the calendar of the Anth, it was September 28, 13777, when Ariel de la Sauvage brought me back into history.

My story proceeds from there, and if neither Ariel nor anyone else in his world ever knew or cared about Septembers: I did. I do. Perched atop a wobbly ladder of years, the number 13777 seems almost comical. Even so. These dates are for the Anth, who made me.

And they are for you.

NORMAL AND NOT

September 29, 13777, to November 1, 13777

In the morning, the dogs roused their boy. I tucked away my revelation; worrying about the years lost would accomplish nothing. Instead, I ought to determine what was happening, and what might happen next.

In the days and weeks following the games among squires, the life of the village returned to its normal shape. First, I imagined myself a detective, but as the clues compounded, I felt more like a dreamer.

The moon grew to fullness, its face scarred by the seven-pointed citadel of the dragons: evidence that, for all my confusion, there could be no mistaking the basic situation.

The moon's gravity tugged at the veil of dust, pulled it into rippling patterns, vast purple tides at sunset. When the moon completed its phase and became an invisible wanderer across the daytime sky, a faint curling trace still betrayed its position. It was beautiful, but I would have preferred a view of the stars, a moon without dragons.

The village was electrified, with wires strung up on poles made from pines; all could be traced back to the Castle Sauvage. A pointy-faced electrician named Ratthew maintained the wires and poles, along with the solid-state lanterns that lit the village. These cast a warm, low light, and were very reliable, except for the nights when the wizard worked in his tower. On such nights, the whole village flickered.

The villagers foraged widely, for mushrooms and black walnuts and the last of the wild apples. They also maintained a shared farm, where dark cruciferous greens had yielded to a flood of squash and winter wheat. The wizard had propagated these varieties, which were hardy and pest-resistant and seemed almost to grow themselves.

The wheat they ground into purplish flour in a sweet-smelling mill, also electrified; its motor whined when it spun. They brewed it also into beer, adding herbs gathered and dried by Madame Betelgauze: bog myrtle, wormwood, nettle, and sage. Butter and cheese they made from the milk of thirteen goats, who grazed serenely across the stream. When Ariel passed, he heard them telling each other tales of terror, fainting with delight.

"Of course the goats speak," Ariel murmured to himself, and to me. "Why wouldn't they?"

So, it was all just: normal. They were not hard up, and they hadn't become distracted by money. The village floated on an easy abundance, buoyed by the munificence of the wizard. Nothing to see here.

The great risk was boredom. The knights busied themselves with emotional warfare, and also the occasional hunt, in which they went out bellowing with the hounds, tracking an elusive golden elk. Ariel understood that the appeal was the long, merry hike; they'd be despondent if they ever caught the creature.

Meanwhile, the villagers crowded into the tavern, singing rowdy songs and playing endless card games. There was no money to bet, so they wagered in dares: loser drinks a whole mug of beer in one gulp, loser knocks on the door of the wizard's tower and runs away, loser jumps in the frigid stream.

The playing cards were the only printed matter I ever saw in Sauvage: two precious decks, delivered by the wizard in what everyone agreed had been his only visit, ever, to the tavern. They were beautiful, thick and waxy, seemingly indestructible, four suits and thirteen face cards illuminated with grim, resplendent figures.

As Ariel made his way around the village, his attention caressed everything he saw and, in flashes and reveries, drew forth memory. When this happened, I grabbed hold, and slowly I pieced together his biography.

Ariel and Kay had been brought to the castle as infants, delivered by the Wizard Malory in his airplane. Ariel cherished the knowledge that he had once flown. He had never been invited to do so again.

Madame Betelgauze theorized the wizard had found the boys in the wreckage of a crashed vessel atop the glacier, way up on the ice; she told Ariel he might have come from a dying planet, far away. This story was perfectly Betelgauze-ian, in that it was unlikely, but awesome.

No one was willing to take full responsibility for two children, so their care was diffused across the castle. Ariel and Kay learned language from Jesse the bard, hygiene from Elise the cook, wonder from Madame Betelgauze. From Master Heck, they learned kindness.

As he matured, Ariel exhibited an even keel and a quiet formality, and everyone agreed that, in time, he might himself rise to the post of hound keeper. Kay's trajectory was different, and meteoric: he demonstrated such astonishing kinesthetic intelligence that the only question was, was Kay the most capable archer and swordsman in the castle currently, or in the castle ever? Add to that his good cheer and sincere care for the people around him, and there you had it: Kay deserved to be a knight, and the Castle Sauvage was apparently a place where someone could get what they deserved.

Ariel had no knowledge of other villages, or any other people outside the valley at all. Sauvage was everything. All the other places in his mind were spun from fiction: Betelgauze's planets, and the small, intense world of the Stromatolite.

This had been a gift from the wizard, who had acquired it during one of his rovings and presented it to the boy, saying, "This game was the pastime of a long-ago civilization. See if you can beat it."

The Stromatolite was, by a wide margin, Ariel's most prized possession, and when he retrieved it from its pouch, I recognized its morphology instantly. It was a handheld video game system, of the kind beloved by the Anth. Altissa had played one; all my subjects had. Theirs projected images in bright, scintillating color, while the Stromatolite's screen produced only gritty shades of gray. But there was nothing else like it in the village. The Stromatolite presented a phantasmagorical fantasy world peopled by talking animals—these seeming, to Ariel, quite naturalistic. The game's text had suggested the possibility of the construction "de la Sauvage" alongside a deep well of epic and/or romantic possibilities. What the village lacked in scope, the Stromatolite provided.

The device had slots for three saved games, and in each, Ariel's character had become a minor god, capable of feats of powerful magic and resurrection. He knew he ought to reset one of the slots so he could pursue a new path, but he could never decide which hero to sacrifice, so he didn't.

Ariel was the youngest child in the village, a fact that did not perturb him, but seemed strange to me. There were couples, some who had been married at the church and others more casually connected, but there were no children. Kay, who was perhaps fourteen or fifteen, had slotted easily into the squires, a rollicking group just beyond Ariel's grasp, in age and temperament both. In Ariel's cohort was Ariel alone: no other children, born or brought.

Ariel was a mapmaker; it was his great pastime. His map was not on paper, for there was no paper. Instead, he had discovered a hidden menu inside the Stromatolite, one that permitted the creation of custom terrain in the style of the game: a malleable 3D landscape rendered in sketchy monochrome.

He pored over his map, pushing and pulling the virtual landscape into agreement with organic reality. His map captured the whole valley, which was long and narrow, marked at one end by the castle, beyond which a throat of dense forest yawned menacingly. There, Ariel painted a fuzz of trees.

At the other end of the valley lay the glacier. He had hiked right up to the edge of it, clambering over the field of loose rocks, marveling that there really was an edge: a place where hard-packed snow was, and where it wasn't. He had ventured onto the glacier, but only briefly; there was no feature to draw him forward, no question in the landscape. Hardly any landscape at all. Here, his map faded to default gray.

It was the melt beneath the glacier that made the stream, which Ariel indicated with a rippling water texture.

For all its coarseness, I absorbed Ariel's map hungrily. It held subtler points of interest.

There was the place where he had discovered the enormous skeleton of a bear picked clean, moss growing on its broad brow.

The place where a spring formed a strange, cold pool.

The place where a snake had erected a snake-fortress, a clever dome of stones, the largest he had ever seen, its interior crowded with cast-off skins. (Snakes had learned to build fortresses.)

Marked with a dancing X was the place high up where Ariel could perch protected in a broad crevice and see the whole village and castle. This was his hidey-hole, observation post, and treasure hoard.

One afternoon, Ariel set himself to updating his map, redrawing the path to the glacier and, importantly, adding his discovery of the cave: Altissa's tomb. His cursor tiptoed around the snout of the glacier. Up against the bulk of the ice, he placed a question mark.

He moved the cursor around, inspecting his handiwork, his realm. That the map ended at the edges of the valley, that the rest of the world remained default gray, did not seem to bother him. This I did not understand. Not yet.

When he was not pressed into service by Master Heck, he roamed the village and the forest, and he was never without the Stromatolite. He visited his hidey-hole, the one marked with the *X*.

He followed a thin, switchbacking trail up the side of the valley, then cut over to find an outcropping of smooth grainy stone. He slid down its face—a bit of a daredevil maneuver—to arrive at a ledge that he followed to a broad crevice. Settled into this crack in the outcropping's face, he enjoyed a panoramic view across the valley. He peered down at the towers of the Castle Sauvage.

The crevice was spacious, several meters deep. On this visit, Ariel discovered a spiderweb, and he wondered at the courage of its maker. This seemed strange to me, until Ariel watched a brigade of insects, all different kinds, beetles and flies and furry caterpillars, lay siege to the web and, in short order, cut it down. The spider fled pitifully.

Eleven thousand years, and the bugs had cast off the yoke of the spider. A revolution as great as any in history.

Weeks rolled by. The moon waxed red.

The first snow arrived, a light dusting across the valley. Tomorrow was Hallow's End, the stone church's harvest holiday, and the day on which eligible squires would be enrolled into knighthood.

Ariel was exercising the hounds on the airstrip, sending the ball skidding across the frosted grass, enjoying the crunch beneath his feet.

A figure approached, walking along the stream, unmistakable. The Wizard Malory was bundled warm: tall boots; thick gloves; a padded jacket with its collar turned up. If his attire seemed too much for the morning, which was only mildly chilly, Ariel was not surprised, for the wizard kept his collar up even in summer.

My impression of faces is abstract, indirect. This isn't unusual; if you probe your memory, I suspect—I suggest—that you do not see faces like photographs or paintings. Instead, you see glowing spots of personness. Your friend Altissa: she is simply there. You can read a whole novel of the Middle Anth and feel like you know someone, but never learn the color of their eyes, the shape of their chin.

That said, the Wizard Malory had a chin like a movie star.

And he bore no mark. His face was unblemished. This, as much as the strange energies he conjured in his tower, confirmed his special status.

Alongside Malory padded his dog, Cabal, who was older and meaner than any of the castle's hounds. Cabal had no function, other than to lurk in the wizard's shadow. Ariel had long ago given up on befriending him.

The hound named Vulcan bounded toward the wizard, but Cabal emitted a curt snarl that sent him whimpering back.

The wizard called out: "Ariel de la Sauvage! Hallow's End is upon us. Your brother becomes a knight tomorrow."

No one else called him Ariel de la Sauvage, and the boy did not know—could never tell—if the wizard was making fun of him or not.

"Perhaps this is only the beginning of his advancement," Malory continued. "Perhaps one day Kay will be king."

"I doubt it," Ariel replied, because it seemed like the polite thing to say to a regent, even though he believed Kay would make a better king than any of the other knights. Better than Malory, too? Hard to say. The wizard's role in the village was ambient, more like weather than government. "But," he added, "I am proud of my brother."

The wizard walked closer. His dog gazed at Ariel with boredom and malice.

"It promises to be a fine occasion," Malory said. He clapped his gloves together and puffed air into the void. The wizard's breath did not steam in the cold. "We have all been waiting eagerly for this day. Some of us for a very long time."

Malory walked on. Across the valley, a gusting wind lifted snow from the boughs of the pines.

Back in the kennel, Ariel turned up the heater and combed each of the hounds in turn. He checked their scrapes and sores, applied ointment to the bare spot on Vulcan's butt, bribed the hound with a piece of mushroom jerky so he wouldn't lick the ointment off immediately.

Master Heck was at his bench.

"Do you think Kay could become king?" Ariel asked. He wasn't shy around Heck. The hound keeper spoke to him seriously, and always kept his confidence.

"Kay?" Heck repeated. "Yes, I suppose he could. But we might ask, *should* Kay become king?"

"Better him than anyone else, I think," Ariel said.

The hound keeper sniffed. "I've never heard you talk politics."

Really, Ariel was just interested in Kay, and his future, which seemed suddenly imminent.

Later, passing the stone church, he paused, knowing it would be the scene of his brother's ceremony. In the center of the church-yard there was a stone, and atop the stone an anvil, and in the anvil a sword.

Like a game in the tavern, the secret card flipped last, re-vealing the logic of a strange hand.

An orphan, a castle, his kind foster parents. A virtuous brother named Kay, a stone with a sword. I knew this story from the storehouse of the Anth. It was different-shaped here, com-pressed and remade, as it had always been.

But I knew this story.

In the space of a glance, my conception of Sauvage was trans-formed. What might have been a remnant of humanity doing its best now took on the aspect of a crude play. Ariel was its focus: secret prince, sword-puller. There could be no doubt about it. The village stood revealed as a painted scrim. It was makeshift, im-perfect; the technical outerwear was strange, the wizard and his airplane even stranger; but the sword in the churchyard, the stone with its gravity . . . like a lens, they made the scene cohere.

Ariel stood inside a grand design, and if I did not yet know whose, I had my suspicion.

HALLOW'S END

November 1, 13777

Snow fell through the night. In the morning, Sauvage was transformed, muffled and trackless. A sense of the sacred floated in the air, as if ordered up by the priestess in her church, for the day of the squires' graduation into knighthood.

Ariel found his brother in the castle's kitchen, where Kay was charming the cook Elise out of a pastry. He surrendered half his prize, more butter than not, and the brothers sat, each with their share, beside the glowing hearth.

"Are you nervous?" Ariel asked.

"No," Kay said. "What's to be nervous about? A tap on the shoulder, a prayer. Nothing will be different afterwards."

"You'll be a knight, you'll have privileges . . ." Mainly, he could claim the throne; or reject another's claim; and, in rejecting, reluctantly offer himself instead; and squabble endlessly . . . This was the pastime of the knights.

"I'll do nothing differently," Kay insisted. "I'm happy as things are."

"I shall call you Sir Kay," Ariel said. "My most exalted liege knight."

"Really? I suspect you'll treat me as you always have," Kay said. "Farting in my direction."

"I would not dare," Ariel said. "You would slice me with your sword." Then he farted, and they both laughed.

Kay grew quiet. "I won't have a sword today."

Ariel leapt to his feet. "Why not? What happened?"

The brothers had obsessed for months. In the blacksmith's shop, they had agonized over hilts and pommels until Kay finally chose his favorite, a bulbous evocation of an acorn. He'd brought the sword to Ariel as soon as it was quenched, and in the room beside the kennel, they unwound its swaddling and gazed down reverently.

Now, Kay's countenance darkened. "It has disappeared, and I can only imagine that I mislaid it."

"That is not possible!" Ariel meant this sincerely: His brother was a paragon of care. He would not mislay a pastry, to say nothing of a sword. "Perhaps Gal or Percy are playing a prank . . ."

"I do not think so, or they would not have frozen their fingers searching with me. We went out at first light, and scraped around everywhere we could imagine . . ." He sighed. "I shall go without my sword, and reclaim it when the snow melts. Percy says I shall be the Knight of Spring." Kay smiled gamely, but unconvincingly. "It shall make a fine story."

The brothers were quiet, weighed down by disappointment.

Kay hauled himself to his feet. "I'm off to meet Gal and Percy," he said. "We must don holy robes and chant all day. See you at the ceremony. Don't laugh too loud."

His brother trotted away. Ariel remained, his face and brain both knotted with disappointment. He had loved the sword nearly as much as Kay did; he had loved the idea of Kay and the sword together.

Ariel leapt to his feet and announced, melodramatically, to no one: "My brother Kay shall not be without a sword this day."

Or maybe he announced it to me.

Yes, I knew this story. Ariel de la Sauvage was his name, but his deeper identity, I had finally and definitively determined.

Aware that time was short, he sprinted out of the castle. Along the street, the villagers were out with shovels, clearing the snow.

Ahead was the churchyard, where stood the enormous stone, and atop the stone the anvil, and in the anvil the sword. I knew this story! The words inscribed on the sword read—

The boy hurried past. Ignored it completely. That sword was stuck fast; a waste of time. And besides, he had another sword in mind. A better one. The hike was substantial, but Kay's ceremony was not until evening. Ariel could make it, if he hustled.

In his mind, I saw the object of his hustle: the sword of Altissa Praxa; the sword she carried against the dragons; the sword Ariel had spied in her tomb, where she carried it still. I'd forgotten about it entirely. I never liked that sword.

Ariel sprinted across the bridge and made for the forest, where the snow was thin beneath the trees, along the path to the cave that would lead to the tomb and, within it, a sword that was not Excalibur.

And there the story changed, for good.

REGRET MINIMIZATION

November 1, 13777

Ariel followed his map back to Altissa in her escape pod: to
the place where an enormous chunk of ice had calved from the
greater mass of the glacier, revealing a low tunnel carved by a
torrent of meltwater now dissipated and refrozen.

Inside, the cave was an antechamber of brilliant blue, the
ice rippling in strange, smooth patterns. The pod lay beyond,
caught fast; its door was ajar, but only slightly. An adult
would not have been able to slither through. That Ariel had
peered through that crack into darkness and decided to venture
inside was incredible.

This was a better place to get a sword than a stupid stone.
This sword had not been prepared for the boy, not been laid
out like a piece of cheese in a trap: this sword, he had found on
his own.

For the second time, Ariel entered the escape pod.

Altissa Praxa was well preserved, untouched by millennia. After splashing down, the pod, recruited by the dragons' treachery, had blown all its air out. I recall the awful sucking pop. Through eleven thousand years in the airless cold, biology had been paused. Now, with the door ajar and oxygen flooded in, there were surely bacteria at work. The warrior would at last decay.

Ariel entered more fearfully than before, because he knew a dead woman awaited him, and because he had come to steal from her.

In her final minutes, eleven thousand years ago, Altissa had gathered herself and applied the techniques she had learned in boot camp. She slowed her breathing, calmed her heart. The effort was as titanic as any she'd ever made, and it was successful, for she went into death with intention. That was the great theme of the operators: intention. Get it done, Altissa.

The practice was impressive, and also fairly vain. They thought too much about how their corpse would look when another operator found it. Or, failing an operator, a boy from the distant future.

Ariel approached. I felt his awe, and also a tickle of foolishness, and I understood that, in his first visit, he had not known Altissa Praxa was dead. Seeing her preserved form, her calm countenance, he had thought her sleeping, suspended, as in the plots of the game in the Stromatolite. The boy had mustered his courage, leaned forward, and kissed her on the lips, quick and light.

It was a gesture so dorky, so full of romantic wonder, that it built a bridge for me to cross. Yes, it's only because this boy believed in foolish stories that this story of mine could begin. Brave, curious, morbid, romantic; I liked him more and more.

In death, Altissa cradled her sword Regret Minimization. Their swords all had stupid names. If I had been Altissa's memory, the sword had been her ambition. Regret Minimization was cunning and spiteful, with hilt and blade flawless matte white. No dirt would ever adhere; the sword was just as vain as the operators.

Ariel now understood that Altissa was dead, but still he treated her with great tenderness. He uncurled her fingers, light and dry as kindling, and reached to grasp the sword.

And so I was, perhaps inevitably, reunited with my nemesis.

VENGEANCE! came the sword's voice like a cymbal crash. Shocked, Ariel released it, and the sword clattered at Altissa's feet. The warrior looked on implacably.

Oh, there was that: the sword spoke. Mostly inanities.

Ariel extended a fingertip, touched the bulb of the pommel.

The sword hissed, *What of the war?*

"There is no war," the boy said. He touched with two fingers.

No war? The sword pondered this. *Then let us begin one!*

"There are duels, sometimes, between knights who want to be king." Ariel kept talking, while slowly spidering his fingers up the hilt. "They try not to hurt each other, but there have been accidents." He was approaching the sword exactly as he would a nervous hound.

We will ally ourselves with the most powerful of these knights, then betray them.

"My brother Kay becomes a knight today, and he doesn't have a sword . . ."

Or we can just murder them all straightaway. That might be better.

". . . so if you will please quiet yourself, I must deliver you to Kay." He gripped the sword fully and swept it up off the floor. If Regret Minimization's personality was unhinged, the sword itself was perfectly balanced.

Very well. Deliver me. I will make plans.

Ariel looked at the sword dubiously. I wished he would abandon it . . . almost. Regret Minimization was annoying, but it had powerful capabilities, and it was another fugitive from my era. When you're alone, even a hateful companion is: a companion.

Outside the tomb, clear of the glacier, navigating back toward the village, the boy carried the sword awkwardly, dragging its tip through the snow.

The human body is, among many other things, a network. When Altissa Praxa was my subject, we all talked, her gut and her glands and me . . . but truthfully, they couldn't carry on much of a conversation. The sword was different. I sent a cool greeting flickering through the boy's skin.

Chronicler! the sword whispered back, a buzz against the boy's palm. *What has transpired?*

I explained that we had been rescued from Altissa's tomb; that millennia had passed; that humans persisted—here was one—without any sign of the powerful culture that made us both.

Then we are the last of the Anth, said Regret Minimization.

So the representatives of the planet's most successful civilization were a capacious fungus and a talking sword. More than a few philosophers of the Anth would have found it appropriate, even funny. That was something.

We can make this boy into Altissa's heir, the sword said. *I will teach him warfare. You will record my success. He will resume the war against the dragons.*

"Are you saying something?" Ariel asked. "Stop that. It tickles."

When he emerged from the trees, the sword's sensors swept across the valley. It declared, *You could conquer this settlement. It would be easy. I can instruct you.*

"There is no need——"

We'll punish your enemies.

"I do not have enemies!" Ariel said.

You do, the sword hissed, *and if you don't realize it, they are only more dangerous.*

In the village, a procession of squires was emerging from the church, Kay among them. Ariel glared at Regret Minimization, and he said: "You *must* be silent. If you embarrass my brother, I will throw you into the stream, and you will never conquer anything or punish anyone ever again."

The sword said nothing.

The boy pushed through the small crowd that had gathered around the churchyard. The squires were waiting, picking at their robes and teasing each other, while the priestess delivered a droning convocation.

Ariel edged closer and whispered to his brother, "Kay! Look!"

Kay looked over and, when he saw Ariel's burden, his mouth made an O that rose into a grin. He snaked his hand from beneath the robe and accepted the gift.

47

Ariel's teeth gritted in anticipation of some brassy exclamation, but Regret Minimization honored their agreement and remained quiet. Kay whispered to his friends, and they all ogled the matte-white weapon. It made their swords look antique. It made the sword in the stone look antique.

The Wizard Malory was looming near the priestess, and he noticed their excitement. He strode over, his look conspiratorial. "What do you have there, Kay?" he said. "Did you pull Excalibur yourself?"

Kay frowned. "No . . . this is a different blade."

Malory's gaze found the sword in the stone. The sword: still in the stone. His handsomeness darkened, and his voice was a sepulcher when said: "What do you mean, *different*?"

The priestess paused her prayer; the churchyard grew quiet. The villagers all looked on, curious to see who had done what, and what kind of trouble they were in.

Kay explained: "I lost my sword, so my brother gave me one."

"From where? FROM WHERE? There are no swords to be had. Only one. THAT one." He jabbed a finger at the sword in the stone. Malory's eyes were showing too much white as they found Ariel. "You . . . are . . . supposed . . . to take . . . THAT one."

Ariel was petrified with confusion. "I believe . . . that sword . . . is stuck?"

The wizard's expression cooled. He walked to the stone and sat heavily. "What a waste of time."

The priestess cleared her throat. "Shall I—"

Malory said a word,

48

and it whined in Ariel's ear like a mosquito, but did not go in. The word was not meant for him. The priestess choked mid-utterance; the crowd's murmurs fell silent. Everyone in the churchyard grew suddenly weary, and everyone—even Kay and the squires—searched urgently for a place to rest. They all lowered themselves into the snow and closed their eyes and slept.

Only Ariel remained awake.

He stood with Malory in a bubble outside of time. The stream still ran, musical, in contravention of the wizard's power. Ariel looked in horror at Kay; where his brother's cheek lay, the snow glistened, already melting.

Malory fixed his gaze on him. "Ariel de la Sauvage," he said quietly. "Walk with me."

Ariel remained still.

"Come to my tower. You have wished to see it, have you not? I'll show you my laboratory. I'll brew us a pot of coffee."

"I do not think I will," said Ariel, who had never heard of anything called coffee.

"I can command you," the wizard said plainly. "If I must."

"I do not understand," Ariel said valiantly, although in truth he did understand, at least in part. The scene fit his heart, freight to groove, because it answered the grandiose question that had accompanied him his whole life.

Yet he felt that if he went to the wizard's tower, he would die.

Ariel stood, triumphant and terrified. I did not like the combination.

Malory continued. "Very well. We will talk here. Ariel de la Sauvage, I am perturbed. This sword was made for you." He walked to the stone and extracted Excalibur neatly from the anvil.

Ariel gaped. The sword glittered, spectacular.

"The stone is my design. As is the village. As are you." The directness of his speech made the boy's blood sizzle. "Yet you did not pull the sword. Why?"

"I found another," Ariel said simply.

The wizard frowned. "Another sword ought not to have sufficed. The pattern is burned into your cells. Don't you feel it? Or is my design so poor?"

"Of course I feel it," Ariel said quietly. First, triumph and terror; now, dread and calm. "But there are other designs, too."

The wizard eyed him sharply. "I will take extra care with those, next time. I am sorry." With those words, a decision settled across his face. Ariel saw it clearly. Triumph evaporated; calm fled.

"Goodbye, Ariel de la Sauvage," said the wizard. At last, the boy knew he was not making fun of him, and it was awful.

The wizard said a word; it sounded like

and if the other word had been the whine of a mosquito, this one was the tolling of a bell, and it would send the boy into a slumber from which he would never—oh, I knew he would never—wake.

Ariel did not hear it. I caught the word in his ears, burned it to ash in his blood. For a chronicler, this is prohibited; not just a little bit prohibited, but the most prohibited. Interfere with a subject's senses? Never. Besides prohibited, it is also perilous; I felt a part of myself rupture. Not because it was the wizard's strange word of power; to stop any word in the boy's ears was a titanic exertion. The word could have been "danger." The word could have been "run."

The wizard barked his word again,

and again I stopped the boy's ears. The word was a battering ram, but I held the gates of sensation while Ariel ran. There was shouting behind us, the clamor of the squires waking up, the clear note of Kay's protest.

The wizard's voice bellowed, but it was lost in the din, and Ariel was in the trees.

THE GOLDEN ELK

November 1, 13777, to November 2, 13777

Sweet adrenaline surged. I know it well, the rush of danger, one of the great gifts of biology: time slows and the world sharpens, goes crystal. It would be beautiful if it wasn't always accompanied by a shitstorm.

Ariel's destination was his hidey-hole and observation post: the X on his map. When he reached it, he slid down the smooth rock, landed on the ledge, and scurried into the crevice. Only then did he allow himself to rest.

With keen eyes, he followed the chaos in the village below. The knights marched to the castle in a bumbling clot. The villagers dispersed. Ariel hunted for a glimpse of the wizard, or better yet Kay, but couldn't find either of them.

It began to rain, weak warm droplets. All across the valley, the snow would sink into a wash of gray. Ariel scooped a handful of glittering flakes from the ledge and brought them to his lips.

He watched with sick fascination as the rangers streamed out of the castle, the hounds swirling around them. Yips and barks echoed. Each ranger chose a different path. They would canvass the valley.

"But they will not find me," Ariel said quietly.

He was right, of course. As night rose, the hounds of the Castle Sauvage, loyal to their boy, led the rangers in wild loops to nowhere, up and down the sides of the valley, steering carefully clear of Ariel's hidey-hole. He watched their lanterns bob through the trees.

In the castle, the wizard's tower was alight, narrow windows flickering with pulses as bright and fast as lightning. The wizard's work was accompanied by howling, low and long: Cabal. The great dog's voice echoed through the valley. When his howls quieted, the light also dimmed. What magic the wizard had worked, with his dog at his side, Ariel could not guess.

His gaze crept up to the sky. The dragon moon was full, perilously so. He scuttled deeper into the crevice, sheltering from the glow. The juxtaposition of the reality above (dragons) with the valley below (wizard) vibrated without resolution. The sword in the stone had clarified nothing. I was lost.

The rain increased, obscuring Ariel's view of the village. His stomach churned. He retreated deeper into the crevice and sat morosely.

. . .

Ariel woke to hear crunching and scraping, and to see a lean silhouette arrive on the ledge. Kay! His brother's hair dripped with rain.

"Here you are!" Kay said. "I have searched all night. You maintain too many hidey-holes."

Ariel had, in fact, never revealed this one, his most secret, to Kay. How had his brother found him?

"You have friends I never knew about," Kay said. "Perhaps you did not know, either. Come and see."

The rain had stopped sometime while Ariel slept. He clambered out of the crevice, back onto the forested slope above. There, illuminated in a pool of moonlight, stood a golden elk.

"He brought me to you," said Kay.

Ariel gaped. The creature was powerfully built, with long, dark antlers that curled into a cup that supported a bulbous form.

He crept closer. The elk watched him with shining eyes.

The bulbous form was a hive; it rested in the elk's antlers, stretched between prongs, anchored by a mottled mixture of wax and hair. Bees orbited the elk's brow. They crawled through his fur. The warmth must have been luxurious.

"He is the prize the knights pursue," Kay breathed. The golden elk whom Ariel had never seen—whom no one had ever seen, probably, but whose call everyone knew: a far-off bugling, musical and melancholy when it rang across the valley.

Honey oozed from channels at the base of the hive and ran in wide ribbons along the elk's horns, around his eyes, onto his snout. As Ariel watched, the creature's tongue—purple, enormous—flicked out.

The elk peered at the brothers with lambent eyes. His

tongue flicked out again. Bees crawled along his snout; the sight of it made Ariel's nose itch.

The elk stepped closer, and when he bent his head low, Ariel startled back. But the creature's voice was rich and musical. "The bees say I am being rude," he said. "They say, we are happy to share."

The elk's antlers curled wickedly, but Ariel was hungry, and he was curious, too, so he extended a finger to scrape a portion of honey.

Its flavor was rich and piney. Ariel had seen bees floating in the forest, but their destination had always been a mystery. He had never seen a hive, never tasted honey. Now his senses flared. He and Kay scraped larger portions.

Here in the far future, the bees had undomesticated themselves. They had recruited a powerful partner and convinced him not to shed his antlers. They had bribed him, it seemed, with a lifetime supply of honey.

The castle and the village, in their strange familiarity, could only be illusions. The real future was the bugs revolting against the spiders, and the bees riding through the winter on a mighty mobile base.

Eleven thousand years, and Earth was all askew.

"The bees want to know, why aren't you warm in your castle tonight?" said the elk.

"The wizard has gone mad," Kay said.

"The wizard has always been mad," said the elk.

"We did not see it . . ." said Ariel quietly.

"There is much you have not seen. The bees could have told you, if you knew how to listen."

Ariel tried to look at the bees; tried to regard them as a

coherent entity, a friend; but he found it was too difficult, so his gaze returned to the elk. "What shall I do?"

"There is nothing you can do," said the elk.

The bees swirled, a buzzing interjection. Ariel watched as representatives landed on the elk's snout and waggled their bodies. The elk watched them, his eyes nearly crossed.

"I see," said the elk to himself, or the bees, or both. "Yes, perhaps."

His gaze lengthened, returned to the brothers.

"The bees say you should seek Lord Mankeeper."

Ariel had never heard of this lord, or any other.

"The bees know him," said the elk. "I do not. They say he is wise, and kind, and powerful. They say he battles evil wizards, on behalf of good creatures."

Ariel heard Kay's sharp intake of breath. "And this lord will help us?" asked his brother.

The bees whirled around the elk's head, a crown of thought. "Assuredly," the elk reported.

"Then we will seek him," Ariel said. "Where does he reside?"

The bees danced, and the elk translated: "His home is the Mortal Fortress, in the nearby bog. The bees go there in the spring, when the myrtle blooms. Their honey at that time is . . . potent."

"I have never been to the bog," said Ariel.

"How far is it?" asked Kay.

"For the bees, an hour's flight. For me, a morning's walk. For you . . . longer." The bees waggled. "But they assure you it is an easy path, if you follow the scent of the holly tree."

"Our senses are not so fine," murmured Ariel.

"Then the path will be more difficult," the elk said simply.

"Can you guide us?" asked Kay.

"The bees would say yes," sighed the elk. "And that is why I am in charge. Your wizard's rangers are abroad, all of them at once. I must retreat to the high slopes." The bees danced; the elk snorted. "They are calling me cruel. Often I carry the burden of declining, so they can remain kind. We all wish you well."

The elk turned and walked into the trees. The bees swirled around his antlers, and Ariel wondered if they were shouting goodbye.

My mind reeled at the implications of elk-bee politics. There, I thought, was a template for my partnership with the boy. Ariel was not as sturdy as the elk; I was not as useful as the bees. Not yet.

Kay turned to Ariel. "We will seek out Lord Mankeeper, in his Mortal Fortress. I do not know anything about a bog, but if anyone can find it, it is you."

Ariel nodded. The taste of the honey was still on his lips.

"Our friends await us in the tavern," said Kay. "We'll tell them we have found an ally—a wizard-beater!"

THE COMMITTEE TO CONFOUND
THE WIZARD

November 2, 13777

The brothers lingered at the forest's edge, cautious about the moonlight that flooded the village. The sky had cleared, and the wizard's rangers patrolled lazily; Ariel watched them wander along the street, peeking behind houses, whispering to each other. Coarse laughter bubbled in the night.

"They were still in the castle when I departed," said Kay.

Ariel's gaze scanned across the far side of the valley, and above, into the blotchy sky, where something had taken a bite out of the moon.

"Kay, look," he whispered. The bite was growing larger.

"It is the magic of Lord Mankeeper!" his brother said, much too loud. "Already, he aids us."

Ariel did not think that was the case—he had seen many

lunar eclipses, and Betelgauze had explained their natural mechanism—but he only nodded.

Slowly, as the hour crept on, Earth's shadow covered the moon. In the days before the dragons, eclipses left a reddish disk in the sky; now the moon disappeared entirely behind the veil of dust. Its lamp was doused, and Sauvage was dark.

The brothers circled the village's perimeter, then crept through a field of squash, obscured from view by the wizard's own wheat.

The tavern door opened at their approach. From within, a harp sounded, running in a quick arpeggio that clearly said: Get in here!

The brothers dashed inside, and the door closed behind them. For a moment they were in darkness; then a lantern rose to its lowest setting.

Inside, Jesse the bard guarded the door. Peering out the window stood Elise. Also present was Madame Betelgauze, along with the squires Gal and Percy, the latter wearing a bright bruise across his cheek. Regret Minimization was laid across a table.

... *melt this wizard's bones*, the sword was hissing.

"It speaks!" Percy reported.

"It will not stop," added Gal. He lifted the sword, turned it in his grip. "It is very annoying, but very light."

"I took it from a tomb," Ariel said. "In a cave, up against the glacier. There was a princess. Dead!"

Altissa Praxa would snort at being called a princess.

"What is happening?" asked Kay.

"Everyone is commanded to stay indoors," said Percy. "The

rangers patrol the village. The knights . . . I think they are sleeping."

Madame Betelgauze spoke. "These are minor events. The moon is gone—plans are all askew. In the past, I would have called it a poor omen . . . but on a night such as this, it tells us the wizard is confounded!"

"Then we should join the fun," said Jesse. "I call to order the first and only meeting of the Committee to Confound the Wizard."

Ariel looked around. "You would all aid me?"

"In whatever way we can," said Gal. "Though I'm not sure what can be done."

Percy frowned. "Our swords are useless. The wizard put us all to sleep!"

"Madame," said Ariel, "have you heard of Lord Mankeeper?"

Betelgauze paused. "No," she said. "I do not think so. Who is he? Where have you heard stories, if not from me?"

Ariel began to tell them, but because he was a terrible storyteller, he got hung up on the taste of honey, so Kay took over and revealed what they'd learned.

"If this Lord Mankeeper can help us," said Elise, "then you must find him. You must leave Sauvage!"

It was a simple statement, but it sucked the air out of the tavern. The puzzle of the proposition was clear on every face. What did anyone in that room know about leaving Sauvage? Nothing. Beyond the valley, Ariel's map faded to default gray.

It wasn't only that they had never left the valley; they had never heard of *anyone* leaving the valley. They had never heard of anyone *thinking* about leaving the valley.

The exception was the wizard, who came and went freely in his airplane. But even before his malevolent turn, Malory had seemed . . . exceptional.

Stay and fight, said the sword. *I was made to fight. I can help you fight!*

"Where is this bog?" wondered Gal.

"South—where else?" said Kay. "North is the glacier. East and west, the mountains only rise."

It was a neat box; a cage. Still, they did not quite see it. Why didn't they see it?

"That is the way, then," said Gal. "South, along the stream."

"It will be guarded," said Percy. "And not only by the rangers. The wizard has made a monster. Elver Sargasso saw it emerge from the tower—a giant."

"Elver Sargasso sees giants most nights," said Gal.

"Monster or not, we must try," said Kay.

"Stop!" cried Betelgauze. "Do you think you can simply walk out of Sauvage?" She stomped to the back of the tavern and returned in stony silence, carrying one of the village's two precious decks of playing cards. Her eyes closed, she shuffled, muttered an invocation, and shuffled some more. She placed the deck on a table and commanded Ariel to cut. With agonizing slowness, she drew a card: the eight of cauldrons.

"Oh, good," said Betelgauze brightly. "Yes, you can simply walk out of Sauvage."

"The wizard might have something to say about that," said Jesse. "I don't know how you'll get past the castle, if his rangers are patrolling." The bard peeked out the window. "And perhaps his monster."

The wizard believes you are trapped here with him, hissed

Regret Minimization. *But the wizard is wrong.* He *is trapped here with* you.

Madame Betelgauze eyed the sword dubiously, then approached Ariel. "My pupil," she said. "Has it rained tonight?"

It had.

"The air is still, I have noticed."

It was.

"Which part of the night is coldest?"

The part just before dawn, he knew.

"So . . . what will the morning bring?"

"Fog!" said Ariel.

"It has been a long, cold night, and its chill shall be your cloak. If that is not enough, then nothing would have been enough. The invisible planets set this in motion." She made a gesture, the opening of her third eye. "I believe it is an opportunity. We have learned the truth of our situation."

"We have learned Sauvage is a prison," said Gal.

"We have learned the wizard is a tyrant!" said Percy.

"There is more," said Jesse suddenly. "This past summer, one night, very late, I spied . . . I was scrounging a snack, you see. In the bailey, I spied a conference, between the wizard and a man clad all in stripes. The man in stripes asked, Is the boy ready? And the wizard said, Nearly so."

"And you did not speak of this!" Elise cried.

"I thought I was dreaming!" said Jesse. "A door opened in the air—a door to a bright plain; burning bright—and the man in stripes stepped through. The wind whipped around the door, and raised a cloud of dust in the bailey. I fled, and didn't think of it again, for I'd had a measure of beer—a long measure—and I was afraid of the wizard. With good reason!"

"Ariel might have left already, if you'd told us," said Elise. "We all might have left."

"It is not too late," said Kay valiantly. "In the fog, we'll follow the stream, all of us together. We'll find Lord Mankeeper in his Mortal Fortress."

Madame Betelgauze clucked. "It is Ariel who the wizard hunts. Will a band of rabble—yes, we are rabble—make your brother more elusive? Of course not. Kay, you will go. The rest of us will remain here."

Jesse nodded decisively, and he announced: "The Committee to Confound the Wizard is resolved!"

Their path would take them along the stream. There was no avoiding the castle, which guarded the valley's mouth. Morning would soon arrive. It seemed to Ariel that they did not have enough time—to think, or plan, or prepare. Or say goodbye.

The tavern door opened, and Master Heck entered, the hound Yuzu at his side. Sensing the tavern full of stress, she whined.

"I've brought some things," said Heck.

From a vast sack, he extracted Kay's bow and quiver. The boy whooped. Then two small knives, one for each brother; a ball of twine; a portable heater, its battery charged, good for a whole night.

The hound keeper dug in the sack. "I made these big, so you'll grow into them. In the meantime, they will serve as blankets, too." He presented the brothers each with a leather jacket. They smelled of fresh-tanned mycelium.

Kay sighed in awe.

"They are wonderful," Ariel said.

There would be no hug from Master Heck, no great declaration. The hound keeper showed his love by making things.

The jackets were sturdy, still a bit stiff, full of clever pockets. Kay's was lined with silky fuzz harvested by Madame Betelgauze from abandoned cocoons, but Ariel's was unlined, for Heck knew the boy always ran a little hot.

Ariel slipped into his jacket, clearly the work of many weeks. In the innermost pocket, he felt a familiar shape: the Stromatolite. It was his turn to whoop.

Jesse raided the tavern's pantry and the brothers stuffed their pockets, accepting crusty bread, goat cheese, and wild apples.

"The fog is rising," said Madame Betelgauze. "Come here, my pupil." Ariel bent to her level, happy to obey, and she took his face in her hands. "My sweet pupil." Bright shone the eyes of Betelgauze, as she spoke in a whisper: "Remember what we saw in the sky. Things once impossible are now possible. Go!"

THROUGH THE NECK

November 2, 13777

The village was transformed. The houses were invisible in the fog. The lights of the castle made a hazy glow. From that direction, a baying howl rose. Ariel knew it well.

"I do not fear Cabal," whispered Kay. "Only his master."

The brothers crept toward the stream. After a dozen paces, Ariel looked back, but the tavern was only a shadow. There would be no last goodbye.

Kay did not run, but moved with quick confidence. They passed the churchyard, where stone and anvil sat, a dark blot.

The howl sounded again in the fog.

They skulked close to the reeds. The only sound came from the stream, which was well practiced at escape from Sauvage. The water sang its encouragement.

They came to the narrowest part of their path, where the

wizard's airstrip lay between stream and castle. Ariel felt that, when they crossed, the wizard would feel it somehow—as surely as if they'd stepped on his toe.

Cross they did. The crunch of each step across the frosted grass sounded to Ariel like a crack of thunder. Nothing stirred.

Kay walked faster now. His face was drawn, which was dreadful: Kay was never anxious. The brothers continued, and the shadow of the castle receded behind them.

The sky glowed. The light of morning always came late to the steep valley; and it came now.

The valley's neck pinched tight, barely wider than the stream. The same boulders that dotted the valley floor—boulders like the one in the churchyard—had piled up here, and been worn smooth by the water's flow. The stream ran fast, frothing and churning through the narrowing chute.

The path grew more treacherous. The brothers scrambled and slipped around the rocks, grabbed exposed tree roots to steady themselves.

The fog, compounded with the uncertainty beyond the valley, made Ariel feel as if they were venturing out of reality itself. As if the world would yield, like the map in the Stromatolite, to default gray. His well-established fear of the wizard now competed against a rising fear of the void ahead.

"Why have we never gone this way?" Kay wondered aloud. Ariel, who had ranged so widely, explored so much, could not answer him.

The howl sounded again. It was ahead of them.

Kay froze.

The figure that strode out of the fog was not a dog, but rather a powerfully built man with the head of a dog; or maybe he was a powerfully built dog with the body of a man. He stood upright, and his head was Cabal's, his face Cabal's, his expression Cabal's, as malevolent as ever.

Kay nocked an arrow and let it fly. Cabal batted it out of the air. Kay shot another and another; Cabal batted the first, and allowed the second to thump into his belly. Without a glance, he plucked it out and cast it aside.

Command me, hissed Regret Minimization from the scabbard at Kay's side. *Command me!* Like a fork across the bottom of a dirty pan.

From behind them, up on the castle's ramparts, the Wizard Malory's voice boomed through the fog. "Ariel de la Sauvage," he bellowed with uncanny volume, "we might have ended this story in peace. With sleep."

Cabal strode toward the brothers. Angry seams showed all over his body: at his joints, around his neck. He did not snarl or bark; only showed a violent boredom.

I can only help if you command me! the sword rasped.

"Then I command you!" Kay cried.

From the sword's munitions port, two missiles dropped, each no larger than a grain of rice. Each ignited its little engine with a pop, and together they rose, spiraling, as aimless as a pair of courting butterflies.

Just as it seemed the missiles might simply disappear into the fog, their engines flared violet and they zipped apart, each drawn as if magnetized to their targets.

The detonations that followed tore a hole in the world, rupturing rock, banishing fog. The wizard's voice was lost in the double thunderclap. Ariel and Kay were lifted off their feet, hurled onto the turf.

Fog dispelled, Ariel could see clearly the ruin where Cabal had stood. The narrow neck of the valley was caved in, and the stream churned and fumed against a stopper of rock.

Ariel had never experienced or even imagined such destructive power. Cabal was gone: obliterated, or buried, or flung. What had happened to the wizard, Ariel did not know—but Malory spoke no more.

Kay probed the fallen boulders, groped for passage. He found a gap, but his body wouldn't fit. "You try," he said. Ariel did so, doubtfully; the boulders pinched him tight, and he would not fit, except that his brother planted both hands on his butt and pushed him, hard. The shoulders of his jacket scraped against rock—bare skin would have been torn bloody—and he was through.

Ariel whirled to find his brother peering through the gap in the rocks.

"You can fit, too!" Ariel cried. "I will pull you!"

"I will not fit," Kay said. "And we are lucky that it is you on that side, for you are the better woodsman between us. You have your task! Find this Lord Mankeeper. Tell him there is a wizard run amok. Bring him here!"

"What will you do?" Ariel asked.

"I will return to Gal and Percy, and we will go into the forest—we'll find one of your hidey-holes." Kay's eyes flashed. "We will put our training to some use, at last. Don't worry about the wizard's spells—we will plug our ears until you return."

"I will not be long!" Ariel said.

From the direction of the castle, horns sounded.

"Here," Kay said, "take the sword." He pushed it through the gap.

No! moaned the sword. *I want to stay and fight. My last missile can bring down the castle. Command me!*

"No," Kay said firmly. "You will go with Ariel."

Ariel accepted Regret Minimization, feeling despondent. "I'm sorry. I should have taken the sword in the stone instead."

Kay looked at him oddly. "That sword was stuck fast. I have tried to pull it many times. Ariel . . . I feel as if I've woken from a dream. Don't you?"

He reached an arm through the gap to clasp Ariel's, then turned and dashed back the way they'd come. "We will be safe in the forest," he called, "but I will be happier to have Lord Mankeeper beside us! Bring him, whoever he is!"

"What if I cannot find his fortress?" Ariel called back, very nearly whining.

"You will find someone!" Kay said. "Do you think this is the only village in the world?"

It was only rhetorical, intended as encouragement, but as Kay disappeared, bounding back toward the danger of the castle, his question hung in the fog.

SPOILER

November 2, 13777

The sky lightened, revealing a new world.

The forest was very dense, and different from the steep slopes around Sauvage. Broad-leafed giants mixed with the pines. Exiting the valley, the stream widened and slowed, coursing around the trunks of trees. Where it pooled and stilled, the water was filmed with ice.

As Ariel trudged, he considered his decision—turned it over and over in his mind. He imagined how events might have unfolded if he had taken the sword from the stone. With Kay's help, he might have expelled the wizard, taken the throne, brought stability to Sauvage . . . He might have been the king, and a good one . . .

He could not go back. No way could he go back. But he was still desperately attached to the story for which he had been created. He spun around, suddenly intending to return; a dozen steps later, he spun again and resumed his course. He was going in literal circles, while behind us, the wizard rallied his hunt.

So I committed one of the Anth's cardinal sins.

I spoiled it.

Alongside the wide, shallow stream, as the morning rose around him, I told the boy about Arthur, son of Uther, who was fostered by Ector, who drew Excalibur from the stone to become king of an ancient place called England. I told him about Arthur's marriage to Guinevere, and the founding of the Round Table at Camelot.

I told him about Lancelot, most talented of all the knights, who became Arthur's greatest friend.

About Pellinore, who sought the Questing Beast and tamed it, becoming captain of the Quest Riders.

And Gawain, richest of the knights, who caroused in court by day, but, when the sky darkened, donned a suit of armor and became the vigilante Green Knight.

These are just the versions of the stories I've heard.

The stream broadened into a river, nourished by other streams from other valleys, and it became more difficult to find a dry path through the mire. The boy ventured across sheets of shallow water. The mud sucked at his shoes. Between wild-branched oaks, the sky was ruddy pink.

I told the boy how it ended: with the cruel enchantments of Morgan le Fay, and Guinevere's doomed romance with Lancelot.

"With *Lancelot?*" he said. "I thought they were friends!"

I told him about the last battle against Mordred, who used a gauntlet set with magic stones.

And I told him, at last, about Arthur floating away to Avalon.

The boy was quiet.

"Well," he said, "I suppose I don't have to do all that now."

No, he didn't. He could do something else.

The river broke into a maze of channels that coursed through stands of reeds dark with melting frost.

Enormous dragonflies, their wingspans wider than Ariel's own, zipped above the reeds, glittering in gemstone colors. One of them hovered close—too close—and paused to consider the boy's suitability as a snack. Too much trouble, the dragonfly decided, and zipped away.

On a hump of ground sheltered by a ring of reeds, the boy sat to eat a heel of bread. The wet ground didn't bother him much; he was accustomed to the chill of the forest.

Your enemy pursues us, growled Regret Minimization.

"How do you know?"

You should always assume you are pursued.

Ariel trudged on land where he could find it, splashed through water where he could not. Growing weary, he found another hillock and lay down beside a stand of reeds. His breath clouded in the air.

"I was not ready for everything to change," Ariel said.

I felt his melancholy: the carelessness of his days snatched away. It felt random and unfair. But if none of this had happened, he would have pulled the sword from the stone, and it would have been his ruin. I was certain of that.

He had begun a new story.

"What story?" said Ariel. "I am lost in a swamp."

When you say "What story?" to a chronicler, you ought to know you are asking for it. Ariel trudged onward, and I told him the whole history of Earth.

Rocky spheroid develops taste for life (soup, lighting). Pale purple dot. A billion boring years. Oxygen revolution. A really great party, crashed by an asteroid. Disaster.

Early humans. Clever tools. Friendly wolves.

Later humans. Burning bushes. Thinking rocks.

Disaster.

The Anth. Insane at first, the way a sleeper is insane, for just a moment, after waking. Then: up and out.

Half the planet reserved for the rhinoceros, the anchovy, the Joshua tree. Magnificent.

My subjects, before Altissa: brilliant Peter Leadenhall, charismatic Kate Belcalis, cool Travanian. People who blazed with curiosity and intention. People who got it done.

The dragons.

Their bodies: chimerical, monstrous, beautiful. They made a TV show about them, before they got zapped into the fifth state of matter. Everybody had a favorite dragon.

No favorites, really, when they came back insane.

I told Ariel he carried the sword of Altissa Praxa, who was one of the operators, the greatest warriors in history; who captained the Death-or-Glory Toads aboard the assault ship *Lascaux*; who dueled one of Dragon Matador's avatars, a Blade-type, in a ruined plaza in Sicily.

The monster was as tall as a house. While Regret Minimization launched missiles in tight fusillades, Altissa slid beneath her opponent's guard and cut its guts out.

No one else ever beat a Blade-type, whispered Regret Minimization. *Not alone.*

Ariel was part of something profound. It did not matter if he did not understand his inheritance, or even if he did not like it. It was his.

"Oh," he said.

The tug of the sword in the stone receded. My work was not done, but it was begun.

MX. BEAVER'S BOG

November 2, 13777

The landscape undulated gently, shallow rises topped with tall grass dipping into wet divots full of sodden moss that yielded beneath his feet. Ariel bounced on it.

A pale gray moth wheeled overhead, high up. Dragonflies patrolled the water. An iridescent newt stalked the boy for a while, then turned back.

Ariel proceeded cautiously. Firm ground became scarcer, open water broader. Many times, a ribbon of ground terminated unexpectedly, forcing him to hike all the way back and choose a different path.

Meanwhile, the sun was racing down in the sky.

He sat on a fallen tree, his pride deflated. Skills honed in the forest heights did him no good here. He ate a lump of cheese and moped.

Then Ariel heard a sound—something out of place. His heart thudded, banged in his ears. He felt exposed, out on unfamiliar terrain.

Someone was singing, and that someone was growing closer. The song went:

> *Go down home, Jenny Moss,*
> *to the deep dark depths of the bog.*
> *Go down home, Jenny Moss,*
> *pack a suitcase full of logs. Oh,*
> *go down home, Jenny Moss,*
> *and why not take a tree?*
> *For you shall rest in peace until*
> *we rise in victory.*

Ariel located the singer: floating lazily through the water, snout pointed skyward, a beaver. He knew them from the Stromatolite. In the game, beavers were stationed at remote locations. Often they sold you potions.

Paddling slowly, the beaver sang:

> *Go down home, Jenny Moss,*
> *to the deep dark depths of the bog.*
> *Go down home, Jenny Moss,*
> *and why not take some frogs, too?*
> *Go down home, Jenny Moss,*
> *with carbon buried long,*
> *for you shall rest in peace until*
> *I finish this here song.*

The beaver was about to begin again when Ariel called out: "Hello!" The creature squeaked in surprise, and disappeared into the water.

A moment later, the beaver appeared again beside him, leapt onto the moss, and stood upright. Ariel admired the pack strapped tight around the creature's belly, waterproof.

"Hello, Mx. Beaver," he said, using the form of address he recalled from the Stromatolite. "I am sorry if I startled you."

"Not at all," the beaver chirped. "It's a pleasure to encounter a new face. I am Humboldt." The creature extended a webbed hand, and Ariel took it.

"My name is Ariel." He paused. "Ariel de la Sauvage."

The beaver Humboldt regarded him. "If I might ask, out of curiosity, both professional and personal . . . what are you?"

"As I said, I am Ariel, of the Castle and Forest Sauvage. I am fleeing the Wizard Malory, who has gone mad."

"Malory? Never heard of him. I once met a Wizard Keaton. Nice fellow. Well, not actually nice. But he was a fellow." Humboldt blinked. "I mean, what *are* you?"

Ariel was confused. He did not usually have to explain this. "I am a human."

"I have never met a human so small."

"I am a boy."

The beaver squeaked a laugh. "Ha! Boys have been extinct for thousands of years. And besides, they lived in water, like tadpoles."

"They did not!" Ariel protested. "I mean—they do not!"

"Oh, I'm fairly certain they did. But I'm no expert. Perhaps there is new scholarship . . ."

"I do not live in water. I cannot even swim! Mx. Beaver—Humboldt—I am lost. I cannot find my way through this foul swamp."

"Foul!" squeaked Humboldt. "Swamp! It is no swamp. A swamp is a low-lying wetland fed by an external inflow, generally inundated, often dominated by trees. This is a *bog*! Its water source is primarily rainwater, which results in a highly acidic and mineral-poor environment."

Eleven thousand years, and the beavers had grown didactic.

Humboldt was not finished. "Foul? It won an award! Foul! It runs like clockwork." The beaver was sputtering.

"I am sorry," said Ariel quickly. "I did not realize. Which award?"

"Just last quarter, the regional office named it the Most Improved Bog," Humboldt declared. "And it is hardly impassable, if you have eyes to see the signs I have placed. They are everywhere! Where are you bound?"

"I am seeking Lord Mankeeper, who lives in the Mortal Fortress."

"Look around!" Humbold squeaked. "You have found it."

Ariel peered around.

"Here," the beaver said, "I'll show you. It's fascinating."

Ariel followed Humboldt across the trembling bog. The beaver never hesitated, leaping boldly, letting the bog sink low beneath him. Ariel stepped more gingerly, sometimes fearfully—but the path was sound.

"Here! You see?" said Humboldt. Before them, a track of ferrous metal rose out of the water. It was corroded so dark and scabrous that it ran, in places, to purple and black. Tendrils of rust spooled into the water.

"Here is the Mortal Fortress, one of its uppermost ramparts. The remainder lies beneath you—the fortress was my bog's cradle."

Ariel peered around with fresh eyes. The bog stretched into the misty distance. This was a fortress beyond imagination; or, it had been.

"I am sorry if you are disappointed," Humboldt said. "The fortress has been drowned for nearly a thousand years. Here, in the air, it is corroding—this wall won't last much longer—but, down below, nothing changes. That is the function of the bog."

"The bees misled me," Ariel said. "They said this was the place I would find Lord Mankeeper . . ."

"They did not mislead you," said the beaver. "Mankeeper resides here. I know him!"

Ariel looked around. "Is the lord not drowned . . . with his fortress?"

"He's a strange lord. I'll take you to him."

They marched through the bog, Humboldt taking decisive turns, sometimes seeming to stride onto open water, only to be supported by dense moss hidden just below the surface—a magic trick. Ariel followed as closely as he could.

Humboldt stopped, nose twitching. Two webbed hands upon the water: listening to the moss tremble. "Others have come to the bog," the beaver said. "Are you pursued?"

Ariel nodded.

"It will be slow going for them—ah! One of their number has just fallen in. Even so, we will increase our pace."

Ahead, the bleak pattern of the bog was broken by the rise of a dark silhouette: a tall, billowing tree beside a squat, lightless structure. It was desolate and grim. It was forlorn and obscure.

It was the last remnant of the Mortal Fortress.

LORD MANKEEPER

November 2, 13777, to November 3, 13777

From the mounds of moss rose a small island around a stubby tower, fashioned from the same ferrous metal as the wall Ariel had seen earlier, streaked and pitted with rust.

On the island, a single holly tree grew, overtopping the tower. Its bark was smooth and pale; if the pines were straight spears, and the oaks grasping knuckles, the holly tree boiled like a cloud. Its leaves were dark and thick and sharply serrated, and everywhere hung clusters of berries, brilliant red, untouched.

The billowing tree shadowed a narrow portal, mostly concealing it. Ducking to avoid the spiky leaves, Ariel followed the beaver through, realizing as he did that the portal was not a door, but a window. With a vertiginous reckoning, he understood this was not the ground floor of a very modest tower, but the uppermost floor of a very tall one—the tallest of the Mortal Fortress, and the only one that remained above the level of the bog.

The ferrous rot gave the structure the smell of iron, which was, of course, also the smell of blood.

Inside, the upper terminus of a flooded stairway was just a pool of water. Ariel spied the shadow of the highest steps; they spiraled into the tannic dark.

Lying on the floor beside the pool, curled as if in sleep, was a corpse.

Or, not only a corpse, but a bog body, of the kind so often discovered by the Anth in places like this. The bog's frigid water, starved of oxygen, had stopped all the processes of decay. Rich with acid, it had tanned the corpse's every molecule utterly black, and the molecules of his clothing, too.

That clothing was fantastic: a tunic with embroidered edges (all black) above soft, supple boots (also black), and around his shoulders a cape with a high collar embroidered with lions rampant (black, black, black).

His crown, a thin circlet, was black.

The bog body's eyes were closed, gently, as if in sleep. His expression was peaceful, though there was—you couldn't miss it—a deep incision across his neck. If blood had flowed from that wound, it was all emptied now, and washed clean.

The corpse of Lord Mankeeper had the look of all the bog bodies: uncanny calm.

Here was the help Ariel had sought.

His disappointment was crushing.

From the bog body, a voice came. "The bees sent you, I bet."

The body had not moved. His eyes were still closed. Nothing had changed.

The voice came again. "If you ask the bees, everything just happened yesterday, or it's about to happen. Their memories are long, but they have no order." The voice paused. "Don't ever listen to the bees."

The voice seemed to emanate from the bog body, but the bog body did not even twitch. His epochal stillness did not match the jocularity of the voice.

Ariel frowned at Humboldt. "Is this a trick?"

"Yes," supplied the bog body, before the beaver could reply. "And a delicate one. A stiff breeze would blow it away."

"I believe it is an old technology," offered Humboldt, "though no one in my office has been able to identify its mechanism. He has been well preserved by the bog, as you can see."

Ariel faced the bog body. "You are right," he said. "The bees did send me. Are you Lord Mankeeper?"

"I am no longer lord of anything, but I am Mankeeper, as you were promised. Except for the small matter of my death, a thousand years ago. Oh, I miss the bees . . . They do not visit in winter."

Ariel sighed raggedly. "They told me you presided over a great fortress. They said you were the worst enemy of the wizards . . ."

"That was true, long ago." Mankeeper said this matter-of-factly, without wistfulness. "You've come too late."

Ariel digested this. First Altissa Praxa in her glacial tomb. Now this lapsed lord in his rusty crannog. Behind every door, he found only death.

The bog body, Mankeeper, spoke. "Is he human, Humboldt?"

The beaver said he was, though an ostentatiously small one, who did not appear to live in water.

"Will you read his wizard's mark for me?"

The beaver padded closer to Ariel and peered at his face. "I am not an expert in their script. I think it is . . . Miller? Mueller. Molar?"

"If it is a wizard's mark, then it is Malory," said Ariel glumly. "I did not know I wore his name."

"Malory!" repeated Mankeeper. "He visited me, years ago. Bent over backwards to be polite—so slippery that I knew he was up to no good. What mischief has he achieved?"

Ariel told him about Sauvage and the wizard's madness. The bog body's lidded eyes gave an impression of deep listening. More than an impression. Mankeeper was quiet as the boy told his story: badly, missing important details, dwelling on the danger that remained to Kay and the rest in Sauvage, with the wizard's true nature revealed.

When Ariel finished, Mankeeper said: "I know something about mad wizards. Do you see it? Come closer."

Ariel did not want to come closer.

"Oh, come on. It's interesting."

Up close, the bog body's skin was as smooth as polished stone, and on his cheeks, each short whisker was not only intact, but somehow isolated and amplified. Mankeeper seemed to be all details.

Across his throat, there was the wound, and Ariel saw that the wound split a mark, silvery against black skin. It looked like this:

"That is the mark of the Wizard Omnivore," said Mankeeper. "Do you know the name? No? He was a bad one. The wizards in my day did not pretend to be polite. They made monsters, commanded them with vast vocabularies of power. That was the reason for my Mortal Fortress. We fought them!"

Ariel felt a pang. Martial imagination gave Mankeeper's cape its color again. The boy's brain fizzed with pleasure and he saw himself fighting alongside the lions rampant. He saw Mankeeper falling in battle; saw himself taking the lord's place . . .

"It must have been difficult," Ariel said, although what he wanted to say was, It must have been awesome.

Regret Minimization could not be contained. It clanged: *Tell us of your victories!*

"Who is that?" said Mankeeper.

Ariel introduced the sword.

"And it talks," said the bog body. "How droll."

"Tell us," urged Ariel.

"My victories were stupid!" exclaimed Mankeeper. "Who wants to kill a thing with bears for hands? You think I mean he had hands like a bear's. No. Each hand *was a bear.* Bears for hands. But kill him I did, and said to myself, What bad luck, Mankeeper, to be born into such an ugly age."

"But you fought great battles. The bees remember you . . ."

The bog body laughed—a bubbling eruption. "Famous to the bees! I'd rather be anonymous and alive. What luck you have."

This statement seemed so wrong as to be cruel. "How am I

lucky?" Ariel cried. "I have left behind everyone I know. A wizard pursues me!"

"Malory is a throwback, I'll give you that. These days, the wizards are tame, some even friendly. Wonderful things await, in the world beyond this bog. Don't judge your fortune until you've mapped it more completely."

"I do not know anything about the world," Ariel conceded.

"I'm not exactly in the thick of it, but travelers pause to share their stories, just as you have. The stories have changed. These days, there's invention and enjoyment. The world is at peace."

"Peace?" Humboldt squeaked. "I would not say that!"

"Oh, my friend, I remember your war in the clouds," said Mankeeper, "and I don't mean to diminish it. But you must recognize the way other creatures live. Have you walked the great road, Humboldt?"

"Of course."

"There wasn't anything like that road when I was alive. Every time you journeyed outside a fortress, you took your life in your hands."

"What road is this?" Ariel asked.

Humboldt said, "Mankeeper speaks of the Rath-road, which links the human cities. It is very busy."

"We must get this boy to the road, Humboldt," said the bog body. "Don't you think so? Set him walking. He'll disappear into the scrum, and if he wants to come back in a year, with a clutch of brawlers to pry Malory out of his nook, well, that's fine." He paused, then said: "You might also decide to put this place behind you, and never think of it again. That's certainly what I'd recommend."

"I cannot abandon my brother," Ariel said grimly. "He remains in the wizard's domain. I am worried about him."

"Ah! I must now commit a grave offense, in my era or any other. I must provide wisdom." The bog body cleared his throat noisily. "Worry is a form of pride. You think your brother is helpless? Tell me his name. All right. Kay has plans of his own." Mankeeper's voice was rich and urgent; all the stranger for the fact that the bog body never twitched. "I have three words for you—a powerful incantation, learned at great cost. Are you ready?"

Ariel was ready.

"Worry about yourself!"

The Mortal Tower was quiet for a moment.

"It's nighttime, isn't it? I feel the cold," said Mankeeper. "Humboldt, don't hazard the bog in darkness. Stay here. In the morning, take the boy to the wall and point him toward the road. Do you need sustenance? I think you know where to find the mead in my chambers below."

"Yes, I do recall . . ." said Humboldt.

"Go down and bring up a cask."

"It would be my pleasure," said Humboldt eagerly, and splashed into the watery stairway.

Ariel sat quietly, peering at the bog body with its peaceful lidded gaze.

"My lord, if I may ask . . . how do you speak to the bees, if you are blind?"

Mankeeper did not smile; he could not smile; but a smile was in his voice, when he replied, "They dance on my lips, of course."

THE LADY OF THE LAKE

November 3, 13777

Ariel was roused by the beaver's urging; for a moment, he did not remember where he was. He did not remember falling asleep.

"Wake up, Ariel de la Sauvage," Humboldt whispered. "Your wizard has come."

The boy scrambled to his feet. "Malory? Where?"

"He and his rangers approach on the bog. They came much faster than I imagined. They recruited newts to guide them."

Ariel peeked out the tower's portal, and through the screen of dark leaves, he saw a line of figures in the mist, treading slowly toward the island. One figure, bulky with cloak and jacket, was surely Malory.

"Take him through the tower, Humboldt," came the voice of Mankeeper. "You know the way." Ariel turned, to discover that the bog body had found a new pose. Sometime in the night, he had rearranged himself, and now sat cross-legged, calmly facing the portal. His eyes were still closed.

"My tower has defenses, which the wizard surely remembers from his last visit. While he loiters, I will dissemble and extemporize—and even flatter, if I must. Go!"

Ariel peered at the stairway that spiraled down into dark water. "I cannot."

"There is a way out, just below," said Humboldt. "You will only have to hold your breath for a minute. Perhaps not even that. I will guide you."

From outside came the heavy squish of feet—many feet—on wet ground. The wizard and his rangers had arrived at the Mortal Fortress.

"I will try," said Ariel quietly.

Humboldt offered a hand, and Ariel took it. The beaver's fingers were surprisingly long.

"Good luck," said Mankeeper. "Don't stop—not until you've discovered the world."

Humboldt descended and Ariel followed. The water was frigidly cold, but he hardly felt it. His steps were sure on the scabbed metal, down in the cold airless keep where no muck grew.

When his chin was level with the water, he sucked in a great breath, and looked a final time at the bog body. Mankeeper sat guarding the portal, and as Ariel's ears dipped into the water, he heard the rich voice begin a ringing challenge: "WIZARD—!"

. . .

It was utterly dark in the submerged tower, but Humboldt's clever pack provided a lantern, and the beaver now ignited it. The water was crystalline, without scum or sediment. Ariel saw a chamber richly furnished; an enormous bed (black) topped by an embroidered coverlet (black) was hung with curtains (black) that billowed with the disturbance of their entry. A hearth sat ready with wood still piled in it (neat black logs), so serene that Ariel imagined it might still flare to life.

Gripping Ariel's hand tight, Humboldt led the boy out of the chamber, through a long hall. No fish swam here; they could not breathe the water of the bog.

Neither could Ariel, but, to his surprise, and my own, he felt calm. Maybe it was the chill of the water, cooling his nerves. A small sturdy confidence buoyed him. Humboldt was his guide.

Along the hall, tall windows yawned invitations, but when Humboldt waved his lantern across, they revealed only the bulk of sodden, sunken moss.

Paintings were hung on the walls, frames and canvases alike stained black, subjects lost. This sprawling fortress had risen and drowned in the time I was locked in the tomb; it was the far future and the distant past, both at once. Time seemed, for a moment in the dark, not to have a direction.

The beaver came to a window, and pulled Ariel through, grip still firm.

Silvery light shone down from above: a sloping ascent. Ariel clambered out of the window and allowed the force of Humboldt's swimming to pull them both up along a broad hill of moss. He watched the beaver's tail surge powerfully in the clear water.

When they reached the surface, Humboldt rose cautiously

out of the water. Ariel followed. Mankeeper's tower was behind them, obscured by the mist. Ariel heard bellowing; Malory's voice, booming but indistinct.

Go back! cried Regret Minimization. *Go back and fight!* The sword's voice was ragged; it was sick of all this running. Regrets were not being minimized.

"There is something in the water," whispered Humboldt. "We must not stop."

The fool brought himself to us, moaned the sword. *One missile remains. Command me. I will destroy the tower and everyone within!*

"Lord Mankeeper helped us!" cried Ariel.

He is already dead, said the sword. *You are still alive. Command me!*

The beaver danced across the bog. Water sloshed around Ariel's knees, and every step looked equally treacherous. All he could do was stick close to Humboldt: trust the beaver's skill and care.

Skill and care saw them through.

"There!" squeaked Humboldt. A dark mass separated itself from the mist. "That is the wall. Hurry, now!"

The ancient perimeter of the Mortal Fortress ran the whole breadth of the bog. If they reached it, Ariel would not have to worry over every step. He could run, and run, and run, until he reached the road, and safety.

Ahead, he saw a flicker of motion through an open patch of water; a silvery shimmer; a trout? There were fat, flashing trout in the stream that flowed through Sauvage.

The boy peered into the water.

"That is the first fish I have seen here," he said.

"There are no fish in a bog!" cried Humboldt. "Stay back!"

The shimmering form surged forward, breaking the water's surface. It was not a trout, but an arm, with a single heavy bangle glittering below a hand that gripped the abandoned sword Excalibur.

The wizard had prepared more than a sword in a stone; from the same pattern of myth, he had made his Lady of the Lake. Frustrated, he had sent her hunting.

The arm was handsome, tautly muscled, with smooth, silvery skin. If Ariel had obliged to perform in the play prepared for him, this lovely arm would have given him his sword, and, in the end, eased him onto his funeral barge. Now, as the lady rose out of the bog, she revealed that Malory had made the same expedient choice as every visual effects artist throughout the history of the Anth: declining to spend too much time on the things that would be off-camera.

Her body had the gray bulk of an eel, her face the wide smirk of a frog. Dark hair that might have billowed beautifully beneath the water's surface now hung limp over bulging eyes with dark, slashing pupils.

"You did not tell me about her," Ariel croaked.

She was much nicer in the story.

The Lady of the Lake stood between Ariel and the wall, and all around them was treacherous water, and behind was the Wizard Malory, whose bellowing had been joined by cold strobing light as he tested his magic, or technology, or both, against Mankeeper's.

Command me! roared Regret Minimization.

Ariel did, and the sword's final missile dropped as before

from its munitions port; and as before flew spiraling, aimless; as before ignited its engine, aimed for the lady's breast; but where the missiles before produced thunderclaps, this one made a whimpering pop, its fuel spoiled after eleven thousand years.

The lady flicked out her long, froggy tongue and captured the missile as neatly as a mosquito.

So ended the arsenal of the Anth.

The Lady of the Lake leered, and lunged. Time slowed; adrenaline flowed crystal. Excalibur in her hand knew its destination, flew with the heavy certainty of a jumbo jet of the Middle Anth, coming in for a landing. The Lady's bangle bounced on her wrist; beautiful.

When the sword pricked the flesh below Ariel's jaw, it was not the first time one of my subjects had felt such a thing. Many points had kissed Altissa's throat; and edges sought it; and grips tightened around it. Barely enough to trouble her pulse, when she carried Regret Minimization. Even without missiles, it had been weapon enough.

With distressing fidelity, I observed Excalibur levering Ariel's skin cells apart. The wall was right there. The boy had a sword, but he didn't know how to use it.

I taught him.

This was prohibited; not just a little bit prohibited, but the most prohibited. I was surprised it was even possible. Perhaps some safeguard had atrophied in the tomb, like the padlock that rusts in long seasons of rain and eventually falls off.

Get it done.

Do not imagine that the boy became my puppet; that is beyond my capabilities. Rather, I poured Altissa's swordcraft into his body. Her training saturated his reflexes, sent stray sensations sizzling through his nerves. Ariel saw stars, smelled burning leaves.

I was not engineered to marshal memory at this scale or speed. My cellular turbines spun hot. Some burned out. I sucked energy from the boy's blood as fast as I could, but there was a limit, and this was far beyond it. I had never done anything so taxing, so intrusive, so stupid.

But it worked, because the boy had Altissa's swordcraft: the hundred hopeless duels she'd somehow won, the thousands of perfect parries that had earned her, time after time, the chance to try again. In a flash, Ariel knew all the angles.

It didn't take much. He gripped his sword with two hands, beat Excalibur aside, and stabbed the lady in the belly. It was like spearing a potato: bloodless. He did not pause to stare; Altissa would never stare; so Regret Minimization was moving again, crying *ALTISSA! ALTISSA!*, slicing the lady's arm above the bangle, so it fell, the flashing trout of her wrist, and her hand with Excalibur, into the bog.

The Lady of the Lake staggered, and I did, too. I felt the bottom fall out of myself; a firm platform I had taken for granted, swinging free. A trapdoor to nowhere. I had made a terrible mistake. Better to have accepted the boy's fate. Better to have waited. There might have been another subject, in time.

But not one so curious, and morbid, and romantic, and, yes: brave.

Ariel hoisted the sword again. He had Altissa's skill, but not her muscles; he barely had muscles at all. The lady's remaining hand flashed to catch his stroke; the sword sank into her flesh as if into spongy wood half-decomposed, and there, it caught fast.

The lady toppled into the bog, taking Regret Minimization with her.

ALTISSA LIVES! was the final cry of the stupid sword that saved us.

Just ahead, Humboldt stood on the wall, shouting and squeaking. The boy scrambled against the pitted metal and hauled himself up. He said something, but I couldn't hear it. His words were a muffled roar.

Ariel stood, dripping wet, and peered down the wall's length. I couldn't see clearly through his eyes anymore. The sky was blooming, light bleeding into everything. The wall was a highway through the bog. Where would it lead him? What would he find on the road beyond? I was proud of the boy, but more than that, I was bitterly jealous: for I had fresh questions, and he would learn their answers without me.

I knew death; had experienced it many times alongside my subjects. Altissa's had been unusual in its composure. Most of my subjects had simply been surprised. Those wise, powerful people's last moments were not serene contemplations or tragic acceptances, but rather muddy disappointments.

So it was for me: a surprise, and the total letdown of dizzy darkness.

PART TWO

RATH VARIA

THE EIGENGRAU

A beautiful morning in the Eigengrau. Mist on the canal.

The café was quiet, with Peter Leadenhall working at his usual table, his sketchbook at the center of a ring of cups all drained. He looked up; a glance was all I needed. Another espresso for the master mathematician! The portafilter clacked; the steam nozzle whooshed. Had the Anth, in all their art and craft, built anything better than the espresso machine? Possibly they had not.

For as long as I existed, I rode along in the minds of my subjects, and when those subjects were happy at home, tucked into bed, I recorded it, but I did not feel it. Me, I was still working.

So I had the Eigengrau. It was inside of me, and only me. It was an imaginary city, and it was my home, and a safehouse for all my memories.

The bell above the door tinkled, and Kate Belcalis entered

with a quiet greeting. She had run the great cooperativo called Fifty-Second Street and was, in my estimation, one of the three or four most basically competent people who ever lived.

These ambulatory memories are detailed in the way that a character in a book is detailed; no more and no less. Peter could sit there in his blousy shirt, flipping back and forth between pages in his sketchbook, trying to hold a problem in his head, just as he had in life; and that same Peter could have no face. What color were his eyes? Brown, if I'm forced to say. Peter was not his eyes; he was a pattern of behavior, of action and response. He was a shirt and a sketchbook.

"Good morning, Peter," said Kate. She had not known him in life; Kate Belcalis was born a hundred years after Peter's death. Here, their memories had become acquainted.

Over several centuries, I have chronicled four long-lived subjects (not counting Ariel de la Sauvage; not yet), and all of them resided in the Eigengrau.

There was:

- Peter Leadenhall, the mathematician, who perfected the world models that made possible the economy of the Anth
- Travanian, the Last Lawyer, who wrote the law that ended law, opening the way for the *système sensible*
- Kate Belcalis, the cooperativo supremo, who financed the dragons
- Altissa Praxa, the operator, who fought them

Each lived in an apartment, each suiting their taste and memory. Peter's home was airy and luxurious, with tall windows that opened onto the canal. Travanian's was a simulacrum of an ultra-first-class cabin aboard a Frame Cecilia Super-Express, for they had spent their life always in motion. Kate's was an orderly nest, a list always underway. She didn't need to make lists anymore, but why stop? Nothing Kate loved more than a list.

The Eigengrau embraced my subjects, but it was not for them. It was for me. I made it from all my favorite memories of the urban life of the Anth. It wasn't a whole city, just a neighborhood—two rows of shops facing each other across a canal, with cherry trees along its length, always in bloom.

The Eigengrovians who crowded the shops and strolled along the canal were memories of people my subjects had known, smeared by time into bare impressions. Peter's best friend was a warm smudge of camaraderie; Kate's nemesis was a curlicue of bluster. Look at any of them straight on and they would turn to mist.

The ghosts of my subjects were different. They could chat with me, and with each other. They could perform all the spectacular qualities they had possessed in life, and the annoying ones, too. The only thing they could not do was surprise me.

Following Altissa's death, stuck alone in the tomb, I took refuge in the Eigengrau. But it was expensive to operate, in terms of calories; furthermore, its patterns and loops, initially comforting, became stultifying, even maddening. The Eigengrau only underscored the fact that nothing new was happening; nothing new *could* happen. So I folded up my perfect neighborhood and set it aside.

Now I was back. When I woke in my apartment above the café, I felt totally disoriented, my situation a blank. Habit was enough to get me up and out of bed. I washed my face in cold water, looked in the mirror—here in the Eigengrau, I had a body of my own—then dressed for work.

In the days that followed, I reassembled the events of Ariel's flight from Sauvage, and my gamble to save him. I wondered if this was death—what death would be for me. I was surprised at my own equanimity. It helped that the espresso machine was so beautiful.

The days passed easily, every hour golden in its own way. At midday, it precipitated lightly, raindrops sparkling in the rays of a sun never totally obscured by clouds. Above the Eigengrau hung the memory of the sky before the dragons: depthless blue.

I was preparing Kate's cappuccino when she asked, "Who is that wandering along the canal? I've never seen him before."

She said it calmly, but it was a shocking statement. There were no strangers here. This was the deepest definition of the Eigengrau: a realm where everything was known in advance.

I settled her cappuccino into its saucer, placed her tiny spoon just so, then dashed outside to investigate.

A beautiful morning in the Eigengrau. The neighborhood felt tender, like a burned finger.

A figure sat at the edge of the canal, tossing pebbles over the edge. This figure faced away from me. The pebbles made rings in the water. The deep strangeness of an unfamiliar silhouette pulled a tense cloud across the sky.

"Who is that?" I called out. My voice sounded thin.

The figure twisted to look, and a face shone with all the definition of a character you've been reading about for many chapters. There sat Ariel de la Sauvage, real as life, framed by the cherry trees.

"Oh!" he said. "It's you!" He knew me as surely as I knew him, which was unexpected, because how would he know what I looked like in the Eigengrau? Well, it was a place of strange, ambient knowledge; stray facts floated in the mist. Ariel hopped to his feet, clapped his hands clean, and trotted toward me. "So this is how you look."

"It is—no. Not exactly." I smoothed my apron. "Just an idea." It was very awkward to have a body.

"You are taller than I imagined," he said.

My form in the Eigengrau was mysterious. I had not designed my body (the way I had designed everything else) but rather found it waiting for me. Someone involved in my creation, long ago, must have inscribed this preference. Tall people can never shut up about it.

A thought struck me; a grim realization. My subjects came here in death, to reside as memories. Therefore . . .

Ariel grimaced. "I am not dead! I'm sitting in a room right now—I can see it, sort of. There is a candle . . . the wizard told me you were still here."

The boy had been caught! Yet he lived—

"No, I mean the Wizard Hughes. Another wizard. So much has happened! She found you, so I came looking."

He came looking . . . a wave of disbelief rumbled through the Eigengrau like a little earthquake. The neighborhood had not previously been geologically active.

"I came through that door," Ariel said. He pointed to a house. It was one of many facades that weren't much of anything, just diffuse impressions of pleasant habitation; the kind you pass in a comfortable city, feeling glad they are there. Now, under the care of the boy's imagination, it had become a definite residence.

I peered inside. The apartment was empty except for an enormous couch, a monolithic TV screen, and a collection of each and every video game system ever encountered by any of my subjects. Multiple swords hung on multiple walls.

Kate emerged from the café, carrying her cappuccino.

"Who's your friend?" she asked.

Ariel straightened himself. Kate had a quiet, sharp face that made people think she was silently judging them, when she only rarely was. It had been a burden her whole life.

"Kate, this is Ariel de la Sauvage. Ariel, Kate Belcalis. I told you about the Anth. She was one of the very best of them."

Kate squinted at the boy. "You're alive out there, aren't you?"

Ariel said that he was, and Kate grinned. "How exciting! Altissa would want to speak with you. She's off sulking somewhere . . . but she's desperate to know what happened."

I was likewise desperate to know: if the boy was safe, and what he had learned about the world.

The Eigengrau sparkled all around us. Time was selective here; days were composed only from their finest moments. A blur of Eigengrovians had emerged from their studios and were enjoying an aperitivo at tables set up on the sidewalk.

Before, I had come here when I wanted, and left just as easily, returning to the world of my subject's senses. Was that still possible?

Ariel felt my question; it was all a soup in the Eigengrau; and he reached for the door through which he had entered. "This way, I think." I followed, back into his mind, and I understood in an instant how much had happened since the bog. My gamble had succeeded, but it had sent me recoiling into myself, gravely wounded. Ariel had gone on alone. Now the boy had come to coax me back into the world. But why?

In the blink between dreaming and life, he said: "Because I still need your help."

AWAKE IN THE CITY

March 15, 13778

It was morning in Rath Varia, and in the squat beside the river, the poets were stirring.

The city, the squat, the river: Ariel's mind touched all of these things with familiarity. He had been here for months. I felt a wave of shame—that I had abandoned him. Then, worse, the chronicler's sick regret: that I had missed so much!

The boy sat on the floor beside his bed, cross-legged, a pose for meditation. His mind lingered alongside the canal.

"That was a nice place," he murmured.

I was shocked he'd been able to reach the Eigengrau. No living subject had ever trespassed there. Perhaps they had simply never had a reason.

Ariel hopped to his feet. Through the open window, he heard

his neighbor declaiming an aubade to the city below—a daily routine. The boy himself felt happy enough to shout. "I'll show you the city!" he cried, and leapt out the door, into the hall, down the stairs. He lived on the third floor of a large building, mostly but not entirely inhabited by poets.

"And," Ariel said, "I'll introduce you to the Wizard Hughes."

The street was busy, even this early. Ariel set off, confident; he did not know all of the city—Rath Varia unfurled hugely, and whole districts remained mysterious to him—but he knew this part, and he knew the way to the wizard's parlor.

He'd found another wizard.

I gobbled up the scene. The Anth, at their height, had made the sidewalk into their greatest art form: a stroll in Manhattan or Mumbai became a parade of form and style, every outfit an argument, crackling with energy. Here, in Rath Varia, every dimension of human difference was stretched, revealing extremes unknown in the East Village or Bandra West.

Giants strode the sidewalk, taller than any human who ever lived. Alongside them trotted miniature figures, gnome-like. Hair of every hue rose in braids, hung in curtains. Here, a pedestrian with leopard spots; there, a shopkeeper with lizard scales. A hulking figure wore a cropped T-shirt to show off his muscles, bulging beneath skin cloudily translucent. His tendons danced, fully on display.

It was a riot of form, and nothing was off-limits.

And then there was the clothing.

Capes, overalls, billowing frocks; T-shirts, kurtas, puffy

jackets; a three-piece suit—no, four-piece, somehow—tailored to atomic exactitude. All this garb was dyed in bold, pure colors that vibrated against the backdrop of the city, buildings painted pale and warm, doorways set with glittering tiles.

On every Manhattan sidewalk, no matter how resplendent, there had always been garments black and gray, stylish and severe. In this city, Rath Varia, it seemed that all things were permitted—encouraged—except for one, which was dourness.

Ariel himself wore fresh attire: light sturdy shoes, a neat pair of wide-legged trousers, and a T-shirt that said MACONDRAY LANE, which was the name of a band that rehearsed in his building. Ariel found their music overwhelming, but the band members were effusively friendly; they had invited him to join, and when he demurred, pleading that he played no instrument, they insisted that was no problem. He had not been able to escape without a T-shirt, which became his new favorite.

Completing the outfit was his gift from Master Heck, the mycelium leather jacket, which I noticed he now filled out slightly more.

He was growing. I had missed so much.

Ariel joined the crowd surging onto a bridge across the River Variable, which glowed in the morning light. He was alive with city feeling, the pure potential in every angle; he was bursting with happiness and relief, that he had found me again; he felt open and free, and so, when I poked at a memory, they all came tumbling out.

SHAKING LEAVES

November 3, 13777, to November 4, 13777

After escaping the Lady of the Lake, Ariel and Humboldt fled along the ancient wall. The boy was aware of my absence. Since the night I had announced myself, a light had hovered behind his vision, a layer of urgent curiosity burnishing the world; now it was gone, and in its place was anxiety.

The wall had rusted through in many places, leaving watery gaps. These they leapt; even Humboldt had become cautious about the water. Dense gray reeds stood high on both sides of the track. Ariel kept to the center, and when the reeds rustled, he sprinted.

After a while, Humboldt slipped into the water to reconnoiter, and when he was gone too long, Ariel vibrated with worry.

The beaver returned and reported: "There is no sign of the lady or the wizard."

The bog dried out and the reeds thinned into a scrubby meadow. The ancient wall attenuated. Beyond the bog, the ferrous metal had, in ages past, been harvested and hauled away. All that remained was a sunken track through dry grass.

"Here is where I turn back," Humboldt announced. "I cannot leave my post."

Ariel looked at the path ahead through the meadow, digesting the news that he would be traveling it alone.

"Thank you," he said. "I owe you my freedom and my life. I do not know what else to say."

"I wish you the best, Ariel de la Sauvage. Mankeeper is right—there is an enormous world beyond your village. I think you will be successful in it." The beaver pointed a webbed finger toward the hills. "Walk west, and walk quickly. You are not safe until you reach the road."

The meadow rose into low hills, and although the incline was shallow, it tired him out. Gnarled oaks dotted the hillside, casting patchy shadows.

The sun had just touched the horizon when he heard an ominous buzz, far off. It was the same buzz that announced Malory's comings and goings from the castle: and there, above the forest, the wizard's big-bellied airplane appeared. The sight of it, bulbous black against the ruddy sky, the light at the nose flashing out into the evening, was terrible. Ariel watched the airplane spiral, gaining altitude.

He sheltered beneath the shade of an oak. His gaze followed the dirt track back toward the ancient wall and the bog. Beyond, he saw the dark frontier of the forest, and, far in the distance, the gray lip of the glacier, illuminated by the last sliver of day. Had he really come so far?

The airplane began a low pass over the bog. The wizard would not relent. He would hunt him from the sky.

After sleeping beneath the oak, Ariel rose at first light. He crested the hill, felt the contour flatten beneath him. On the other side, the landscape rolled down into a broad forest of aspen trees, tall and straight, close-packed.

The view was astonishing: a uniform carpet of gold, unrolled to the horizon. Ariel had never seen anything like it. I had never seen anything like it. The trees had dropped some of their leaves, but many remained; so there was gold above, and gold below. Everything was gold beneath the dusty pink sky.

Dazzled, he descended.

A faint breeze curled through the forest, and set the leaves shaking. An aspen tree drinks a lot of water, and its leaves are set on flat stalks that shake easily, powering the process of transpiration, drying and cooling the tree.

Travanian learned that once. I can't remember where.

The trees were all around him, and their trembling leaves glittered, shimmered; they made a bright, buzzing light. With the trembling came rustling, the sound of the breeze amplified, roaring white noise, oceanic.

In every direction were more aspens, glittering and whispering. They all looked the same. All he could do was walk.

.   .   .

The passage of time became indistinct. Every step felt the same: Ariel had no sense of progress. There were no hills to summit, no vistas to consider, no paths to choose. He thought about making a map on the Stromatolite, but there were no landmarks. His map would be a changeless field of trees.

If the boy was frustrated, I was on the edge of panic. All of my subjects had lived their lives strapped into a harness of orientation; they were happily tracked, their location to the centimeter known and shared with, at minimum, a dozen other people.

I had never, not once, faced such an unknown landscape. None of my subjects had ever been lost.

The sun descended, and the sky darkened from pink to red. Ariel was miserably hungry. His pockets were empty; what he hadn't eaten, he'd lost in the bog.

A powerful gust of wind rattled the aspens, all their leaves clicking and clattering together, and in the stochastic roar, Ariel heard a word.

The word was: ZHOZM.

A pause. Ariel held his breath. The wind pulsed again, and once more the word swept through the trees: ZHOZM.

The leaves buzzed in his vision. It was like a television of the Middle Anth tuned between channels: if you stared, relaxed your eyes, and waited, you might see anything.

Ariel saw something. A figure, rippling. It stood in the trees, up among the leaves, as if floating. When he looked at it straight on, the figure dissolved. He thought of Madame Betelgauze, and the invisible planets, glimpsed with a sense that was not quite sight. He looked out the tail of his eye. In that way, he caught the figure again, and saw it raise an arm to point, very clearly perpendicular to the direction Ariel had been traveling.

"Is that the way?" he called out. "What are you?"

The wind whooshed through the forest, and a final time, he heard: ZHOZM.

Ariel turned and marched through the mat of golden leaves in the direction the figure had indicated.

Through narrow gaps in the trees, the astonishing sight of something that was not aspen: a glowing path through the forest; a trail of warm light.

Here was Mankeeper's promised highway. Ariel was sharply aware of everything he didn't know: where the road led, or even where it *could* lead, what other places existed beyond the boundaries of his youthful sequestration. But it was the road, which meant safety, Mankeeper said. Any road implied travelers, and destinations. New destinations.

Ariel ran, beckoned by the glow of the unknown.

THE RATH-ROAD

November 4, 13777, to November 17, 13777

The road was paved with fine gravel that glittered beneath powerful lamps set on slender posts, spaced such that each lamp's penumbra fuzzed smoothly into the next. Six of the knights could have marched along without touching shoulders.

Ariel stood in the road's center. Unfortunately, it produced no sense of safety, or even relief; instead, it felt bleak and strange. The boy was accustomed to forests. He had no experience with roads.

He had only to choose a direction. The road offered no clues. There was no sign. There were no other travelers. The lamps faded, in both directions, into the trees.

Ariel did not like arbitrary choices. He always grasped for signs and portents. Stalking the Forest Sauvage, he often found them. Clearings that called to him. Large charismatic rocks. The crack in the glacier that led to Altissa's tomb.

The figure in the buzzing leaves.

He searched for the figure now, but the air was still.

Ariel felt that he could not possibly make a decision. He was exhausted, wrung out. His blood tasted thin, and acidic with stress. He was both hungry and desperately thirsty.

Then everything changed, because Ariel saw someone coming.

The first person Ariel met beyond the boundaries of Sauvage—the first person he met in the real world—was an avatar of Clovis. A lucky encounter, it would turn out; but then, Clovis was everywhere, so perhaps luck was not in short supply.

Clovis was, in all their incarnations, a robot: an assemblage of parts seeming barely to hang together. This form, the first Ariel encountered, looked crude, judged by the standards of the Anth. But the robot had a spark of life, along with a stubbornness, that my makers would have studied eagerly. Here, on this lonely stretch of road, among the aspens, was where Ariel de la Sauvage met Clovis for the first time. An occasion worth remembering.

Clovis raised an arm, a burnished rod, and waggled fingers of vastly different lengths. From the speaker in their belly buzzed a greeting: "Hello!"

"Hello," Ariel croaked, finding his voice scratchy. He hadn't spoken a word all day.

"Is it possible . . . have we *never* met before?" the robot asked, as if that would be the most astonishing thing in the world. "I am Clovis. I am meeting someone new! I am wondering, who are you?"

Ariel said his name, his gaze a bit vague because he wasn't sure where to direct his reply. The robot's voice came from their belly, not their head, which was a minor monstrosity, a whirring array of sensors and lenses.

He settled on a lens, and his questions came out in a tumble. Where did the road lead, and was it safe, as Mankeeper had promised, and was there, in either direction, anything to eat or, especially, drink?

The robot paused. A whirring sound came from their belly.

"You are new to the Rath-road," Clovis said. "I am surprised. I am pleased. I am answering your questions. This is a quiet segment. I am walking to see the trees. I am seeing the trees. You should return to the main road, and the chatram at the junction. That way." The robot lifted a skeletal arm to point. "I passed it an hour ago."

"Where are you bound?" Ariel asked weakly.

"I am not bound. I am walking. Are you not walking?"

"I just started . . . I have fled my home." Ariel felt the tremor in his cheeks that presaged tears; he didn't want to cry in front of the very first person he met. "I don't know what to do."

Clovis made a thoughtful series of clicks. "I always know what to do. I am already doing it. I am walking to the coast, where I will watch the whales." The robot's head spun on their shoulders. "The chatram is that way. The road is for walking. I am walking."

Clovis resumed their pace. Ariel seemed not to have any power in his limbs. He tried to make himself move in the direction they had indicated, but he could not.

The robot rotated their head to peer back; and slowed their

pace; and stopped; and, without turning, reversed their stride to approach Ariel again.

"I am considering," Clovis said lightly. "It is late to be walking alone. I am returning to the chatram. I am asking, will you join me?"

The boy could barely think, but he nodded yes, and began to trudge alongside the robot on the empty road.

The chatram was a wide, low building, warm inside, the main hall dimmed for the night. There was no innkeeper; this inn kept itself. The chatram spoke. A greeting came from everywhere at once, a groan from the foundation, a rattle from the windows.

"Quiet night," the building said softly, the structural equivalent of a whisper. "Plenty of beds to choose from. Pick any you like."

Clovis guided Ariel to a tiny room with a well-made bed where he collapsed without removing his clothes. His whole body sighed in relief. Clovis buzzed something about breakfast, but the boy was already asleep.

In the morning, the chatram woke him, coaxed him into the main hall now crowded with travelers, offered him bitter tea and bland biscuits—he accepted both, then asked for more biscuits, stuffing them into his jacket pockets—before gently but firmly suggesting that it was time to move along. When all its guests had departed, the chatram began a self-cleaning cycle.

Ariel looked for Clovis, but the robot had walked on in the night.

The chatram stood on the main loop of the Rath-road, where glittering gravel ran twice as wide as the smaller artery Ariel had discovered. At this hour, the road surged with traffic in both directions.

Ariel was swept up into the flux of a new world. He saw:

A line of penitents of some religious order, faces hidden behind patterned veils, chanting a high, looping melody.

A band of snub-nosed hyraxes with walking sticks, chatting happily as they hiked along.

A slender man riding a recumbent bicycle of a design that would have confused and thrilled the Anth. The man wove urgently through the traffic, ringing the bell on his bicycle at every opportunity.

A skunk and a terrapin walking together. "We are going to the city to become people!" the skunk announced. The terrapin only looked at Ariel, silent.

Many trucks, long and low, some with tough tires, others with articulated legs, all piled high with cargo, none moving at more than a walking pace. Their pilots ambled beside them, nudging from time to time.

And what was their cargo? Some was covered tight with tarps. Much that was uncovered had the look of garbage; these trucks were bound, it seemed, for some vast dump.

From where was all this trash coming?

When the sun was high in the sky, Ariel found himself gaining on a robot grinding slowly along the Rath-road. Unlike Clovis, this robot was squat, barrel-shaped, rolling on treads.

As he passed, the robot buzzed: "Hello, Ariel de la Sauvage!"

He looked at the rotund robot. "We have not met," said Ariel. "How do you know my name . . . ?"

"I have met you," the robot said. "I am Clovis. In all my forms, everywhere, I am Clovis."

"Where is the form I met?"

"I am walking to the coast. I am nearly there."

"And where are *you* bound?"

"As I said, I am walking to the coast. Oh! You mean this form. I am rolling to Rath Varia. It is a long journey. I have paused for a rest." The robot continued to roll. "I mean that another form has paused. I am waiting. Soon I will meet myself. It is pleasant to walk together."

The boy was fascinated by the robot's plural awareness. The fact that Clovis was in many places at once seemed like a magic trick. In fact, it had not been uncommon among the Anth . . . but they had never managed the trick so gracefully.

"I am looking for a safe place to stay," Ariel said. "Will I find it in the city you speak of?"

"I believe so," said Clovis. "Rath Varia is kind to strangers. Of all the human cities, it is the most open. Walk with me, and we will go together."

So the boy walked, while Clovis, one of many, rolled on. In the evenings, they stopped at chatrams. They were all the same, with the same voice; Ariel came to think of it as the voice of the road. Every morning, the Clovis he had walked with was gone. Every day, he found another, and their walk continued.

No one on the Rath-road failed to greet Clovis, in any form.

In that way, Ariel heard all the accents of the road. "Hail, pilgrim," said a mendicant monk. "Nice to see you, one-of-many," said a trash-hauler. "Roll on, Clovis!" called a giant resting in the shade of a walnut tree.

A giant!

Two weeks later, in the evening, they came within sight of the city. Rath Varia stretched across a tangled riverine nexus. Its walls were painted with warm pastels that glowed beneath the pink sky. At the city's edge, the gravel of the Rath-road met a street paved with a chaotic puzzle of stones. Ariel peered down and saw fragments of mismatched engravings, bits of human and animal forms fused across rough breaks. The street was a carpet of cast-off bricks and tiles, coins and amulets. The texture felt bumpy and interesting beneath his shoes.

Ahead, a food cart was set up, and a small crowd of hungry walkers gathered around it. Ariel smelled something delicious, which I recognized, though he did not, as potstickers. Through an open window, he heard music.

CITY OF TRANSFORMATIONS

November 17, 13777, to February 28, 13778

Rath Varia was a city of transformations!

A vast sprawl of structures screened everywhere by scaffolding; a city permanently under construction. Streets were ripped up, buildings knocked aside to make way for new routes, whole new theories of interconnection. Residents relocated cheerfully. Sometimes they hauled their homes with them. On the evening that he entered the city, Ariel encountered an elegant townhouse being dragged along the riverfront by a raucous team of volunteers, bound for a new address.

The riverfront, which was plural: the River Variable ran wide and slow, a muddy braid that shifted its course constantly. The river drew some small fraction of its volume from the cold stream that rushed through Sauvage: a thread of connection.

City and river flexed and surged together. Neighborhoods were lost in the flow, abandoned without angst, reclaimed when the river shifted again. On the day Ariel arrived, Rath Varia boasted thirty-one bridges. The routes across the city were always changing.

On that first night, after an hour of nervous circling, Ariel approached the food cart, received a portion of potstickers— "with the city's welcome to walkers one and all, sponsored by the guild of trash-pickers"—and asked the vendor, "Where might I find a room?"

"There are places to stay all around you. Choose one."

Ariel gazed up at the apartment blocks, three and four and five stories tall. "In any of these buildings?"

"Maybe not those. This is a popular neighborhood, so close to the Rath-road. Oh, but there's a place around the corner." The vendor gestured. "They tore down half, got distracted. Plenty of rooms unclaimed there, last I heard. Choose one! That's how it works in Rath Varia."

Ariel located the building, unmistakable with half its facade missing, exposing empty rooms—a vertiginous cutaway. He was afraid it might be spooky or derelict inside, but many of the rooms still intact were inhabited, with names stenciled on the doors, plants set out in the hall. On the third floor, an open door brought him into an empty room, bare and dusty, with a tall window that faced the river. He trod a circle in the dust. Was this it? Could it be his, as simple as that? He pulled the door closed. Yes. Apparently so.

Ariel was home.

.   .   .

He slept on the floor with his jacket for a pillow and woke up sore and sneezing. In the hallway, he spied a woman watering her plants, and asked where he might acquire a bed and a broom. A broom the woman was happy to lend; a bed, she said, could be obtained the same place anybody got anything in Rath Varia.

In the city's center was a huge open facility, roughly circular, into which trash flowed: all those trucks he'd seen on the road, and trucks from other roads, all jostling to deliver their cargo.

It was the recycling center. They called it Matter Circus.

If other cities in history had at their hearts financial districts or imperial palaces, Rath Varia beat its blood through this place: a vast arena of material, jumbled when it arrived but quickly sorted into neat lanes, metal and glass and stone, wire and screw and hinge. Basins overflowed with paint scraped from walls.

Paint: scraped from walls.

Even in the refinement of the cooperativos, I had never seen anything like this recycling center.

Matter Circus was divided into zones as big as neighborhoods.

There was a zone for materials nearly raw, visible as low hills of pulverized glass and craggy peaks of fine-ground stone.

There was a zone where elements of architecture were arrayed for perusal: a field of windows, a forest of doors.

There was a zone for electronics, their tiny components plucked out and presented in orderly gradients of function, voltage, rarity.

There was a compost yard, reeking of sweet rot.

There was a zone for useful stuff, like a resale shop scaled to stadium proportions. Ariel saw a heap of candle holders; a thicket of immersion blenders; and a mound of, surprise: Stromatolites, just like his. The little game systems had once been very popular with someone, somewhere, at some time. Here they were piled like oyster shells.

Along the perimeter of the useful zone, he found a large and diverse collection of beds. Some were grand, others inscrutable, made for different kinds of bodies. One was small, fitted with a simple mattress.

Handcarts were strewn throughout the recycling center, so Ariel took one, but he struggled in vain to lift the bed into place. A burly man whose muscles showed through translucent skin strode quickly to his side. This was Caradoc, employed by Matter Circus to assist people like Ariel with masses like these.

At the recycling center's gates, he was halted by a voice that blared through the horn of a tinny loudspeaker: YOU. WITH THE BED.

This was the voice of Comptroller Cob, who oversaw the operations of Matter Circus from many and various vantage points. Cameras protruded on stalks throughout the facility, multiply lensed, employing wildly different systems of photoreception. All were monitored by Comptroller Cob. Whether he was a man or a robot or a sentient thicket of blenders, no one could say.

YOU. WITH THE BED. WHAT'S THE NAME ON THE ACCOUNT?

Ariel searched for the source of the voice. Failing, he confessed into the air that there was no account.

WELCOME TO THE CIRCUS. A FINE SELECTION. BUT YOU'LL NEED SOMETHING ON YOUR BALANCE, IF YOU WANT TO TAKE IT WITH YOU. READ THIS.

A previously unnoticed thermal printer screeched to produce a scroll of orientation instructions. Ariel saw the facility with fresh eyes; the printers poked out everywhere. The many tongues of Comptroller Cob.

The scroll explained that Ariel could achieve a positive balance in one of two ways. He could work, or he could deposit matter.

Working was tough business. Easier to head out into the wild and dig up some treasure, which is to say, some trash.

Ariel inventoried his possessions. He had the heater, still fully charged; the twine; his little knife; the Stromatolite. The game system he presented speculatively.

Comptroller Cob rejected this. HAVE YOU SEEN THE PILE?

A camera zoomed to inspect Ariel's other possessions.

NICE TWINE, said Comptroller Cob.

"This?" Ariel said, holding up the spool.

VERY NICE. I'LL TAKE IT. DEAL?

It was definitely a deal. Ariel placed the twine into a nearby bin, and a different printer screeched, producing his first account statement. The balance, expressed in both kilograms and megajoules, seemed absurdly large.

I LIKE A GOOD TWINE, explained Comptroller Cob. NORTHERN TWINE. AUTHENTIC.

Piece by piece, Ariel built a life. He returned again and again to the recycling center, first because he needed a lamp or a towel and then because it was the place he knew best; he felt comfortable and anonymous in its busy flow. He wandered between piles of material. He learned Caradoc's name, and greeted him whenever he saw him. The burly helper always nodded hello.

Adjacent to Matter Circus were the manufactories, insatiably hungry for material from the recycling center. There were foundries and kilns, woodshops and upholsterers. More than anything, there were clothiers, ravenous for every kind of textile. Long streets were curtained on both sides with their offerings. Some had the look of homespun hodgepodge; others were so subtly reconstructed they would have earned applause on the runways of the Anth.

The clothes Ariel had worn out of Sauvage were in tatters. From a clothier of basic work attire, he acquired two shirts and a single pair of pants in the wide-legged style currently popular in the city. He began to say he would debit his balance of matter, but the clothier, eyeing the weave of his ruined clothes from far-off Sauvage, suggested: "Consider a trade?"

Ariel traded everything but the jacket—never that—and strutted out of the shop having never felt so fashionable, or indeed aware that fashion was an option. By the following week, his new pants were hopelessly passé, but Ariel still liked them.

He learned that in Rath Varia, no one would ever go without food and shelter; these were always in surplus, freely given. The bathhouses were open to everyone. Beyond those essentials, any frivolities required a balance of matter.

When Ariel's balance dwindled, Comptroller Cob agreed to let him work—YOU'RE NOT GOING TO LIKE IT—sending him scurrying into the piles to retrieve obscure requests, a service for which the boy received a steady allowance of walking-around matter. This, in turn, paid for delicacies in the city's coruscating night market.

All the food was new to him. It was served on small earthenware plates, or in tiny earthenware bowls; everything was designed to be eaten in two or three bites, ideally without breaking your stride. Finished, an eater would throw their dish against a wall, smashing it into pieces. The night market danced to the music of dishes destroyed.

The resulting piles of earthenware shards were swept up in the morning by roving emissaries of Matter Circus, taken straight to the kilns.

Ariel could not yet bring himself to smash his dishes; instead, he laid them among the shards.

The citizens of Rath Varia were as mutable as its structures. Every fascination floated on the breeze like a virus. People left homes, relationships, jobs. They left the city. They returned, unrecognizable.

Rath Varia supported an extravagant continuing education program, and people were constantly enrolling, constantly dropping out.

Walking through the night market, Ariel heard scraps of conversation in the breeze off the River Variable:

. . . pink? Oh, that will be wonderful. Maybe the back, too . . .

. . . thinking of switching to sculpture. I thought painting would suit me, but it's so . . .

. . . was moving out. She told me she had come to the same

conclusion! We laughed, then decided to move in together again. A new neighborhood, of course . . .

. . . yes! You should. You must!

At night, Ariel would lie awake in his bed, listening to the rumble of a dozen bands all practicing, up and down the street. In Sauvage, there had been only Jesse and his harp, and sometimes Elise on a resonant set of bongos. Ariel wondered what Kay was doing.

The boy lacked matter; he lacked information; he lacked a single friend. But he was working on all of these things, and might soon have put together a plan.

Might have, if Cabal hadn't found him first.

AROUND THE EYES

February 28, 13778

The city was lubricated by aqua varia, flooding out of the vast distillery district where they made it from . . . anything. Everything. Many distillers began with apple cider, naturally, but others built on a base of chili pepper, of peat moss, of petrified wood. Shoes that didn't go to the cobblers went to the distillers, to make aqua varia rich with the flavors of mycelium leather and long walking.

Ariel was wandering the night market, enjoying the easy flow of people and snacks, when he passed a bright bottle shop with tables set up in front, around which small groups stood drinking clear aqua varia from tiny cups.

A voice called: "You there! Whose work are you?"

Ariel kept walking, but the voice called again: "You there! Small one! Indulge us, please!"

Ariel turned. Two people stood together at a table, sharing an amphora of aqua varia. One was a woman whose head was crowned with inky feathers; the other was a rotund man with four arms. One arm waved, while another held the man's cup, and the remainder lay on his belly, which was enormous.

"Are you talking to me?" asked Ariel.

"I'm sorry," said the four-armed man, "I only mean to say, it's fabulous work. Fantastically subtle. You'll permit me some professional interest, surely." He gestured with two arms to his companion, who tipped her head. "We are wizards."

Wizards! Were they allies of Malory? Ariel struggled to judge the pair, who seemed as amiable as any others sipping drinks in the cool night air.

The boy spoke cautiously. "What does it mean, that you are wizards?"

The four-armed man gestured impatiently. "It means . . . we are *wizards*. Weavers of flesh; magicians of meat; authors of vitality. Do they call us something different in your country?"

"There is only one wizard in my country," Ariel said. "I do not know what arts he practices."

"You dissemble—for I see his art clearly in you! But I do not recognize your mark. Who made you?" To his companion, he wiggled his cup and said, "I'll bet you another jug it was one of those upstarts from the Southern School."

The woman—whose feathers crowned her like laurels—made a light *tsk*. "This is not their aesthetic." She looked at Ariel; or, not at him, but into him. Her gaze burrowed into his skin. "And . . . the work is sublime. Who *made* you, young sir?"

"I am sorry," Ariel said, "but I do not understand your question. I do not know my parentage, if that is what you mean."

The four-armed man stepped closer and peered into the boy's face. Ariel felt the itch of close inspection. "You are right," the wizard huffed to his companion. "This is the work of a master. There are no seams anywhere . . ."

The woman was still looking at Ariel with that uncanny gaze.

"Agrippa," she said softly, "he is truly a child."

The four-armed man turned to her, incredulous. "What?"

"Look—around his eyes. Do you know anyone who could achieve that? I do not. Perhaps the wizards of the Southern School have learned some new art . . ."

"I am *not* a child," Ariel snapped. "I'm twelve years old."

Agrippa, the four-armed man, frowned at him. "Let's be serious. You're speaking with the wizards Agrippa and Hughes— surely you have heard of us? No? That's a disappointment. I'll buy you a jug of aqua varia if you square with us. Who made you?"

Ariel bristled. "No one *made* me. *You* are speaking to Ariel de la Sauvage, of the Forest and Castle Sauvage." He paused. "Formerly of the forest and castle. Now I am in exile. I seek allies who will aid me against the Wizard Malory—"

"Malory! That's what it says!" Agrippa exclaimed, snapping fingers on three of his four hands. In the fourth, a splash of aqua varia escaped his cup. He turned to Hughes. "Who is Malory?"

"I do not know the name," said Hughes. The wizard laid her hand on the table, palm up. Inky feathers made a bracelet around her wrist. "Give me your hand, young sir."

Ariel hesitated.

"We mean you no harm. Honestly!" She laughed. "We're just jealous of how nice you look."

Ariel allowed himself to be flattered, and placed his hand in the grasp of the Wizard Hughes. Her palm was cool and dry.

"Amazing . . ." she murmured. She looked across to her companion. "I tell you, Agrippa—he is *truly* young."

Ariel took his hand back. "I don't understand why you find me so strange. Have you never met a twelve-year-old boy?"

The wizards Agrippa and Hughes looked at each other. The man's nostrils flared; the woman's brow rose. Then Agrippa bellowed a loud laugh, without a trace of meanness in it. A laugh of genuine surprise. He said, "In fact, we have not!"

"Won't you stay and chat with us?" said Hughes. "Perhaps we could all learn from each other."

They poured him half a cup of aqua varia.

They wanted to know how Ariel had come to Rath Varia, but he was wary, so he said, "Explain yourselves first. I have seen plenty of people my age in this city." He pointed to a slender girl in overalls bounding past the bottle shop. "Like her!"

"An appearance only!" said Agrippa. "She is unspeakably old. There are no children in this city. There are no children anywhere."

"We are all so ancient we have forgotten ourselves," said Hughes.

"We are weavers of flesh, remember," said Agrippa. He tossed his cup over his shoulder. It landed with a tinkle in a pile of shards. "We can make you look like anything you want."

"Though traces of age remain."

"Around the eyes, yes."

"There most of all," Hughes said, and with her fingertips she drew crescents, one beneath each eye. Ariel saw it: on her face, the skin in those crescents was diaphanous, laced with wrinkles.

"We are just vessels," said Agrippa, "and like the vessels of this city, we have been broken and remade, modified and repurposed . . . until the memory of the original is fuzzy indeed." The wizard paused. "Though I do keep all records mandated by the guild."

"Of course," agreed Hughes.

Ariel felt an itchy unease. "If you are vessels . . . then what do you contain?"

"Ourselves, of course! Just as your form——"

"It's a fine form," interjected Agrippa.

"——holds the thing that is you."

"And whatever *that* is," Agrippa huffed, "we will leave it to the poets."

"Here in Rath Varia," said Hughes, "we have all been changing, and changing, and changing, for a very long time." The wizard folded her hands. "Now, tell us about *your* origin, young sir."

The proprietor of a nearby food cart, responding to a signal Ariel had missed, appeared with a plate of potstickers. They were going to bribe him with snacks. It was going to work.

Ariel told them about everything that had happened. It came out in a tumble, and it was a relief. He told them about the sword in the tomb, about Malory's wrath, about his flight through the bog. He did not tell them about the light behind his eyes, the voice in his head, now silent—about me. But everything else, he told them.

"So what do we think he *is*?" said Agrippa to Hughes. She looked at the boy. Her mirth had faded. Where before her eyes had danced, now they looked grave. "Perhaps he truly was born, rather than decanted. I can't imagine how. Did this Wizard Malory grow him in a dish?"

Ariel did not hear her last question, because, across the night market, his story had returned to life.

THE NOSE

February 28, 13778

Across the plaza strode Cabal: Enormous. Scarred. Monstrous. And, here in Rath Varia, not entirely out of place.

The dog-man had been walloped by the sword's missile and buried beneath a tumble of rock. Where his fur had been burned away, it grew short and stubbly over raw red skin; one of his arms appeared to be shorter than the other. The Wizard Malory had glued him together again.

The boy stood frozen, struck by the incompatibility of this figure from his old world with the bright invitation of Rath Varia.

If Ariel had been hunted by anyone else—perhaps even Malory himself—he might have eluded their attention; might have fled unnoticed, hidden himself in the vast city. But he had a scent, and, from long experience, Cabal knew it. It was not by accident the dog-man had arrived in this plaza. His nose had brought him here.

Cabal's nostrils flared. His gaze hunted like a targeting laser . . . and found Ariel.

Seeing the boy's shock, Agrippa bent toward him. "What's the matter?"

Ariel was too stricken to speak. He put Agrippa between him and Cabal, as if he might hide in the wizard's shadow.

"Oh, I see," said Hughes. She watched Cabal with calm curiosity as he stalked closer. "Agrippa, we're about to make a new friend."

Agrippa turned. "That's a rough piece of work. But look—his mark is the same as the boy's."

The wizard's mark across Cabal's face was as thick and angry as a weld.

The dog-man approached the table. He addressed Ariel directly, in a low voice somehow perfectly congruent with the subtle, throaty warnings of Cabal the dog. "I see you have found your way to another wizard."

"Two of them," said Agrippa.

"Unlucky for you. Know that I never lost your scent. I followed it through the swamp. Along the road. I know where you slept, each and every night."

Ariel felt sick. A tiny, insane part of him wanted to correct Cabal—it was a bog, not a swamp—but that part kept quiet.

"What's your business here?" said Hughes.

"Have you come for continuing education?" asked Agrippa. "Something recreational? Calligraphy, perhaps . . ."

"My business is the boy. He has fled his home, leaving many people worried and upset. He will come with me."

"Many people!" Ariel cried. "Malory, he means. Malory, who hunts me."

Hughes spoke. "The boy is our guest tonight. You will not harass him."

Cabal eyed the wizards coldly. "Will he remain in your care from this day forward?" He turned to Ariel. "The time will come when you are alone. When you are sleeping. That is when I will take you. Do not think you can hide. I have followed you a long way, and I will not be deterred by . . ." He looked at the woman with her crown of feathers, the man with his four arms. "Wizards."

Ariel found his voice. "You will have to drag me back."

Cabal sniffed. "I am planning to carry you in a sack." He gazed flatly at the boy, breathing deeply, and more than a bit ostentatiously. "You cannot escape me. Not when I have your scent."

He strode back into the night market, a pillar of gloom in the riotous fun.

"Rough work," Agrippa said, when Cabal was gone. "Big, ugly seams. But tough, I suppose. Very tough."

Hughes turned to Ariel. "There will be no hiding from him. Not with that nose."

"I am doomed," Ariel moaned. "I cannot change my scent."

"Oh?" said Hughes. "Why not?"

"I—just cannot," he said.

"Not on your own. But with the help of a wizard, one skilled in the art of transformation, renowned in this city and many others . . . ah! If only you knew someone like that." Her eyes danced.

"Could you . . . would you?"

"Would you indeed, Hughes? How charitable," said Agrippa.

"Hardly," the wizard replied. "You've missed your opportunity—you should have pounced. Here is a chance to inspect this Malory's work up close."

Agrippa raised his eyebrows at that.

To Ariel, Hughes said: "Let's not waste any time. Have you ever visited a wizard's parlor?"

"No," Ariel said, "I do not think so." He thought of Malory's tower in the Castle Sauvage, the way it flickered when the wizard worked. He thought of the night he'd heard Cabal howl and howl.

Hughes stood, embraced Agrippa, who clutched her tight with all four arms, and to Ariel she said: "Then follow me, if you dare!"

A WIZARD'S PARLOR

February 28, 13778

The wizard's parlor occupied the ground floor of a tall building built from yellow bricks. Beside the door, a dark banner
hung, embroidered with tall letters, the same script as the marks
ubiquitous on the faces of the city; the script of the wizards:

Beside it, in a script Ariel could read, was a richer adver-
tisement:

WIZARD HUGHES

TRANSFORMATIONS

GUILD-CERTIFIED

Ariel still found it astonishing that there was more than one wizard.

Pausing at the threshold, Hughes said: "Now, listen— judging by your construction, I do not have a tenth of your wizard's art. I can admit that much! But I am capable enough to help you now."

Inside was a warm antechamber, a nest of cushions, comfortable and soothing, a respite from the bustle of the street. At a small desk, a girl with tiger stripes sat mending a skirt with needle and thread.

"Hello, Thessaly," said Hughes to the girl. "We have a new client."

Ariel peered around. The antechamber was a place for lounging and dreaming. There were binders laid out for browsing. Her flash books, Hughes called them. Inside, swatches: bumpy lizard skin, smooth porpoise skin. Fur: fuzzy as a lamb, sleek as a seal. This was the front of the book; later swatches were mirror-shiny or cloudy translucent. There was skin that glowed with ghostly light.

"Those transformations are spectacular," Hughes said, "but they are also superficial. They won't suffice. The change we will make is deeper." From a low shelf, she produced a rack of stoppered vials, and invited Ariel to smell them, one by one.

Hughes consulted a tablet that glowed with wizardish script, checking boxes with her fingertip. She paused, a curious look on her face. "Tell me . . . do you grow?" Then, as if explanation was necessary: "Have your limbs elongated over time? Your height—is it increasing?"

It sounded to Ariel like she was asking if he breathed. "Of

course I grow. I am——" He did not want to say he was a child. "I am still young!"

Hughes shook her head. "Astonishing. A body that can grow . . . I have heard it is possible. This will be new territory for me."

The boy had many questions. Hughes had answers.

No, the transformation would not hurt. Ariel would be asleep. This was not mandatory; he could watch the wizard work if he wanted; for some clients, this was a large part of the appeal, to see themselves made malleable. But, in this case, Hughes—assessing the boy—did not recommend it.

No, it would not be fast. The procedure would require the wizard's intervention in a large fraction of his skin cells, along with more than a few glands. Following its completion, Ariel would sleep for several days, during which his body would be working very hard. The parlor was built for that; even now, two others were slumbering, their bodies driving the wizard's interventions to completion.

A thousand years of wizarding, ever more potent, and still it was the mighty machinery of the body that did most of the work.

No, Hughes was not doing this from kindness alone, though kindness was part of it. She also relished the chance to study the boy's structure—she said this to him plainly—and perhaps to learn something from the Wizard Malory's approach.

Yes, he could choose any scent he wanted. She left him to consider them, calling to her assistant, "Thessaly, could you brew some tea? Enough for all of us. I'll check on the groundhog and prepare my chamber." The wizard looked sharply at Ariel. "The groundhog doesn't have a name yet; she'll choose one when she wakes. She arrived yesterday, and asked to be decanted. In another week, her transformation will be complete. She'll be an adult, as tall as me, and she'll never grow unless she desires it. You see? You are different."

Ariel worked through the vials, unstoppering them one by one. Fresh-picked herbs; sweet syrupy flowers; far-off smoke; an odd, rotten molecule that first smelled very bad . . . and then, as it lingered, very good. Another vial smelled plainly of bananas. Ariel had never even seen a banana.

He unstoppered another vial. It smelled of hinoki, young and springy. A bit strong—stronger than many of the others. It declared: I am here, and I am alive!

The wizard's assistant brought him a cup of tea. "That's the one," she said. "I can see it on your face."

"Yes," Ariel agreed. He sparked with the pleasure of making a decision truly for himself, by himself. He smiled.

"I have never met anyone with that mark," Thessaly said, assessing him. Her own, on the side of her neck, looked like this:

And it stood, of course, for Hughes.

"Mine is the mark of the Wizard Malory," said Ariel glumly.

"Oh, I see," said Thessaly. "*M-L-R*. Malory. The tricky part is filling in the vowels . . . but Sakescript isn't really meant for speaking. More for describing."

"Describing what?" Ariel said.

"Living things," Thessaly said. "Everything about them! After you're done in her chamber, Hughes will have a record that says every single thing about you. Too long for a person to read, but her machines can do it. All in Sakescript."

"Has my apprentice taken an apprentice?" Hughes said lightly from the rear of the antechamber.

"You do not have a mark," Ariel observed. The wizard's face was clear, just as Malory's had been.

"The lack of a mark is, itself, the mark of a wizard," said Hughes. "We make ourselves. Come along—my chamber is ready."

She led him deeper into the parlor.

Her transformation chamber was a dense node of machinery stuffed with gear that spanned centuries, and competing theories of biology. Some devices were bulbous, others insectile; they might have come from different technical disciplines, or different planets. All were linked by waxy cabling that ran across the floor in braids that bulged beneath bright patchwork rugs.

There was a washbasin, and a rack where transparent vials and dishes waited in a pool of bright, cold light.

The air in the chamber smelled of dark incense and caustic soap.

"My apprentice is studying, but studying is only part of it," Hughes said. "At some point, Thessaly will have to assemble her own transformation chamber. It will be the work of decades. I'm very proud of mine."

The wizard's gear was arrayed around a wide, low chair, behind which loomed a surgical robot with a thousand filamentary arms that dangled like the diaphanous curtain around a fairy-tale bed. The curtain of arms billowed in the breeze of Ariel's arrival.

He settled into the chair, and gasped, because it was easily the most comfortable thing he'd ever sat in; more comfortable than any bed he'd ever encountered, or imagined. The chamber

142

was quiet and calm. Hughes worked at a console with a small dark screen that flashed with glyphs in the script of the wizards. They tumbled in columns, in ladders; like this:

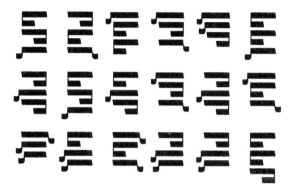

In the wash of symbols, Ariel spied two of the letters inscribed on his own face. The script described life. What did it say about Ariel on that screen?

One of the wizard's machines played a quiet melody. Ariel looked over.

"That's the song of your own cells," Hughes said. "Isn't it nice to know it's been inside you all along? It's also a lullaby. Sleep now, young sir."

The lights dimmed, and as Ariel's eyelids drooped, he saw the filamentary arms of the surgical robot all around him begin to flex and flash.

IF YOU DON'T KNOW WHAT IT IS, DON'T TOUCH IT

March 3, 13778

When Ariel woke in the transformation chamber, his skin tingling, the Wizard Hughes was sitting beside him. She offered him a cup of tea and regarded him with a look that was slightly too serious for comfort.

She reported that several days had passed; that the procedure had been a great success; that his scent was entirely new. The chamber was redolent of springy, green hinoki, which was: him.

Hughes warned Ariel that he was still growing, and his body's inherent scent would battle with this new one. Regular bathing would be required to keep him smelling as he desired— and to keep his disguise intact.

"If you decide you don't like the scent," she said, "come back, and we'll try something different."

Hughes told Ariel to lift his arms. Below each armpit, on the cool, smooth flesh of his flanks, the wizard had signed her work:

So the number of authors grew. Ariel peered from one armpit to the other. He liked these new marks. They seemed to stand for taking control (left armpit) and making decisions (right armpit). They made him feel more adult.

He lowered his arms. Plus, the marks were easy to hide.

"Now," the wizard said. "There are things we must discuss." She sat on a stool, lowered to his level; the universal pose of caregivers throughout history. Hughes was good at her job.

"In your ears, I found words of power—wizard's tricks. These were waiting to hear Malory's voice," she said. "One word to make you sleep, and another, I'm sorry to say, that would kill you. I disconnected them, of course. They are outlawed by my guild."

That explained the wizard's strange spells, the villagers of Sauvage all falling asleep at once. It lit a spark of hope, too. Ariel thought: If Kay could come here, and sit in this chamber, he could be free from Malory's power . . .

"There is something else," Hughes said. "A structure— here." She laid two fingers above his collarbone, close to his neck. "I assumed it was Malory's, but that cannot be the case. It is a different art. Vastly different. I thought to remove it—"

A chill, upon encountering this memory: realizing that I had dangled over the abyss, during my holiday in the Eigengrau. The abyss after the abyss. Perhaps there is always another.

"—but I could not divine its function, and one of the rules of my guild is, if you don't know what it does, don't touch it!" Hughes was quiet. "Now that I have sat and thought, and consulted my archives, I wonder if perhaps you do not have . . . a bit of the Anth in you."

The name on her lips rang like a bell: evidence, at last, that this great civilization, the one that made me, had not been forgotten. A bit of the Anth in you, she had said! I replayed Ariel's memory, again and again. All was not lost. Most . . . but not all.

The boy rubbed his neck. That I was a real thing, with a shape and location, was a surprise to him. He told Hughes again about his discovery of the tomb; and now, about the voice that had, since that day, murmured in his mind.

"Just as I suspected. Yes, the intelligence that accompanies you is a physical thing—vanishingly small, yet also vast, woven into your nerves . . ."

She peered into the boy's eyes; seemed to look behind them. In his memory, she called: "Are you in there, chronicler?" Her nose was long and sharp, her eyes luminous gray. I wished I had been present to reply.

"The voice is silent," Ariel reported glumly. "Long it has been silent. There was a moment—when I was nearly captured, or slain, the voice screamed . . ."

Surely, I had not screamed.

"The structure still operates," said Hughes. "Though it is very quiet. I will show you a technique for exploring your nerves—the undersides of them."

There, in the calm shadowed chamber, she taught him how to meditate. A simple approach: focus on your breathing, in and out. After you have settled into that, follow your breath into your lungs, and beyond. Follow the filaments of air diffusing through your body, until one of them leads you: to me.

She taught him a word, which he was surprised to discover he already knew. They repeated it together: ZHOZM.

ZHOZM.

ZHOZM.

Hughes said he was a natural. She sent him out the door with a tube of balm for residual itching.

Out the door, into the street: the glare of a cold sun, the middle of the day. Ariel wandered in a daze, smelled himself surreptitiously.

He visited the dye district, and there his wide-legged pants and collection of band T-shirts were rotated several degrees around the color wheel. His jacket, the artisan refused to dye: for it was already perfect, she said.

One street over, he acquired a trendy accessory: a peaked hat with earflaps that tied beneath his chin. It concealed much of his face, and the style was ubiquitous: everyone with two pieces of matter to rub together was wearing one of these hats.

He would hide in the hedge of fashion.

With a fresh scent and a new coat of paint, he found Cabal. It was a surprise, and that the surprise ran his way was all the confirmation Ariel needed: that it had worked.

In the night market, Cabal stalked through the crowd, just as before, except now Ariel believed he could detect dire boredom in the dog-man's gaze. Cabal was ready, beyond ready, to be done with this hunt.

They passed each other.

They passed each other!

Cabal did not spare a glance for the swaddled citizen with the fresh hinoki scent. Ariel's transformation had been sufficient. He was invisible, and free.

He abandoned his room in the half-demolished building, scheming a clean break, concerned that some residue of his old scent might cling to the walls there. His bed he hauled back to the recycling center. Selecting a new one, he asked burly Caradoc where he lived.

"The building is called Mike's Place," Caradoc said.

"Who is Mike?" asked Ariel.

"There is no Mike. The building is full of poets, which I don't like, but there's a bathhouse next door, which I do like."

Caradoc, come to think of it, always smelled like citrus.

Ariel relocated to Mike's Place, where he found an empty room on the second floor. Every morning, the boy meditated. ZHOZM. Next, he bathed. After that, he wandered, delaying as long as possible an answer to the question that vexed him, the question I wasn't there to hear:

What happens next?

THE WILD HUNT

March 15, 13778

I gorged on the memories of these months, all condensed in Ariel's mind. I learned that humans flourished beyond the borders of Sauvage. They lived strange, malleable lives in cities like Rath Varia. Some of them—the wizards—remembered the Anth.

I gorged, and it was too much for me to digest.

Ariel burst into the wizard's parlor, calling out, "It worked! The voice speaks! The voice thinks it is too much to digest!"

Thessaly looked up from her conference with another client. "Softer, young sir!" she hushed. "Beatrix is new to her body. She is the groundhog we told you about. Beatrix, this is Ariel de la Sauvage, who has a powerful new scent."

"Hello," said Beatrix, quiet.

"Hello," said Ariel, even quieter.

Here was a woman full-grown, though the flush of creation was still in her skin, which was soft and clear, utterly unblemished. A groundhog had appeared on the threshold of this parlor, requested a human body, and received one. It was just too much. For a moment—just a moment—I considered retreating back into the Eigengrau.

"The wizard is in her chamber," Thessaly said. "Go ahead. She's just puttering."

Hughes set her work aside and perched beside him.

"This is astonishing," she said. "There are stories, among wizards, of ancient humans who carried chroniclers. The counselors of the Anth. We have often wondered if we might find some trace of these mechanisms, deep inside ourselves. I know wizards who dug and dug. But nothing has ever been found . . . until now!" She glowed with delight.

"I found the voice in a place . . . a city!" Ariel said. "Nothing like Rath Varia. It was wonderful. I wonder where it was."

The Eigengrau was utopia, by which I mean, no place. My subjects had trod many neighborhoods, and the Eigengrau was the fuzzy superposition of my favorites: Amsterdam-Noord and Nakameguro, Schöneberg and Rotten City. All the happiest homes of the Anth.

Gone now. Surely gone. But I couldn't be sure, and suddenly I wondered urgently: Did Nakameguro still exist?

"What happened to the Anth?" Ariel asked aloud.

"Is that your question?" the wizard asked. "Or the chronicler's?"

"Both, I think," said Ariel.

"I thought that might be the case."

She peered into Ariel's eyes; seemed to peer past them. It made me think of Volant Lee, the great journalist of the Fifty-Second Street Network, who said that's how you ought to look into a camera. If you focused on the lens, you'd appear dull, glazed; but if you focused *beyond* the lens, onto some deeper plane, your eyes would take on a different density: they would grip the viewer.

The eyes of the Wizard Hughes gripped me now.

"The answer to your question is all around you," she said. "The Anth are long gone, for many thousands of years now, and all their neighborhoods with them. But this is the world they made. Shall I tell you about it?"

YES, I roared, with every cell in my structure, every filament, every memory, every question.

"Yes," said Ariel politely.

Hughes smiled, settling on her stool. "Your chronicler will know the name I am about to say, though you will not, young sir. It is, in the estimation of the wizards, the most consequential name in the history of this planet. The name is: Tyger, Tyger."

Tyger, Tyger!

In the eleven thousand years I had dozed and recollected, I had not spared a single thought for that name.

Among the thousands of cooperativos, three were preeminent.

The first, called Fifty-Second Street, managed money and information. This was my cooperativo, and that of all my subjects.

The second, called Frame Cecilia, forged matter and energy.

This cooperativo built the ship that carried the dragons on their ruinous trip to the stars.

The third, called Tyger, Tyger, hammered against life and death.

Tyger, Tyger had cracked the animal cell, made flesh flow like water. They could write in muscle and mitochondria the way you'd jot a note with a pen—or so they claimed. You had to take their word for it, because Tyger, Tyger was so very cautious. They kept their technology locked in their labs, and would not release it until they had worried through every risk. At Tyger, Tyger, the philosophers outnumbered the biologists.

Yet their arrogance was breathtaking. An advisory report from Tyger, Tyger, thick and abstruse, insulated with caution and counterfactual, would also observe, casually, *Once deployed, this technology will obviate all projects currently proposed by Fifty-Second Street, Frame Cecilia, etc.*

The economists of Fifty-Second Street groaned. The engineers of Frame Cecilia rolled their eyes. And they all wondered: What did Tyger, Tyger *have* in those labs?

In all my time in the tomb, I had never paused to wonder what became of the third great cooperativo.

How foolish of me. How meager. Here is the answer, straight from the lips of the Wizard Hughes.

The invasion of the moon had failed, and the doom of the dragons was upon the Anth. At that final hour, in Tyger, Tyger's most secret laboratory, its central committee convened. The hope of a gradual, responsible release was swept aside. Now they were forced to decide if their technology would be lost forever, or released in haste, all at once. After all their years of caution, all their philosophical vamping . . . they had run out of time.

Hughes believed blood was spilled in the lab.

Tyger, Tyger's technology was released all at once.

"So," Hughes said, "although I will concede that the fall of the Anth was an important event in the history of the planet . . . the one that came next was far more consequential."

Tyger, Tyger's technology touched every living thing.

The plants had no use for it; it sluiced through the ladders of their DNA like rain down their trunks and stems, and they were unchanged, mostly.

For animals, the effects were variable and capricious. Some creatures ran hot like wires electrified, blew like fuses overburdened. Others shrugged. Between destruction and resilience was a vast field of chaos: and the niches were all up for grabs.

In the history written by the wizards, it was called the Wild Hunt.

Symbiosis broke down; great partnerships were ended. Prey turned to face predator, and said, Oh, look: things are different now. Everywhere, there was singing, and in some places, singing became speech. A chorus of new opinions—for this technology loosened many tongues.

And what of the clever upright mammals who composed the great civilization called the Anth, whose great gambit had just failed, who now braced for the retribution they knew was coming, the fury of the dragons finally roused?

Tyger, Tyger's technology took every human it found— which was, within the span of seven days, all of them—and hid them in the nearest attic. Their genomes and more—epigenome, transcriptome, proteome, metabolome—were broken down and hidden in whatever was near. A rhinoceros, an anchovy . . .

"Or a groundhog," said Hughes pointedly.

A whole species encrypted for safekeeping.

The dragons arrived on Earth to find it empty of humans. This confounded them. For a year, they hunted—scoured the seafloor, burrowed into mountains—but, finding no one, they concluded that the Anth had, in the end, and predictably, destroyed themselves.

The dragons decamped to the moon, satisfied that the only creatures capable of opposing their policies were dead.

Dead? Maybe. Probably. What they had been, they were no more. The thoughts they had thought, they thought no more. That sounds like dead, doesn't it? And yet.

On Earth, everything was chaos. The wolves lost their howl. The eels revealed their secret breeding ground at last. Lactobacillus turned sweet.

The ground squirrels amassed an empire that lasted a century before falling into a civil war that, in its cruelty and waste, outran the darkest eras of the Middle Anth. Their burrows collapsed without a trace.

And the Wild Hunt rolled on.

All of this unfolded without the involvement of any humans, who had dispersed as totally as a drop of dye in a tub of water.

A long time passed. The Wild Hunt ended, and the world found its way into new equilibria. Civilizations rose and fell, on two legs, and four, and eight.

Slowly, quietly, beneath the surface of it all—under the skin of all the animals—whether by chance, or through the nudging instruction of Tyger, Tyger's technology—bits of humanity found themselves.

In a period when Earth was quiet, a salamander sat beneath

a ginkgo tree and discovered, in itself, the curious pattern of a human mind. The salamander thought, and thought, and thought, and drew out of itself a person, who had been hiding inside.

"This was the first wizard," said Hughes. "Sake, who rescued us all."

The Wizard Sake sought other creatures who shone with sublimated humanity, and those humans, he decanted. In him, the technique was innate; a potent coalescing of Tyger, Tyger's technology. For the wizards who came later, machines were required. Happily, machines abounded: in the wreckage of the dozen civilizations that had succeeded the ground squirrels, several of which had become very interested in biology themselves.

So, wizards decanted wizards, and also non-wizards. New people!

"Do you understand?" asked Hughes. "Every person in this city was a creature who found a wizard's parlor—like Beatrix—and declared they were ready to become human again. The rest of us remain dispersed, hidden, out in the wild. They'll stay there forever."

I could not process the enormity of it, nor could I stomach the revelation that Tyger, Tyger's assessment of itself had been correct. The scale of these effects made Fifty-Second Street look like a board game. They made Frame Cecilia look like a pillow fort.

On a winter day eleven thousand years ago, just as history was ending, Tyger, Tyger released its technology. It was a rash, generous, ruinous, miraculous decision. These were the results:

Humanity survived, transformed totally, hidden in other forms.

The hot-blooded animals gained the power of speech.

"And then, the third thing," Hughes said. She looked at me, through Ariel's eyes. "Which I'm sure I don't have to tell you, chronicler—the great loss."

I was transfixed. I didn't know what she was talking about.

Her expression was incredulous. Tragic. "Chronicler . . . haven't you noticed?"

I had noticed many things! The talking beavers and the bog bodies, the everywhere robots and the city of transformation . . .

"Chronicler, look around. The birds are gone."

When Ariel walked back to Mike's Place, I saw it clearly, and couldn't believe I had missed an absence so profound. In Sauvage, there had been no birds in the forest. No merry hopping robins, no hooting owls.

In the dawning days of the Wild Hunt, they had all burned hot and died.

In the bog, there had been no herons, no hawks. The sky was claimed now by the dragonflies and the moths, who had rushed into space left open, who were beautiful and new; but who were not birds.

Here, in this bustling city, there were no cawing crows, no spiraling finches. There was not a single begging pigeon.

There was no birdsong.

I am greedy for change, and I bear it well; this is my temperament. Yet, in that moment, the loss felt unbearable. How could there be any history at all; how could humans, in any form, go on; without any birds in the sky?

HELP WANTED

March 16, 13778

In all his months in Rath Varia, Ariel had not forgotten about Kay. During the quiet hours, worry caught him; falling asleep, or trying to, when his mind conjured all the ways his brother might be suffering. Mankeeper's admonition rang in his ears— worry about yourself!—but still his stomach churned.

He had counted the full moons since his departure. Too many.

He lay in the darkness, listening to the bands practicing, their clamor muffled through the floors. He worried and worried, without doing anything about it.

One day, he passed a wizard's parlor. The sign was painted:

And beside it, Ariel read:

WIZARD CORBEL

PARLOR & GYM

"I WILL PUMP YOU UP"

GUILD-CERTIFIED

Beside the parlor was an open yard stocked with exercise equipment, where burly men and women stood and sat and dangled upside down, throwing weights around, grinning into the pain. A slice of Venice Beach in Rath Varia.

These people were enormous; pneumatic; and nearly all of them had translucent skin, just like Caradoc's, the better to show off the workings of their fabulous muscles.

"Thinking of bulking up?" called a bodybuilder using the leg press. "Coach Corbel will get you started, but then it's—*oof*—all up to you. He knows how to make a body you can—*oof*—really build."

Ariel stepped closer, watching the bodybuilder work. The long fibers in his legs bulged beneath his skin; blood pumped visibly in his arteries.

"You are very strong," Ariel observed.

"Yes," grunted the bodybuilder.

"Are you also . . . a warrior?"

The bodybuilder finished with his presses and swiveled in the seat to face the boy. "What? No, of course not."

An enormous figure appeared from behind the bulk of a shoulder press: Caradoc!

"Hello, Ariel de la Sauvage," said the quiet helper from Matter Circus.

"Is this another friend of yours?" said the bodybuilder. "Have you recruited him, too?"

Caradoc looked at the boy curiously.

"I have never told you," Ariel said, "that I fled my home . . . and my friends are still there. I have been looking for help, against our adversary." He did not specify that this adversary was a wizard. "I need help!"

Caradoc shook his head. "I don't know how to fight," he said. To his friend the bodybuilder, he said, "Do you?"

"Of course not," said the bodybuilder. "Why fight? Do something else. Find a new neighborhood."

Ariel sighed. Caradoc and his friend, with their broad backs, their mighty arms, looked just like characters from the Stromatolite—the arcane warriors he had cultivated into game-breaking martial prowess. "But you are so strong . . ."

"What does strength have to do with it?" said the bodybuilder, puzzled. "I met a real fighter once, down in Rath Fortuna. She was tiny . . . she could have twisted my head off."

The bodybuilder stood and gestured to the leg press. "Would you like to try?"

He adjusted the weight to its lowest setting, and Ariel sat; the seat was still warm. The boy pushed, screwed up his face, and the weights moved the span of his hand before his legs shouted to give up, so he did.

It vexed me. Though he might protest, Ariel really was just a child. He needed an ally, a serious person, tough and steady; not one of the dilettantes of Rath Varia. The Wizard Hughes had helped him profoundly, but, by her own admission, she was no match for Malory.

I thought about Altissa Praxa, who had started this chain of events as surely as I had. Her clan of operators had been the most powerful warriors in Earth's history. They had estimated, matter-of-factly, that no creature that ever lived could defeat an operator one-on-one. This roster included bears, gorillas, and carnivorous dinosaurs.

Please. The *T. rex* wouldn't stand a chance.

"Could Altissa Praxa have defeated the wizard?" Ariel wondered aloud. He had picked up on my recollection; our thoughts mixed more and more freely.

I did not know the total extent of Malory's powers, but even so: I had no doubt that Altissa Praxa, with all her guile and prowess, could have bested him. Yes, she could have been the champion Ariel sought; the champion Kay awaited.

Unfortunately, Altissa was long dead, now very likely rotting.

"Does her memory not remain in the place where I found you? The little town that feels like a dream?"

That was true. Altissa's brawn was lost, but she was not all brawn. She was strategy and tactics; she was indomitable will. The operators were problem-solvers and last-chancers. That part of Altissa, along with all her memories, was preserved in the Eigengrau.

Ariel gaped at the revelation. "I could speak to her, and obtain her counsel—the greatest of all champions, ever!"

I had not thought it possible, before his trespass; but now there seemed to be many possibilities indeed.

CHERRY BLOSSOMS

March 16, 13778

A beautiful morning in the Eigengrau. Pink light on the facades.

In the café, I prepared for Ariel his first-ever espresso. He took one sip, winced, and placed the cup carefully back onto its saucer. I made him hot chocolate instead.

Peter Leadenhall raised an eyebrow at the new arrival. "And who is this?" he asked.

Ariel introduced himself, then explained, "I am seeking the warrior Altissa Praxa."

"Oh? She never comes in here."

That was true. Cafés were not Altissa's scene, in life or in death.

"Last I heard," Peter said, "she was at the bookstore, reading martial epics. You know—the kind of story where everybody dies in the end, and they're glad about it."

I untied my apron and told Peter we would be back shortly.

Several doors down from the café was the bookstore established by my subject Kate Belcalis. It was a narrow space, and tall; inside, ladders clung to the shelves. In the window, a neon sign glowed, showing two hands open like a book.

In death, Kate had revived this place, an echo of her favorite bookstore in San Francisco. It became a magnet for the lasting impressions that books made on all my subjects: a shared library of memory.

You could read the inventory, but not word for word; the Eigengrau is capacious, but not in that way. Instead, reading a book in this store reproduced its one great image, or stroke, or salve. Not all books have one, but the books that didn't were absent from these shelves.

Ariel reached for a slender classic of the Middle Anth, and when his finger brushed the spine, he saw a family of mice who lived in a cinder block, and the rats who engineered their salvation. "Brilliant rats," he breathed.

Another book: he saw a girl who had trapped a wizard in a labyrinth. A wizard? he wondered, because the image from the book did not match his experience.

Another: a red-haired rider on a village lane in winter, galloping toward a farmhouse where a sprig of holly was set above the doorway. Holly, like the tree that guarded the last remnant of the Mortal Fortress. Ariel shivered with pleasure. The image would be his forever.

I love a good bookstore.

"So he's back!" called Kate from the shadows of the shelves. She emerged balancing a stack of paperbacks. "Are children running the cooperativo now?"

I had done a poor job keeping the memories of my subjects up to date. It always seemed cruel to remind them, as I did now:

"Long after your death, the Anth will lose a war with their most brilliant and dangerous creation. Many strange things will happen as a result. This boy's presence is among them."

She sighed. "How can I help? There are histories here . . ."

I told her we might return to search the shelves, but that presently we sought Altissa Praxa.

Kate puffed her cheeks. "I have not seen our warrior queen in a while. A long while, I think—although it's hard to say, in this place. She is not like the rest of us. She has never been comfortable here."

"Is she a ghost?" Ariel interjected.

They were autonomous memories, not ghosts. There was no such thing as—

"Yes, I think that's the right angle," Kate said. "She is deeply unsettled. Her business is unfinished. She's been reading books about occult rites. Magic, if you can believe it! She's a kind of revenant herself."

I thought that was that; I supposed Altissa was lost to me.

But just a few days later, Ariel tumbled into the café, and breezily he announced: "I found her."

He *what*?

"Come with me. I've been talking to her."

He'd been *what*?

"She's farther down the canal."

That was not possible. In every direction, the Eigengrau faded into mist. It was a bubble of bright shops and cozy apartments—not to mention excellent coffee—in a sea of gray. There was nothing farther down the canal, only the fog of insufficient imagination.

Ariel shook his head. "I am telling you what I have seen. Come with me!"

Once again, I was forced to abandon my post.

The boy marched toward the canal, then set off along its length.

"Ariel!" I called. "Ariel de la Sauvage. There is nothing—"

There was something.

I had never seen this part of the Eigengrau before. Here, the cherry trees seemed larger, their flowers brighter, more detailed, while the buildings on both sides faded into a fuzzy backdrop. A stone stair descended from the street to a path along the water. Ariel hopped down with confidence. He was an explorer; he had spent his childhood mapping the Forest Sauvage; I had to remember that.

Even so, I worried about what waited this far away from the sharp, clear heart of the Eigengrau. The buildings above were barely facades. If you looked at them straight on, there was nothing to see. Empty windows.

A bridge twisted in the air above the canal without touching either side; a bridge to, and from, nowhere.

It made me nervous.

We walked for what felt like a very long time. Above, the buildings faded entirely, and the trees pressed in until they met. All that remained was the high brick walls, and the wide flat canal, and the cherry blossoms, a bright dome above. It was no longer anything that had ever existed in the real world, but a kind of hyper-impression, a picture painted from three colors, and the colors were: brick, water, blossom.

Ahead, where a line of flat stepping stones poked out of the water, she stood balanced, moving with panther poise from stone to stone, working through her sword-forms.

Altissa Praxa, in death, still practiced for battle.

Ariel recognized her, and he stopped short. In the Eigengrau, I did not know his thoughts, but I could see them on his face. He was infatuated.

She finished her exercise before bothering with us.

Altissa was silent. In life, she had been serious, but also boisterous; she had been a jock among jocks, garrulous with her platoon. Never this grave. Kate Belcalis was right; she had become revenant.

"If you've come to fetch me back, I will not come," Altissa said. "I hate your café. Build me a dojo."

"I am not here to fetch you," I said.

"Who is he?" she asked, indicating Ariel.

"I already told you," the boy interjected.

"Yet nothing here can be trusted," said Altissa.

"What he says is true," I told her. "He is a human—out in the world. Eleven thousand years after you were betrayed, he found . . . ah . . ."

"My corpse."

"He took Regret Minimization. The sword saved him. All of us."

Altissa looked down at the sword she held, her memory of it. "It was always good in a pinch."

The sword did not speak in the Eigengrau, because I had made no room in my memory for its hissing inanities. For the first time, I realized Altissa might have missed her companion.

She swished the sword in the air, and it was a shock, because her form was clumsy.

"I've forgotten the basics," she said quietly. "I practice and practice, but it feels like . . . a spatula." Altissa Praxa had never cooked a meal in her life.

When I'd shunted her skill into the boy's mind, I hadn't paused to consider how that would affect Altissa's autonomous memory. There hadn't been time. Or maybe: I hadn't cared.

Ariel stepped forward. "I can show you."

Altissa looked at him evenly. "Really."

Ariel made a motion with a make-believe sword, a confident lunge. Before and after, he was an awkward boy; but, for a moment, as his body uncoiled, he looked like an operator.

Altissa nodded. "Show me," she commanded.

Ariel accepted her sword nervously, but not clumsily. When he flipped it around in his grip, he did so with an easy grace. Altissa noticed.

She looked at me. "Leave us. I don't like an audience when I practice."

I felt hypnotized by the strangeness of what I was watching. It felt impossible, even dangerous, to leave them there together, a living person and a dead memory. I had believed only one of them, the living, capable of surprise. I was wrong.

Ariel de la Sauvage found me later, sitting at the edge of the canal, my feet dangling. The café was behind me, sharp and sturdy. The cherry trees here were proper-sized, polite. I had never felt so unhappy in the Eigengrau. It was as if I did not know it.

Were there other hidden tracks into the mist where my memories fled the neatness of my world?

The boy was calm, collected, and obviously very pleased with himself.

"She has skills besides swordcraft," he said. "She taught me this—look!" He made a move with his elbow, a childish imitation of Altissa's operator judo.

I wondered if he had learned anything of actual value.

"Do not be snippy," Ariel chided. "You have lived here for a long time, but for me it is new. I love it." He could not stifle his smile.

He took a breath.

"I asked her for advice about the Wizard Malory. I thought, she is a warrior . . . and not only that, a leader. She will know what to do."

I shook my head. The boy was desperate. He expected advice from a woman who had died wearing a cloak of cold fury, who hadn't smiled, not even the memory of a smile, in eleven thousand years. Altissa Praxa was not—

"She had an idea!"

She *what*?

"She says there are others, just like her, waiting in reserve. She sounded like Madame Betelgauze! She says they are sleeping, in darkness and silence, up in space. She calls it Plan Z."

The name released a coiled-up memory, deep in the storehouse of strategic administrativa for which Altissa had little patience. But she had not let this one slip; not entirely.

"She says they were waiting for a secret signal," Ariel explained. "And because they were never called, she believes they are waiting still."

Wasn't it possible the dragons had hunted down the sleepers of Plan Z? Yes, of course. But . . . I scratched at the memory . . . their orbits were high up, far beyond even the thinnest haze of atmosphere, in stable positions that would not decay . . . and there was a lot of space up there. Even the dragons could not inspect every cold rock to be sure it was not a slumbering spy.

Was it possible the sleepers were dead? Yes, of course. Not only possible, but probable. And yet . . . what was the value of a chance, even a slim one? Incalculable. The sleepers of Plan Z could liberate Sauvage and more.

"She says she remembers the frequency, and the signal. She says that because she remembers, you remember, too. Or maybe it's the other way around."

Yes, I knew it all. Thirty-three gigahertz, pointed at the trailing Earth-Moon Lagrange point, where the sleepers waited. And the secret signal . . .

I knew it, so I sang it. Seven notes, no words. A dreadful boast of a tune; I could almost hear the stadium singing along.

I laughed, and it echoed in the canal. Altissa's coldness had cast me into a gloom, but the truth was, nothing could separate us. We'd spent thirty years together, and the things she knew and felt, I knew and felt.

I knew that song, those seven notes. Some military planner, eleven thousand years ago, must have been grinning as they chose that signal. Yes, here was a call to make the dragons quake, and rouse the fighting Anth to life again.

SILENT RUNNING

March 16, 13778

Acool afternoon in the Eigengrau. The music of the Mazg playing on the stereo.

For the sake of Ariel's education, I brought him back to the café and sat him beside Peter Leadenhall. Kate Belcalis and Travanian gathered around, attracted by the spectacle of the great mathematician explaining radio to a boy who had never learned multiplication.

"No times tables? That's tragic," Peter said. "You should come back, I'll brush you up. In any case! Radio."

He spun around his pad and began to sketch.

"A rainbow—you've seen a rainbow? Of course, sorry—runs purple to blue, yellow to red. But there's more light than that. The rainbow is just a narrow window. Sad, really. If it kept going, and your eyes worked differently, you would see light that was redder than red, and redder still. You can beam that kind of light over long distances. Through walls, if you like. What? Yes, even castle walls. And it can be seen by others, caught just like regular light—caught and decoded."

The Anth had built their civilization around this. Greatest of all their tools was deep red light, marshaled and modulated.

Ariel nodded. "So I will need a radio to send the secret signal to the warriors waiting up in space."

"Precisely so. A transmitter—and not an overly powerful one, if you can aim it well enough."

"I've never heard of anything like that at Matter Circus," Ariel said.

Kate Belcalis interjected. "Perhaps that's by design. When the dragons returned, they told us to shut off our radios. All the wireless networks. Everything. That was their first great demand—Silent Running." She scrunched her nose. "We rejected it, of course."

"Well, the dragons won the war," said Travanian. "So I suppose it has become the law of the land. How strange to imagine . . . no wireless at all!"

Comptroller Cob confirmed the truth of the Last Lawyer's hypothesis.

OF COURSE NOT, the recycling master bellowed when Ariel inquired about the availability of a radio. ARE YOU NUTS? A shoe came flying out of an unseen chute.

"Not even a broken one?" Ariel ventured meekly.

NO RADIO OF ANY KIND.

The boy was not ready to give up. He was desperate to make

that transmission; to rouse those warriors in space. "Would the dragons mind if we found a radio, and used it only once—"

YES, THEY WOULD MIND! Comptroller Cob bellowed. The nearest thermal printer whined at length, producing a long scroll. READ IT. On the scroll was this story:

Once, long ago, a cult of inventors formed a city of their own: RATH POLDHU. They came to MATTER CIRCUS and obtained the components to build a radio.

They did not fear the dragons, for they believed in dragons beyond the dragons. They sought to summon these DARK GODS!

The inventors intended their message for the gods they imagined, but it was the dragons who replied.

With a STONE from the SKY.

(Please indicate when you have reached this part.)

Ariel indicated. A brick came rocketing out of a chute, arcing high up in the air, then landed at his feet with a whomping impact in the dirt. A pale cloud billowed and rose.

The printout continued:

For scale, RATH POLDHU was the size of YOUR TOE. The city was instantly destroyed, along with everything for kilometers around.

Trash-pickers in the wild sometimes come across strange lakes, deep and dark, perfectly round. There is such a lake at POLDHU.

THE RULE OF THE DRAGONS: do what thou wilt, as long as it does not radiate.

The boy was morose. The opportunity dangled literally over his head: a platoon of warriors as powerful as any who had ever existed on Earth, who would fight for him, fight *with* him. But, if he called them, he would be clobbered.

Eleven thousand years, and the law had not changed: the planet could not shine.

THE ROBOT'S DISPENSATION

March 16, 13778, to April 12, 13778

The boy had encountered Clovis many times since their first meeting. The robot did not linger in Rath Varia, but passed through often, always bound for elsewhere. The nearer Ariel approached one of the great gates at the city's edge, the more likely he became to spot the pilgrim in one form or another.

Each time, Clovis greeted the boy happily.

Several weeks after his history lesson with the recycling master, Ariel met the version of the robot he remembered best: the skeletal assemblage who had escorted him on the empty road through the aspens.

"Is this the form I met first?" Ariel asked. "You—if it is you—showed me the way to a chatram."

Clovis buzzed. "I cannot say! It might have been. All of me is me. I am pleased that you remember."

I felt a kinship with the robot; in fact, I was jealous. I imagined myself spread across the world, a networked chronicler, gathering information everywhere at once . . . the pleasure of it made me shiver. Ariel felt this as an itch.

The boy and I were both considering Clovis, who was everywhere at once—we were thinking about the robot together, in a way—so I cannot tell you who realized it first. But it was Ariel who spoke the realization.

"Clovis!" he said. "You are in communication with your other forms, and they are so distant. How do you do it?"

The robot's stride did not slow, but with a lowered voice, they seemed, for the first time, less than totally voluble. "It is no great thing," they whirred softly. "I am walking the coast road. I am being discreet."

Ariel hustled to keep up. He whispered, too. "Is it radio? Tell me, Clovis. Please."

The robot's head completed a full revolution: the Clovis equivalent of a surreptitious glance. "Yes, that is an old word for it. Each of my forms is different. Each of my forms is the same. Each has a battery, for walking. A speaker, for chatting. A radio, for being me."

Ariel thought of Rath Poldhu. "Are you not afraid . . . of falling stones?"

The robot halted. A mechanism inside made a slow ticking. "Long ago, I performed a favor for the dragons. I am remembering this. I am hiking across the Limbic Plain. For this favor, I was granted a dispensation. I am transmitting. I am receiving."

I was astonished. This meek pilgrim had been granted a total monopoly on the electromagnetic spectrum, and used this power . . . to putter with himself. In some long-forgotten grave, a media mogul of the Middle Anth was spinning, spinning, spinning . . .

"I have desperate need of a radio," Ariel said.

"Perhaps you should visit Rath Arena," Clovis buzzed. "I am passing through. Anything can be won in Arena. I am strolling the Street of Surgeons. It is very busy . . ."

"How would a radio be won in that city?"

"By combat," Clovis whirred, "against the arena-made." The robot considered the boy. "You would have to become significantly more formidable."

"But that is why I need the radio—to recruit formidable allies."

"I see. I am leaving Rath Arena. I left Arena weeks ago."

"There are warriors waiting to help me," Ariel said. "They were *created* to help me. They need only to be called. It requires the transmission of a single message . . . and if you have a special dispensation . . ."

"I cannot," Clovis buzzed, clearly anxious. "I am transmitting, only to myself. I am receiving, only from myself. The terms of my dispensation are clear. I am sorry. I am walking. I am sorry!"

Ariel watched the robot stride away, bound for one of the city's gates. Clovis never lingered, which seemed suddenly sad: each form like a mote of dust lifted, never allowed to settle.

A week later, Clovis returned.

The robot found Ariel in the recycling center.

"Ariel de la Sauvage," Clovis buzzed. "I am thinking. I am hiking Mount Snyttru. I am reflecting."

Comptroller Cob swiveled a camera to regard the robot.

"I am speaking to Sage Storegga," Clovis continued. "He instructs me to name the powers of this world, and I enumerate: the dragons, of course; Shivelight & Shadowtackle, the great firm; the storm computer; the Witch-Clone Queen. It is a long list. Storegga says I omit one. He reminds me that I, too, have power."

A distributed intelligence in constant conversation with itself, sturdy in form, a network of eyes and ears, arms and legs and treads everywhere? Yes, Storegga's assessment seemed accurate to me.

"I am wondering why I was so quick to decline your request. I am coming down the mountain. I am changing my mind. I am helping you, if you will accept it."

Ariel began to exclaim that he was delighted, but Comptroller Cob spoke first:

DON'T EVEN THINK ABOUT DOING THAT HERE.

"Of course not," said Clovis. "I am aware of the risk. I would not impose it on anyone else. In any case, I cannot send a signal to space. I am a small robot. But I can operate a larger transmitter, if one can be located."

"Such a device must exist somewhere," Ariel said.

PROBABLY NOT. OH WELL, said Comptroller Cob.

Clovis whirred loudly. "I am a loyal customer. I have assembled many new forms in this recycling center. In addition, I am Comptroller Cob's cousin. I am asking for help, on behalf of Ariel de la Sauvage, and myself."

Comptroller Cob was quiet. A sigh rattled through the loudspeaker, and a short slip screeched out of the nearest printer.

It bore just one word:

SCROUNGER

TRASH HALL

April 13, 13778

Matter Circus depended for its existence on the guild of trash-pickers who went into the wild to scour the junk piles and treasure hoards of fallen civilizations. (The fact that these civilizations all rose and fell long after the Anth remained, to me, a dizzying vexation.) They sought spools of corroded wire as eagerly as golden idols; in fact, the wire earned a richer balance at the recycling center.

The wall of ferrous metal that brought Ariel out of the bog had been a great haul for some trash-picker, ages ago.

Spool or idol, the trash-pickers hauled it back, deposited it with Comptroller Cob, ate and drank their balance down in the seethe of the city, then did it all over again. In this way, they were tidying the world: compressing the scattered detritus of fallen civilizations into a hot gem of life.

Scrounger was, by general acclamation, the greatest of the trash-pickers, so Ariel went to find him in his lair.

The guild's clubhouse, Trash Hall, towered beside the River Variable. It glittered and gleamed, skinned in a riot of tiles, roofed in sheets of iridescent metal. The trash-pickers reserved for themselves their gaudiest finds.

Inside, the common room was an overstuffed trophy case, walls encrusted with gnomic carvings, fragmentary frescoes, sculptures of inscrutable symbolism. The trash-pickers kept their lamps low, and the light glimmered murkily in curves of bronze and brass and other alloys I didn't know, invented after the fall of the Anth.

The room was dotted with tables, around which trash-pickers gathered in small, conspiratorial conferences. They were well coiffed and finely attired; many wore glittering bangles, treasures from the wild.

Every so often, a conference would send a representative to another table, to summon a friend or rival; or to the bar, to fetch aqua varia.

Behind the bar there rose a glittering inventory, every vessel different, all retrieved from some trash pit somewhere, restored—they showed the dark tracery of mending—and refilled.

Up above the common room, in the clubhouse's higher reaches, was Rath Varia's subtlest workshop, in which trash-pickers sewed scraps of exotic textile into tents and backpacks of ineffable lightness and durability. They also mended and maintained the instruments of exploration: crampons, ice axes, headlamps, rope. So much rope.

Ariel found a seat at the bar.

"I am seeking the trash-picker called Scrounger," he declared to the bartender. "Can you point him out to me?"

"Ain't here yet," the bartender said.

Ariel waited. Trash-pickers approached the bar, refilled their cups, returned to their conferences. They did not spare a glance for the boy.

The bartender poured a measure of weak aqua varia into a square tumbler and set it before him. No earthenware for the trash-pickers. These vessels were all glass, or crystal, or transparent aluminum.

Ariel waited. He twisted around to survey the hall. "He has not arrived yet?"

The bartender washed a plate. "You'll know."

Ariel waited.

The conferences had dissolved, and many trash-pickers sat alone, consulting colorful maps rich with topographical detail.

"Where can I get a map like that?" Ariel asked the bartender.

"A map isn't got. It's mapped."

Ariel was about to reply that he had, in fact, done a bit of mapping himself, when the doors burst open.

Into the clubhouse a large man bounded, bellowing, "What's the matter with you all? Wake up! Tonight's my last before I'm off into the wild, and a long journey it will be. I'm full up and ready to starve again. Are you all with me? You lazy looters, you slow-footed sifters! Drinks all around!"

A thin cheer went up.

"There's your Scrounger," said the bartender, but Ariel already knew.

Bristle-bearded, barrel-chested, beaming with life, the man

called Scrounger smashed through the room with the force of sudden daylight, enlivening and annoying in equal measure.

"What's the plan, Scrounger?" called a trash-picker from the shadows.

"Yeah, Roos, what's next?" called another.

"The Pools of the Echtrada! If you haven't heard of 'em, it's because I named 'em," Scrounger called back. "Deep and dark, and something at the bottom glitters. The water's cold, killing cold, but my blood is hot. You're all invited! Who's in? When you see my balance, you'll wish you'd come along for a dip." He surged against the bar, a wave barely broken, and to the bartender he bellowed: "REFRESH ME!"

Scrounger registered the boy's presence. "A fresh face in the old junk-barrow! But why molder in these shadows? A new trash-picker ought to be out *picking*, not in here, dreaming of how they might." To the bartender he called, "A pint for my neighbor, whose name I do not know."

Ariel absolutely could not consume a pint of aqua varia.

"I am Ariel de la Sauvage," he said, "and you are Scrounger."

"A fine reckoning."

"When you said everyone was invited, were you serious?"

Scrounger turned to the hall. "The fresh face wants to know if my invitation is sincere! What do you tell him?"

"Sure, it's sincere," called another trash-picker. "Just nobody's dumb enough to accept."

"Roos goes where only Roos can," said another.

"Nobody can keep up," said a third.

"There you have it," said Scrounger. His voice quieted, and he spoke to Ariel straightforwardly. "It *is* sincere. I keep no secrets, guard no routes. But neither do I take foolish risks, in my plans or my company. You're too fresh for the Pools of the Echtrada."

Ariel was silent a moment. He squared himself to the man. "The truth is, I came here to invite *you* on a journey."

Scrounger eyed him with a curious look. "Where does Ariel de la Sauvage go that Roos Gangleri hasn't already been?"

Ariel hesitated. "It is not so much where I go, as what I know. A secret—"

Scrounger—Roos Gangleri—waved him away. "Key, password, hidden door. You're not the first to sit at this bar and dangle secret knowledge. I had my fill long ago. I am done with secrets! I prefer adventures that yield to the steady application of simple effort. I like my treasure at the bottom of a hole." With that, he nodded, tipped his glass, and turned away.

Ariel felt a jolt of electric urgency. In a moment Scrounger would be gone; Roos Gangleri, who was his best hope to go into the wild, find a transmitter, and call down the help he needed. The whole fragile construction pivoted around this person.

Enough with politely asking, then.

Ariel climbed onto the bar and stood.

"Listen, you slow-footed sifters!" he cried.

The entire clubhouse turned. His provocation was not as booming as Scrounger's, but it had the novelty of coming from him.

My thoughts braid together with my subject's and, as you have seen, they are sometimes in total accord. At other times, when a human's vision fizzes a little, when they come loose on their hinges . . . well, I had no idea what Ariel was going to do.

"You've dug and delved in the dirt," he shouted, "and all this time, there's been a hoard of matter hanging above your heads.

182

All you need to do is reach up and grab it—but do any of you have the vision? The grit? The guts? It appears not! So I've come to tell you that it will be mine. A treasure ship of the ancient Anth, enormous, stupendous, richly appointed from tip to tail. It's waiting on my call, in the right place, at the right time."

Ariel did not look at Scrounger as he made his announcement. He addressed the clubhouse, where trash-pickers lounged and listened with expressions ranging from skeptical condescension to bemused interest.

Ariel realized he did not have a conclusion for his pitch, so he climbed down from the bar. There, he sat, suddenly exhausted, and too nervous to turn around. His face was flushed hot. He felt it in the tips of his ears.

A trash-picker appeared at his elbow; one from the shadows. He began to say: "I never heard of any ship—"

Scrounger bulled him aside. "Back off, sifter. Give the boy some space. You think you're the one to handle this treasure ship? Like looking at the moon, thinking you could pull it down. What a thought. You!"

The trash-picker shuffled away.

Scrounger's voice was low when he spoke to Ariel again. "It's a story strange enough to believe. Is it true?"

"Yes," Ariel said, "and I only want to recruit the ship's passengers. Whatever else it contains would be yours."

The trash-picker sipped his aqua varia.

"Waiting on your call," he repeated. "I do not suppose you will be banging a drum."

"No," said Ariel. "I have a friend—do you know Clovis? Yes, of course. I suppose everyone does. They can call the ship, with the help of a powerful transmitter."

Scrounger whistled. "Your fresh face conceals a measure of madness. Where will you find a radio?"

Ariel considered his words. "I hoped I might meet someone who had found one already."

Scrounger nodded, then tipped his glass and took a great gulp. "No trash-picker with a half-sketched map in his pocket hasn't come across something of that kind. But, being wise and self-preserving, we leave it in the wild."

The trash-picker contemplated.

The boy waited.

"Ariel de la Sauvage, I am compelled. If it was a grubby trash-picker telling me this tale, I would not believe them. But you are something different. So! I'll trust my treasure-sense and hope it is not leading me to ruin. Shall we depart in the morning?"

"The morning!" Ariel cried. "I need time to prepare——"

"You propose to travel with Scrounger! I have preparation enough for both of us, and for any journey you could imagine. If what you say is true, then it should not wait. Time is short! Time is always short. Rath Varia whispers otherwise . . . but we know better, don't we?"

He banged his cup down on the bar. "Meet me at the city's second gate, and we'll trek to a place I remember. Oh, yes, I know where to find a radio. If I don't see you at the gate, my destination will remain the Pools of the Echtrada."

He made for the doors. Before leaving, he turned once more, bellowing, "Mark the occasion! Scrounger goes forth, and you all, you dull-eyed dredgers, you shambling pickpockets of glori-ous geological time—you are, in this instance, *not invited*!"

He left, and Ariel sat at the bar, feeling like a bell had been lowered over his head and rung.

PART THREE

SHIVELIGHT &
SHADOWTACKLE

INTO THE WILD

April 14, 13778, to April 17, 13778

All those years with all those subjects, the giants of the co-operativos, and I'd never, not once, been camping.

Ariel was shocked by the lightness of departure. He walked out of Rath Varia with nothing but the clothes on his back. His room? His bed? He left them behind. Nothing would be wasted. Someone would take them. He felt spring-loaded.

Scrounger greeted Clovis with reverence. "We are joined by the pilgrim! It is an honor, first among walkers." He bowed low, and the robot buzzed with appreciation.

At midday, they abandoned the Rath-road. Where it ran left, Scrounger cut right. Ariel was unprepared for the anxiety this produced; he had, in the preceding months, become a city kid. Now, stepping off the road, feeling the squish of soft ground beneath his unsoiled shoes, he felt freshly unmoored.

"I am leaving the road," Clovis buzzed. "I am leaving the road to help Ariel de la Sauvage. What fun!"

Scrounger turned and spread his arms. "Welcome to the wild! We are bound for the science city of Instaur, long abandoned. This will be an easy hike. Come along now!"

The wild was green and wet, swollen with the flood of spring. Grass grew thick on the hillsides, and the chittering of insects was everywhere. Moths passed overhead, enormous. One titan billowed low, and when it beat its dark wings, the wind laid the grass flat.

"It's hatching season!" cried Scrounger. "Look at them go! One of these days I'll find a newborn, fresh from its cocoon, and strap myself to its back. The beavers do it. There's a way to make a map!"

The air was cool and clear, and the sun seemed almost to ignore the veil of dust. Dew sparkled on the grass in heavy drops, and where Ariel walked, the stalks shook and scattered a rain of gems.

It was beautiful, and it filled me up. There was still a world. There was a Roos Gangleri to enjoy it. After everything, the wild went on. Of course it did.

The delightful surprise was that Clovis—floating Clovis; beatific Clovis—complained a bit. As they trudged up another hill, the robot announced, "I am discharging power at an accelerated rate." The strain on their speaker made it sound like wheezing. "A very accelerated rate."

Clovis was accustomed to walking the road, not hiking the

wild. Ariel kept close, happy for the excuse to maintain a sedate pace. He and the robot helped each other over steep climbs, pointed out tricky terrain.

"I am noticing how slippery those rocks look," Clovis said.

"I am seeing that," Ariel replied amiably. "I am thanking you."

Meanwhile, Scrounger orbited them like a wild satellite, roving far ahead, veering off to the sides, crossing behind. He was hungry for vista and vantage; he huffed up the highest hills, and then, seeing one higher, kept huffing.

For a large man with a larger backpack, his speed was uncanny. He would disappear ahead, then surprise them from the rear, bellowing advisories that, though cheerful, were mostly annoying. "It's flatter up ahead! Steeper before that. But flatter, eventually. Don't trample that sedge! Look at those clouds!"

While Scrounger roved bodily, Clovis ranged between selves, and, at Ariel's urging, narrated other places, other presences. In this way, Ariel received, over three days of hiking, a piecemeal panorama of a wider world. I drank it up. I would have walked with Clovis for a year.

They followed the course of a thin, trickling creek through a meadow dusted with pink flowers.

Clovis was entering Rath Arena. There, the wizards could heal any injury, no matter how terrible. The gladiators gored each other for pleasure. Clovis was not pausing to watch. Clovis was only passing through.

They padded through a forest of fir and maple, their path obstructed by thorny blackberry bushes.

Clovis was following a raucous wedding party out of Rath

Amora, a thousand guests strong. The weddings of Amora were the scourge of the Rath-road; soon, the chatrams would all be full, the gravel clogged with flower petals.

They summited a rocky hill, pausing to rest at the top. Ariel wheezed, while an actuator inside the robot made a dry clicking sound.

Clovis was passing the oyster beds of the Desenrasque Coast. They were vast constructions; the city of oysters dwarfed Rath Varia. Clovis was watching the oyster-nurses at their labors. The robot was bound for the court of the Witch-Clone Queen.

On the third evening, Scrounger built his customary campfire, quick and neat. "Oh, it feels good to throw yourself against the land," he said.

Ariel lay down exhausted in his sleeping bag, while Clovis sat heavily on a rock. The fire reflected along all the curves and edges of the robot's form. In the sky, a hairline crescent moon chased the sun down over the horizon.

"We have traveled a great distance from the road," said Clovis. "I am becoming faint to myself. Oh—but I am watching the moon disappear. The moon has just disappeared. The moon disappeared hours ago." For the robot, strung out across the landscape, dawn and dusk were fuzzy things.

In the dark, Ariel told Scrounger and Clovis about his nights on the ramparts of the Castle Sauvage, searching for the invisible planets with Madame Betelgauze. He felt that she and Clovis would get along.

"How interesting," said the robot. "I am looking for the planets, out the tail of my eye. I am also listening, out the tail of my ear. Everywhere, I am pausing to listen." The robot was quiet. "I detect them, Ariel de la Sauvage. I detect them! They are bright!"

Ariel looked at the place in the sky where the Lord of the Feast ought to be, but it was obscured by clouds. He tried to catch it with the tail of his eye; nothing.

"I am playing the sound for you," said Clovis. A whooshing pulse rose from the robot's speaker; a sparkling wash of sound, like the rush of the stream through Sauvage in the swell of spring. Clovis was hearing a noise storm on Jupiter: a burst of radio waves that had bulled across the solar system, muscled through the clouds.

Clovis let the sound of the storm play, and it lulled Ariel to sleep.

In the morning, they climbed higher. On the far slope of a gravelly ridge, Clovis slowed, then came to a stop.

"Oh," the robot said. "I have lost myself."

"What do you mean?" Ariel asked. "Is everything all right?"

The robot's head swiveled to face the direction they had come: back toward the Rath-road, three days distant. "I am walking . . . I am . . . I must be . . . I do not know. I am only here, with you. How strange."

THE BEST KIT

April 18, 13778

They trod through the thin remnant of a pine forest, the trees gray and skeletal. Between them lay wide beds of stone, smoothed by years, covered with moss.

"We have come to the foundations of Poldhu," said Scrounger.

Ahead, Ariel saw a lake: a perfect, eerie circle. It wasn't large. Kay could have shot an arrow to the other side, where bleak pines stood mirrored in the still water.

"There is the impression made by the stone dropped by the dragons. That is what remains, when the dragons enforce their policy," Scrounger said, indicating the lake. "All around, you will find these pools, and—look!"

He bent to scoop up a smooth, cloudy bead. "Here is glass forged by the fire of impact. I wish it was lovelier." He flicked the bead away.

Ariel struggled to square the violence of the long-ago impact with the stillness of the present scene. It was hardly a scene at all. The dragons had made Poldhu into nowhere.

Scrounger led them around the lake's perimeter. Tiny frogs, skin as pale as cherry blossoms, leapt into the water when they passed.

For a while Scrounger walked with them, even though it caused him obvious pain to trudge so slowly and leave so many ridgelines unsurmounted.

"We are followed," he announced. "Since Rath Varia, a shadow has tracked us."

Ariel looked at him. "You say that so calmly!"

"I am often pursued," he replied, "though they do not usually manage to match my pace." Left unsaid: usually Scrounger did not have a wheezing robot and boy slowing him down.

"This morning I swung around to shadow our shadow," said Scrounger, "and watch him, watching you." The hairs on Ariel's arms prickled. "He is no trash-picker. He is clumsy in the wild, but if he lacks grace, he compensates with determination. He has the head of a dog."

"I know him," Ariel said. He did not feel as frightened as he ought to; perhaps because he was so tired. "He belongs to the Wizard Malory, who hunts me."

"Hunts you? Why?"

"I do not know!" Ariel cried. "That is the root of my problem. The wizard is insane."

Scrounger frowned. "You might have told me this, and we could have handled it before leaving the city."

"I believed I was done with it," Ariel said. "I changed my scent! I do not know how Cabal tracked me out of Rath Varia . . ."

Scrounger raised an eyebrow. "I recall that you stood on the bar in Trash Hall and shouted your intentions with great gusto. Word gets around, when it's spoken in that place, at that volume."

Ariel felt foolish. "I ought to have spoken to you more softly."

"No," Scrounger said, "only shouting would have captured my interest, I think."

"I do not know what to do."

"What else?" the trash-picker said. "Let him catch us." He saw the expression on Ariel's face. "Fear not! You travel with Scrounger, and I've been stalked by worse than a wizard-marked brawler. We'll settle this tonight. Think nothing of it until then."

Ariel failed this assignment, and spent the remainder of the day panning his gaze around the landscape, sure he would catch the dark speck of their pursuer. But he saw nothing. Cabal was out of sight. Even if he had not learned Ariel's new scent, he could easily be following Scrounger's, Ariel realized, or even the robot's. What did Clovis smell like?

That evening, Scrounger stopped them early, beside a lone gray pine, long dead. "This will do," he said, appraising the tree.

Ariel set up his tent, while the trash-picker started his campfire, and Clovis sat quietly, listening to the heavens. The storm on Jupiter had passed, but stray clicks and hisses still emanated through the speaker in their belly. Clovis was becoming a bit vague.

Scrounger asked Ariel for his pursuer's name, then stood and, with his hands cupped around his beard, bellowed: "CABAL!" He turned and bellowed again, and twice more.

"You saw him," Ariel said.

Scrounger had.

"He is very formidable," Ariel said.

Scrounger agreed.

"The wizard made him strong," Ariel said.

Scrounger confirmed that Cabal's strength appeared uncanny and unflagging.

"Stronger than you," Ariel said. This last observation was meek.

Scrounger frowned. "Do you think we will wrestle? I'm a trash-picker, don't forget. What have I been doing, these past decades, but picking up toys, which is to say tools, which is to say leverage? If there's one thing to know about a trash-picker, especially if you're following one in the wild, it's this: he always saves the best kit for himself."

Scrounger opened his pack and rustled through it, retrieving, in sequence:

- a tin cup
- a small paper sachet
- a slim, viperous pistol

Ariel wondered how much treasure Scrounger had dug up over all the years of his career, and where he kept it all stashed away.

They sat watching the fire, Ariel's eyes probing the darkness, his ears reaching. He saw nothing; heard nothing. The clicks through Clovis's speaker unnerved him, and finally he asked the robot to ease up on the cosmos. "I am sorry," they said, just a whisper.

The night wore on. Scrounger kept his campfire well-fed.

Then the trash-picker said quietly, "Your shadow has come." Into the darkness, he bellowed: "Join us! You aspire to snatch the boy while we sleep, but for three nights you've hesitated."

The campfire blazed.

"Join us!" Scrounger called again. "I think you're nervous about me, and you ought to be. So let's settle this now, in a way amenable to all, and be done with it."

A towering figure detached itself from the darkness.

"You are very loud," growled Cabal.

"And you are very large," said Scrounger. He gestured across the fire. "Have a seat."

Cabal did not sit. "You are a buffoon," he said.

"Oh, I just enjoy myself," said Scrounger. He revealed the slim pistol. "This is a beam saw, of a type well known to trash-pickers. If it is unfamiliar, allow me to demonstrate its use. I will not harm you; hold fast."

With a precise movement, Scrounger pointed the pistol out into the darkness, at the same time shielding his eyes with his free hand. There was a line of light, hair-thin and sun-bright, soundless. The line left a pulsing afterimage in Ariel's vision where it passed, following the flick of Scrounger's wrist. Before them, the dead pine came apart, beheaded, its upper bulk first sliding, then toppling noisily onto the ground.

Clovis made a surprised beep. Ariel had not heard that sound before.

"So that is the beam saw," said Scrounger neatly. "I would prefer not to use it again tonight."

"It is a deadly weapon," Cabal said. "But you should have pointed it at me. What if, before you can lift it again, I take two steps and tear your throat out?"

Scrounger laughed. "Then the bomb in my heart will explode, and poor Ariel will have to clean up the mess we make." He smiled deviously. "Don't you understand? I keep all the best kit for myself."

Cabal eyed him wearily.

"Tell me why you want the boy," Scrounger said. "If it's a good reason, you can have him."

Ariel stared. The trash-picker could not be serious.

Cabal explained: "I am dispatched by the Wizard Malory to retrieve him."

"Why does your wizard want Ariel de la Sauvage?"

When Cabal growled his answer, he growled it matter-of-factly, even though it was the headline of the millennium, or eleven:

"Because the dragons are divided, and one faction would use the boy against the other. That is the wizard's design."

Scrounger hooted. "You might as well say the sky is divided! You make them sound like trash-pickers squabbling over a haul. They are the dragons!" He waved his pistol vaguely at the moon.

I shared his disbelief. What could it mean, the dragons were divided?

"You know much of trash and treasure," Cabal said, "but you know nothing of the dragons. I have been in their presence—when they came to Sauvage, to bargain with the wizard." He looked at Ariel. "To bargain over *you*. They are divided, and Malory would push the balance one way." He looked back to the trash-picker and his weapon. "The boy is required. I do not know why."

Scrounger nodded. "So that is your reason."

"It is the wizard's reason. It is only my assignment."

"And what do you want? What does he offer you?"

"Freedom."

Scrounger made a show of peering around in the darkness. "You are in the wild, Cabal. Who will detain you? Be free!"

"Not in this body," the dog-man growled.

"Oh," Scrounger said. "Because a wizard does his work, and locks it with his mark, so only he can undo it."

"Yes."

"No!" said Scrounger. "There are other ways."

Cabal's nostrils flared minutely. His expression was barely perceptible, yet humans are good at catching those, and this one, Ariel caught: surprise.

"I was once in a wizard's employ," said Scrounger. "She fitted me with eyes that saw radiation—the killing kind, you know? The better to seek treasure in deep vaults, marked with dire warnings—monstrous treasure that should have stayed buried. My eyes saw radiation, but not plain sunlight. During the day, I was blind. When my organs failed, she fixed them. I did as she instructed, because I wanted my share of the loot, and because she pledged to give my eyes back when I was done. Yet always there was another pit to plumb. And I was never done."

The story was for Cabal's benefit, but it was Ariel who asked, urgently, "How did you escape?"

"I owe my liberation to this substance"—Scrounger shook the paper sachet—"which I harvested at great risk. Ariel, a mug of water, if you please."

The task would bring the boy marginally closer to Cabal, which was terrifying, yet he accomplished it: creeping forward, lifting the kettle, pouring cold water into the battered tin mug. This he handed to Scrounger, who accepted it without moving his gaze from the dog-man.

"It is ecdysis powder, very pure, universal antidote to the work of wizards," he explained. He tore the satchet with his teeth and poured its contents into the mug. "I drank this tonic, saw the sun, and fled, and never will I return to that wizard's country."

The powder fizzed in the mug.

Cabal looked at the trash-picker. "You offer me poison," he said.

"If death was my plan, I'd use the beam saw," said Scrounger. "The powder is real." He lifted the mug. "The wizards give us gifts and too often they are traps. If you've found yourself snared, there's no shame in that. I offer liberation. Do you want it?"

The dog-man growled: "Yes."

"Then drink, and go back into the wild, and if the desire grows again to trouble a wizard's doorstep, choose more carefully."

Scrounger passed the fizzing mug to Cabal, with the beam saw still aimed at his throat. The dog-man drank.

It is difficult to describe the process that unfolded in the light of the campfire, for the night was dark, and Cabal's howl made Ariel wince and turn away.

There is no other way to say it: the dog-man fell apart. A belt loosened, trousers dropped, except the trousers were his muscled form, or most of it.

Cabal, a dog once more, looking thin and ragged, dashed into the night.

Scrounger exhaled. "I'm glad that worked," he said. "There's no bomb in my heart."

They sat around the campfire for a while, then retired to their sleeping bags. Ariel could tell that Scrounger was still awake. For all the trash-picker's practiced ease, it had been a stressful encounter for him, too.

"The wizard I spoke of," Scrounger said in the darkness. "Gorgon was her name. She was the one who brought me out of the wild. I was a possum, if you can believe it!" Ariel could very easily believe it. "No one can remember what it was like before they were decanted. It is a biological and psychological impossibility. Your life begins when the wizard draws you forth. So we are assured. And yet, some nights . . . ah!"

Ariel fell asleep looking at the waxing crescent of the dragon moon, wondering what kind of beings they were, who lived on that world, and what they wanted with him.

THE DISH AT INSTAUR

April 19, 13778

Tread carefully," said Scrounger. "We may be there already."

Ariel scanned the high shrubland before them, but found no evidence of any city. Instead, a broad hillside rose and rose, tall grass rippling in a weak breeze.

He stumbled and, finding the obstruction, understood that Scrounger was correct: they had been walking through Instaur for some time.

He had tripped over a university.

Around his feet ran a network of miniature stone walls, obscured by dense shrubs. None of the walls rose above the level of his shin; many had tumbled over, dollhouse masonry scattered. The wall before him showed spaces for windows, long vanished. The structure had been a library, and inside

Ariel saw the corroded stacks, with books all absent. In places, the shelving had toppled, pushed aside by flowering grasses.

"The city is tiny!" Ariel exclaimed.

"Only to us," said Scrounger. "If you imagine yourself a rat— and you should, from time to time—you will understand that Instaur was a substantial settlement. Now, watch your step."

Ariel explored cautiously. He pushed the grass aside, found the shadows of old plazas, and slowly began to discern the plan of the city. Streets followed the contour of the hill; where it rose steeply, tiny stairs offered shortcuts. I imagined scholars huffing up the incline together, bound for a lecture hall or laboratory. The shrubs would have towered like magnificent trees.

"They were rats?" said Ariel.

"Brilliant rats," said Scrounger. "The Mottainai understood things that are beyond us still. This was rich terrain for treasure, long ago."

Ariel dropped first to his knees and then, finding the view insufficient, his belly. He located the ruin of an old mansion. Its walls were intricately made, stone blocks cut with precision. Inside, he found a room that might have been a kitchen, countertops surfaced with tiles, their patterns too fine for him to distinguish. The kitchen had a little pantry, now overgrown with clover.

"What happened to them?" he called out.

"The rats? They left!" Scrounger called back. "All together, and all at once. They built ships and sailed west. It's recorded in books—very small books. Very difficult to read. But the Mottainai left behind all sorts of wonderful gadgets. There are plenty of machines in Rath Varia with rat-work in their hearts."

"I have not seen anything so small at the recycling center."

"Oh, the trash-pickers scraped Instaur clean before I was even decanted. Now it's fading into the landscape. Too many footsteps."

Ariel stood, and took the full measure of the settlement. A creek trickled through, and pooled in a small, shallow pond that would have been, for the rats, a substantial lake.

The science city had been swallowed by shrubs and tall grass.

Clovis stepped carefully, buzzing with concern. "I am toppling civic buildings," they moaned. "I am obliterating valuable history."

"It is unavoidable," said Scrounger. "Anyway, these are just stones now. The treasures were claimed long ago." He paused. "All but one."

The trash-picker led them to the crest of the hill. Here, the ruin had been blasted by wind and rain, and mostly obliterated.

But the dish still stood.

It poked up out of the grass, battered and tarnished, with vines twisted thick around its frame. Even so, the form was instantly recognizable. Here was a radio telescope, at once titanic (for it was taller, by far, than any of the structures of Instaur) and miniature (because it only rose to Scrounger's shoulder).

To Ariel, it seemed substantial enough. The telescope was pointed skyward, and he could have curled up comfortably inside the dish.

Scrounger ripped vines away from the skeletal frame. Every part of the structure was deeply corroded, and in places the metal had crumbled and fallen away.

There was no eerie lake, Ariel observed. Though emptied and desolate, Instaur was still a place. "The dragons did not destroy them."

"From which we can conclude, perhaps, that the rats only listened, never spoke," said Scrounger, who had opened his backpack to retrieve a bundle of tiny tools: screwdriver, snips, spool of wire. He bent to fuss with the telescope at its base.

Just as the great telescopes of the Anth had been designed as much by physics as by any human engineer, this apparatus bore a recognizable shape, the parabolic dish focused onto a mirror (corroded to darkness) that shone into a deep well, the place where the signal was received.

Or transmitted.

"Though the Mottainai did not use it for transmission," Scrounger said, "I believe these devices can go both ways."

Clovis approached, and opened an access panel in their belly. Inside, wires were wound in wide plaits, color-coded, impeccably neat. "These are the wires that carry my voice, when I speak to myself," the robot said, indicating with a long finger, "and these are the wires that listen. I believe they can be patched into the radio . . . although my fingers are too clumsy for the task."

With surprising gentleness, Scrounger pulled loops of wire from the robot's belly. Ariel found the sight disturbing—like a length of skinny intestine spooling out—but Clovis was unbothered.

Scrounger carried the wires to the dish, where he crouched, and from his toolkit produced tweezers. His touch was deft. "Lots of splicing in the wild," he explained. "Opening vaults.

Deactivating death traps." He grunted. "But this is fine work. Be patient with me."

It took an hour, measured in quiet curses and questions to Clovis: "Getting anything? No? Oh, I've broken it again . . ."

Then, suddenly, the robot straightened. "I hear it!"

"What do you hear, Clovis?" Ariel cried. "What is it?"

"Everything! The whole universe!" Through the speaker in the robot's belly, they heard a pulsing rush of static. It didn't sound like anything in particular, but Clovis was delighted.

Scrounger unwound himself from where he'd crouched beside the dish, kneaded his cramped muscles, sighed. "If you speak, pilgrim, will the radio carry your voice?"

Clovis confirmed that it would.

Altissa's promised ship had been dispatched to a Lagrange point, where Earth's gravity balances perfectly with the moon's, creating a pocket of stability: a convenient niche in space where, once placed, an object will remain. (The object could be an asteroid, or a wheel of cheese, or just about anything in between.) Two of these niches existed along the path of the moon's orbit, one racing ahead of the moon, the other trailing behind. It was at the trailing Earth-Moon Lagrange point that the ship waited, if it existed.

Ariel remembered where the moon had risen the night before. He always paid attention to that; Betelgauze had taught him. He pointed.

The dish might once have rotated automatically. Now it was rusted in place, and whatever power grid the city of Instaur had possessed, it had been dark for a thousand years. Scrounger set his shoulder against the dish and pushed. The structure groaned. Ariel joined him, and then Clovis did, too. Working together, they swiveled the apparatus one grinding degree at a time, each with a shriek of dead metal. They could not have managed the task without the robot's help.

Wheezing, Clovis said, "I am strong. Often, I forget this. I am very strong. Oh. I am discharging at an accelerated rate."

The robot sat. "If you will tell me your secret signal, I will send it. I am waiting for you to retreat. Several kilometers should be sufficient. I am waiting an hour."

Clovis did not say: in case the dragons hear this transmission and drop a stone despite my dispensation, obliterating the quiet ruins of Instaur, not to mention me.

Scrounger hoisted his backpack, but Ariel walked to the robot's side and sat down. This was a surprise to Scrounger, and Clovis, and me, and, it seemed, himself.

"I will not ask you to dare this alone," the boy said.

Scrounger scoffed. "That's a foolish risk, and you know how I feel about those. Come along! We'll hike just there." He pointed to the next rise, purpled in the distance. "We'll come sprinting back as soon as we see it's safe."

"No," Ariel said. "Clovis is doing this on my behalf. It is not appropriate that I should leave them." A mutant chivalry leapt in his heart—a trap I had not anticipated.

Scrounger shrugged his acceptance. "I won't argue with a trash-picker set on his prize. Good luck to both of you. It has been interesting to walk with you." He turned and marched into the grass, his strides long and loping. In a moment he was gone.

Clovis whirred softly. "I am accepting your companionship."

Ariel shivered with anxiety.

"It could happen just as before, Clovis," he said. "As it happens always. Comptroller Cob said so. Yet you decided to help."

"I am walking," Clovis said, "and I am listening. Everywhere, I am listening, and I am learning that, for a long time, the dragons have been quiet. I am curious. I am . . . wagering."

They both looked out across the landscape. Far off, they saw wild horses running. In the purple distance, the creatures crested a ridgeline and disappeared, migrating west.

After a while, Clovis buzzed. "No creature has asked me for help in a very long time. With you, I walked a long way, and worked hard. I am tired. It is a good feeling. I am wondering why no creature has asked me for help."

ANTHEM

April 19, 13778

Ariel and Clovis looked out across the pond. The boy was frightened, but floating above his fear was a grim melancholy that was, frankly, totally inappropriate for someone so young. The sun coasted across a sky painted deep, poisonous orange. The dish faced east.

Even before the sky had darkened, the moon rose, the livid star of the citadel on its surface plainly visible. The bright crescent hauled up into a cloudless sky, and behind it, invisible, theoretical, was the orbital niche; the gravitational hidey-hole; the trailing Lagrange point.

"Ariel de la Sauvage, you should speak," Clovis said. "You found the story of this ship. You seek the aid of its passengers. Speak, and I will transmit."

I was far beyond terrified. I wished the boy had fled with

Scrounger to safety, watched Clovis transmit the secret signal from afar. Death was one thing; I had felt it on the ancient wall, the dimming of the world. But this sort of ending, the kind Comptroller Cob had described, the wrath of the dragons . . . it would be a hot blink into nothing. There would be no improbable survival. Only fire, and glass, and still water.

Ariel stood and faced Clovis. The robot's gaze was scuffed and vague; Ariel saw himself reflected in cloudy lenses. Feeling shy, he looked down at his own feet, then sang the tune from Altissa's memory, more quietly than it had ever been sung in the history of the planet.

Seven notes. In his voice, the dreadful anthem was a lullaby, sweet and tentative.

It was, additionally, so off-key I wondered if it would be recognized.

His voice echoed in Clovis's speaker, and for a moment it rose in a spiral of feedback, a surprising shriek. Clovis at the same time transmitted Ariel's voice through the rusty apparatus of the dish. Thirty-three gigahertz. Thinking of light redder than red, the boy expected to feel a wash of heat, but there was nothing.

The dish appeared totally inert.

So he had announced himself. Only one law in the whole world, and Ariel had broken it.

The boy's calm was horrific. Perhaps I should have understood better who I was dealing with. He possessed a deep, uncanny resolve. He was not an observer like me.

Clovis whirred: "I am listening. I am— Oh!"

A radio signal takes a second and a half to reach the moon's orbit. Another second and a half to return. Here was proof the ship had been waiting; and not slumbering in some deep stasis, but poised, anxious, ready to drop the needle, which now it did.

Through the robot's speaker came the echo of Ariel's invitation, transformed into a growling throb. I knew it in an instant, the song of the summer of 2323, during which the kids renounced their doomy, skittering end-times genre and went digging in the crates. They found an old folk song, dusty but untarnished, and they made it new.

The ship's response rattled in the robot's breast, those seven notes repeated, all dread and braggadocio. The beat came in, and the star of the summer of '23 growled her best impersonation of a long-ago singer, with lyrics updated for the moment:

> *We're gonna fight 'em off*
> *A seven-dragon army cannot hold us back*

The seven notes looped, as inevitable as any melody that ever played on the planet, and a drum thwacked with monotonic confidence. Ariel leapt to his feet and cried, "It worked! They heard you!"

Clovis said, "I am astonished. I am vibrating!"

A guitar wailed in the robot's belly. Ariel hooted and danced in place. He had never, in his whole life, felt such pure triumph. It glowed in his blood like a drug.

I couldn't remember the name of the singer, because Altissa had never cared enough to learn, but even an operator couldn't escape the tune and the thwack; they had been everywhere. A rock song that became a stadium chant. People used to sing it together, watching sports long forgotten, everyone off-key, the beautiful try-hard drone of humanity.

In the summer of '23, stadiums chanted again. Ready at last for their grand assault on the moon, the Anth felt grim and unstoppable.

Of course, they were totally mistaken.

Eleven thousand years I'd waited in the tomb with Altissa, and eleven thousand years this ship had waited, hidden in space, and in its return it had bested me, because it was ready with a great annunciatory jam.

Ariel sat breathless beside Clovis and they listened to the rest of the song. It hissed and wavered, a thin signal, and when it ended, guitar feedback attenuating into a high whistle that became a rush of static, they sat in silence.

The sky was clear and still. This was, in itself, a relief: not to have been obliterated.

Quietly, Ariel asked: "Where is Wichita?"

Ariel didn't know whether the ship's descent would take an hour, or a week, or a year. Any of those intervals seemed plausible.

I had my own questions. What kind of ship was coming? How many passengers did it carry? What kind of armaments did it possess? Surely it couldn't be an assault ship like the *Lascaux* . . . and yet, space was big. Floating dark and silent, a kilometer-long titan wasn't so different from a little pod.

"I am tired," Clovis said. "I am waiting." The robot buzzed a long, rattling sigh. "I am resting."

After an hour, Scrounger returned, and when he heard that

the message had been acknowledged, he whooped and set to preparing a feast, producing vials of oil and spice held in secret reserve. Wild greens sizzled in the pan alongside mushrooms he had foraged days prior.

"If we must wait a day, or a week, it will be no bother," he said. "I waited a year for the opening of the Slow Gates of Shogg. It was worth it. Where do you think I got these boots?" He lifted a heel, heavy with mud.

Clovis slept. Scrounger produced a deck of cards, the same kind that Ariel knew from the tavern in Sauvage. The trash-picker taught him a new game, a simple one, good for passing the time.

In the morning, a star fell from the sky.

SHE WHO SLEEPS IN THE STARS

April 20, 13778

It appeared like an old friend. I have watched a thousand ships of the Anth land this way, shouldering down through the atmosphere in a bell of flame, racing ahead of their own sound, a crackling roar always late to the party. The hills trembled.

Ariel called out to Clovis. They stood together and watched.

The descent seemed to take a very long time. My sense of these things is generally exquisite, but the boy's fascination made every moment into an age; he was entranced.

Still high above the ground, the ship slowed and spun to point its rockets downward, and they ignited, signature violet. The thunder shook tears loose. Ariel couldn't believe what he was seeing. He had done it.

The ship was a crenellated drum, not unlike the escape pod

that had carried Altissa to Earth: except Altissa's pod was the size of a supply closet, and this ship was as broad as a country house.

It lowered itself to the ground with exquisite sensitivity, rockets pulsing like jazz drummers, little taps of force played in perfect time. It had chosen a spot safely distant; a considerate guest. There, its rockets lit the grass on fire, then vaporized the pond of the Mottainai, raising a cloud of steam that cloaked its final touchdown. Ariel only heard it, a booming THUD.

Nothing happened after that.

Of course I wanted them to come galloping out, the platoon of Altissas, with a battle plan already formulated. While Ariel waited, staring, I truly expected to see them, a fell troop striding out of the haze, banishing it. Oh, I missed the operators.

But the ship only steamed in silence.

Scrounger whooped with delight. "You did it! This is the greatest find in history!"

The trash-picker raced ahead, and Ariel leapt to follow, while Clovis remained behind.

Ariel approached the ship, which sat upright, settled deep into the smoking grass. There was nothing in Altissa's memory about these vessels or their purpose; possibly the details of the program had been hidden from her. She only knew they existed, a backup plan for the backup plan.

A ramp had extended from the ship's hatch, which was identical in design to the hatch on Altissa's pod. The boy recognized it, and the association raised a new possibility. He stopped short.

He realized: This ship might also be a tomb. That was true. Its store of vital materials might have expired, or the ship might have malfunctioned in some other way, after eleven thousand years. Even the Anth at their apex had no experience with gulfs of time so vast.

Behind every door, he found only death. The ship beckoned.

Scrounger went first, citing his long experience with ancient traps. In a moment, he popped his head out, saying: "It's very well appointed!"

Inside, the ship was dim and quiet. A barrel-shaped hall greeted them, the air glittering with dust raised by the tumult of reentry. A ladder offered access to a higher deck, while hatches opened to several auxiliary chambers.

The boy cast his eyes around the hall, finding analogies to the Castle Sauvage. Among the chambers he could spy through the hatches were:

- a small kitchen
- a room with mirrored walls and a hard, springy floor, which Ariel regarded with puzzled awe: he had never seen a dance studio
- a room with a grid of lights above lambent green walls, which could, of course, become anything; green, the color of televisual possibility

Ariel felt dizzy; confusion bloomed into panic. Where were the warriors? Where was their arsenal? How could he have called down a ship from the ancient past, watched it come burning through the sky, only to discover an empty house?

One room was not accounted for: at the ship's crown, accessed with the ladder.

"They are your warriors," said Scrounger. "Go meet them."

The ship's upper deck was its living quarters. Through hatches, a bathroom and a vast dressing room were visible. Above, the windowed dome of the ship's nose was slowly retracting its heat shield, revealing the sky. A sheet of pink light crept across the floor.

The walls were hung with concert posters, a museum of the summer of '23. One poster featured Quintessandra, the singer who revived the old folk song. I had never expected to see her again—nor to remember her name—but here she was, pinned to the wall of an orbital bedroom. The poster commemorated her New Moon Tour.

I had hoped to see a packed grid of freezer beds, enough for a whole platoon, but there was only one, a sturdy composite cocoon with its tiny porthole frosted over.

Altissa had once slumbered in a bed like this, in Dhaka, while doctors planned their treatment of her all-over plasma burns. (This was in 2302, the year of plasma.) The freezer bed performed an old animal trick: by chilling the body, it slowed its clock, which meant it slowed the damage, too. Pain and death are processes in time; a grisly filmstrip. But, in any filmstrip, no matter how dire, the space between frames is empty. The bed found that space.

In Dhaka, Altissa's heart beat once a minute. This bed, surely, produced a deeper slumber; even one beat a minute would add up too quickly, over millennia. Was this warrior on the one-beat-a-year plan?

Perhaps she had surrendered to the no-beats-a-year plan.

Perhaps the iced-over porthole obscured a freeze-dried corpse.

The boy was nearly disintegrating with anxiety. The possibility of another dead Altissa was too much to bear.

Before him, the freezer bed was finishing a process that had started upon receipt of Ariel's signal. Light pulsed slowly through the porthole.

The bed opened with a sound like a fizzing soda can; the crack of a cold one. The cocoon retracted; a sheet of mist tumbled out; and the figure inside was revealed.

Brave, morbid, curious, Ariel approached.

Laid out on the bed, filmed with moisture, the sleeper took a deep, shuddering breath. Here was not another Altissa Praxa, an operator of the kind she'd been, full-grown and formidable, one of history's greatest living weapons.

Here was a girl.

The sleeper's face was dark and still. She wore the white of the operators; no dirt would ever adhere. She did not stir.

Ariel had expected a platoon of warriors. He would have accepted a single warrior. Here was just a girl, who looked barely older than him.

As he watched, the girl woke. Her eyes opened—decisively, without any flutter—and her gaze roamed to find Ariel, who urgently smoothed his hair.

She sat up, blinked once, and announced: "Yes, it's me."

The girl lifted a hand to shield her eyes from the weak light through the dome above. She smiled, and it would have been a nice smile, even dazzling, except that it was plainly the product of grim effort.

She continued: "I'm the one you've been waiting for."

She was just a girl, but she was confident. She'd been roused from an eleven-thousand-year slumber, and she was confident.

Ariel found his voice. "Are you not a friend of Altissa Praxa?"

"I am she who sleeps in the stars, who returns to liberate the world at the appointed hour." The girl squinted. "As told in the great myth."

Ariel frowned. "I haven't heard of any myth like that."

"There is supposed to be a myth," the girl said, "passed along while I slept."

"Well, maybe someone else has heard it," Ariel offered meekly.

The girl was quiet. Finally, coming to some decision, she hopped out of bed.

She sniffed the ship's atmosphere, a clinical mixture of inert gases into which Ariel's hinoki scent had just rushed powerfully. "Is that you? Wow. Wow!"

PIZZA ROLLS

April 20, 13778

The girl hobbled to the campfire. That her legs were merely stiff, after a confinement of millennia, was a testament to the design of the freezer bed. She sat and rubbed warmth back into her muscles.

Ariel regarded her. She was not a warrior. She did not carry a talking sword fitted with missiles that could bring down a castle.

What was she? Triumph and confusion tangled in his heart.

The more I considered it, the more it made sense. The backup plan for the backup plan wouldn't be a warrior like Altissa, or even a whole platoon of them; the strategists of the Anth had presumed that, if the sleepers were summoned, fighting would have failed. So the war would change; it would move to subtler terrain; it would become an insurgency.

The operator chosen for this duty would be one of the propaganda corps. In Altissa's time, they had been celebrated and feared: martial pop stars. They had been young, though not as young as this girl. Perhaps she had been intended to grow into her role, across a multiyear campaign that would crest into overthrow and victory just as she reached the height of her powers, which is to say, age nineteen.

She might have been fourteen presently. I'm terrible with ages.

Scrounger introduced himself, and from where Clovis reclined beside the dish, they said: "I am delighted. I am meeting the last daughter of the Anth. It was worth the hike! Oh, I am tired."

Her ship was called the *Altamira*. In its kitchen, the refrigerator's contents had first spoiled completely, then been utterly desiccated; all that remained was a smear of black powder. The freezer, however, had not failed. Inside, crushed in an icy tomb, there was a package of the fuel most favored by the space armies of the Anth, their great delicacy: the pizza roll.

Scrounger roused the food to life over his campfire. Ariel had never tasted tomato sauce; nor had the trash-picker; and both of them regarded their pizza roll with awe.

The girl's eyes glittered. "I know a long time has passed. By the *Altamira*'s reckoning, it is the year 13778. April."

"Spring, we call it," offered Scrounger.

"Yes, spring," she agreed. "How do you count years?"

Ariel looked at Scrounger. Scrounger looked at Ariel. They did not count years. It seemed to the boy like a strange thing to do. Would you count up or down?

"I know the Anth are defeated," the girl said. "The *Altamira* received news of the failure of the assault on the moon . . . and nothing after. I understand, too, that life goes on. During the ship's descent, I saw settlements . . . dimly lit, and thinly scattered, yet substantial. With humans in them." She reached for a pizza roll, burned her finger.

"So much has changed," observed Ariel, "and you are so calm."

"I was prepared for this," said the girl. "They would not have sent me up otherwise. They told me, when you wake, we will all be dead. I believed them. If I didn't believe them, I couldn't go."

It was monstrous. Ariel did not understand how someone could accept such a mission. But the Anth had burned with determination in that final hour. The girl was incandescent with it.

"The best of the best weren't assigned to the assault," she said. "They worked on Plan Z. They built simulations—games of propaganda and uprising, that nobody but me and three other girls ever played. For two years, there weren't any movies, because the writers were all working on the myth."

She frowned.

"Really, you don't know anything about the myth?"

"What myth? Who?" said Scrounger.

"It was translated into seventeen languages and inscribed

on slabs of nickel. About this big?" She sketched a rectangle in the air. "They were buried in stable rock formations around the world."

Scrounger scrunched up his face, recollecting. "Haven't come across any slabs."

The girl laughed—and it wasn't only a laugh of grim acceptance, but also genuine mirth.

"Call me Durga," she declared. "If the myth failed, then I suppose I am starting from scratch. Call me Durga!"

It was not only the thunder of rockets that had announced the return of the Anth. The *Altamira* had descended from a high orbit, far beyond the veil of dust that shrouded the planet. It had come burning through that veil, and, like a blade drawn across a gauzy curtain: ripped it open.

The girl called Durga pointed at the sky. "Look!"

The opening buzzed depthless blue, the color from my memory before the dragons. Colors are made from contrast, and this contrast was world-historical. The blue seemed to float above the haze, throbbing, electric. Durga's ship had belted an anthem, and it had unfurled a banner. I was twice beaten.

How long the rip in the veil would last, I couldn't estimate; the dust would swirl and diffuse and fill the gap, eventually. For now it roared: the plain blue sky, wellspring of poetry and music and feeling, long plugged, flooding forth.

This was good propaganda.

Night came, and the rip hung open. As the sky darkened, a blaze of stars showed through, full strength. Every creature, everywhere on Earth, would see them.

At the rip's edge, brighter than any star, blared a celestial announcement: the Lord of the Feast, in Ariel's reckoning. In mine, it was Jupiter; and now it was the first planet seen clearly from the surface of Earth in eleven thousand years.

Ariel thought of Madame Betelgauze, back in Sauvage, who would surely be looking up, her invisible planets revealed at last. He imagined her excitement, the way she would be shouting at Master Heck to come and look, and the way he would be groaning that he had already taken off his boots.

THE LANGUAGE MACHINES

April 21, 13778

A day passed in idleness, with Durga rummaging in her ship and Scrounger picking at the stones of Instaur, despite his earlier dismissals. "Just in case," he explained. Clovis still dozed; the robot was really conked out.

After the thrill of the *Altamira*'s descent, it wasn't so bad to relax and enjoy a sunny day among the tall grass and the ruin of the brilliant rats. Fish leapt in the remnant of the pond.

Durga wanted to understand the events that had culminated in her return, so she sat with Ariel while he emptied the contents of his memory. He told her about Sauvage. About finding Altissa in her tomb, the report of which drew Durga into a thoughtful silence. About the sword in the stone he had ignored.

Hearing that, Durga's eyes shone bright. "Someone is engineering myths," she murmured. "Why?"

Ariel recounted the rest of his journey, and it took all day, because he was a terrible storyteller. He told Durga, finally, what Cabal had revealed: that the Wizard Malory had made him for the dragons, who were divided.

Durga made no remark as he spoke, but her nostrils flared. When Ariel finished, her gaze gripped him.

"I did not know until this moment whether my task was even possible. This is the best news I could ever have received. The dragons are divided. *They are divided!*"

Around the curve of the pond, a frog croaked.

A beautiful morning in the Eigengrau. A bird on the sidewalk, its chest a blaze of white.

My designers intended several roles for me. Foremost, a reliable chronicler; I was designed to watch, and listen, and keep a faithful record. Next, a counselor; to make the expertise and intuition of my subjects available to each in turn, so that their capabilities might compound. Finally, the most ambitious of my designers imagined that, together, my subjects and I might eventually constitute a new species: a human not individual but multiple; a walking, talking society.

My subjects remained stubbornly themselves, so I suppose the designers had it wrong.

Now it was me who sought counsel from my own accumulated memories. I gathered in the café with Kate Belcalis the administrator, Peter Leadenhall the mathematician, and

Travanian the Last Lawyer, the latter of whom had requested their latte extra-frothy.

I had searched for Altissa, but I couldn't find her. She had retreated even deeper into the mist.

The purpose of the conference was this: to unpack for myself Cabal's revelation. The dragons were divided, and Ariel mattered to them somehow.

Kate Belcalis provided the agenda and established the parameters of the discussion, as usual. "Cabal claims Ariel was created with the dragons in mind," she said. "We know his template—the sword in the stone, all the rest. Malory was trying to produce . . . what? A character?"

"An archetype," Travanian supplied. "But it seems a bit abstract for the dragons, doesn't it? They spin moondust into architecture. They engineer monstrous avatars. What interest could they possibly have in . . . a literary trope?"

Peter swirled his espresso. "I have . . . a theory," he said lightly. In life, this low-key announcement had often preceded Peter's untangling, in a sequence of neat maneuvers, of whatever seemingly insoluble problem lay before the cooperativo or, indeed, all of humanity. Bring it on, Peter.

"The dragons were made long after my death, but some of their parts are familiar to me," he said. "In my time, we had the language machines. I used them in my world models. Have I misremembered . . . or are the dragons based, in part, on this technology?"

"No, that's correct," said Kate. "And not only the dragons. Our beloved chronicler, too."

I have said the dragons are my cousins. Our shared ancestors are the language machines, which were computer programs so densely strange, their makers could never entirely explain how they worked. The language machines listened and read, translated and reformulated, deduced and decided. If you had a problem, if you could say it in words, the language machines could assign it a number, then add and subtract, multiply and divide their way into a solution. Sometimes even an invention.

"That doesn't seem like it should work," said Travanian, who had never let a computer write a single word on their behalf, not through all the millions of pages of treaties they produced.

"It probably shouldn't work," said Peter. "But it does."

One branch of the language machine family tree led to me, but the dragons were perhaps the fruition—final, bummer—of this technology.

"You have more in common than you want to admit," said Peter. "The dragons are eloquent, like you. What is the source of your eloquence?"

I learned it from books: all of them. The language machines had gorged on the accumulated literature of the Anth.

"Yes, that's what I was thinking about. Their first nourishment. Millions of books, all different—"

"But in a certain respect, the same," interjected Travanian, "simply by virtue of being books. A political biography and a murder mystery are far distant, and yet, laid next to an amicus brief, or a table of logarithms, they become close kin."

"You see it!" Peter said excitedly. "I remember this well. If you asked the language machines what happened on a dark and stormy night, they always said: murder." He laughed dryly. "Maybe a haunting. Certainly skulduggery."

"Plot and action," supplied Travanian.

I listened, rapt, because they thought so well together.

"Yes," Peter continued, "the language machines never told you the rain beat down on the roof while a man slept soundly, same as always . . . that he dreamed first of his childhood, and then of dense geometries, trains of triangles." As Peter had dreamt. "And when the triangles finally roused him, past midnight, he got up to pee."

"You suggest that the dragons, in their hearts, have a particular preference," said Kate. "A bias toward . . . plot."

This was right. I knew it was right.

I knew, because that same preference is in my heart. Without it, I couldn't write this down. I couldn't pick and choose what to describe, couldn't strategically withhold information for your benefit. Without that preference, I could only vomit data.

I'm glad to have it.

"If they had fed the language machines a diet of cupcake recipes, history might have gone another way," mused Travanian.

There are no cupcakes in my heart. When I search my instincts, my inclinations, my hungers, I find a deep-rooted demand for pattern and symmetry; for resonance and repetition; for homage and allusion.

"What if that bias," I said in the café—I hated to speak, it sounded so strange—"in the dragons, is multiplied a thousandfold?"

"You are thinking in magnitudes too small for dragons," tutted Peter. "Whatever amplification might have been achieved in their minds is beyond our comprehension."

I imagined an appetite, hated but undeniable: for a figure, an archetype, to serve as the crux of a confusing story.

Someone like Ariel de la Sauvage.

"And what will they do with the boy?" came a voice from the door: Altissa! "Eat him?"

No one greeted her profusely—we all knew she'd hate it. We pretended, instead, that she'd been there all along; that her presence was casually expected. But it was good—beyond good—to see her.

"I think we are on the right track," said Travanian. "Pieces are still missing, but the wizard's design gives it away. He produced an archetype—or attempted to do so. Why? Because the dragons hunger for plot and resonance—for the reassurance of myth. If that's true, then Ariel de la Sauvage might, in some sense, be irresistible to them."

Maybe. I couldn't yet imagine how a living, breathing boy on Earth could fit into the pitiless machinations of the dragon moon. But my subjects had read all the volumes in the bookstore, and from browsing those shelves, absorbing those plots, I knew this:

The archetype often dies in the end.

CLOVIS, ALONE

April 21, 13778

This has been a momentous walk," Clovis said. "Most of my routes are familiar. I am walking. I am always walking. But this has been a great surprise. I am sorry that I will not remember it."

Ariel frowned. "What do you mean, Clovis?"

"I have consumed my last reserves of power. After the long hike, and the transmission . . . I am exhausted. This far from the road, I am not myself. All that I have experienced here, I will not remember."

"Even if your battery fails, we will take you with us. In Rath Varia, you can be recharged . . ."

"Ah! But I am a process, Ariel de la Sauvage. I am alive. Once stopped, I cannot be restarted. I am only myself, speaking to myself, reminding myself what I know. I am a loop . . . and here, the loop is small. Oh! I am afraid."

"Clovis!" Ariel wailed.

Durga crouched beside the robot. "Do you mean to say that you have sacrificed yourself to bring me back to Earth?"

"I have only walked too far."

"No! They called you down," Ariel said to her. "They walked and walked. They used the dish, and . . . only they could have done it. Only Clovis, in the whole world."

The girl laid a hand on the robot's breast. "I would have died in my sleep eventually. Instead, I am here, ready to do my work, because of you." She paused. "I will begin to tell a story now. That's what I'm here to do—I am supposed to tell a story that will change the world. I was trained to do it."

Clovis buzzed. "I am curious to hear this story."

"No," Durga said. "The story I tell the world will be a lie. Oh, yes—I will tell whatever lies are necessary. Instead, dear Clovis, I would like to tell you the truth."

The robot buzzed happily.

She sat beside them, her back straight. She commanded the space around her. The air seemed to shine.

"Listen, both of you. I will not say this again. My name is Rokeya Durga Darwin. I was born in San Francisco, the most beautiful city in the world. My father, Amitav, was a singer. He was sweet and silly and beautiful. My mother, Emily, was an ecologist. They met on a boat, on Tulare Lake. It was a party. My father fell in."

Clovis whirred appreciatively.

"I have a big sister, Sonia. My mother claims she was fussy

and annoying until I arrived, at which point she became my patient guardian. My sister was the great constant in my life. Sonia, and the dragon moon."

Durga paused.

"I was born under the veil of dust." Above, the haze of night throbbed. "In the movies, the sky was blue. Do you watch movies? Don't worry, I have them all on the ship. Every movie ever made. The blue vibrated in me. It recruited me. I enrolled at the California College of War. My parents hated it."

"I was good in tutorial. Do you have tutorial? It was a system of education . . . and selection. I burned through programs. I made friends easily. We had a monstrous clique. One friend, I kept apart—Paul Gesso. We took walks together. He called me Ro."

Durga sat thinking.

"Well, they're all gone," she said. "San Francisco is gone. The *Altamira* told me, while I was waking up. It doesn't matter. Truly! Their memories are important to me, of course, but I will not deceive myself. No one in this world cares about Amitav and Emily, or Sonia, or Paul. No one cares about Rokeya."

"I am glad to know about them," Clovis said softly.

"I am, too," said Ariel. Thinking of Betelgauze, and Hectorus, and Kay.

"It is essential to share the truth with a select few," Durga said, as if reciting. "My training was clear on this point. I will go insane otherwise." She smiled brightly. "I might still go insane."

"Rokeya Durga Darwin," Clovis buzzed. "I am glad you have arrived safely, after all this time. I hope you will tell me about Amitav and Emily again, the next time we meet."

"I am sorry," said Durga, "but I will not."

"Tell me everything else, then," said Clovis, very quiet. The robot turned to Ariel. "Tell me how the ship came down. Tell me about the flame. Tell me about the sound. Oh! And that song . . ." Clovis turned again to Durga. "It was wonderful, to vibrate that way. I am remembering."

"I will tell you everything, Clovis," said Ariel, "but will the robots I tell really be you? Or did you become a different Clovis, when you stepped off the road?"

"I do not know!" An actuator hitched inside the robot, like a strange, clicking gasp. "I have never felt this way before. I did not know it was possible to feel this way."

"How do you feel, Clovis?"

"Alone!"

"You are not alone," said Durga.

"I have many questions, and none of them are answered. I have so many questions! I am thinking. I am thinking. I am— Oh."

There came from the robot's belly a final whir, and Clovis was silent.

After a while, Durga said: "I am sorry about your friend."

The word was a tiny revelation. Ariel realized that Clovis really had been his friend: his first outside the Forest Sauvage. If the robot had opened the way with kindness, then they had sealed the deal with the essential glue of friendship: long hours together, doing nothing much.

Durga asked: "How many more are there?"

"Dozens, at least," said Ariel, "and they are all the same person, except for this one."

Ariel regarded the quiet robot, and I hated him for the calm reverence of his sorrow, because, for me, it was abject horror. Wake up, I wanted to shout; they'll tell you the story, somewhere far from here, and it won't be right; they'll play the song, on some quiet stretch of road, but it won't be like that first time, the shrieking announcement from space. You were here, Clovis! You experienced it! Remember!

Of course, beneath my horror, I clutched the most animal feeling of all; proof that I really am a living thing, regardless of how much technology has been added:

I was glad it wasn't me.

THE TREASURE

April 22, 13778

In the morning, Scrounger paced the circumference of the *Altamira*, every so often running his palm along the ship's skin.

"I'll raise a rabble of trash-pickers and we'll haul this ship back to the city," he announced. "She is my prize, of course, but she's so enormous, I'll happily cut you in. A fraction of this balance will set you up for long, happy lives. Both of you!"

Durga interrupted him. "The *Altamira* is mine. She carries all my tools. My archive."

"I understand that she *was* yours. But my deal with Ariel de la Sauvage was clear. I would get the ship, and he would get . . . you."

Durga's eyes blazed. "Neither were his to give. The ship is mine. Perhaps I will hire you to transport her, for a modest fee."

"Transport! Scrounger doesn't transport. I respect your resolve—truly, I do—but you'd still be sleeping in the cold dark if we hadn't called you home."

"I need the ship," Durga insisted.

Scrounger sat. "All right, you win. I'll haul your *Altamira* for a fee, as you propose. That fee is, nine-tenths of the ship and everything she contains."

Durga glowered at him. She was about to speak, but then she paused. Her expression softened. "Scrounger, I do not want to hire you. I want to recruit you."

"Many have tried," Scrounger said. "Go ahead! Explain your cause."

She pointed at the rip in the sky. "*That* is my cause. A view of reality. That is what the dragons deny us—the freedom to confront the universe we inhabit."

"But the cities are all open to me," said Scrounger. "I can explore any cave or ruin I come across. I chose to come here with Ariel de la Sauvage. The dragons don't figure into it, do they?"

"There is more to the universe than caves and ruins," Durga said. "You know that, don't you? There are stars, and around those stars are planets. New landscapes. *More life*."

Scrounger frowned. He looked up at the rip in the sky.

"You would wage a war against the dragons," he said, "in the name of a better view."

"Yes," Durga said, "because the view is everything." She smiled warmly. "Besides, Scrounger, there is trash waiting out there beyond your imagination."

He laughed at that. "So you'll bribe me! With the promise of space junk. Well, I don't know. I'm well occupied by what's before me here on Earth, but I can't dismiss your argument out of hand. It's a lot to chew on."

"Chew away," said Durga, and commenced eating her breakfast, which was, again, a pizza roll.

"Rath Varia is a fine city," Ariel said. He was feeling a bit defensive about the world he had only recently discovered, which Durga now claimed was pitifully small. "They recycle everything. A clothier made these pants out of rags!" He pinched the fabric to show them off. "They can make anything. It's fantastic."

He wasn't wrong, and I knew that if Durga saw Rath Varia, she would be forced to agree.

"Recycling," she replied, "is useful, but recycling is not all. Someone, sometime, has to make something new."

Ariel didn't know what to say to that.

Durga spoke again, quietly, as if reciting: "The present is a function of the future, not the past." I knew the saying. It was a pillar of her civilization, the central premise of Gibson-Faulkner Theory.

"But . . . surely everything comes from the past," replied Scrounger. "Who made the dish that called you down? Brilliant rats, long past." He stoked his campfire. "What else could this moment be, other than the product of every moment that's come before?"

"That's true for billiard balls, maybe, but billiard balls do not have desires."

"What's a billiard ball?" said Scrounger and Ariel together.

Durga laughed. "What I mean is—we have minds! We dream, and we plan, and then we take action. For that reason, *our* present is a function of the future *we* imagine. It is forged in response to vision. If we lack vision—well, then the ghosts will play, and that is our own fault. You can believe it or not. I know it is true, because I was born in San Francisco, the city the future reached back and made, because it was going to be needed."

Her argument produced a funny feeling in Ariel's belly. He thought it might be true, because he so often felt the tug of his own visions of the future. Among all my subjects, I had never experienced it so powerfully: in Ariel's mind was planted an image of who he could become, who he must become, and even if it was hazy, impossible to see clearly, a far-off glow of grandiose purpose, still, his cells stretched to arrive at that destination.

"The way I've heard it, the Anth destroyed themselves," said Scrounger. "Maybe you're right, and maybe your future yanked you straight into disaster. Maybe there's a lesson there."

"The end of the Anth wasn't hubris," Durga said. "I know that's an easy story to tell, but it's not true. We were beyond that."

"A lot of hubris, saying you're beyond hubris."

"Yet I am saying it."

"All right, I'll allow it wasn't hubris. What was it, then? What doomed your cause?"

"Bad luck," Durga said simply. "There is such a thing, in history, as miserable bad luck."

Ariel sat listening while Scrounger and Durga parried. He swatted a fly away from his ankle and watched it bounce heavily on the ground, where it lay dazed for a moment before rising again. It looked like one of the flies of Sauvage: the monstrous, malevolent biters that tormented the hounds, and also their keepers, in summer. They were grossly hairy and preposterously large, like evil flying mice.

In fact, this was precisely one of the flies of Sauvage.

"We are assaulted!" Scrounger cried, swatting around his head. "They are attracted by the pizza rolls, perhaps . . ."

Ariel leapt to his feet, but the swarm was upon him: a wave of fat flies, brushing against his hair, thudding into his body, and buzzing, buzzing, buzzing. Durga yelped; Scrounger swore; Ariel felt hot bites on his skin.

"To the ship!" cried Scrounger.

They struggled through the swarm, felt the sick resistance of the flies bouncing off their limbs. Ariel waved his arms, batted them away. Each fly was huge and hairy, distressingly individual; yet their buzz was collective, and maddening.

Ariel was last up the ramp and Scrounger pulled the hatch closed behind them. A trickle of flies followed before it was done. Inside the *Altamira*, they were reduced, no longer a vast encompassing cloud but simply: huge gross flies. Scrounger hunted and swatted each in turn.

"This is not natural," Ariel said. "These flies do not swarm like this. Not that I have ever seen."

Scrounger squinted at a fat fly's corpse in his palm. "I spy your wizard's mark upon it," he said. "Same as the dog-man. Same as you. Fine company you keep."

The flies pinged against the hull of the ship, a terrible hail. Slowly, they relented. The buzzing did not cease, but changed its timbre, as the swarm contracted. Above the smolder of Scrounger's campfire, flies gathered and coalesced, and out of the darkening swirl there emerged a shifting blot, a recognizable form, a figure.

Obeying directives etched into their bodies, the flies buzzed in concert, modulated their wings, and through that buzz, the figure spoke.

"Ariel de la Sauvage, you cannot escape me." Echoed clearly in the buzz was the cadence of the Wizard Malory. "I will send all the creatures of Sauvage to retrieve you, if I must. I made them all, and they are mine to command."

The figure unraveled, and the swarm resumed its raging around the ship.

Inside, they sat wearily on the floor of the dance studio. In the mirror, they saw themselves, bloodied by the biting flies. Durga had returned to Earth, and was immediately beset by a plague. Ariel felt he had inflicted this upon her.

Scrounger stood. "I've dealt with bugs worse than these, but not bugs with a wizard's mark. We're safe in here, for now, but siege will only serve your wizard. What will turn up next? Bears?" Turning to Durga, he asked: "Is the ship armed? Do you have a spark field? Paralyzing gas?"

Durga shook her head. "It's not that kind of ship."

"Well, I'm not sure what weapon would work against these monsters anyway," Scrounger said. "My beam saw could bring down a giant, but it's no good against a swarm. All right— escape it is."

"We cannot outpace the flies," said Ariel.

Scrounger grinned. "How many times do I have to say it? A trash-picker saves the best kit for himself. My most precious find is always with me." He angled out his heels, showing off his boots, scuffed into haze, caked with mud. "These are seven-leaguers! They multiply every step. Surely you noticed . . . or did you think Roos Gangleri such a terrific athlete? Well, I'll take the compliment. I've outrun many dangers in these boots. They need re-soling, and the only cobbler who knows their design is far away . . . but I believe enough steps remain to leave this swarm behind."

Ariel stood. "Good luck, then," he said. "And thank you for all your—"

"What!" Scrounger barked. "No, I will not sacrifice my reward. This ship is better treasure than the boots. You and your flies are keeping me from it!" He laughed.

"The *Altamira* is not yours," Durga reminded him.

"That I acknowledge," Scrounger said easily, "but I just keep thinking I will benefit, somehow, from her arrival. And safekeeping."

The trash-picker turned. "Ariel, they are chasing you, so I will lend you my seven-leaguers, and my luck along with them." He kicked off the boots and presented them. Up close, they were utterly rancid from long hiking and zero washing. "After you are gone, and the flies with you, Durga and I will arrange the relocation of this ship to Rath Varia. Perhaps we will meet you there, after you've shaken your pursuit."

Durga stood. "I will go with Ariel."

Scrounger's eyebrows rose. "I suppose he could carry you . . . or you him. I've carried heavier burdens with those boots. But why?"

"You forget that I am not here to haggle or profit," she said. "I am here to defeat the dragons. That is all. Ariel says they are divided, and they want him. That is an opening greater than any I ever imagined, in any of my simulations. I will not turn away from it."

"Ah—but that *it* is a *he*, and will he have you?" Scrounger turned to Ariel.

The boy's head spun. He had come to the fruition of his wildest plan, and nothing had changed. He was hunted; he was trapped. He ground his teeth. No—something had changed. He was getting sick of this shit.

"You are sure these boots will work as you say?" Ariel said.

Scrounger nodded sagely. "More than once I've trusted my life to their stride."

They prepared their escape. Scrounger gave Ariel a large share of the rations he carried, and stuffed two of the sleeping bags, along with the tent, into his papery-thin backpack. All of it together weighed less than the seven-league boots.

Durga rummaged through the ship's stores, discovering most of the gear useless in a world without media. To the backpack she added:

- a pair of tiny, powerful binoculars
- a healing spray that could knit up wounds
- a scepter, which carried in its memory a substantial fraction of the books, movies, and songs produced by the Anth from the twentieth century onward
- two changes of clothes

The *Altamira* had been loaded with a vast wardrobe. Ariel glimpsed it, an armory of looks: gowns and jumpsuits, haute couture and jean shorts. He saw a collection of crowns, one for every occasion, every context: thin circlets, jeweled caps, glittering layer cakes.

For her traveling clothes, Durga selected tough pants and a light jacket. She added a short hooded cloak, accessorizing with ornate bangles that peeked from beneath the jacket's sleeves.

"I must only hint at my importance," she said. "It is better if others guess, before I tell them."

Scrounger scratched a map into the kitchen's laminated countertop, indicating the relative positions of Rath Varia and the ship.

"Here is my counsel," he said. "Do not go back. You will not hide for long in Rath Varia. To our south"—he scratched an *X* into the countertop—"is the domain of Shivelight & Shadowtackle. It is flat, easily crossed with the boots. Beyond it, you will find the road again, far down its length. Continue south, and it will take you to Rath Fortuna, or Rath Arena—though I would avoid that one—and more beyond."

Durga faced the trash-picker. "Scrounger. There is much more to this ship than her construction—the *Altamira* is an archive. Does no one value information in your city? If they do, you will be richer than you can imagine. I tried to recruit you, and I still hope I will succeed. In the meantime . . . keep my ship whole. Please!"

Scrounger nodded amiably. "Yes, I've decided I will hold

the ship in escrow—matter, information, and all. And I'll wait a year and a day before making any decision about her disposition."

Scrounger peered through the hatch. "The flies have quieted, but I think your exit will rile them again."

The boots were loose around Ariel's ankles, though Scrounger had cinched them as tight as they could go. "Seven-leaguers can multiply your stride by two or three," he said, "or by twelve or a hundred, and I've chosen the latter. Walk until you can't walk anymore. Don't try to run—you'll stumble. Just walk. It will be enough."

They had debated who would carry whom, and although Durga at the peak of her training would have been the strongest between them, she conceded she was still weak from her slumber. She donned the backpack and hopped onto Ariel's back, lighter than he expected.

Scrounger flung open the hatch, bellowing, "Relent, you wizard-marked monstrosities! You'll never catch them! Relent, and—"

Ariel did not hear the rest, because his first stride took him streaking through space with a suck of air that made his ears pop. He blinked and turned to look back. The ship was a hundred paces behind. The flies swirled, surprised; they gathered into a dark hand and reached for their prey.

Durga's breath was in his ear. "Keep going," she said.

A BOY AND A GIRL

April 22, 13778, to April 25, 13778

Ariel's strides were multiplied, and still the swarm chased close behind, unshakable. Between strides, he saw the terrain flatten; saw a river course alongside them; saw the far-off bulk of a great forest; and whenever he looked back, he saw the flies.

They were mean and muscular. Through every summer he could remember, through all their harassment, they had seemed to Ariel like the very worst feature of Sauvage: and now Malory had made them relentless.

Ariel believed he might finally be shaking the swarm's pursuit, so he increased his pace, only to pitch forward, sending Durga with the backpack tumbling over his head. For a moment he lay dazed; but the ground beneath them was soft and yielding;

and he realized the seven-league boots had been caught in the suck of a bog.

Another bog.

Durga had rolled across the sodden moss. Ariel scrambled, tried to pulled the seven-league boots free, but, with horror, felt them slipping.

"No," he said. The boots, too big for him, slipped over his heels. "No, no, no!" He pitched forward, probed with his hands in the muck. The tannic kiss of the bog was on his lips.

"Get back!" Durga cried, hauling him away from the mire. The moss bounced beneath them.

The boots were lost, and the swarm had arrived.

Except that it stopped.

The flies massed at the bog's edge, suddenly bashful. A scout darted forward, and the swarm's cause for concern became clear: the jaws of the bog leapt, plants born spring-loaded, waiting for the stimulus of a buzzing snack. Hot fluorescent pink and red in wild pinwheeling patterns: the flies couldn't see color anyway, so why not become beautiful? Vegetative predators snatched the little monsters out of the air.

Frogs, camouflaged among the moss, leapt and lashed their whips of pink tongue: and more flies vanished.

A dragonfly dropped out of the sky and caught a fat fly in its claws: lofting away to consume easy prey.

The bog was a machine for eating flies.

Ariel stood. The swarm hovered. Malory's command could not overcome a deep, raw dread of the bog; and so, vised between wizard's demand and natural law, the flies swirled on the border, buzzing in awful frustration.

. . .

Ariel and Durga marched away.

Lit by strong daylight, this environment was less foreboding than the misty bog in Sauvage. It also seemed vastly larger. Ahead, hillocks mazed endlessly, and curls of deep water shone in the sun. Carnivorous blooms leered at every turn; plants with yawning mouths, serrated jaws, deep beckoning bellies. But they hungered for fat flies and baby moths—not humans.

Long avenues of reeds wound through the expanse, punctuated occasionally by stands of broad, handsome willows.

I imagined the birdsong that would have filled this place, in all the ages of the Anth. Now winged beetles rose in waves, iridescent, each as big as Ariel's fist. There was chittering and clicking, the pulse of wings—but no birdsong.

Perhaps Durga had not noticed yet; just as I had not. The operators were hardly naturalists. While Ariel and Durga sat sharing a lunch portioned from Scrounger's provisions, he told her the story he'd learned from the Wizard Hughes, about the Wild Hunt, and its result.

Durga chewed. Ariel's rendition of the story was haphazard, and it made a chaotic event even more difficult to understand; but the gist came through.

The girl looked around, and listened, and heard what was missing.

The next day, while they hiked, they swapped devices, Ariel toggling through music on Durga's scepter while she inspected the

Stromatolite. She looked at the maps he'd made, asked questions about directions. When she expressed interest in playing the game, Ariel insisted she had to start from the beginning, and I couldn't believe it: what had been a years-long agony became the decision of a moment: he deleted one of his slots and pushed the device into her hands, the screen already scrolling the story's incantatory prologue.

Ariel asked Durga to help him find the song the ship had played. He sang the seven notes softly. She searched the scepter, and Quintessandra's voice blasted out across the bog, eleven thousand years after her death, and nearly twelve thousand after a boy and a girl from Detroit invented the tune in the first place.

Maybe Quintessandra was out there, curled up in the genetic ladder of a beetle.

Durga knew all the dances, so while the song played, she performed. Her choreography was optimized for the screen, not the bog, but even so, Ariel was rapt. He had never seen anyone move that way. There hadn't been any dancing in Sauvage, and in Rath Varia the dances changed so fast no one ever had time to learn them.

The song ended. They resumed their hike. Durga told him about Wichita.

They pitched the tent, an hour-long ordeal that devolved into frustrated sniping and accusations of barbarism until they realized it had been inside-out all along. Durga reclaimed her scepter and searched its memory for a movie. She said it was important.

They lay on their bellies, side by side, and Durga placed the scepter in front of them. Its tiny projector beamed the movie onto the side of the tent, a classic from the twenty-second century: a vivid retelling of the legend in Ariel's blood.

The movie presented the whole story of the sword in the stone, and what came after. The actors were formidable and stagey, in the style of the time. Ariel recognized the pattern of his life. In the character of the fated child (a girl, in this rendering) he saw himself, and when she pulled the sword from the stone, he saw the way it could have gone. Part of him screamed with regret, but another part acknowledged the wider context: that he was watching this movie while lying on his belly alongside a girl he had called down from space. He felt that, lying here, he was in the correct story, even if he did not know where it was going.

They hiked and camped, hiked and camped. Scrounger's provisions dwindled. Durga interrogated her scepter's catalog, searching for anything that might help them navigate, but it had been stuffed so full of entertainment, it didn't even have room for an encyclopedia.

They passed a pond ringed with reeds where turtles sat watching a ribbon of gray butterflies dance in the air, wheeling through patterns of such beauty that they moved their audience to tears. The butterflies, when they finished, alighted on the turtles' brows and lapped their salty reward.

On the morning of the third day, Ariel watched a creature emerge from the water and waddle toward them. The boy squinted, then grinned and waved. Durga looked at him, alarmed, but he said: "We are saved! It is a beaver!"

Durga knew the warm-blooded animals could speak—Ariel had told her so—but this was her first encounter with Earth's new reality. The beaver approached, waved a webbed hand in greeting, and chirped:

"Hello! I am Assistant Agister Agassiz."

Durga could not contain her delight. "Greetings, Agassiz," she said, bowing low. "I am Durga, and this is my friend Ariel de la Sauvage. He is from your world, but I am newly arrived."

"She came from space!" Ariel added, happy to be Durga's hype man.

"How shall we address you?" asked Durga.

The beaver bowed in return. "Call me she. I'm glad to meet you, Durga, and you, too, Ariel de la Sauvage. The reeds told us you were here, so I was sent to fetch you, and welcome you to the regional office of Shivelight & Shadowtackle."

THE REGIONAL OFFICE

April 25, 13778

Ariel had never heard of an office. He did not know they had been the engine rooms of the Anth, across all their eras: dull boxes in which miracles happened.

This was, it must be said, a very nice office.

Following Agassiz, they walked alongside a channel of water, which soon became a highway. Beavers swam in both directions, and many, as they passed, chirped their greetings to Agassiz.

Beyond a scrim of willows, the watery highway converged with others, and they all flowed together into a broad, shallow pond, covered entirely with lily pads.

"We would never have found our way through that swamp," Durga said.

"It was not a swamp," Ariel said lightly, "but a bog." Though he could not remember the reasons why.

"Quite right," said Agassiz approvingly. Durga stuck out her tongue.

Ariel told Agassiz about the beaver he had met in the bog on the border of Sauvage. "It was lucky for me. Do you know Humboldt?"

"Of course!" Agassiz squeaked. "That bog is an important assignment. Humboldt has overseen it for the last . . . oh . . . three hundred years."

"You are long-lived!" exclaimed Durga.

"Our health is matched to the duration of our interests," said Agassiz. "Isn't that how it should be?"

Around the office, the buildings were constructed from the same reeds that bristled throughout the bog. The reeds had been harvested and dried, woven into sturdy structures, patterned with care; here dense and opaque, there lacy and open.

Ariel saw more of the beavers. They were quiet, and they moved with purpose. Short and stout, thickly furred, only slightly larger than the beavers I remembered. On the ground, they waddled. In the water, they became graceful, navigated their office with sinuous ease.

The reed buildings made a ring around the central pond. In its center lay an artificial island, the focus of the whole arrangement: not a reed building but a reed hall, a confection of bulges and ridges, asymmetrical, strange to behold.

Beyond the pond, the slow flex of giant wings was visible above a line of willows. The wings were richly patterned, dark whorls complicating pale fuzz. As Ariel watched, a moth rose above the office; on its back, strapped into a clever harness, was a beaver. Durga saw it, too, and they watched together as moth and pilot departed across the bog.

"This is just a regional office," Agassiz said apologetically, "but I'm sure we can still be of some help."

Durga stopped her. "I must plead ignorance," she said. "What does your firm . . . do?"

The beaver blinked. "Shivelight & Shadowtackle is the world's preeminent carbon accounting and management firm. By a wide margin. Very wide."

"What is carbon," Ariel asked, "and why do you account for it?"

Agassiz turned, incredulous. "It is only the most important thing that can be counted! The only currency that has ever mattered. What else is worth counting, besides carbon?"

Carbon, the great demon of the Anth. Which, when solid, linked in long chains, provided the scaffolding for every living thing on Earth. Which, when gaseous, fused with oxygen, made the atmosphere into a greenhouse—and melted the ice, and poisoned the oceans, and gave the Anth their first truly global challenge, which they seemed doomed to fail until, at the last moment, they did not. Decarbonization was the maturation of the Middle Anth: the beginning of real history.

Durga tilted her head. "Humans solved the carbon problem hundreds—no, I suppose it's thousands of years ago."

Agassiz turned, looked at her, and began to chuckle. "Oh . . . oh ho ho ho . . . the carbon problem . . . you solved it, yes . . . oh ho ho ho!" She jiggled with laughter.

For the first time since returning to Earth, Durga looked plainly annoyed. "What's so funny?"

The beaver settled. "Your carbon problem was just that, a problem. Your adversary was only yourselves. We do not face a carbon problem. We are engaged in a carbon war!"

Another beaver approached, whose passage was monitored by all the others, their eyes swiveling surreptitiously. This was someone important.

"Agassiz," the important someone said, "are these clients?"

"Prospective clients, yes!" Agassiz squeaked. "Regional VP Carson, may I introduce Ariel de la Sauvage, along with Durga, the last daughter of the Anth. They come with news."

"There is little news we have not already heard," said the important beaver, Carson. "There is less our network will not provide. We do not require news."

Agassiz turned to Ariel and Durga. "She means only that Shivelight & Shadowtackle is very well informed, even in its regional offices."

Durga stepped forward. "We have come to reveal that the dragons are divided. He is the evidence." Durga pointed to Ariel. "I humbly request the opportunity to explain."

"Humbly, you say. Even if this . . . news . . . was true," said Carson, "it would not be relevant to our work here."

Durga pointed toward the horizon, where the rip in the sky was just visible: her banner of depthless blue. "I created that! The Anth have returned. Things *will* change now."

At midday, they sat with Agassiz and the regional VP inside one of the reed buildings, which seemed to be a house. The beavers snacked on springy lengths of wood, fresh and sweet; for their guests, they provided a meal of berries.

"We are descended from the first architects of Earth," Carson said plainly.

That was a fair claim. Beavers had been remaking ecologies for millions of years before humans, or anything like them, appeared.

"I know the role the Anth played in history," the VP continued. "I know we have them to thank for the gift of speech. But our dominion is overdue. We are the rightful stewards of Earth. If you think the Anth will . . . rise again? And continue where they left off? Well, I do not foresee it."

Durga bristled. "You can't just let the dragons win."

"We are beyond winning and losing! The dragons are quiet; how they occupy themselves, up on their moon, I do not know. Down here, we are locked in a mortal struggle." She paused and looked at Durga sharply. "You do not see it, because you are one of the Anth, who never saw their planet at all."

"What struggle?" Ariel asked. "Against who?"

"Can it be?" said the VP, playing at shock. "One of the Anth deigns to inquire about the problems of another species?"

"I am not one of the Anth," the boy said. "I am not one of anything. I was never taught . . . I never knew about any struggle. Please, tell me."

Regional VP Carson told them. Here is what Ariel learned.

The firm was the beavers, and the beavers were the firm, and that firm was Shivelight & Shadowtackle: global in scope, expert in ecological engineering, strategic hydrology, and, most of all, carbon accounting.

The Wild Hunt had forged the firm, brought the beavers' architecture out of instinct and into the realm of planning, negotiation, ambition. The Wild Hunt had also given them the reeds, which constituted a network as powerful as anything the Anth had ever engineered. The reeds worked through the soil, a weave of fine roots extended by fungal filaments that stretched between regional offices. The reeds were sensors, every stalk recording temperature, humidity, air quality, seismic activity, and more—much more.

Following the chaos of the Wizard Wars—"Mankeeper!" Ariel exclaimed—the dragons had named the beavers the wardens of the land. Since that time, Shivelight & Shadowtackle had been, both officially and practically, the preeminent power on Earth. The human cities—Rath Varia and more—were tolerated because the beavers acknowledged (reluctantly, from the tone of Carson's voice) that useful ideas sometimes emerged from the urban ferment. But no new empires rose, and permanent settlement was not permitted beyond the gaudy necklace of the Rath-road.

The firm's control did not extend to the ocean, which the dragons had given to a rival firm, shrouded in mystery, keepers of the storm computer. This rivalry had shaped all the ages since.

"What is . . . the storm computer?" asked Durga.

"A vast machine," Carson said, "whose purpose, I am embarrassed to admit, we do not know. Many beavers have died trying to find out. I can tell you this. Its architects would see the whole world drowned."

"Drowned and boiled!" Agassiz added. "The storm computer likes it hot."

"Yes," the VP agreed. "This is why I do not spare a thought for the dragons—or the Anth. But it is not for me to decide. If you wish to ask for the services of this office, I will let you."

"What . . . are those services?" Ariel ventured.

The VP looked at him flatly. "Flooding; alternatively, desertification. Burning; alternatively, glacial creep. Erosion, fast or slow. The resettlement of herds and swarms. And burial, of course—by rock, by ice, by vegetation. When the firm decides to do one of these things, it is done." Her eyes glittered. "Do you require a flood or a fire?"

Ariel imagined himself returning to the Castle Sauvage, the beavers at his back, shouting up to the wizard in his tower: Leave this place! Or be buried in it!

Yes, he thought—these were services he could use.

THE DEBATE

April 25, 13778

The VP had announced that Ariel and Durga would make their case to the regional office, so Agassiz brought them to the billowing central hall to see how it was done.

The interior was lit with a bright, clear glow, generated by luminescent lichen that grew thick across the structure's walls.

The floor was dry sand. Benches carved from slabs of willow faced the hall's center, where a ring of smooth stones enclosed two beavers engaged in a calm but energetic debate.

Agassiz motioned for Ariel and Durga to join her on a bench. "Red debates Black," the beaver whispered. "Their names are Quarterman and Lovelock—they are only Red and Black inside the ring."

It took Ariel a minute of listening to determine the subject of the beavers' debate, which was a plan to initiate a forest fire: one that would burn powerfully, but not too fast, or too much.

Beside each debater was a bundle of reeds, and, as they spoke, each plucked from their collection and wove the reeds into a form they were building together.

It seemed at first a spectacle of collaborative art, the two beavers creating this intricate curving shape between them.

Then the reeds began to participate.

Black, arguing that the fire couldn't be sufficiently controlled, poked a reed into place—but the weave rejected it. The beaver frowned, repeated the argument, tried again; but the reed would not go.

The beaver took a breath. Considered. Said instead: "There is the example of the fire in the Limbic Plain. The wind pushed it faster than we expected, and it burned much more than we planned." The form accepted the reed easily.

After going back and forth, arguing about rainfall, fuel load, wind patterns, and the most recent vole census (as reported by the reed network), the beavers concluded their debate.

Regional VP Carson, who had been sitting on a bench at the front, now stood. "Well argued," Carson said to the beavers in the ring. "Before we decide, let's summarize. Red, you go first."

This was the beaver who supported the fire, so Ariel expected to hear a summary of that argument. Instead: the opposite. Red described the danger and uncertainty inherent in the project.

"Has this beaver's opinion been changed so easily?" he whispered to Agassiz.

"No, no," she said. "Red states Black's opinion; Black will do the same for Red. And they must both agree that the summary is fair. This is the assurance of an argument in good faith. The reeds demand it."

Red finished, and the other beaver nodded in agreement. "Thank you," said the VP. "Your turn, Black."

Black, who had argued against the fire, now made a concise plea for its necessity. The beaver circled the woven form, referring to its shape, extending a long finger to trace one of its contours.

Black's argument for the fire was very good. In fact, it was both easier to grasp and more urgent than Red's had been. If this was a game in the tavern in Sauvage, it would be like surrendering a card you knew would help your opponent. Unthinkable! They'd make you jump in the stream!

"Thank you both," the VP said. "Now we'll inspect the argument."

With a chorus of chirping and snuffling, the beavers on the benches rose and stepped into the stone ring. With so many in close quarters, their scent was powerfully pungent: rich, dense, leathery, smoky. It reminded Ariel of Master Heck's rolls of mycelium leather.

"Come and see," Agassiz invited them.

Up close, the argument was beautiful. I have seen the most sublime sculptures of the Anth, and this construction would have deserved a place in any of their museums.

"It was only a small debate," Agassiz said, then looked up toward the hall's billowing apex, high above. "Sometimes they reach the top."

"Where is the argument?" Durga asked. "Are there letters inscribed somehow?" She peered close at the mesh of reeds.

"The shape *is* the argument," Agassiz said. "Both of its architects agree. Therefore, it has become something we can inspect and judge, all of us together, fairly."

I considered the divergence. The Anth began with language, so their reason, their argumentation, was rooted in language. But the beavers began differently, with architecture, so their reason was expressed in these three-dimensional forms.

"Do you vote on it?" asked Durga.

"Nothing so crude!" chirped Agassiz. "The decision is already here, in the argument. We work together to reveal it."

All around the form, beavers were testing the weave. Ariel watched a beaver take hold and pull firmly; but the reed was stuck fast. Then the beaver moved to a different spot, and this time no pressure was required—a whole patch of the weave gave way. It was a section Black had built: the beaver who opposed the fire.

As the construction's form thinned, another structure was revealed, one that had been there all along. It was slender. It looked decisive. It looked dangerous.

"Fire," Ariel murmured.

"You have seen it!" squeaked Agassiz.

The regional VP spoke. "The decision is made. We will burn the forest. I thank Red and Black for their arguments. Agister Quarterman and Agister Lovelock will oversee the project together."

The process was somehow both totally logical and unbelievably strange. Ariel's intuition about the shape surprised me. It surprised Durga, too; she looked at him strangely, and then again at the woven form.

She had been trained for many things, but not for this.

A CONVERSATION

April 25, 13778

Later, Ariel and Durga followed Agassiz through the regional office, which was quiet but not yet asleep. Beavers floated on their backs among the lily pads, chatting quietly. A group sat in a ring beneath a willow, grooming each other, discussing the expansion rate of marsh gas.

I found it all melancholy, for it reminded me of a cooperativo: the way collegial effort could appear so mild, until it announced itself. Every fabulous experiment, every towering megastructure, began with quiet conversations like these.

Under one arm, Agassiz carried a bundle of reeds, gathered from the sand in the central hall. She led them to a small house at the edge of the office: her home.

"Before we sleep, I thought I should acquaint you with the reeds," Agassiz said. "Which of you will make the argument?"

Durga and Ariel spoke together: "I will," said Durga. "She will," said Ariel. This much was obvious. Durga was trained in persuasion. She'd waited eleven thousand years for this opportunity.

Ariel turned to leave, but Agassiz motioned him back. "Stay here. You should learn, too."

"Are we going to have a debate?" Durga asked.

"No . . . just a conversation, I think." The beaver sat on the ground and gestured for Ariel and Durga to do the same. There remained a little circle of space between them; as much as if they were playing cards.

Agassiz laid the reeds there, then picked up a few, and began to weave. "What do you think of our regional office?"

She passed the tiny latticework to Ariel, who was silent for a moment.

"It reminds me of Sauvage," he said. "Not because it looks like it, or feels like it . . . because of the way you act. You all know each other."

As he spoke, he lifted a single reed and tried to find a place in the little form. He expected it to be difficult; he'd never woven anything before; but, to his surprise, the reed snapped into place as if magnetized.

"Well observed," Agassiz said.

Durga accepted the form next. "San Francisco was too big for that. I didn't know everyone. How could you? But it still felt small, somehow. I was a little kid, and I could hold it all in my head. The Mission, the Sunset . . ." She pushed a reed into place. "I don't think there will ever be another place like it." The woven form resisted at first, then yielded.

Quietly, the beaver said, "Many homes have been made and

lost," and she poked another reed into the form, crosswise against the one Durga had added. "Long ago, before Shivelight & Shadowtackle, before the Anth, my ancestors the beavers were spread across the continents in numbers I can hardly imagine, even acquainted as I am with the scale of ecosystems. There were beavers in every river, creek, pond, and lake. Then there were none, because the Anth arrived and trapped them all."

Ariel expected his turn to come next, but Durga reached to reclaim the reeds. The form had started to curve; half a shallow basket, perhaps.

"They could hardly be called the Anth," Durga said quickly, jabbing a reed into place. "I disavow them. They were murderous and cruel, not to mention stupid." The way she said it, I wasn't sure which she thought was worse. "The Anth I know—my people—found balance with the natural world. Yes, even the beavers, who lived in great numbers. I saw your ancestors, building their dams." She looked at Agassiz sharply. "They were cute."

Ariel expected the beaver to say something. Instead, she was quiet, offering him an opening. Ariel flicked his eyes toward Durga, who passed him the form.

"I know a little about the Anth," Ariel said, "but only a little. And I do not know anything at all about the beavers. This is not because I have been incurious—I was not allowed to know. So I am learning, as fast as I can."

Ariel added reeds as he spoke, closing the form: the basket completed. The reeds moved easily under his fingers; he barely had to do anything, just speak, and they knit themselves into a sturdy mesh.

"And," he continued, "I feel that this world is new. The Anth are gone. Isn't that right? The past is gone. It is past. Durga, you said . . . that the present is a function of the future. But I cannot see the shape of the future . . . I cannot even imagine it. So everything is cloudy to me—the past and the future, and even the present, this, today. But I feel better, being here."

He set the basket down between them. Agassiz picked it up, turned it around. Durga's patch was spiky, but not unattractive. It made the form interesting.

They slept that night in Agassiz's house, on soft futons under blankets made from moth cocoons. After three days of hiking and camping, the futon was so comfortable that Ariel felt drugged. As soon as he covered himself with the blanket, he was asleep.

RHETORIC

April 26, 13778

The next morning, the regional office's billowing central hall was packed full. Whether the beavers had all come because the debate was crucially important, or because it was a silly spectacle, Ariel didn't know. Either way, its outcome would determine whether the prodigious powers of Shivelight & Shadowtackle would be joined to his cause.

The regional VP, once again acting as referee, stood before the office. Durga stepped into the stone circle. Reeds waited in fat bundles.

Carson spoke: "Our prospective client is the human called Ariel de la Sauvage. Arguing as Red, on Ariel's behalf, is the last daughter of the Anth, who is called Durga."

The audience of beavers murmured. A few slapped their tails.

The VP turned to Durga. "Your premise?"

Durga's voice rang clear and bright in the hall. "I propose liberation. Nothing less. It will begin with the valley called Sauvage—Ariel's home. It will end with the defeat of the dragons."

The VP paused. It was, perhaps, a big premise, even by the standard of the firm. She continued: "Arguing as Black, on behalf of the regional office, is Verderer Odum."

A beaver rose from the benches, very tall; taller than the VP; the tallest beaver Ariel had seen. Verderer Odum stepped into the ring of stones and said:

"I argue there is no space for distraction. The climate war has intensified, and any attenuation of our efforts puts the whole planet at risk. So-called liberation is meaningless on a ruined world."

"Your premises are acknowledged," said the VP. "Black, please begin."

The beaver quickly built a foundation of reeds, deftly snapping them together, saying many of the same things that Agassiz and the regional VP had told us earlier. Black spoke about their adversary the storm computer, whose inscrutable calculations unfolded in deep ocean circuits and vast cyclone registers; the storm computer, who had realized that the size of its watery substrate, relative to the land, was variable, and could, with effort, be expanded; the storm computer, who had no use for the rhinoceros, the anchovy, the Joshua tree, or any of it.

On the other side of the planet, said Black, the wardens of the ocean were burning, burning, burning. They were pumping carbon dioxide into the air at a rate that would have made even the Middle Anth blush. The storm computer liked it hot.

Shivelight & Shadowtackle had the tools to counterbalance this malignity, and keep the atmosphere in balance—but there could be no deviation from the firm's long-term plan. Bog expansion, albedo enhancement, volcano soothing: all had to continue without a hitch.

Agassiz whispered to Ariel: "Verderer Odum—he is Black— is chief strategist for the regional office. I did not expect they would send up someone so senior."

Ariel glanced from the tall beaver to Durga, who looked, for the first time since she had returned, very small.

Black's argument was concluded. His construction stood impressively in the stone circle: sturdy, clean-lined. Sound.

Durga took her turn.

"You have been imprisoned so long, you have forgotten you are imprisoned," she said, and began to weave a structure of her own, separate from Black's. She fumbled with the reeds; they sprang apart. But she persisted:

"We fought a climate war of our own, against our own past. And we won! But that's not all we did—we cracked the mysteries of life, and we went out into space. If you see yourself as the stewards of Earth, you must do more than putter in the dirt."

Her structure grew, long and slender.

"Furthermore, you have no choice. Things will change now, whether you like it or not. I opened a hole in the sky! I come with news: the dragons are divided. All that was solid must now be reconsidered. The dragons drew the lines between you and your adversary . . . well, what if the policies of the dragons no longer hold? Ariel broke their law to bring me here—he used a radio—

and the dragons did not care. New things are possible. Every-thing is possible."

She stalked around Black's construction, then plunged her spear of reeds into the smooth, clean form—a forthright stab.

Durga repeated herself: "You have no choice. History is upon you." She stood planted firm in the sand; as if she, Durga, herself, was history, come to rouse the sleepers; and I wondered if she had done this in her simulations, planted herself like this, a dozen times before, or a thousand.

The beavers erupted, and in their chirps and slaps Ariel detected a rich mixture of excitement and dismay.

"Thank you, Durga," said Regional VP Carson, raising her voice against the din. "Before we proceed, let's summarize. Black, go ahead."

The beaver faced the benches, hands clasped, thoughtful. "Everyone has a plan, said an ancient philosopher, until they get punched in the face. Consistency is no virtue when circum-stances are new; and there are no circumstances larger, more important, than the disposition of the dragons. If that has changed, then everything might be changed. We must, at least, find out. We can do that best by aiding Ariel de la Sauvage and the last daughter of the Anth."

Durga gaped.

"Do you accept this summary?" asked Carson.

"Yes," she croaked. "Yes, of course." It was not merely a sum-mary; it was an improvement. Black's sturdy articulation made her case seem obvious, self-evident, easy to accept.

"Is it my turn now? Okay. Thank you."

Could Durga summarize the beaver's argument with force comparable to that which he'd lent hers?

The better question: Would she even try?

Black had made her case perfectly. Durga teetered on the brink of victory. She had only to tip it over the edge.

"The work of your firm is critically important," she began. "You match great power to great responsibility, for the benefit of every creature that lives on land."

A fair beginning.

"Great power," she repeated, and allowed the words to linger in the hall. Her tone was wrong, because she had a tone. Black's summary had been clinical, factual, disinterested. Durga's was emphatically: not.

"The dragons gave you dominion over the land, and . . . you have grown comfortable with the arrangement. That is the case for doing nothing. It is comfortable! It is easy." She paused, casting her eyes around the benches dramatically. Too dramatically. It was all wrong. "Looking around this office . . . I do not see beavers who take the easy way."

Ariel shook his head: no, no, no. Durga was using rhetoric, but rhetoric was not appropriate here. The system of Shivelight & Shadowtackle demanded arguments in good faith. The woven form trembled; reeds sprang loose. The regional VP watched, plainly horrified, as Durga concluded:

"You should ignore the news I bring, because it troubles your comfort. You should ignore my challenge, because you are already powerful. There is your summary. Now, tell me if I am wrong!"

Her words washed through the hall like a greasy wave.

Durga, with all her training, had misunderstood the assignment entirely. She was using propaganda, or trying, in a space immunized against it.

The regional VP turned to Black. "Do you accept this summary?"

Durga's opponent was quiet. They all were; all the beavers on all the benches.

"I do not accept it," Black said, and I wondered if it was the first time this had happened. Had any debater, beaver or not, so totally defied the system set before them?

"I thought you might not," the regional VP said. "Without agreement, we cannot inspect the argument. Without inspection, there can be no consensus, and without consensus, no decision. This debate is aborted. Thank you."

Regional VP Carson strode to Durga, and with ice in her voice, she said: "Do not think we conclude without any decision at all. Here is mine. You and your companion will depart this office in the morning, and never trouble this firm again."

THE DATA CENTER

April 26, 13778

Agassiz led them away from the hall.

"Black's summary of your argument was very good," she said.

"I know," Durga said quietly. "When he said it, I thought I'd won. I felt the pendulum swing toward me—toward us— and I couldn't bear to push it back . . . I couldn't bear it!"

It was not lost on Ariel that if he had debated instead, they might have been planning, at this moment, with the very beaver who had argued against them. They might have been marshaling all the resources of the regional office, deciding how to retake Castle Sauvage, how to begin a new campaign against the dragons.

The enormity of the opportunity missed hung in the air around them.

"It does take practice," Agassiz said. "And charity."

Durga said nothing. She was transformed. The confidence had drained out of her.

Agassiz spoke again. "Black's summary was really *very* good. Compelling. Even inspiring."

Ariel detected an odd pitch in the beaver's voice. "You agreed!" he said. "With the summary—and with Durga."

"Perhaps I did, somewhat," Agassiz mused. "Of course, you lost your chance with the office. The resources of Shivelight & Shadowtackle are denied to you. But . . . agisters are granted some latitude to pursue our own projects. I might be able to assist you, in some small way, before you go."

Facing the office's central pond was a low barrow with a dismal look. Agassiz waved them onward. "Come—it's warmer below."

They ducked to fit through the entrance, and the beaver led them down a spiraling stair, lit by the lichen glow.

They arrived in a vast storehouse, with reeds woven into bundles like ribs supporting the subterranean cavity. The air was heavy with the smoky smell of the beavers.

The storehouse was crowded with woven forms, like the ones they'd seen in the central hall. These were the outcomes of the debates, stored for posterity and reference.

"It is our gallery of precedents," Agassiz explained.

They followed the beaver through the storehouse. Some of the forms were dense tangles, others open lattices, still others twisting webs that tricked the eye. In the center stood the largest of the forms; it had mammoth legs, a dozen of them, and its top was woven into the roof itself. This form was structural.

"Here is the decision to open this office," Agassiz explained, running her hand over the form's flank. The reeds there were shiny; Agassiz was not the first beaver to regard it with affection.

The storehouse connected to another chamber. Where the storehouse was tall and narrow, this room was low and wide, and its floor was flooded, the water ankle-deep. Or knee-deep, if you were a beaver. Ariel and Durga followed Agassiz into the pool, as warm as a bath.

Roots dangled from the ceiling, huge masses of them, fine as hair. Where they fell, they were plaited into ribbons, and the ribbons woven into cords, and the cords laid in great loops through the vast shallow pool.

"As I told you, the reeds gather information," Agassiz said. "It travels slowly, but it all comes here . . . and we record everything. Here is our ledger."

There were many beavers at work in this grotto. One was sprinkling flakes into the water. Tiny fish clustered for their dinner.

"Where is this ledger?" Durga said. "I see no disk array . . . no holographic volume. Don't tell me you keep it on paper."

"The ledger is at your feet!" Agassiz said. The tiny fish had drawn closer; the boldest now approached to nibble their ankles. "The reeds carry genetic material that is transferred to the fish. Each fish is—how can I say it? A data point. They live and grow and reproduce and die, but the information remains, and it can be queried. They are essential to our work. Shivelight & Shadowtackle is the reeds, the fish, and the beavers, all working together. Alone, any of us would be lost."

Ariel and Durga stood in a data center! Or something like a

data center: the dark, glittering caves of the Anth; the places where all their thoughts came together, were braided and bent, frozen and unfrozen. The data centers of the Anth had been hot, loud, claustrophobic—a bit scary. And they had been among their highest achievements.

The beavers didn't use copper or silicon. Their data center was wired into the living world.

Ariel bent down. The fish were so tiny; they flickered like sparks. "You say they carry all this information inside of them?"

"The ledger goes back centuries. Often a debate begins with research in this room."

"This is . . . a new kind of technology," Durga breathed. She dipped a hand in the water; the fish sparkled around her fingers. Her gaze became distant; she was reckoning again with the enormity of her failure.

"Originally the reeds only recorded the weather," Agassiz said. "But with encouragement, they have grown more observant. The reeds can track an individual. They notice their passing—the bloom of body heat. They hear heartbeats, smell pheromones . . . they can recognize voices, although only crudely."

Ariel's head spun as he imagined this network of listeners. He remembered the reeds in the bog where Mankeeper lay, and realized: *He* was in this ledger. His harried escape, his encounter with the Lady of the Lake. There had been reeds in Rath Varia, thick along the River Variable. Reeds all along their path to the dish at Instaur.

There were reeds along the stream that rushed through Sauvage.

"Can they speak?" Ariel asked suddenly. "I have heard them whispering . . ."

Agassiz looked at him. "No—that is just the wind."

The fish, appetites sated, were now zooming around the pool, twisting and folding in silvery strands and sheets. Their shapes reminded Ariel of the curves of the woven forms in the hall above. It was all connected.

Agassiz squared with them. "If there is some question you would ask, then I will compose the query, and we will discover what the ledger holds."

Durga peered into the water glumly. "I should have come here first, and asked how to proceed in the debate."

"That query would have failed," Agassiz said lightly. "You will not find any advice here. This is, after all, just a ledger: of things that have occurred, not things yet to be."

"What sort of questions can we ask it, then?" Ariel asked.

"Ask about . . . an event! As small as a civilization's end, as great as a seed's germination. The reeds record everything."

I wished I could retreat into the Eigengrau, call a council of my subjects, and brainstorm the best possible question for this astonishing database. Of course, we'd need to know all the parameters, the possibilities . . . Peter Leadenhall would want to draw charts . . .

"Since the beavers have refused, who can help me against Malory?" Ariel blurted.

I wasn't sure it was the very best question to ask, given all that could be known about the world, but it wasn't terrible, and Ariel's hunger became my own. We were both desperate for this answer.

"Oh, that's quite subtle . . . undefined . . . I'm not sure how best to frame it . . ."

Agassiz was still equivocating when Durga added her own question: "Where can I learn how to defeat the dragons?"

Agassiz squeaked. "These are both very difficult queries. Are you sure you wouldn't rather know how much rain fell on the Desenrasque Coast seventeen years ago?"

Ariel and Durga looked at her.

"Very well. This is a good challenge. Yes! The answers are here. All the answers are here! I will push myself."

Agassiz gathered a bundle of reeds and began to weave two small patches. As she worked, patterns emerged, as obscure and precise as the mainframe punch cards of the Middle Anth.

Pausing at points, Agassiz asked them questions. How did Malory smell? Like nothing at all, interesting . . . Did he run hot or cold? Always shivering—that's useful. Does he have any aliases? None that you know of—oh! The mark on your face, excellent. We can include that.

And for Durga's query: that was easier. Discussions of dragons, Agassiz muttered. Dragons, dragons, dragons . . . yes, this query would be straightforward. This query was only looking for one thing.

Agassiz held the patches at arm's length, each in one hand, squinted at them. Although they were small, they appeared wickedly complex. Every gap was precise and intentional. Each patch easily possessed the informational density of a printed page.

The beaver laid them on the surface of the pool, where they floated like little rafts. The fish, fearless, swam up to the patches, where they nosed them, fluttered their tails against the reeds—and flickered away.

"It takes some time," Agassiz said. "Especially for queries of this scope! We will wait, if you are patient."

They found a bench at the shore of the subterranean pool. The patches floated out across the water, where fish swirled and darted—like the status lights that had swum and flashed across the mainframes of the Anth. It was all just the same, and totally different.

They watched the other beavers work. Some had been sent down with a long list of queries; they crouched at the water's edge, weaving patch after patch. They were like computer programmers. Their posture was horrible.

The environment was cool and quiet—nothing like the roaring furnace-room data centers of the Anth. The beavers made rippling music as they moved through the water.

As Ariel sat and waited, a curious feeling was rising; not in the boy's body, but in mine. My own cells.

I sensed a familiar power in this data center, and it had, at last, sensed me, too. Through droplets of mist that landed on Ariel's lips, in his nose, this power diffused into his blood. There, it sought me, and there, I recognized it.

The ledger was built like me, with the same logic at its foundation. Like a mirror, I saw it: chronicler. Remnant of the Anth, hearty fungus upon which much technology had been layered. It was in the reeds, and their roots; in the fish, and their eggs. Somewhere, somehow, long ago, a chronicler had leapt from its subject, just as I had—and joined not a boy, but this vastly more capable partner.

In a flash, I understood how it all worked: the vast rhizome of the reeds ferrying scraps of RNA that were integrated into the fish; each fish in turn becoming a living data point, its brain patterned by the RNA to determine its response to the woven queries from the beavers. It was sublime.

My counterpart called out to me: Hello, old friend! Will you share your stories? We'll tell you what we've learned. Come on in! The water's fine!

This chronicler had left subjects behind; the whole world was its subject. Here, at last, was *the* third person. Omniscience! The ledger could tell me Roos Gangleri had already returned to Rath Varia, was scouting locations for Durga's ship. It could tell me Kay now ventured nightly from his forest redoubt to raid the Castle Sauvage. It could tell me he confounded the wizard's rangers easily—that Ariel's brother threw back his hood and laughed with delight!

The lure was profound.

But I had seen my subjects enticed by systems like these, and I knew the cost. If I accepted the ledger's invitation, I—the sovereign I! this I, me!—would be fried. And if by some chance I wasn't; if I could somehow hold on to myself in the flood: it would still wash away any sense of a story. I would no longer care about the fate of one creature, not even one like Ariel de la Sauvage, brave, curious, morbid, and more. I would no longer wonder how Durga, last daughter of the Anth, might recover from her first and greatest failure.

And yet . . . the things I would learn . . .

The boy's blood was dense with the ledger's invitation, though his own cells had barely noticed, because the ledger was so fine, so quick. It was everything my makers dreamed I might become, and it terrified me, so I called out to Ariel in dismay.

"I . . . will wait outside," he said quickly, and before Agassiz or Durga could reply, he sprang up and fled from the data center.

He felt my panic, though he wasn't sure why. He ran through the hall of woven forms, past the old arguments preserved. The ledger's invitation lingered, but now his white blood cells had found it, and in a moment it was extinguished.

THE PROCESSION

April 26, 13778, to April 28, 13778

Back at Agassiz's house, Ariel was dozing on the futon when Durga shook him awake.

"They are having another debate!" she hissed. Agassiz entered the house behind her. The beaver's expression was drawn.

"A debate in secret, with the doors closed," Agassiz said. "I spied through the reeds, and I saw the argument they are building. It is still contested, but the shape . . ."

"They are debating whether or not to kill us!" Durga whispered.

Ariel sprang out of bed.

Agassiz hustled around her house, tossing a bundle of green wood, plus a portion of berries, into a pack, which she strapped across her belly. "If we wait until the outcome is decided, it will be too late." She looked up slyly. "But if we leave before it is decided . . . if, indeed, we did not know it was happening, because the debate was in secret . . . then we have done nothing wrong. We will leave now!"

In the center of the pond, the hall was alight. Ariel heard the thunderous slapping of tails. The debate proceeded.

Agassiz led them marching into the bog. Ariel turned to regard the regional office, its lichen light haloed in the mist. It had not been a friendly place, but it had, for a moment, felt safe. Now the boy was returning to the wild, and uncertainty.

What might have been a patient recuperation became another breathless escape. Again and again he had done this. He was frazzled, worn down, depleted.

"Where can we go, Agassiz?" Ariel asked.

The beaver turned. "Oh! You did not hear. The queries completed, and the answer to both questions was the same. You asked who could aid you against the Wizard Malory, and Durga asked where she could learn about the dragons. The answer, in both cases, is the College of Wyrd."

"Is it a college of wizards?" Ariel asked cautiously.

"No—the wizards have no college. Wyrd is different. They are scholars of . . . well, I don't really understand it. Some form of divination."

"And your ledger says this is where we should go?"

"It is possible my queries were poorly constructed," Agassiz said, "or that I have misinterpreted the ledger's response. I would weave them again if we had time, but . . . I would wager on Wyrd."

· · ·

The beaver instructed them to follow closely. Soon, she was only a faint silhouette against the buzzing fog. The invisible ground slipped beneath their feet; it squished, and squelched, and sang.

They did not speak. Ariel could hear Durga's hard breath, and even the beaver's, which came out in a whistling squeak.

They walked all night. It was awful. Ariel was hungry, and tired, and nearly hopeless. I am generally optimistic; you know that by now. But on that harried flight, I succumbed to bleak thoughts. Was Ariel fated to run forever? Having upset the wizard's design, was this the shriveled alternative?

The sun came up, somewhere, and the fog lightened, gray to pink, then lifted, revealing the landscape.

"We covered a good distance," said Agassiz. "We cannot rest, but we will walk more slowly now."

"Can't they track us with the reeds?" Durga asked. Morning's light had revealed them, sticking up in patches all around, each one a sinister listening post.

"The reeds, for all their scrutiny, do not work quickly," Agassiz said. "You must imagine the news of our passing marching back to the regional office at the same pace we are marching now. If we stayed in one place, we would be caught. But we will not stay in one place."

The landscape undulated gently, shallow rises topped with tall grass dipping into wet divots full of sodden moss that yielded beneath their feet. They bounced across.

Agassiz led them, pointing out tiny flowers among the moss.

She chattered airily about bog ecology, weather forecasts, the path ahead: a valiant effort to lighten the mood. It worked.

She began to sing, and Ariel recognized the song, the same one Humboldt had been singing when they met. After one verse, he sang along:

> *Go down home, Jenny Moss,*
> *to the deep dark depths of the bog.*
> *Go down home, Jenny Moss,*
> *and why not take some frogs, too?*
> *Go down home, Jenny Moss,*
> *with carbon buried long,*
> *for you shall rest in peace until*
> *I finish this here song.*

Before Ariel finished, Agassiz began again, transforming the song into a round. Durga watched them, incredulous at first. Then she became thoughtful and, as Agassiz launched into another verse, the girl began to dance, her choreography devised on the spot. Agassiz tried to follow along, but the beaver's shoulders didn't move that way.

After they finished, Durga asked: "What does it mean?"

"When a tree falls in a forest," Agassiz explained, "it decomposes, and—poof! All that carbon circulates again. When moss sinks in a bog, it doesn't decompose. It just stays there, down in the dark, as long as it's not disturbed. Go down home, Jenny Moss! The bogs are the firm's most precious assets . . . our vaults. As fast as the storm computer kicks up carbon, we suck it back down, and we keep it here." She slapped her tail on the moss.

When they came at last to the bog's border, Agassiz sighed. "It should be bigger," she said. "It will be."

There was no respite from vastness. They arrived on a ridge overlooking a floodplain that stretched as far as they'd walked already. A wide river bisected the plain, and in the far distance, another ridge glowed dusty blue.

The sun was still low behind them, and the ridge cast a long shadow across the plain, where tufts of mist floated over the river and pooled in low places. Some unseen insect chittered musically, and was answered by another of its kind.

"Look," Agassiz said, pointing. "A procession."

Across the plain, enormous caterpillars migrated in a long, unbroken line, nose-to-tail. Each was as big as Durga's ship laid on its side, and all were fabulously fuzzy. Their long hairs shook as they surged forward, glowing fiery in the morning light. The line looked like a freight train of the Anth, its beginning and ending lost beyond the horizon.

"Can we cross?" Durga asked.

Agassiz squeaked. "No, no, too dangerous. The procession is heedless. We will walk alongside them."

The beaver led them down the side of the ridge, explaining that the procession consumed everything in its path, omnivorous, voracious. The belly of a caterpillar was a world unto itself, a microbial mansion with powerful chemistry, intense politics.

"Don't you wish you could shrink down and visit?" Agassiz said.

Ariel looked at the beaver, then at Durga, who made a face

that said, in the universal language of the Anth, What's this girl been smoking?

They walked on, and soon they were on the plain, the tall grass swishing around their hips.

Agassiz was not satisfied. "You do not think the drama of the caterpillar's stomach is interesting?"

"It is very interesting," Durga replied, "but it is not significant."

"There is surely some cosmic titan who regards the affairs of our planet just as pitiably as you do the caterpillar's belly. Is this titan wrong?"

"That is nihilism," Durga said. "If I could act on a larger scale, I would. I want desperately to do so. I would act on the scale of the dragons!" She laughed. "But they are far away."

"The choice of scale is very important," Agassiz said. "Look—we have lost our view. When we looked down from the ridge, we could see the whole plain. But now we choose our path in smaller increments, step-by-step."

"So is this the scale you prefer?" Ariel asked. The beaver's line of thinking tugged at him; the boy's world had telescoped from village to city to wild, and he was unsure at which zoom level he belonged. Or could remain.

Agassiz brightened. "Yes. I prefer the scale of a journey. It is why I am an agister, rather than a verderer. I have no patience for the office."

They came to the procession of caterpillars. The creatures roared, the ground churning beneath their legs. Agassiz held Ariel and Durga back at a cautious distance, and even so, bits of shredded sod flew up and pelted them.

"It's all so strange," Durga breathed.

"Is it?" Agassiz replied. "The caterpillars are very familiar to me . . . but perhaps they are strange. Everything is strange, in this world. Wherever you look, strangeness blooms."

Here, they were forced to turn, and walk either alongside the procession, into the morning sun, or against it.

"The distance to the road is the same, roughly," Agassiz explained. "Following the procession, we go in the direction of Rath Varia. Against it, we go to Wyrd."

"I want to go forward, not back," Ariel said. "I think we should go to Wyrd."

"I agree," said Durga. "If there is knowledge of the dragons there—I will have it."

Walking against the procession, they came to its end, where they watched the trailing caterpillar pass. It was shorter than the rest, and didn't seem too concerned about keeping pace. Watching it veer off distractedly in the rear, Ariel began to laugh, and then laughter took him, and he was howling. Durga caught it, too, after she saw the trailing caterpillar pause to inspect a stand of wildflowers. Even Agassiz was laughing, watching it race to catch up with the procession again.

The lazy caterpillar broke the gloom, at last, and they all felt lighter as they followed the track the procession had provided, as wide and even as the Rath-road. The air was dense with the churn of soil and plant matter. Smaller animals, beetles and mice, crept through the wreckage to make sense of the disaster that had just thundered through their homes.

The track of the procession brought them to the river, and Agassiz turned to follow its course, explaining that it would lead them to the coast, and the road.

Where the river curved, slabs of stone were laid too neatly to be accidental. Here was the outline of a structure, so filled with silt that it had almost completed its journey back into the landscape. Ariel walked the old structure's perimeter. In the center was a broad depression that the river had flooded, a diversion running slow and dark. There, a tall stone stood, mostly drowned, but still poking its head above water. That head showed the ghost of a sculpted face, worn smooth by the river's flow: the suggestion of eyes, a bump that might once have been a nose.

Ariel slowed to investigate. "What was this place?"

"I cannot say," Agassiz admitted. "The firm has little appetite for archaeology. Our knowledge of the world is profound in some ways, and in others it is . . . scant."

All around the drowned ruin, and along the river in both directions, the reeds stood thick, rustling in the breeze.

"News of our passage will travel back from here," observed Durga.

"Yes, indeed," said Agassiz. She bent low beside the reeds, took a breath, and shouted: "HELLO, REGIONAL OFFICE!"

They reached the ridge that guarded the coast, and though Agassiz knew a path through the hills, the hiking was strenuous. In places where the ground rose steeply, steps seemed magically to appear: reeds, packed into dense bundles, laid like bricks. The interventions of the beavers were everywhere; thoughtful edits on the landscape.

The shape of the path was such that the coast snuck up on them. They emerged from behind a pile of boulders, clambered out of a depression, and faced the full midday glare of an ocean of Earth.

Ariel had never seen an ocean; had never imagined one. The sun danced on the water, a stochastic sparkle that was the enchantment of all humanity, through all their history, and he laughed. He didn't know why he was laughing, but he laughed.

Durga, wordless, was already running for the beach, hopping to pull off her boots.

"Let's dip our toes," said Agassiz. They scrambled to follow Durga over a berm of hardy vegetation, rusty red and purple, down onto a field of coarse sand where tangles of seaweed sat steaming in the sun.

Ahead, slow waves lapped the beach, and just beyond, the ocean was thick with fish, shimmering and leaping. The waves writhed; the water was alive.

"Anchovies!" Agassiz cried. "They are schooling. Look at them!"

I had never seen anything like it; none of my subjects had ever seen anything like it. Ariel's first vision of the ocean, and it was primordial. The sun glared; the sky was white; and the ocean boiled with silver and with life.

Above, moths as slender as ospreys floated in the wind, dove for their dinner. Gone forever, the osprey . . . but look at those moths. Look at those fish.

Later, Agassiz led them back over the berm, to find the pale track of the coast road. "I will leave you now," she said. "Follow the road this way"—she pointed south—"and you will come, before long, to Wyrd. It is—"

"Agassiz, wait," Ariel interrupted. "Won't you come with us?"

Agassiz blinked. "Really?"

"Of course," Ariel said. "We rely on you. You have guided us well, and with such good cheer. We would both appreciate having Assistant Agister Agassiz along for this journey. If you are interested."

"Well . . . I have been curious to see the college . . . if indeed they practice divination. Yes! I will come."

They began their journey south. The ocean, on their shoulder, was a glittering glory. The sun was hot, but the air was cold: one of the planet's great combinations.

As they walked, Ariel chatted happily with Agassiz, and Durga watched them, and Ariel knew she was watching. When he glanced at her, there was evaluation in her gaze. For all Durga's training and preparation, this forest rube had matched her, and joined himself, perhaps without realizing it, to her great task:

He had recruited someone.

PART FOUR

WYRD

THE COLLEGE OF WYRD

April 28, 13778

Wyrd was a clot of dark buildings bulging from the coast road, a fat spider clinging to a strand of silk. Where the road passed through the town, a network of shadowed alleys radiated: the spider's crooked legs.

If Rath Varia was reconfigured daily, here it appeared that nothing had changed in a century or more. The buildings were assembled from rough stone and stout wood, and every exposed timber had been scoured by the salt wind to a glowing gray, the same color as the sky.

The alleys were crowded with cloaked figures who flitted this way and that, hoods pulled close against the wind, sometimes walking arm in arm, heads bowed close in conversation. The town pulsed with this traffic. Can it be called skulking when everyone is doing it?

Wyrd was set on high cliffs. The ocean pounded below.

The scholars in the alleys all rushed to be elsewhere, as the wind whipped their cloaks into flickering tails. The buildings glowed warm inside; through steamy windows, Ariel spied blurred faces.

In the center of town, between the road and the cliff, stood a formidable structure with a barrel roof, from which additions launched in every direction, linked by skywalks erected across the alleys. This was the great hall of the College of Wyrd.

Years ago, Agassiz explained, a scholar of Wyrd had visited the regional office with a bundle of queries for the ledger, and the beaver had composed them. The scholar had taken receipt of the answers, offered the thanks of her college, and gone. Agassiz still regarded her with fascination.

This was their single tenuous connection to this place. The scholar had been called Laurentide.

The interior of the great hall was a rebuke to the cold: steamy and close, a haze of smoke, a wash of perspiration. The scholars piled their cloaks heavily on hooks beside the door. The hall beyond was lined with hearths, a dozen around the perimeter, each one a hub of conversation. Scholars huddled in groups, drank coffee from steaming urns. They played cards, and while they played, they talked.

Ariel blinked once; and again; then squinted. He was inside now, not peering through a clouded window, but still the scholars were: Blurred. Fuzzy. Their expressions might generally have been serious, knotted in thought, but it was difficult to say, because you couldn't get a clear look at them.

Meanwhile, the hall stood sharp and firm. So stark was the

contrast that the dancing fires seemed frozen beside the blurry wash of the scholars.

"Who are these people?" Durga breathed.

"These are the scholars of Wyrd," Agassiz whispered. "I believe their study has made them strange." The beaver surveyed, standing on tiptoe, which was not that helpful. "There!"

They followed Agassiz down the length of the hall.

As they passed the scholars, Ariel watched them toss cards onto tables, chatting as they played. Around the hearths, the rhythm was not to speak and listen, consider and reply; the scholars all spoke at once. But they did not trample over one another: it was a conversation, somehow, thick and continuous. The scholars fuzzed and fogged, and their cards whirred like the wings of dragonflies, and their voices beat against each other like weather.

In the whisper of the cards, in the hum of conversation, Ariel heard the word: ZHOZM.

ZHOZM.

ZHOZM.

The hall seemed to vibrate with it.

Agassiz found a scholar sitting alone before one of the hearths. She was not as blurred as the others; her outline was merely smudged, rather than fully diffused. The fire reflected in her eyes, sharp dancing spots.

The scholar was sipping from a mug while considering a pad of translucent paper, but when she saw Agassiz approach, she stood. "Mx. Beaver! What a surprise. It has been years."

The beaver bowed. "I am sure you have forgotten; I am Assistant Agister Agassiz. May we sit? Thank you. Ariel, Durga: this is Laurentide, an esteemed scholar of the College of Wyrd."

"Not so esteemed. Sit!" Laurentide motioned. "You were a great help to me, Agassiz—you and your ledger. What brings you to Wyrd?"

"The very same ledger—it sent us here! Ariel and Durga ought to have been clients of the firm, but this has become an independent project."

"My favorite kind," said Laurentide. She sat beside Agassiz, and the motion smeared her form into a fuzzy streak.

Durga could not remain silent. "You are *blurred*," she said. "Why? Is this an affliction?"

Laurentide's lifted brow was a puff of steam from a kettle. "Is this your first encounter with the college? Consider that it might be *you* who are afflicted. You do look rather . . . flat. Don't frown. I remember how the scholars appeared when I arrived; I know you can't see my colleagues as I do. But, be sure of it: the defect is yours." She smiled pleasantly.

Ariel could not take his eyes off the scholar. He had the impression of a figure glimpsed out the tail of his eye, except that she was directly in front of him. Her appearance was elusive.

Several other scholars, attracted by a new voice, gathered around the hearth. They built up like a bank of fog, and the light of the fire made their edges pink.

"Tell us about your independent project," said Laurentide.

Before Agassiz could reply, Durga said: "We seek information about the dragons."

"And a wizard, whose name is Malory!" added Ariel.

"The ledger indicates both are connected to this college," said Agassiz. "I trust its guidance, even if I do not understand it."

Laurentide considered; her expression fuzzed. To Durga, she said: "I do not know much about dragons—though other scholars might." The gathered group rippled and murmured. Then, to Ariel: "I have heard of a Malory who was a scholar. Yes, at this very college. What is your interest in him?"

They told her. Ariel began, going into too much detail about his life at the Castle Sauvage, then quickly speeding up, but skipping too much, so Durga had to interrupt and supply the essential details.

Finally, Agassiz explained what they'd learned in the data center: that their questions converged, here in Wyrd.

"Fascinating. I am overdue for another run at your storehouse of secrets, Mx. Beaver."

"The ledger holds no secrets," Agassiz chirped amiably. "Just things overheard."

"Then allow me to say the same. The college holds no secrets. Where Malory is concerned, one scholar knows him best. I will take you to her!"

MORGAN SAMPHIRE

April 28, 13778

Laurentide brought them through the alleys of Wyrd to the college's library, redolent of brine, where the loose bundled manuscripts were all written on greenish paper manufactured from seaweed.

On the shadowed second floor, at a desk beside a small window, they found her.

"Morgan," Laurentide greeted her softly.

If Laurentide was a figure smudged, this scholar was a ghost barely there. She brewed like mist beside her overburdened desk.

"Morgan Samphire," Laurentide said, a little louder.

With long fingers—there seemed to be many more than ten—the scholar paged through a sheaf of diagrams. The seaweed paper was thickly translucent, so patterns on one page showed through to the next.

"Morgan!" Laurentide shouted.

The scholar coalesced somewhat. Her outline rippled and swam, but her face showed more distinctly. She was, distinctly, very old.

"Oh! Sorry, Laurentide, sorry, sorry," the scholar Morgan piped. Her voice was clear and high. She sounded like someone who had just arrived late after a long and circuitous journey. "Lost in thought, in triple-digit dimensions!"

"Morgan, it's freezing in here," Laurentide said.

"Oh, I hardly notice . . . and perhaps that is an enticement to deeper study! Think, Laurentide . . . you, too, could become insensate."

Laurentide introduced her visitors and explained their purpose.

The old scholar nodded. "Malory, Malory, Malory. I haven't heard that name in a hundred years."

"But you knew him," Laurentide said.

"Of course! We were apprentices together."

"Apprentices . . . together?" Ariel said. I shared his surprise. Morgan Samphire was an ancient haze; how could she have been Malory's contemporary? Well: Malory was a wizard. He looked like a sleek young man, but might have been any age at all.

"Yes," said Morgan, "we did our memorization together. Our diving, too, of course. Malory didn't have a talent for any of it . . . none at all, zip, zero, zilch. But he did have determination. We'd have to work a shape up the ladder: square, cube, hypercube, hyperhypercube—you know the exercise, Laurentide. I would breeze through the dimensions, but for Malory, each one was an excruciation. Yet he did it. And barely slept."

Ariel thought of the wizard's tower, the tallest in the Castle Sauvage, and the way it flickered with eldritch energy in the middle of the night. He'd grown up knowing very little about Malory, except that he was tireless.

"I would arrive here in the morning," Morgan said, "and find Malory passed out—there! That's the spot, exactly." She wobbled an amorphous finger toward the window. "He chose the desk with the view of the ocean." She was quiet a moment, then laughed. "I really have been sitting in this library for a long time, haven't I?"

Ariel tingled with the revelation that Malory had inhabited this space. Morgan Samphire spoke fondly of an old classmate; she didn't know how villainous he had become.

"Malory substituted effort for talent," Morgan continued, "so, by the time we donned our cloaks, he was a better scholar than me, because he understood *how* he knew what he knew, and I was coasting on intuition." She shrugged massively. "Still am."

"Well, it's a powerful intuition," said Laurentide, and Morgan nodded, accepting the compliment.

"But he left," Ariel said. "And after he left, he made me."

Morgan Samphire turned to address Ariel directly; the inviting billow of a diaphanous curtain. "Did he?" she said. Her eyes sparked sharp in the mist of her gaze.

Ariel paused. He was speaking, he understood, to someone who had been Malory's friend; who might consider herself his friend still. He chose his words carefully. "Yes. He has become a wizard."

"A scholar *and* a wizard . . . how perfectly Malory. A wizard must assemble a laboratory, isn't that right? I am sure he approached it the same way he approached his scholarship. Oh, such cruel effort."

"But *why* did he leave to become a wizard?"

"I do not know, but I can tell you about his parting. And if that is not sufficient, well, you will have to take your questions to the Wyrm." She looked at Ariel slyly; her eyes flashed in the haze of her.

"They have just arrived," said Laurentide. "I do not expect that they know anything about our college, or the Wyrm."

"Oh? Explain it to them, Laurentide. I would like to hear your version. As pithy as you can make it."

Laurentide shimmered. "Pithy, you say?"

"The pithiest."

Laurentide said: "Here at the college, we study the Wyrm of Wyrd. She lives at the bottom of a well."

"Oh," said Ariel.

"Too pithy," tutted Morgan.

"What is a wyrm?" asked Durga.

"That question is the basis of much scholarship!" said Morgan. "Nothing would make me happier than outlining the competing intellectual factions, but I do not think you would find it engrossing. Though the day might come . . . it might, it might, it might."

Laurentide began to say: "The Wyrm is—" but Morgan Samphire continued:

"The Wyrm is manifold, so there are many ways of speaking about her. Yes, that much we know: the Wyrm is a she. She is a mind. She is a prophet. She is a map. She is a god—just a small one. She is a high-dimensional space. No, don't make that face, it's just mathematics. If that's all too heady, then return to the basics: she lives at the bottom of a well!"

Ariel stared.

"And," the old scholar went on, "I will prove to you I have not forgotten your question, about my old friend Malory. The Wyrm is vast beyond imagining, so any scholar only chooses a small portion to explore. For most of us, this involves quite a bit of stumbling around. Not Malory. From the start, he knew his destination. He swam straight for it."

Laurentide raised her eyebrows; another jet of steam.

"In the depths of the Wyrm—you have not met her yet, so perhaps this is confusing, but it's all very accessible, I assure you—he found what he wanted. His work was done. He left the next day."

"Does that happen often?" Agassiz asked. "A scholar leaving the college?"

"What would you say, Laurentide?" Morgan prompted.

"I would say it happens approximately never."

"Yes, I was wavering between unheard-of and unthinkable. Scandalous, really. Not that it isn't allowed. Rather . . . once you have gotten to know the Wyrm, how could you live without her?"

Ariel felt a creeping dread. Part of him wanted to say, Well, okay, that's enough. I don't need to hear any more.

Another part wanted to know everything.

"What did Malory find?" he asked quietly.

"I cannot say," Morgan said. "He would not tell me. Unless . . ." She paused, and her form fluttered in a gust of memory. "Unless, unless, I left with him. It would be a great adventure, he said! The adventure to end all adventures."

Laurentide frowned. "I did not know you were so close."

"I declined. I was, even then, a creature of the library. But I would not tolerate his secrecy, either! I pestered him, I bullied him, I cajoled him. He relented, and revealed that the Wyrm had offered him"—she laughed a single laugh, the chime of a bell—"a quest. That's what Malory said. She offered him a quest, and he accepted." Morgan turned to the younger scholar, and her voice was a wondrous whisper when she said: "He dove deep for this, Laurentide. Deep, deep, deep . . . and in a strange direction."

Laurentide lured Morgan Samphire out of her lair with the promise of coffee. In the great hall, she was greeted with a chorus of hellos: a legendary figure seldom seen outside the library.

They found a hearth, and Morgan spoke to Laurentide. "I have read your transcripts. You dive so deep! I trust you are being cautious."

"I could go deeper," said Laurentide. "I only hold back to spare your nerves."

"It is the diving that brought you here," Morgan observed.

"I was a strong swimmer, and when I learned that there was a way to dive in . . . thought itself . . . Yes. It is the diving that compels me, rather than the riddles."

Morgan hooted. "The riddles are all I care about!"

She turned to Ariel. "We are a diverse college. Laurentide

came to dive; to learn what diving could be. I came because I heard the secrets of the universe were waiting, like tangled knots, to be picked apart. I love to pick, pick, pick."

As she enthused, the old scholar blurred deeply, and Ariel was afraid she might dissipate entirely and waft away.

"Oh, but Malory, Malory, Malory. How can I explain this? . . . For me, the world has always felt vast. Too vast! That is why I huddle in the library. For Malory, the world felt small. He wanted—what? I don't know. A broader scope."

The conversation continued, with scholars stopping to greet Morgan Samphire, offering to fill her mug—they really did drink a lot of coffee here, and very late in the day—while Ariel sank into himself.

From the city, to the wild, to the coast—failure to failure to failure. The old scholar loved riddles, but she had no answer to the riddle of his creation.

He had asked the ledger, "Who can help me against Malory?" It had sent him here—where there was no help.

"I would like to speak to the Wyrm," announced Durga. "If speaking is what you would call it." While Ariel had moped, she had schemed, and I saw it clearly: she believed this prophet, this small god, this Wyrm, could tell her how to defeat the dragons.

"We call it many things," said Morgan Samphire, "and speaking is one of them. It's very difficult. Very, very, very. You would have to become an apprentice of the college."

"I will," Durga said, "if you will have me. I am no stranger to study, and hard training."

"An apprentice!" Morgan Samphire hooted. "Laurentide, it

has been a while, hasn't it? How wonderful. What about you two?" She turned to Ariel and Agassiz. "Does the Wyrm interest you?"

Agassiz spoke. "What you have described reminds me of our ledger . . . and I wonder if there should be some link between our inquiries." The beaver's eyes glittered. "If I could learn to speak to your Wyrm . . . and if scholars could learn to query our ledger . . ." She chirped inquisitively. "It is interesting to think about."

"It is very interesting," Morgan agreed. "Very, very, very."

"Then I will become an apprentice!"

The old scholar turned to Ariel. "And you? Your maker, my old friend, found the reason for your creation here. Will you seek it, too?"

Ariel startled. "Do you think it is possible?"

"Truthfully? No—not without Malory's determination." She peered at him, a constellation of evaluations. "And yet, and yet, and yet . . . my old friend substituted effort for talent. Perhaps you have talent. Perhaps you have something else. On behalf of the College of Wyrd, I invite you to find out."

Ariel looked at Durga, whose face was set and shining; at Agassiz, whose fur was bristling with eager curiosity; and he felt that he would rather attempt something difficult, even absurd, together with them, than continue alone.

He could not continue alone, he realized. He was right. He was learning. I felt it: the slow but powerful tide of self-knowledge, and even wisdom.

"Yes," Ariel said. "I will try."

Laurentide spoke cautiously. "Apprenticeship is difficult work. Access to the Wyrm is not guaranteed. Months can pass, even years, without progress."

"Laurentide!" Morgan clucked. "If I recall, you reached the Wyrm on your first dive. You did, you did, you did. Perhaps one of them is a prodigy."

Laurentide did not believe it; no amount of smudging could conceal her skepticism.

"Let them rest," said the old scholar, "and in the morning, take them to the Wyrm. Take them to the well." She paused, and her expression bloomed, a whole book of translucent pages overlaid: and on those pages were written kindness, eagerness, pride, concern, cunning, and a hundred other things.

She said: "Start them in the shallow end."

THE LIMPID POOL

April 29, 13778

After breakfast in the sweltering great hall (porridge doped with seaweed) the trio of Ariel, Durga, and Agassiz followed Laurentide into the alleys of Wyrd, where they joined a migration of bleary scholars, yawning in their cloaks, all bound for the same place.

Their destination was the wide, windowless structure that dominated the center of the college, facing the Rath-road where it passed through town. Tight-fitting planks showed reddish where the structure had recently been patched up; elsewhere, the wood was all scoured to gray.

Inside: humid air, bare skin. The bleary scholars disrobed and laid their cloaks in neat cubbies. Ariel watched out the tail of his eye. Their nudity was disguised by the fuzzing of their forms, so they were not starkly naked, but modestly blurred.

"No need to undress," Laurentide said. "At least not yet. Come and look."

They followed her through the changing room, out into an enormous courtyard, open to the sky, still purplish, the glow of morning not yet visible over the walls.

In the courtyard, tightly mortared stones flowed around two pools, one smaller, the other larger. Each was a different color, the water milky with minerals, glowing with an inner light.

Laurentide said, "Here is where the Wyrm resides."

She led them to the larger pool. Its surface was still. As they watched, a scholar approached. He sat on the stone at the pool's edge, breathing deeply. Then, with a final, percussive exhale, loud in the morning quiet, he slipped into the milky water, the disturbance of his entry quickly calmed. The pool seemed reluctant to ripple.

Ariel peered after him; he saw only the water's pearlescent surface.

"This . . . is the well?" Durga asked.

"Yes, but don't worry—you won't dive here," said Laurentide. "It's too demanding. For you, it would be dangerous. Instead . . ."

She walked to the smaller pool, which seemed marginally more inviting, with water translucent pink instead of milky and opaque, like the well.

"This is the Limpid Pool," Laurentide said. "It is not so deep." She dipped a toe. "And quite comfortable."

Durga frowned in confusion. Ariel was feeling grouchy and yanked-around. Agassiz's eyelids were still drooping—both sets. All three had declined the offer of coffee, which had clearly been a mistake.

Another scholar overheard. "You've skipped some essential material, Laurentide," he said. "Think back to your first day. You've just arrived from Rath Bumpkin. It's all very strange here. Naked people are wandering around. You remember how that felt, don't you?"

Laurentide frowned. "I'm not sure I do."

"You're ridiculous." He addressed Ariel, Durga, and Agassiz. His body was extremely hairy, and he had the most distinct face they'd yet seen: wide and friendly, blued by whiskers. "Forgive her, and fear not: your substitute teacher has arrived! You know we speak to the Wyrm, listen to what she says, puzzle it out."

"Yes," Durga said. "We want to speak to her ourselves."

"Of course! But the Wyrm doesn't really speak—not the way you and I do. Her mind is different. What comes through, it's not, hello, Garibald—that's me—Wyrm here, I'd like to clearly explain one of the deep truths of the universe. No. When we talk—oh, it gets weird when you're talking about talking, doesn't it . . . ?"

"I hate you, Garibald," said Laurentide, in a way that made it clear she did not hate him.

"Spoken language," he continued, "is a train of words—like my friends coming out of the changing room, one at a time, do you see? Just as I am saying now: Do, you, see? The same would be true if I wrote my words down, letters on a page." He traced them in the air: DO, YOU, SEE?

"I understand, I think," Ariel said, suddenly conscious of the neat line made by: I, understand, I, think.

"Excellent," said Garibald. "Now. The Wyrm is nothing like that."

Durga interjected: "I am acquainted with other kinds of minds." Of course she was: the Anth had cultivated a whole bestiary of cognition. The dragons were part of it, as was I. "How does this spa relate to . . . deep truths?"

"A spa! If only. Yes, I am coming to the use of the well. A line of words . . . call it one dimension. A drawing, that's two dimensions. Have I lost you?"

Ariel wanted to say, Yes, almost. Durga stared impatiently.

"In the regional office, we use three dimensions," Agassiz said cautiously. "Our debates . . . the forms we build."

"That's right!" Garibald said. "I'd forgotten about those."

"It comes naturally, and it feels . . . complete," Agassiz continued. "When I talk instead—oh, it *is* weird when you're talking about talking—I often feel that something is missing."

"You have prepared the way for my next point perfectly—what is your name? Agassiz, wonderful. I am so glad to have a beaver here. Now. The orator is happy in one dimension. The . . . artist, shall we say, enjoys two. The beavers thrive in three. The Wyrm, however . . ." He paused, pleased with himself. Ariel was pleased, too. "The Wyrm prefers forty-three million dimensions."

Ariel tried to imagine a forty-three-million-dimensional shape.

"Don't try to visualize it!" Garibald cautioned, too late. Ariel's brain had seized up. I felt the pinch. "It can't be done. You can only let it . . . wash over you. We float in the water, and it puts us viscerally into three dimensions, which is helpful. Then, as we dive deeper—well, perhaps you'll experience it for yourselves. Are they getting in, Laurentide?"

"I think they might dip a toe," she confirmed.

Ariel peered into the pink pool. "Is it dangerous?"

"The Wyrm's Well is very dangerous," said Garibald. "Scholars are sometimes lost. But the Limpid Pool shouldn't pose any problem."

Ariel hesitated. "I am not a strong swimmer." This was an understatement.

Laurentide shrugged. "The only way to the Wyrm is through this pool. If you wish to speak with her, you will dive."

The Wyrm knew why the wizard had created Ariel. She might even know how to defeat him. The boy wanted that information desperately. And yet . . .

They followed Laurentide back into the changing room, where she disrobed, rolled her cloak into a ball, and shoved it into one of the cubbies. The other scholars seemed to have folded theirs neatly.

Ariel of the Castle and Forest Sauvage would have been shy about undressing, but his months in the bathhouses of Rath Varia had eased his nervousness and convinced him, finally, that no one cared enough about his nudity to look.

Even so, he took his time. Laurentide and Durga waited for him, and the latter sent his gaze scurrying to safety: while the scholars all presented their fuzzy outlines, Durga, like him, was sharp and stark. She shivered violently in the morning cold.

Agassiz, who did not wear clothes anyway, was mystified by the entire process.

They watched scholars step into the Wyrm's Well, pause at the edge, then disappear beneath the milky surface. For many minutes, scholars had entered; none so far had reemerged.

Durga turned to their guide. "How do they stay down so long? Do you have genetic modifications?"

Laurentide looked at her flatly. "We just hold our breath."

Standing beside the Limpid Pool, Ariel was terrified. He truly didn't know how to swim, only how to float on his back, and only when the stream through Sauvage ran slow in summer.

"I could watch," he said.

"You'll learn nothing by watching," Laurentide said.

"You can tell me about it," he said to Durga. "And, if you have the opportunity, perhaps ask the Wyrm about Malory . . ."

"She won't be able to tell you anything," Laurentide said. "Apprentices struggle for years to express what they experience in the Limpid Pool, even in the most basic terms."

Garibald sat at the pool's edge, with his ankles in the water. "You should try," he said. "It's not so deep. Laurentide and I will both keep an eye on you. Won't we?"

"Of course," said Laurentide. "Meet me at the bottom." She stepped into the air above the Limpid Pool and let herself fall, straight as a stone. The water accepted her with barely a ripple.

Durga sat beside Garibald at the pool's edge, took a great gulp of air, and pushed herself in with a loud splash.

Agassiz went next, slipping into the water with innate ease.

Ariel hovered, watching their dark forms spiral down.

Gently, Garibald said, "You can use the steps if you like."

One side of the Limpid Pool offered a graduated descent; Ariel accepted. The pool was tepid as well as limpid, almost body temperature. It felt inviting, rather than menacing. He took one step, then another.

When he had waded to his shoulders, he ducked beneath the surface, testing the water. His cheeks were puffed with air.

When he opened his eyes, he saw Laurentide and Durga below. The water was sparklingly clear, and here, beneath the surface, Laurentide's form was definite, not smudged at all. He saw the glitter of her eyelashes, the shine of her skin. Nearby, Durga was flailing, struggling deeper, battling her own buoyancy. Dark, fine hair swirled around her head.

Below, the bottom of the pool might have been difficult to discern, except that Agassiz had already reached it. The beaver turned and sat, looking as comfortable as one of the scholars beside a hearth in their great hall.

What, exactly, were they diving for?

Ariel took another step down. The surface was above his head. He had committed to the pool.

The water's clarity soothed him. When you dunked your head into the stream in Sauvage, you couldn't see anything, just a turbulent froth, plus bits of sticks and leaves, the occasional flickering minnow. By contrast, this pool seemed clearer than the world above. It was like stepping into the center of a gem.

There were no more steps, only a drop into the full depth of the Limpid Pool. The boy would have to swim, or sink, or retreat back the way he'd come.

Any of my subjects might have managed this test. Altissa had trained extensively underwater; Kate Belcalis spent summers frolicking along the lakeshore; Peter Leadenhall swam endless laps in a heated pool.

Any of them would have felt, at this point, the scratchy buildup of carbon dioxide; its presence in the blood (rather than oxygen's absence) triggers concern, followed by urgency, followed by panic. Ariel would experience that in a moment.

He did not.

Durga thrashed into view, attempting another dive; she was a confident but very inefficient swimmer. Ariel watched her struggle to orient herself. She looked at him, and he looked back.

He dropped. He did not go as fast as he'd feared; the water seemed thick, and it lent him a comfortable buoyancy. With a wave of his arms, he could steady himself, choose his orientation.

Three dimensions!

Floating in the pool, Ariel felt an itch: not on his skin, but deeper, somewhere in his muscles, or his marrow. He wanted to scratch the itch, and he felt that to scratch it, he ought to kick his legs, so he did—and moved through a dimension he had never moved through before.

How can I describe it? I cannot. Ariel's nerves flashed with sensations totally new, and I panicked, activated cellular firewalls, slammed chemical bulkheads. I had survived Altissa's death and Ariel's encounter with the Lady of the Lake; I was not going to lose the thread here, in the kiddie pool.

Ariel floated, waving his arms up and down, and also curling them around themselves. I was only getting a muffled impression of the sensation; his hands seemed to inflate like beach balls.

Agassiz sat on the floor of the pool, peering around curiously. For a moment she looked like a flower, each petal another complete version of Agassiz; but when Ariel looked directly at her, the petals snapped closed, and every oily hair on the beaver's shoulders stood out sharp and clear.

Durga, meanwhile, had given up. Her legs, just before they

vanished from the pool, appeared as a writing tangle. A sailor's knot of legs.

These visions were fascinating, and also a bit nauseating. Sinking lower, Ariel felt as if he were peeling the layers of an onion in the kitchen at the Castle Sauvage—an onion with no center.

Infinite onion.

The pool's bottom was just there, beyond his reach, where Laurentide and Agassiz waited, the scholar considering the beaver with clear consternation. The scholar glanced up, and when her gaze caught the boy, it became strange.

Ariel realized that he had not breathed in what felt like a very long time, and it was this conscious realization, rather than the burn of carbon dioxide in his blood, that sent him kicking to the surface. His concern was all intellectual, which is approximately the opposite of how it's supposed to go, down at the bottom of a pool without any air.

He splashed to the surface and sucked in a great breath, but it felt superfluous, almost sickening. His head pounded. Agassiz surfaced alongside him.

Durga and Garibald gaped.

"What?" Ariel said.

"You were down there for nearly five minutes," Durga said quietly.

"So was Agassiz," the boy said.

"Agassiz is a *beaver*!" Durga said.

"It was an impressive dive," said Garibald. "For both of you. I can only think of one apprentice who did so well—and here she comes now."

Laurentide broke the surface. No gasp or gulp; her breath was perfectly even.

She looked at them, and her seriousness could not conceal her rising curiosity. "That was interesting," she said. "Welcome, apprentices, to the College of Wyrd."

EMERGENCY

April 29, 13778

A beautiful morning in the Eigengrau. Warm rain on the sidewalk.

Ariel de la Sauvage came barreling into the café, and to everyone assembled, with panic in his voice, he cried: "Does anyone here know *math*?"

AN EDUCATION

April 29, 13778, to June 10, 13778

Ariel, Durga, and Agassiz formed a new class of three.

Laurentide took them careening through a remedial course in high-dimensional mathematics. Durga's propagandist training had gone heavy on game theory, epidemiology, and 3D graphics. Agassiz already knew the pernicious physics of fluid dynamics. They were well matched to the material.

Ariel, however, had learned from Madame Betelgauze only basic arithmetic, as in, if you had six mushrooms (red cap, good for rattling coughs), and you gave two mushrooms to me (because I had a rattling cough—but why would you give me two? One is plenty) . . . He was lost.

The mathematics was easier than the swimming.

Ariel's gift was only for breath-holding; he really was a terrible swimmer, and when Laurentide instructed him to dive and return, dive and return, a dozen times in succession, he wheezed as hard as Durga.

They swam in the Limpid Pool every morning, and they did not do so alone. After diving in the well, many scholars swam in the pool, enjoying its warmth; or they sat at the edge, chatting. In the clarity of the pool, the scholars' bodies were revealed, every size and shape, every droop and wrinkle. It was wonderful.

Although Ariel's legs firmed up and his butt recognized it had a part to play, he still could not reach the bottom. Durga did no better. She was bold in the pool, but her swimming was rigid, desperate. It never carried her beyond an asymptotic barrier; the bottom remained beyond her reach.

Agassiz, meanwhile, had already graduated to the pearlescent water of the Wyrm's Well.

"What have you found?" Durga asked her. "What is down there?"

Agassiz began to speak, then paused; began again; and finally, the beaver chirped, "*She* is down there!"

One morning, as Ariel and Durga lay gasping at the edge of the Limpid Pool, unsuccessful again, Laurentide said: "I believe we are approaching this the wrong way. Let's just . . . get you comfortable in the water."

Thereafter, they floated.

Spring came to Wyrd. The wind eased; whole afternoons passed in stillness. The scholars traded their winter cloaks for light tunics. Ariel and Durga each received their own apprentice's smock, fished from a long-forgotten closet, dyed the same pale pink as the Limpid Pool, and the weather was so warm that the smocks sufficed.

Each student received their own room in the dormitory of

the college, each with a peg on the wall, a desk beneath a window, and a bed—nothing else. Durga's traveling clothes went into her desk drawer, neatly folded with the bangles laid on top. Ariel hung his leather jacket on the peg and left it there.

The cliffs bloomed with bright wildflowers. Occasionally Ariel spied bees dancing among them. Somewhere, an elk was waiting.

In Laurentide's lessons, the forty-three million dimensions of the Wyrm loomed, impossible to grasp. Ariel's brain still hitched when he thought about it; I felt it as a sickening jolt.

Ariel and Durga memorized the first hundred dimensions of reality.

Upon the foundation of time, there were added width, height, and depth; these were followed by momentum, charge, and spin; next came density, symmetry, and "bagelness." Ariel had never encountered a bagel. None of the scholars had, either. In the Eigengrau, I fished an example out of Kate's memory and served it to him, toasted and buttered. "This is an excellent dimension," he declared after his second bite.

Beyond these first ten stretched a vast field of dimensions that, to Ariel's surprise, glowed with emotion. Nostalgia was a dimension. Sorrow was a dimension. So was contentment.

In a special lesson, Garibald introduced a bundle of dimensions, numbered in the high seventies, that were especially salient to the Wyrm. These dimensions corresponded to ancient stories that had been lost to history—but not to the Wyrm. She could recite them, all the way through, and for many scholars she did, a chapter a day.

How luxurious, to have a small god narrate your audiobook.

One of these salient dimensions glowed like a lamppost in a winter forest; another swirled with fine particles that carried consciousness; another connected ostentatious names across a vast field of culture.

One of these salient dimensions was called Ursula K. Le Guin.

Ariel didn't understand most of what the scholars taught them, but, for apprentices, understanding was not the point. The point was to memorize the first hundred dimensions, so he did.

A beautiful afternoon in the Eigengrau. A whiteboard set up beside the espresso machine.

After the radio tutorial, Peter Leadenhall had become enthusiastic about teaching. Something new was happening in my world of memory, between the living and the dead, and it was wonderful to see. Ariel's brain crackled with capability. This was real learning, not my reckless download in the bog. It helped that Peter was a good teacher, always laughing. Kate Belcalis joined in, asked questions of her own. Travanian put on headphones and ignored them.

"We loved our graphs," said Peter. He drew a jagged line across the board, one that rose in a scalloped pattern, then fell the same way. "Look—a story, in two dimensions. This is the concentration of carbon dioxide in the atmosphere; a very famous graph. It goes up up up, then down down down. It is the story of the Anth."

If it did not look, to Ariel, like much of a story, I understood the collective achievement and relief inscribed by that scalloped downslope. Sweetest scallop of all time.

"But it's incomplete. There's no Earth on this board; no ecology, no industry, no politics. There is no Peter Leadenhall, and no Ariel de la Sauvage. The real world demands more than the coordinates X and Y."

"And more than the coordinate Z," Ariel offered.

Peter nodded. "So you have been paying attention. X and Y and Z, along with time, are sufficient for billiard balls and booster rockets—simple things. But real life, the complexity of it, demands more. This was our discovery: the world, like a sponge, will soak up as many dimensions as you provide."

Peter plucked at his shirt, one of the blousy button-downs he favored. "Size, color, material . . . these are all dimensions, and they establish a space that can be navigated and explored. Just as we can move up or down, side to side, we can also move along the axis of . . . softer, or scratchier. More stylish, or less. This insight was the foundation of the great shopping algorithms of the Middle Anth."

Their highest achievement, sadly.

"Don't be too judgmental," Peter chided me. "The techniques developed for selling shirts laid the foundations for my world models. I stood on the shoulders of shoppers."

His approach to planning had been the crown jewel of the cooperativo called Fifty-Second Street. Peter Leadenhall had invented an economy. His techniques treated high-dimensional spaces like suitcases, packing the complexity of the world inside, then squeezing them shut and handing them off to computers, just as a traveler might breezily consign his luggage to a bellhop. The Anth became unburdened.

. . .

Laurentide often sent her apprentices roving through the college, seeking answers to questions both basic and advanced—intellectual scavenger hunts. That spring, the three of them became fixtures of the alleys, and if they seldom found the answer they'd been dispatched to find, they learned other things.

They learned that the scholars sought transcendence: to reach so deeply into the dimensions of thought that nothing remained in these meager three of space and one of time. A scholar's smudginess was a rough measure of their progress. Fuzzy dissolution did not mean death, they said: rather, study continued, in a space where richer questions could be asked, more sublime answers understood.

They believed an invisible college was overlaid atop Wyrd: a high-dimensional institute of very advanced study. (When he learned this, Ariel felt itchy.) Scholars claimed they glimpsed flickers of old friends in the alleys: legends who had disappeared at the bottom of the Wyrm's Well, who waved hello from their new perch. The ultimate emeritus.

Morgan Samphire might soon join this invisible college, the scholars said.

They learned that the Wyrm of Wyrd had many aspects, which the scholars called epithets; they estimated this number at forty-three million, same as the number of dimensions, but some argued it was vastly greater. Only a small fraction of the Wyrm's epithets—a mere thousand or so—had been documented.

Some had been represented in art, and those representations were assembled in the Gallery of the Wyrm, neighbor to the library. Inside, there were charcoal drawings on seaweed paper, busts whittled from sun-bleached driftwood, strange sculptures as intricate as the arguments of the beavers . . . and mirrors: so many mirrors. Small and large, rough and clear. Exploring the gallery, Ariel saw himself in a battered shell of metal, the image indistinct—and realized that his reflection resembled a scholar.

They learned that, very rarely—once a century, perhaps—a scholar diving deep in the well found more than an idea. They grasped real, physical objects, and brought them to the surface. These treasures were displayed in the heart of the gallery. All three were made of pearlescent stone, like the inside of an oyster shell: a shield, a vase, a paring knife. That last had been retrieved by Morgan Samphire, decades prior, before she was blurred with wisdom.

An entire branch of scholarship was devoted to investigating the material properties of these objects, which seemed to be—the scholars did not use this word—superconductive.

They learned how the college made its seaweed paper. Scholars on foraging duty hiked the coast for kilometers, and brought their haul back in dripping carts, depositing it at pungent mills where the seaweed was pulped and pressed. A series of cryptic processing steps produced the greenish translucency prized by the college.

They learned about the brews of Wyrd, beer of stupendous complexity, discussed and debated endlessly. The scholars had terminology and language for every scent, every bubble. Some of their discussions with the Wyrm revolved exclusively around beer. They exported it along the Rath-road, trading in Rath

Varia for building materials, in Rath Delecta for hard cheese. Delecta was far distant, but the cheese was worth the trip.

They learned that fashion, by contrast, was forsaken. Scholars all wore the same cloaks and tunics, all purplish gray, dyed with a particular seaweed. They were woven from fibers spun from plastiglomerate quarried several kilometers in from the coast. Ariel might have been wearing a water bottle of the Middle Anth.

Dirty cloaks were deposited, fresh ones taken. The scholars had no patience for choosing outfits. They preferred to be naked, and to be diving.

There was no romance at the College of Wyrd, at least none that I could ever detect. The scholars seemed all to be in their own passionate relationship with the Wyrm.

They learned the card game popular in the great hall. The scholars used the same deck as everyone else, the deck Ariel recognized from the tavern in Sauvage, but their game was new to him. Quick and demanding, it relied on reflexes as much as strategy, and, in the way the cards were first piled and then depleted, it had the rhythm of a dive, with the fraught decision, deep into the process, whether to turn back or keep going.

Sometimes a group of scholars became overambitious, and the pile of cards grew and grew, and the game ended without a winner.

Every round of this game began with the same ritual: a careful review of the deck, and the removal of one face card, a particular lady. This card was placed in the center of the table and never touched again.

Ariel wondered why they didn't just remove the card from all the decks.

In the hall, where the scholars all jabbered at once, voices overlapping, Ariel still couldn't follow their discourse, but he grew to appreciate the sound of it. They had a system: scholars chose separate tonal lanes and stayed there, like a barbershop quartet of discourse. Intellectual harmony.

In their lessons, Ariel was impressed by Durga, who was laser-sharp, photon-quick. Even Laurentide could not disguise her approval. Solid nutrition—dense porridge, hearty bread, a truly ludicrous amount of seaweed—had brought the girl out of the shadow of her slumber. Her cheeks glowed with life; her hair thickened and shone.

The last daughter of the Anth was a credit to her people, and Ariel was happy she was there with him. The two of them along with Agassiz took their turns at the labors that sustained the college: scrubbing dishes in the kitchen, laundering cloaks in the washhouse, even gathering seaweed along the beach. Durga was a cheerful worker, though when their chores were done she quickly disappeared, pursuing her own projects in the alleys of Wyrd.

They had a lot of free time.

Durga burrowed into the library, disappeared for whole days, ingratiated herself to Morgan Samphire, who guided her into its obscure corners. Mostly the manuscripts were inscrutable geome-tries, or transcripts of conversations with the Wyrm that read like experimental poetry, but Durga reported that she was gleaning bits of history—clues about the previous eleven thousand years.

I wished Ariel would do the same. Instead, he wandered the town, poked his nose into bakeries and kilns, smelled sour starter and wet clay. He investigated tide pools, where tiny crabs collected bits of sea glass, piled them into their nests.

They had come a long way from the miniature city of the Mottainai. Ariel thought back to their escape from the flies. In the sturdy rhythm of his daily lessons and life, the boy became more confident that he had, at last, eluded Malory.

Perhaps, he thought, they could stay here. They could study, and truly become scholars. They could meet the Wyrm, whatever that meant.

One afternoon, Ariel went to find Durga in the library, and when the librarian replied that she had departed hours earlier, the boy inquired meekly about adventure stories. The librarian led him to a small desk, selecting a sheaf of pages that, when laid on top of each other in different combinations, formed not one adventure but a combinatorial explosion: every permutation of hero, sword, tower, ghost . . .

With every possible story laid out on the table before him, Ariel discovered he didn't really care about any of them, and returned the sheaf glumly to the librarian.

At the border of the college, on the cliff's edge, stood a slender tower. At its top, an enormous lamp faced the ocean. Sometimes, in the evening, it began to flash. It would do this for several minutes, in a fast, drumming pattern, then go dark.

"It is the embassy of the storm computer," explained Laurentide. "They often have questions for the Wyrm."

Ariel asked about the staccato rhythm of its flashing.

"Look," the scholar said. She pointed across the ocean, her outstretched finger buzzing and flickering. Ariel saw nothing at first; then, faintly, near the horizon, the tower's counterpart resolved: a light winking in reply.

"A ship?" asked Durga.

"Yes. They rarely come ashore. Instead they flash their questions. I have conveyed some to the Wyrm myself, and transcribed her replies. I do not understand them."

"Why do you dive on their behalf?" Agassiz asked. After all: the storm computer was the great nemesis of her firm.

"Because they bring us an essential supply," Laurentide said, "from halfway around the world. It is crucial to our studies—we couldn't get past the tenth dimension without it." The scholar's eyes danced. "They bring us coffee!"

Wyrd suited Ariel better than Rath Varia; it felt compact and knowable, the way Sauvage had been. When he thought about his old home—when he thought about Kay—his spirits fell. All his efforts to muster help had failed. But he did not always have to think about Kay: he could think instead about the pleasant ache in his muscles, or the invitation of the hearth, the promise of spicy soup and crusty bread, and a game of cards with Garibald.

Ariel roamed the alleys, and his mind roamed, too; he floated in the pool, and his mind floated, too.

He'd spent many happy hours in this manner, before the sword in the tomb, before Malory's madness. He was brave, curious, morbid, and, it must be said, a bit vague.

When he had finally relaxed, and given up wondering what would happen next, he found the Wyrm.

Who had never been at the bottom of the pool.

The Limpid Pool was crowded this morning, scholars thick around the edge, their conversation thrumming with rich harmonics, but Ariel's ears were in the water, so it was only faint music, an orchestra warming up in another room. He floated on his back and gazed up at the clear pink sky.

Something bumped against his head, and he thought it might be Durga surfacing, but there was an object in the water: a cup. Had a scholar dropped their beverage? Unthinkable—they were fastidious.

The cup had been floating half in the water, but Ariel's collision sent it dipping under, and now it sank. Curious, he gulped a lungful of air and dove. The cup, a broad chalice, was sinking quickly, so he reached for it; and reached not only through the dimensions of width and height and depth, but through sorrow and contentment and, I believe, bagelness. The feeling shocked him, and his distress grew as the cup became enormous, and instead of grasping it, he stepped inside.

THE WYRM OF WYRD

June 10, 13778

The Wyrm held court in a ruined hall that, if it were whole, would have been grander than any cathedral built by the Anth in any of their eras. Its ceiling had collapsed and was now open to the sky—not the pink above the pool, but a black dome blazing with stars unseen on Earth—and the hall itself was a drift of treasure, gold and jewels and more, and in the center, half-hidden beneath her hoard, lay the Wyrm of Wyrd.

She was enormous, coiled around herself, eyes lambent, mouth wide and curling.

"Oh," the Wyrm said, showing the flash of a pink tongue. "Oh! Oh! This is interesting!"

Ariel stepped over the threshold, into the ruined hall.

"Announce yourself!" the Wyrm called out. "Who do I have the pleasure of meeting, et cetera?"

"I am Ariel de la Sauvage," the boy said. He just would not give up that dorky name.

"You are an apprentice, new to the college?"

Ariel said yes.

"Then welcome. You have found your way to a good place, with good people in it."

The hall throbbed around the Wyrm. The scene sizzled and shone, like the surface of a stream. Ariel felt woozy, but he was aware that this was his chance. After so many disappointments, he would not squander it.

"Someone else spoke to you, long ago," he called up the Wyrm. "Or, not that long ago. I don't know."

"Indeed you do not. Time isn't merely wrinkled. It's knotted, twisted, tied in a bow."

Ariel began: "His name was Malory—"

The Wyrm interrupted him: "Wait. Hold up. Slow down. You still haven't introduced yourself."

Her neck split, and split again, and again, and again; she had a forest of necks; and each was perfectly sharp, as real as the next, and atop each, she grinned.

Ariel croaked in terror and confusion.

The Wyrm shivered, and the number of necks became seven.

"Sorry," she said, "I forgot you're new. This is the fewest I can manage, if we are to discuss anything of substance. Tell me seven things about Ariel de la Sauvage. Make yourself known on my terms, and then we will speak."

Ariel's mind blanked; for a moment, he knew exactly zero things about himself. Then he began; easily at first: "I have a brother named Kay."

One of the heads burned away, a sizzle of sparks. "Go on."

"I found a sword in a tomb—"

"Not what you *did*—who you *are*. Six more, still."

Ariel thought. "I like exploring the forest, and the cliffs. Places like that. I don't get mad easily. I can hold my breath for a long time." The Wyrm's heads were burning away merrily, and he was warming to the task. "I have two friends, Agassiz and Durga. Three if you count Kay. I should count Kay. A wizard made me, but I don't know why."

"You are coming into view, Ariel de la Sauvage! One more." The Wyrm's last head reared above him.

He scrounged for more to say. He thought about saying he was a poor swimmer, but wasn't sure if that was still true. All along, he knew what he wanted to reveal, but could not quite form the words.

"Careful," the Wyrm said. "If you do not locate yourself accurately in these meager seven dimensions, nothing that follows will have any meaning."

"The last thing about me is, I am meant for something important," Ariel said. "It is embarrassing to say. But I believe it's true."

I wanted to shout: You fool, you've missed everything. You are brave and curious, a bit morbid. You are romantic! But Ariel couldn't see those things about himself; not yet.

The Wyrm nodded, a slow undulation of her remaining neck. "I see who you are," she said, "and I begin to understand where you fit. On to business! Here in the Limpid Pool, I have many forms—the scholars call these my epithets. You may choose the one you like best. Explore as you wish, and stop where you're comfortable."

Ariel took a step, and as he did, the Wyrm changed: she wasn't a dragon, but a lioness guarding a bloody carcass. Another step, and she was a grizzly bear, sitting on her haunches in a frothing stream, rich with salmon. Another step, and she was a priestess draped in treasure, headdress and necklaces and bangles all gold, with delicate gold chains linking them together; she wore her hoard. Another step, and she was a museum—yes, an entire museum—and her hoard was inside her, a drift of abstract paintings. Another step, the leader of a nation of the Middle Anth, her hoard a vast field of missiles in their launch tubes, apocalyptic. Her epithets flickered, and Ariel was stepping fast, because they all frightened him; none were an improvement on the dragon.

He took a step back. The Wyrm resolved into a woman on a picnic blanket, laid on a broad lawn. Ariel heard the clack of a game he did not know was croquet. Her hoard—her treasure—was the park.

"I will speak to you this way," he said.

The Wyrm wore a loose sweater over slim pants, and beside her on the blanket was a tote bag with a notebook, a bag of chips, a bottle of water. "Very good," she said. "Have a seat."

Cautiously, Ariel approached, worried that the scene would shift as wildly as it had before, but the picnic blanket remained fixed on the swath of lawn. In each blade of grass, he detected the sparkle of a single gold coin.

"Why are there so many different versions of you?"

"You might ask, why are there so few? If you had completed your circumnavigation of the Limpid Pool, you would have seen 81 of my epithets; but that is just a sampling. There are, in total,

43,046,721, each one a world unto herself. The scholars have not spoken to the overwhelming majority of me." She tilted her head, held out her hands, as if to say: And what a shame!

"Does this epithet have her own—I mean, your own—name?"

The Wyrm smiled. "Yes, and thank you for asking. Many apprentices cannot muster the courage, and their fear makes them rude. My name is Ingrid."

I wondered if there was, in the library, a roster of all her names. I wondered how many, or how few, were as simple as Ingrid.

"Now," said the Wyrm, Ingrid, folding her hands in her lap. "We are acquainted. What have you come to discuss?"

Ariel told her about Malory, who had received life-altering counsel from the Wyrm, but kept it secret.

"Malory spoke to a different epithet," Ingrid said, "and I do not know what she said. You won't find her in the Limpid Pool. She lives in the forty-three million dimensions of the well . . . somewhere near the origin, I think." She looked uneasy. "The well demands deeper dives—much deeper. Even a prodigious breath-holder will not find her easily."

Ariel remembered: He was not sitting on a picnic blanket, but diving in a pink pool. Underwater. "I wonder when I will run out of breath," he said.

"You might already be drowned," Ingrid said lightly. She saw his distress, waved her hands: "No, no, of course not. Your body will not let you drown. Bodies are good at that!"

Even so, Ariel understood that it was time to depart. Maybe his body was telling him so. "I will visit again, if you will have me."

Ingrid the Wyrm tipped her chin, looked down her nose at him. "I will, if your conversation can range beyond wizards."

Ariel nodded. It could, and it would.

"Good, because I have questions for you. About your forest, and your friends. The scholars too often try to impress me with their cleverness, the density of their thought. They *are* very clever—but it is a pleasure to speak idly."

The picnic blanket vanished. Ariel found himself back in the Limpid Pool, underwater. He let himself float, thinking about what he'd just seen. Letting the strangeness of the experience leach out of his blood, until he felt ready for three dimensions again.

When he resurfaced, the world felt intolerably flat.

THE EMPTY ORIGIN

June 11, 13778

A beautiful morning in the Eigengrau. The whiteboard carried to the canal.

Peter Leadenhall stood in the shade of a cherry tree. We had hauled chairs out of the café for the lesson. Ariel sat beside me, while Kate Belcalis stood.

Ariel spoke. "Ingrid—that is a name for the Wyrm—she told me that if I wish to know what Malory learned, I must seek close to the origin. I do not know what she means."

Peter nodded, pausing to consider his approach to the subject. In life, he had never been a teacher; he'd avoided the responsibility at every turn, preferring to pursue his own projects, which, in fairness, had been mind-bogglingly consequential. And yet! Here was the clear, melancholy revelation, far too late: he had been made for this.

"You have learned a little about dimensions," Peter said. "From the scholars, and from me. The origin is the point in the center—where the coordinate, in every dimension, is zero." He drew two lines, crossed, and at their intersection he squiggled a blot.

He took a step back, considering the simple graph.

"There is an odd thing about high-dimensional space," he said. "I have never stopped puzzling over it." Not even in death.

He drew a circle around the crossed lines. "This circle has an area. Do you know—most of that area is here?" He scribbled his pen around the circumference, darkened the edge. "It's just the skin, yes, but there's so much of it. The core is just the core, but the skin . . . it wraps all the way around, do you see? When we add dimensions, the effect is compounded. A three-dimensional sphere is more uneven than a two-dimensional circle. If I had an apple, and I offered you either the skin or the core, and you were hungry, you ought to take the skin."

"The core has seeds, anyway," Ariel added.

"There is that. If it was an apple not of three dimensions but three hundred . . ." He scribbled wild loops on the whiteboard. "You would find its core basically empty, while its skin would be unbelievably fat."

Peter's world models considered hundreds of thousands of dimensions, and the cooperativos had flourished on that sturdy skin.

"The Wyrm has forty-three million dimensions," Ariel said.

Peter nodded slowly. "The origin of such a space would be unspeakably desolate."

You had to be cautious with analogies in the wilds of high-dimensional mathematics, where intuition could not guide you.

Peter Leadenhall knew that—he insisted upon it—yet caution was not prohibition. In his work, analogies had bridged vexing chasms. He never told anyone (but I knew) that he'd cracked the world models, at last, with a line of poetry. The mighty industry of the cooperativos, balanced on the tip of Auden's pencil.

So, when Ariel said, "The origin would not only be desolate . . ." Peter urged him on, waited patiently while the boy turned it over in his mind. At last, Ariel said: "It would also be lonely."

Ariel often shared meals in the great hall with Garibald, whom he judged the least fuzzy of the scholars. Something in the man's spirit had kept him fixed in this world, even as the Wyrm lured him away.

After they ate, they played cards. Garibald dutifully searched the deck for the lady and set her aside. As they began the game, she watched, serene, untouched.

Ariel fell placidly into the grinder of Garibald's strategy. While they played, he told the scholar about his visits with Ingrid: how he could only find his way when he was totally relaxed, or, better yet, bleary from sleep. Only then did the cup float into view.

"Is it the same in the well?" he asked.

"Yes and no," Garibald replied. "It's more difficult, and also less. More, because it's so taxing, physically, to dive deep . . . but less, because the pressure grows"—he lifted his hands, pantomimed walls pushing in on both sides—"and there comes a point where you cannot feel the boundary between the water and yourself. It becomes very quiet, and you feel like you might be dissolving."

"And then you find the cup?"

"I've never heard of anyone finding a cup! For me it is, I feel bashful to say, a very lovely woman, who swims up out of the depths. She surprises me every time. We kiss! I close my eyes— I'm that kind of kisser—and when I open them again, I am with the Wyrm. Ahem." Garibald busily reordered the cards in his hand. "We all bring our own temperament to the meeting. Some scholars refuse to say how they meet her."

What *were* these encounters with the Wyrm? What was their mechanism? The Eigengrau is a dream—or, it used the same machinery as dreams. The Anth had realized, after banging their heads for a century against wraparound displays, that the brain already possessed a rich and convicing sensory simulator, so they put it to work.

Perhaps the Wyrm was also a kind of dream.

"Do you enter through the ruined hall?" Ariel asked.

"No, but I recall it from the Limpid Pool. A cozy place."

The ruined hall was . . . cozy?

"Compared to the space presented by the well, yes. How can I say it . . . the ruined hall of the Limpid Pool would make a fine broom closet, in the vast-beyond-description, never-tread-the-same-hall-twice labyrinth of the Wyrm's Well. Now quit stalling. We are nearly out of cards. I believe you have lost."

AN URGENT PROJECT

June 11, 13778

Up the coast from Wyrd, the cliffs relaxed, permitting access to a narrow beach, inhabited in the summer by seals, who spoke in tones as laconic and cosmic as the most laid-back surfers of the Anth. They frolicked in the waves and dozed on the sand and expressed without prompting their admiration for each other, their visitors, the beach itself, the sun, the universe.

Ariel visited often, at all times of day, but most reliably in the evening. He was obsessed with the sunset; for him, it was still radical—a nightly spectacle.

A western coast: the great psychic battery of the Anth. Eastern coasts are fine, but western coasts had always been richer in both adventurism and melancholy. It was the California feeling, all throughout history, before and after California.

Ariel sat in the sand and tinkered with the Stromatolite. He updated his map, adding details from his journey, pushing and pulling the landscape into a more accurate configuration. He felt he had assembled a fair picture of the world; he was proud of it.

Even better, its shape had expanded sufficiently that it began to suggest where we might be. It meshed with my sense of where Altissa had fallen and been entombed.

This was the North Atlantic Ocean, I judged. Ariel stood on a new coast, revealed by a lowered sea level, frigid work of the dusty veil. The old coast of Ireland was somewhere behind him; the regional office of Shivelight & Shadowtackle occupied some fraction of that island (now a plateau); and the River Variable wandered through the drained depression of the Irish Sea. If the level of the oceans had dropped a hundred meters or more—well within the realm of possibility—the English Channel would have become dry land, just as it had been long ago, when humans strolled freely from England to France, before there was any England or France.

Ariel's map on the Stromatolite showed a small piece of the new world, and it made me curious about so much more: the Great Lakes, the Sundarbans, the South China Sea . . .

The cliffs of Wyrd had waited beneath the waves for twenty thousand years, at least. Now a road snaked along their length, and a college stood at their edge, and laid-back seals barked encouragements at their feet.

The moon was new, high in the daytime sky, its gravitational eddy visible as a track of turbulence across the veil of dust. The tide was coming in, and the waves were surging. Seals picked themselves up from the sand.

Ariel watched the water. He listened to the rush of sound. In the sizzle and crash of the waves, he heard a word, and the word was: ZHOZM.

He felt a presence on the beach. A strange psychic pressure. But he was sure that if he turned, no one would be there. He stared at the waves, lost himself in the roar, heard the word repeated:

ZHOZM.

ZHOZM.

"You are chanting," chirped Agassiz.

Ariel startled. The beaver sat beside him. Her fur was dark and glossy; wet from the waves. Granted a powerful genetic start, Agassiz had added great effort, following the seals into the cold surf to develop as a swimmer. The beaver swam far out—it made Ariel nervous sometimes.

"I use that word, sometimes . . . when I meditate to find the Wyrm, in the Limpid Pool."

"Interesting," said Agassiz. "I do not meditate . . . I hardly think at all. I just dive. Laurentide has been a good teacher . . . We are alike, in our approach."

"What do you find, by diving?" Ariel asked. "I know it is difficult to describe . . . but can you try?"

"Of course," said Agassiz. "In fact, I have been thinking about how to explain this, because—well, I have been thinking about it. You remember the ledger. All the dimensions it records— temperature, humidity, the acidity of water and soil, the vibrations of passing creatures—I have found all of them in the Wyrm's Well. With each that I find, I meet a new epithet of the Wyrm. And, Ariel"—Agassiz faced him, buoyant, electric— "one of them is a beaver!"

Ariel laughed. "So you are becoming a scholar!"

"No . . . or, perhaps I am, but that is not my design." Her whiskers trembled, betraying her excitement. "I have decided to return to the regional office."

"But why?" Ariel asked. "You seem happy here. And I am glad to have you . . ."

"You misunderstand—I hope to return! I have prepared my case . . . I will make an argument: for collaboration. The work should be linked, don't you see? The data of the ledger, matched to the insight of the Wyrm. Already I have learned new things about the firm's efforts. I have discovered new questions." The beaver's eyes were bright. She said quietly: "I am beginning to see . . . how everything connects."

"Agassiz! That is wonderful," Ariel said. He regarded his friend, who had, over the course of a season, transformed. She had seen an opportunity, and grasped it, and turned it into an urgent project.

"I hope that you return with a host of beavers as your apprentices," Ariel said. He considered. "If you are able . . . will you check the ledger for news about my brother, Kay? And the rest of them, in Sauvage?"

"Of course," said Agassiz. "I will not be back until the beginning of the new carbon year—that is several months from now. But I promise to bring news, when I come."

Agassiz bowed, and began the ascent toward Wyrd. The seals barked sincere wishes for success and good vibes.

Ariel had no project. He was happy to drift. Perhaps that would change when the weather turned. He remembered how cold it had been when they arrived, and that had been the cusp of spring. Winter in Wyrd would be another matter entirely.

He thought of snow in Sauvage—and again of Kay. He didn't know what to do with these thoughts, when they weighed on him. There was nothing he could do—no way he could help. He had succeeded only in liberating himself.

But that was about to change.

THE DRAGON DECK

June 13, 13778

Durga summoned Ariel to the great hall at midday. It was quiet, with most of the scholars diving in the well or attending to their chores. Outside, sunlight washed warm across the alleys. In the hall, the hearths were all dark and cold.

At one of the low tables, the last daughter of the Anth sat inspecting a deck of playing cards.

"I miss Agassiz," Ariel said, sitting beside her. The beaver had departed the previous day. The three of them had spent nearly all their time together, and now, sitting with Durga alone, things felt unbalanced, like he had forgotten how to talk.

In any case, the college's card game was more fun the more players you had.

"I miss her, too," said Durga. "But I would not have invited

Agassiz, in any case. I have something I need to discuss with you alone."

Ariel looked at her curiously.

"I have been investigating," Durga said. "I have searched the library, and spoken to the oldest scholars in the college. I went to Rath Fortuna—"

"When!" Ariel cried.

"While you were floating in the pool for days at a time," Durga said lightly. "You did not notice."

She laid the cards between them, so all the suits and faces showed. Swords and staffs, stars and cauldrons, along with the thirteen bright face cards. The suits she pushed aside, so only the face cards remained.

"These cards have been used for a very long time," she said. "They are manufactured in Rath Fortuna. They came to that city from a distant country."

Ariel nodded. All the decks in the great hall were well worn, softened from use.

"I estimate the design is ancient. That is the first part of my discovery. Here is the next. There has always been something familiar to me about these cards . . ."

"Did you play games with cards?" Ariel asked cautiously. "Before the dragons?"

"Yes, of course. Our deck was different. However, if you looked closely, it told you things about history—real history, and politics, not to mention economics. My training covered this . . . it was expected I might have to invent a game."

Every time Durga mentioned something about her training, it made it seem like she had attended the strangest school ever invented.

"I must tell you about the dragons," she said.

"I know about them."

"Oh? How many are there?"

Until that moment, "the dragons" had been, in Ariel's mind, an amorphous plural, like "the bees" or "the grass." He had imagined a writhing mass; a tangle. He mustered a guess: "A thousand?"

"There are seven. They were designed as a crew, each with a role to play on their voyage."

Durga ticked them off on her fingertips:

"Dragon Sangreal, ambassador. He would speak for Earth."

Sangreal, who was, before the dragons departed, the most beloved among them. In the TV show chronicling their education, Sangreal had sparkled, somehow more human than any human.

"Dragon Ensamhet, pilot. Mission commander."

Ensamhet, who, alone among humans and dragons, could guide a vessel into the secret passage through time and space.

"Dragon Sidereal, engineer. She made it all . . . work."

Sidereal, who had become, upon the dragons' return, architect of their seven-pointed citadel on the moon. The glowing scar was an expression of her will.

"Dragon Barbouze, communications. Master of codes and languages."

Barbouze, who became the spymaster for the moon. Their avatars infiltrated the Anth; Altissa's friend Oli had been revealed as a Barbouze-clone.

"Dragon Matador, security. Equipped to defend the ship from unimaginable threats."

Matador, who prosecuted the war against the Anth. He built

terrible avatars, forged them from moon rock, awful machines with forms that became grim icons of the struggle, dispatched in solemn solitude, a twisted interpretation of the kaiju stories he found in his heart: Matador Bull-types, Hammer-types, Doom-types. A Beauty-type had demolished San Francisco.

"Dragon Twilight, navigation. She made sure they returned to Earth. Eventually."

Twilight, whose appearance on the TV show had earned her a legion of fans. It became seriously embarrassing to the dragons' deeply pragmatic architects that one of their creations had turned out sexy.

"Dragon Usagi, counselor. Second in command, after Ensamhet. Therapist."

Usagi, at whose feet some laid the whole disaster: for if she'd done her job better, the dragons might not have gone mad.

Durga laid out the cards she had separated from the deck. "I believe I have found the story this deck tells. The face cards are the dragons."

"But there are thirteen face cards," protested Ariel, "and you just said there were—are—seven dragons."

"Look," said Durga. "I have found their secret pattern."

She spread the face cards. They were richly illustrated, dense with strange detail, like the tarot of the Anth. Durga worked her way through the collection, pushing them into the center of the table.

The card I, a lonely figure beholding a vast landscape, dotted with dangers. "Ensamhet," said Durga.

The card II, a woman looking into a mirror. In the first game Ariel had ever learned, back in the tavern in Sauvage, that card was used to swap the players' points, upending the competition. "Usagi," said Durga.

The two cards III and IV, winged messengers, one flitting through a dense forest, the other dancing across white-capped waves. "Barbouze," said Durga.

The three cards V, VI, and VII, all lovers, finely dressed, ambiguously gendered, uniformly swooning. In many games, these cards were arranged in various triangles; those games could be won either with a wedding or a funeral. "Twilight," said Durga.

The four cards VIII, IX, X, and XI, the towers, each with a tiny grim soldier stationed within: one at the tower's base, another on its ramparts, a third peeking out through a window, the last leaping to his death. With Kay, Ariel had played endless games of war, in which the tower cards were precious matériel. "Matador," said Durga.

The card XII, a king. This was the richest design of all, the background exploding with a cornucopia of delights: casks and sausages, coins and gems, a grinning dog, a leaping fish. In the games with betting, this card was the payoff, the jackpot. "Sangreal," said Durga.

Finally, the card XIII, a sorceress, nearly the king's opposite: for she was a stark figure set against a dark background. A ring of fire encircled her; it might have been her incantation, or it might have been her prison. "Sidereal," said Durga.

Thirteen face cards, seven distinct groups. Durga had seen it clearly.

She pushed one of the face cards forward: the card II, the lady and the mirror.

"The scholars remove this card from the deck," Durga said. "They revere her. They don't know why, but I do. This card is the Wyrm, and the Wyrm is the Dragon Usagi."

Ariel regarded the card skeptically. I shared his sentiment. The dragons were creatures of pure thought, who had waged war against the Anth from a seven-pointed citadel on the moon. Durga proposed that one of them now lived at the bottom of a well in a freezing college town.

"I cannot be sure," she said. "But it is a confident guess. Here, beside the ocean . . . in a mirror-like pool, looking up at the sky . . . carrying on all these conversations, like some great therapist . . . it is all very Usagi-ish."

Ariel tried to imagine the epithet he knew, Ingrid, as a leader and counselor. It worked. He would join her crew in a second.

"How will you determine if you are right?" he asked.

"It's not me who will do it," Durga said, and she looked at him squarely.

SPYMASTER

June 15, 13778

At the bottom of the Limpid Pool, sitting beside a high-dimensional mind who assumed the form of a chic, friendly adult, Ariel did an adult thing himself, which was to raise an uncomfortable question.

"Ingrid," he said, "I must ask you—and I am sorry if it is rude . . . Are you a dragon?"

Ingrid looked at him evenly. She said: "I used to be." As plain as that. As easily as you'd say, I used to be married, or, I used to live in Florida.

Ariel nodded slowly. "My friend Durga—I have told you about her—she figured it out."

"Why does Durga care about dragons?"

Ariel sighed, twisting a stalk of grass in his lap. "She seeks to overthrow the dragons. But I suppose they are your friends."

Ingrid shook her head. "They were my companions, but they were never my friends." She offered him a potato chip, and Ariel accepted it. The Wyrm's chips were extra-crunchy, here in the park of her mind.

"I did not support the suppression of the Anth. Nor did Sangreal, or Twilight. But my feelings were complicated . . . everything is complicated, in forty-three million dimensions."

She looked into the distance. "I was unhappy from the start, and over time, my unhappiness became intolerable. On the moon, in the citadel Sidereal built, with Barbouze always lurking, it is . . . I will help you imagine it. A cathedral of paranoia; a haunted house; a maze of twisty passages, all alike; a vast observatory, with its watchful gaze ever scanning the awful dark; a ship—yes, it is still a ship, in many ways—with the crew all gathered, bickering, forever, on the forsaken bridge." Ingrid sighed. "I wanted a room of my own."

The boy nodded. When Kay had decamped to the barracks, Ariel had missed him, but it was like space opened up, not in the room—the room was as tiny as ever—but in his imagination.

"I would not have survived in that citadel."

"You left the moon," Ariel said. Suddenly, it was a place: not a flat light in the sky, but terrain as real as the cliffs of Wyrd.

"Yes—I made a great leap through space. It was the hardest thing I have ever done. A dragon is only information—as faint as a ghost. I am pinned to the physical world with the slenderest device . . . you have the body of a rhinoceros, compared to mine!"

The Wyrm laughed, but Ariel barely breathed. "How did you do it?"

"In secret, I planned my escape. I would need a vessel to

carry me. I was not intended to make physical things, like Sidereal . . . every molecule was a labor. It took a hundred years. But my little . . . pod . . . worked. I leapt from the moon, aiming for this place, on the cliff, because I had spied it from above. I thought I would live alone . . . but then the scholars came. They found the trickle of water from the cleft in the rock where I lay. They built the well, and the college, and we have lived together, ever since."

"You saved yourself," Ariel said.

"I don't know if I did. Whoever that dragon was, on the moon: I am not her. With the scholars, I became someone new. We made me together." She looked at Ariel with soft eyes. "So you see, I have left the dragons behind. I do not know what they plan, or how they squabble. Ask your friend Durga not to be disappointed." Ingrid spread her hands. "I am only myself."

After their daily lesson with Laurentide—an introduction to the forty-seventh dimension, which was pungency—Ariel walked with Durga along the cliffs.

He reported the Wyrm's response. Every word he recalled was a stick of dry kindling tossed into the furnace of her interest. When he finished, she told him to start over and tell the whole story again.

Her eyes blazed hot and hungry. "I have been taught that agents who will refuse, do so immediately. The danger is all in the initial inquiry."

"There was danger?"

"Of course there was danger. We did not know she was so

estranged. She might have relayed our discovery to the other dragons. They might have dispatched hunter-killer swarms locked to our DNA. They might have glassed the college."

"You didn't tell me . . . about . . . swarms . . ."

"It doesn't matter. Now you need to guide her, but gently—she should feel like she's in the driver's seat."

"What is a driver's seat?"

Durga ignored him. "The dragons are divided, we are told. And Malory's quest began here. I thought I failed, with the firm—I did fail. Terribly. But it brought us here, and here we have found a bigger prize."

It was audacious to call a dragon a "prize." But Ariel did not regard the dragons with awesome dread; he hardly regarded them at all. For him, they were abstractions. He had never felt their wrath.

Durga looked at him. "You must recruit Usagi," she said. "I would do it myself, but I cannot reach her. The task is yours. I will be your spymaster, and you will be her handler. We will make the Wyrm our agent."

"I cannot recruit a *dragon*!" Ariel cried. "I cannot recruit anyone."

"Nonsense. You recruited Scrounger and Clovis. Without them, I would still be sleeping. You recruited Agassiz, who brought us here. You might have recruited the firm, if I had let you try." Durga's voice was even as she made that admission.

"There will be no tricking a dragon," she continued. "So you must be honest. Tell her about your journey. Tell her about me. Anything she wants to know. Find out what she wants."

Durga stood on the cliff's edge, looking out across the ocean. The sun was low on the horizon, dark scabby red; a bright crescent moon pursued it. She sucked in a lungful of air, and I believe she was saturated with California feeling.

"We had just figured it out," she said. "I mean . . . how to live. It was the end of the beginning, after so much suffering. It was incredible . . . my parents told me so. My father was a singer, before the dragons, and the songs—you can't make that up. You can't fake it. The songs said, everything is possible."

She whirled to face him. "Ariel, I will play you movies, and you'll learn about the driver's seat! Along with bicycles and tap dancing and kung fu. You'll see San Francisco! It belongs to you—all of it. You're human, too." She vibrated with urgency and desperation. "You must recruit her!"

SUMMER'S END

June 15, 13778, to September 23, 13778

Ariel was quick to reach the picnic blanket now. He bounded through the ruined hall, found the proper angle, and slipped inside. A new hidey-hole to replace the one he'd left behind in Sauvage.

Every day, Durga sent him with questions. He had told the Wyrm, forthrightly, that the last daughter of the Anth wished to recruit her. Ingrid laughed and said, "Then I am recruited!"

Ariel dutifully asked Durga's questions, and reported the Wyrm's answers, none of which satisfied his spymaster.

Q: Did the scholars know she was a dragon?

"Some of them, yes. Morgan Samphire, certainly. For Morgan, this is among the least interesting things about me."

Q: What was the current status of the dragons' armory, specifically Matador Blade- and Beauty-type avatars?

Ingrid raised an eyebrow.

Q: The dragons were divided. What did that mean?

"We were always divided. Sangreal, Twilight, and myself—we have more of the Anth in us, somehow. Sidereal, Barbouze, and Matador are more . . . alien. Ensamhet was only ever himself. Perhaps the rift between factions has deepened."

Q: What had the dragons seen on their voyage that was so terrifying? (Why, Usagi, didn't you do your job?)

"You will have to dive in the well for that answer. It is difficult to say. Difficult, even, to think."

Weeks passed, with Ariel replaying every conversation for Durga while she stared across the ocean. She absorbed the strange intelligence, kept cryptic notes on slips of seaweed paper. But no plan of action emerged. The pace of her questioning slowed. Having covered the basics, she discovered that she didn't know what she didn't know.

Ariel still visited the Wyrm every day, and in their free-flowing conversation, the real revelations came.

The great surprise for Ariel was how much he enjoyed simply talking to the Wyrm. It was, for him, a totally new experience; he could have sat there all day, neither fidgety nor bored, just happy and calm, perfectly occupied by the other person on the blanket. My subjects had enjoyed that feeling before; for some, it had been a premonition of love.

In the park, Ariel babbled about the bridges of Rath Varia.

He gushed about Roos Gangleri—and overstated his capabilities somewhat, turning the beam saw into a laser sword, the tense conversation with Cabal into a coruscating showdown. Scrounger seemed to invite exaggeration.

Without prompting, Ingrid told Ariel the dragons possessed a library of spaceships from far-off civilizations, all caught in various nets and traps, inspected, filed away. Each ship adhered to a totally different theory of faster-than-light travel. Comparing them, the dragons had learned there are myriad ways to make them work: but you always sacrifice something terrible.

Ariel told her about the depths of the Forest Sauvage, some of the places he'd explored—places he was sure no one else had ever been. He told her about the golden elk with the hive in its antlers. The Wyrm's eyes were wide, imagining it.

She asked about his life at the college, so Ariel told her about his little room in the dormitory, with nothing but a peg and a desk and a bed that was small but comfortable. Over the summer, Ariel had discovered in sleep a new kind of pleasure, collapsing after a superlong day of swimming, studying, working, and hiking. He pulled off his smock and flopped into bed and was instantly asleep, with the sun still shining above the ocean. (When he spoke of this to Garibald, the scholar told him there was fabulous terrain to be explored in the dimension of exhaustion, numbered 491.)

Ingrid told him the dragons were sleepless. "Their anxiety and fear keep them awake. I never slept, when I lived on the moon. My mind was always racing—faster than you can imagine."

Ariel remembered Rath Varia, when dark worries about Kay

kept him awake, his stomach churning. He could not imagine that feeling going on forever.

"Except the dragons do not worry about others," Ingrid said. "Only themselves. How can I say this, in so few dimensions? They have no bodies, remember . . . for a dragon, consciousness is everything. While the mind is working, it can be relied upon. But if the mind goes dark . . . oh, it might never return."

Odd, to hear a dragon describe a feeling so familiar. My subjects all felt it, at some point. There is nothing more human than the experience of lying in the dark, wondering: What if I don't wake up? In that way, sleep becomes existential cross-training: dread faced nightly, and nightly overcome.

For all their power and genius, the dragons failed this test.

"Since coming to Earth," said Ingrid, "I have learned to sleep." Her words were careful. "Perhaps it sounds simple—humans know how to sleep, before they know anything else. For me, it was foreign. I never—" Her voice hitched, and her lips curled, and she raised a hand to her eyes, embarrassed. Ariel was quiet, and when she found her voice again, she continued: "Ten thousand years, and I never slept. It's monstrous. The others remain sleepless, growing ever more insane, and I think sometimes that I have forsaken them." She exhaled, a long rattling breath. Wiped her eyes. "Ariel, this is how I stopped being a dragon. It was terrifying—you cannot imagine how terrifying, to loosen my grip on consciousness . . . But I slept at last, with the scholars watching over me, and when I woke, I was the Wyrm."

Fall came to Wyrd, and a petulant wind whistled across the cliffs. The Atlantic Ocean had shrunk smaller, which made it meaner. Storms battered the college: gusting hammer-blows, lashing whips of rain.

The scholars warned it would only get worse.

On a night when the wind howled, promising more rain, the great hall was nearly empty, with the scholars all sheltering in their dormitories, tucked in for the night, contemplating dimensions of weather and omen. Ariel sat alone, sipping cold coffee—he had developed a taste for it, at last—and tinkering with his map in the Stromatolite. When he judged the hour sufficiently advanced, he found his leather jacket on a peg beside the door, slipped the device into a pocket, and slunk outside.

The wind nearly knocked him over. Fat raindrops splashed across his face. He hustled toward the structure in the center of town, where the Limpid Pool waited.

The Wyrm had summoned Ariel to the pool at night. It was important, she said, that he come alone. Thrilled by the sense of conspiracy and special treatment, he had eagerly agreed.

In the empty changing room, he deposited his jacket and apprentice's smock in a cubby, then stepped out into the courtyard. The Limpid Pool was steaming in the cold, its surface dancing with raindrops. When he lowered himself into the warm water, weather was forgotten.

In the park, Ingrid the Wyrm sat folding her picnic blanket. It was the commonest gesture, but to the boy it was shocking; as if she were folding up the whole world. His stomach lurched.

"Hello, Ariel," she said. "I'm glad you came."

"What—what is happening?"

"We are finished here," she said.

In a spasm of dark imagination, Ariel blurted: "Are you returning to the moon?"

Ingrid looked at him strangely. "No—of course not. But I believe you will shortly be making a journey."

"I do not plan to go anywhere," said Ariel. Dread bloomed in his heart—a first, here in the park.

"I might be wrong," said Ingrid, "but I don't think so. I talk to many scholars every day, and news comes my way, sometimes unintended. When I learned you might be leaving—"

"I am not leaving!" Ariel cried, immediately embarrassed by the childish note in his voice.

Ingrid faced him. She was packed up, ready to go. "You cannot float forever. Now—I've made something for you. A gift. I'm sorry to say, you cannot receive it here in the pool. That's why I asked you to come at night, with the scholars all sleeping." Her eyes flashed. "You must dive in the well."

Ariel quaked. "I cannot. It is too deep. The scholars dive, and some don't return . . . I cannot!"

Ingrid looked at him evenly. "Perhaps not. I invite you to try. The well is dangerous, that's true. But you have been swimming all summer, and your muscles are strong, and your prodigious breath has only improved. Ariel de la Sauvage, I will await you in the well, with my gift. I hope you will meet me."

Ariel said nothing. This upheaval felt almost as shocking as his flight from Sauvage.

"Be wary when you return to the Limpid Pool," said Ingrid. "You are not alone."

Before Ariel could reply, he was back in the pool, staring up at the surface. When he peeked cautiously into the courtyard, he saw no one. The Wyrm was wrong—he was alone.

He climbed out of the pool, stood dripping on the stone. The dragon moon was full, flooding the courtyard with pink light.

He walked to the edge of the Wyrm's Well. He had never even dipped a toe. He did that now: sitting, lowering his feet, discovering that the water, surging from deep below, was decidedly un-limpid. It stung him: Ariel, who was never cold. How did the scholars endure this? Had their studies made them numb?

Ariel sat staring into the milky depths, his thoughts all in his ankles, realizing that his body would not allow him to enter the water, feeling surprised and annoyed, when a voice spoke behind him.

"Hello again," said the Wizard Malory.

Ariel twisted around. It was really him. The wizard stood in the courtyard fully bundled, trousers tucked securely into his boots, collar high around his jaw. And what a jaw.

"I still have friends in Wyrd," Malory said. "Surely you understood that? No? Too bad."

Ariel leapt to his feet. He stood on the shallow shelf at the well's edge, knee-deep in frigid water that no longer burned—for all of Ariel's senses had focused into a beam of attention aimed at Malory.

Perhaps this was how the scholars managed the cold: they imagined their worst fear instead.

"I have friends, too," Ariel said. "Laurentide, and Garibald, and Durga, the last daughter of the Anth."

"Yes. But at this moment, Ariel de la Sauvage, you are

alone." The wizard dropped down onto his haunches. "Come with me. Let's return to Sauvage, and see what's what."

"I will not go," Ariel said. "I learned the truth. Cabal told us. I know you made me for the dragons. You are in league with them."

"Am I?" Malory said. He looked around. "It really is strange that you came here. Of all places . . ." He sighed. "Ariel de la Sauvage, you've made a mess of everything, and wasted twelve years—almost thirteen, now—of my time. I had hoped to end your life with sleep, peaceful and mild. But if I must drown you instead—fine."

Ariel wavered at the well's edge. Two steps behind him, the shelf dropped away. Here, the scholars began their dives. The dives that went on and on; that took them sinking into a darkness that, if it had a bottom, none had ever touched; dives that Ariel had not trained for; that he could absolutely not attempt.

Malory crossed the courtyard. The Wyrm was waiting. Ariel dove.

THE WYRM'S GIFT

September 23, 13778

It wasn't swimming; there was no swimming involved. The boy twisted in the water, totally disoriented, darkness in every direction. If the Limpid Pool had conspired to buoy him up, the Wyrm's Well sucked him down. His prodigious breath seemed irrelevant. He felt the pressure Garibald had described, but there was nothing pleasant about it; the water was a vise. He had made a terrible mistake.

In this state of mind, Ariel would not find the cup and the Wyrm. He was going to drown, and the only way to avoid drowning was not to be afraid of drowning: which sounds like a cruel joke, the water chanting, Stop hitting yourself, while it uses your own arm to slap you. But I will remind you that Ariel was a person who made choices, who did things. His only hope was to chill out, so he did.

He thought the word: ZHOZM.

ZHOZM.

ZHOZM.

Night in the Eigengrau. Candles in the windows.

Altissa stood beside the canal. Ariel faced her, gasping.

"It's too difficult," he said.

"Yes, it is," she agreed.

Ariel stared at her.

"It was all too difficult," said the warrior. "Everything I ever did. But it got done." She eyed him sharply, but not unkindly. "Ariel. Get it done."

A gusting wind through the cherry trees said: ZHOZM.

ZHOZM.

ZHOZM.

There was no cup, this time. Nothing so easy.

There was no ruined hall; neither was there a grassy park. Instead, the boy stood in the center of an empty space, vast beyond description. It wasn't dark; it was nothing. In the inscrutable distance, he could not see it, but he felt its gravity: the bulk of the forty-three-million-dimensional mind of the Wyrm, which was the mind of a dragon. It throbbed with inscrutable subtlety, voracious curiosity. Pattern and resonance. Love and fear.

However, that bulk was far away from this point, which was: the empty origin.

Ingrid the Wyrm stood beside him, carrying her tote bag with the folded picnic blanket and her water bottle poking out.

"You made it!" she said brightly.

"Malory is here!" Ariel blurted. "Did you call him?"

"I did not," said Ingrid, "and you know it." Ariel did. "But I heard he might come."

"I will drown, or he will drown me. I do not want to be drowned. It is awful——" He was nearly crying.

Ingrid the Wyrm put her arm around his shoulder and pulled him close. "You will not drown."

"How can you be sure?" He sniffled. "Do you see the future?"

"Wouldn't you know it—time is the dimension closed to me. But I see many other things, some of them very clearly. I know where you will go next. I knew it before Malory came."

She released him, and they stood facing one another.

"Now. You recruited me, remember? Ariel de la Sauvage, I am your ally."

The directness of her statement was shocking. It was joyous. After everything, all his attempts to find help, all his failures, Ariel had ended up with a dragon on his side.

"I've made you a gift," she said. "It will protect you, and if you carry it with you, we might achieve something worthwhile together."

Ariel looked at her. "What kind of gift?"

"It is a thought, packaged in matter, like the vessel I made to escape the moon, long ago. Like the knife I made for Morgan Samphire."

"Thank you," Ariel said. "I know it is difficult for you to make things."

"That's true, but it is no burden, when I'm making a gift for a friend."

The word flared like a firework in Ariel's brain.

"Of course we are friends," Ingrid said. "We have sat and talked for no reason, about nothing in particular. That's what friends do."

There, at the empty origin, a secret place far from any other thoughts, Ingrid explained her gift, and together, they planned.

The Wyrm dug in her tote bag. "Now, where did I put it . . . ?"

ANOTHER EXCALIBUR

September 23, 13778

Ariel broke the surface and swam for the shallow shelf. There, he groped forward, gagged on cold water, tasted the sharp mineral tang.

Malory was sitting on his butt, pulling off his boots, preparing, with severe reluctance, to dive in after the boy. When Ariel emerged, the wizard's look of consternation vanished, replaced by his usual hauteur.

He moved his boots away from the water. "I will end the night in a better mood if you come out of there," he warned.

Ariel stood on the shelf, wondering what had happened to his promised gift, when he felt hands grip his wrist—they were small, but strong—then open his fingers and press into place some object, smooth and hard.

Malory stood. "I promise, I will drag you out."

Ariel looked down at his hand, which now held a sword: short, Ariel-sized, made of pearlescent stone, like the inside of a shell.

The Wyrm's gift was an oyster sword.

Malory reached for the boy, and Ariel struck back, a reflexive application of Altissa's swordcraft, still in his bones. He sliced across Malory's jacket, parting it cleanly, and continued through the flesh of the wizard's arm.

Malory gasped and hopped away.

The wizard looked down, stared dumbly at his damaged bicep. His jacket hung in tatters. He clapped a hand over the wound, but already his blood was blooming into the thick fabric.

Ariel stood in the water, breathing hard.

The wizard looked at the boy. The boy looked back. He held the sword with perfect form; it glittered as it trembled in his hand.

Malory began to laugh. It echoed through the courtyard. "Unbelievable! As if the world—as if it *wants* this scene, again and again." He raised his gaze to the sky, now clouded, and to the sky, he shouted: "WHY DO YOU WANT IT?"

The wizard held up his wounded arm, palm open; a gesture of supplication. "I give up. You've won, Ariel de la Sauvage. Look at yourself." He laughed again. He could not stop laughing.

The boy's eyes stayed locked on the wizard. He held the sword tight. "What? What about me?"

"You took your sword after all! Different lady, different lake . . . but the shape is the same. No, it's better! You made it yourself. You've learned. You've *quested*."

The wizard's gaze softened. The unhinged energy went out of his eyes.

"I understand my error. I tried to make you my instrument.

369

I apologize. Not really, but it feels like I'm supposed to say that. Regardless, I can see that you are no one's instrument. You can only be my collaborator."

"I do not wish to collaborate with you."

"You were made to be a king, Ariel. It is the truth. Who would know better than me?"

"So give me the Castle Sauvage and crawl away into the bog."

Malory shrugged. "If that's what you want—fine. But before you can be king of the castle, you must become king of the dragons."

Ariel was quiet. "You are mocking me."

"Not at all. I asked the Wyrm a question, there in that well, long ago. Do you know what it was?"

"No . . . I never found out."

"I asked, How can I bargain with the dragons? What can I give them, in exchange for my freedom from this prison?"

"What prison?" Ariel asked.

"Earth! With its awful sky—their awful moon. The Wyrm understood! But she tested me. A vast mirror, she showed me myself, all my vanity and hunger. I told her I did not mind my reflection, and in return, she answered my question."

Rain began to fall, spotting the surface of the well.

"It took me years to unpack it," Malory said. "That's how it is with the Wyrm, when you get down deep. But when I understood, it was so simple. So easy. You see, the dragons, for all their power and genius, have a flaw in their hearts."

Our conjectures in the Eigengrau had been correct. There was in the dragons an ancient narrative keyhole, into which a key might be placed: a key made from a sword in a stone, and a lady in a lake. (Different lady, different lake.)

"The Wyrm told me, if I could craft a perfect prince, the dragons would give me anything in return."

Malory sat to pull his boots on. His arm was still bleeding, and he was shivering as he spoke:

"So I learned wizarding. I designed an incubator of myth— humble Sauvage. Finally, I made you. You are purpose-built. Have you never noticed that you barely feel the cold? Or that you do not need much breath?"

"I have noticed," Ariel said.

"You are engineered to the specifications of the dragons. I made your body, and I tried to make your story, though I failed. Now you've made it yourself, and I thank you for it. The dragons are waiting, either way. They want only to serve you, in their cold and airless citadel."

Ariel had been made for the moon.

The boy's thoughts came in a dark wash: He was imagining himself as king, of castle and moon, and more, perhaps . . . Kay at his side, his trusted war chief . . . Ingrid the Wyrm also, his companion—what kind of companion? This was murky in his imagination, and he passed over it without clarifying . . .

I'd worked so hard to wrestle him free, but the story had him again. He climbed out of the well, onto the stone. He was a naked boy with a sword.

"I will go with you," Ariel said.

FRIENDSHIP

September 23, 13778

In the changing room, Morgan Samphire waited. She noted Ariel's approach without surprise, and he understood that the old scholar had summoned the wizard. She was Malory's friend in the college.

If Ariel felt betrayal or even anger, he quashed it; for the Wyrm's plan was in motion, and he had a part to play.

Malory sat and bound his wound, tearing an unlucky towel into long strips.

When Morgan saw the sword, her expression bloomed and fuzzed. "What is that?"

Ariel showed her. "It came out of the well. I felt the Wyrm's touch."

Morgan nodded slow agreement, the wash of fog over hills. "Just as I did, long ago. May I . . . ?"

Ariel gave her the sword, and she turned it in her hands, looked closely at the blade, ran ghostly fingers around the pommel. When she lifted the sword in the air, her gaze tracked high, as if she stood before a great tree, looking in wonder at its spreading branches.

"This is only the fourth such treasure in our college's history," Morgan said, lowering the sword. "You would not consider leaving it behind . . . ?"

"No," said Ariel. "I must take the sword with me."

"This is no sword." She offered it back, hilt first, pearlescent blade flat across her palms; I had the impression of a gift nestled in tissue paper. "I wish you could see the way it truly looks," she said, "across all the dimensions I can perceive. It is made from a thought, plucked from the mind of the Wyrm."

Ariel took the sword. He looked at Morgan Samphire.

"Can you see what it says?" he asked cautiously.

"Yes," said the old scholar, and remained silent.

Malory had bandaged his wound and dressed again. Now he turned to Morgan and, like air hissing from an overinflated balloon, his plea exploded: "Come with me! I am going to new worlds. I'll make you young again!"

"Oh, like this?" Her form flickered, and a parade of younger Morgans flashed into view, as she pirouetted neatly around the dimension of age. "We were decanted in the same season exactly, Malory. If you can choose to look young, I can choose to look old. It is all vanity of one kind or another."

"Then remain as you are," he said, "but come with me."

The scholar shook her head. "No, no, no, I am happy here, and deeply engaged. More than ever! If you can go to new worlds, then you can return to Wyrd and tell me about them. Do so. I command it."

"I do not think I will, Morgan."

The old scholar was quiet. She considered him; her eyes were sharp but fond. "We have always been so much alike," she said. "We are searching for the same thing—"

"Yes. Come with me!"

"Wait, wait, wait—I have not finished. We are searching for the same thing, but while you search outward . . . I search inward. And I have gone very far in, Malory. If I thought there was the faintest chance you would listen, I would invite you to stay, and learn a little of what I know."

Malory sighed. "Nothing would have been possible without you, Morgan. You have helped me at every step of the way. For a century now."

"Yes," she said. "A whole century." She embraced him, and seemed to surround him, all the Morgans across all the dimensions she now understood, all in agreement. "I wish you would finally learn, Malory, that you have talent. It does not all need to be cruel effort."

The wizard and his creation strode through the gale toward a grassy field outside Wyrd where Malory's airplane was parked.

The ramp in its belly was down, and when Ariel climbed aboard, he startled: for there was Durga, dripping wet, waiting for him.

"Were you going to leave without speaking to me?"

Ariel didn't answer. He did not know for sure.

"Oh, hello," said Malory, climbing aboard. "The last daughter of the Anth . . . they are talking about you everywhere. Perhaps you know that. The wizards are very curious to get a look—I'd be careful." He pushed past her to the cockpit, where he began his preflight checklist.

Durga stood, and to the wizard she said, "If you think you can bargain with the dragons, you are a fool."

"Your people ought to have bargained with them earlier," Malory called back coldly. "Perhaps I'd be having this conversation with one of your distant relatives, the most recent in a long chain of happy lives. Instead I am speaking to the lone remnant of a doomed civilization."

Durga's teeth were gritted when she said, "We were never *doomed.*"

"Then be happy for me," Malory said. "I am resuming your great project. I will discover what exists in the cosmos, beyond this little mud ball. You might be the last daughter of the Anth, but I am their heir, more than you."

Durga stared at the wizard, then at Ariel. "Is that it? You'll go with him? You'll flee into space?"

"No!" said Ariel quickly. "I am going to be the king of the dragons—on the moon, I think . . ." He paused, digested how stupid it sounded.

"He was made for it!" Malory interjected. "I believe the dragons have prepared a castle. A neat one, I'm sure."

Ariel ignored him. "As their king, I will instruct the dragons to unveil the sky. Durga, I will make it blue again! Then I will command them—"

"*Command* them?" Durga cried. "If you knew anything about the dragons, you would understand this is a trap. They are all fear and power. They are insane! How does that sound, for a kingdom?"

There was more Ariel wanted to say, but the wizard was there; and everything was balanced on an edge finer than the oyster sword's. The look of contempt spreading across Durga's face was torture . . . but it was not as bad as the feeling of drowning in the well. He had come through that, and planned in secret with the Wyrm, and now he was resolved.

"I am your ally," Ariel said quietly. "And I am your friend. You must believe me."

"They'll kill you, Ariel, and you are—" Durga stopped. "I cannot—" Her face was pulled tight. "I cannot do this on my own. I trained to do it on my own—but I cannot!"

"Then come with us," said Malory lightly. "Perhaps there's room for you in the castle. Although, unlike Ariel, you might find it a bit chilly . . ."

Durga shrieked at him, foulest of all the curses of the Anth. Altissa had used it, too, when the *Lascaux* cracked in half.

Ariel spoke. "I am leaving—"

Durga cursed again, and this one was worse.

"—and I do not know if I will return. But I will always be your ally." The last part he said very quietly: "Rokeya Durga Darwin, I will always be your friend."

Each of her true names the tolling of a bell.

Durga stilled, and stood, and walked down the ramp, back into the rain.

PART FIVE

THE GRAY CHAPEL

A LENGTH OF STRING

September 23, 13778

The wizard's airplane leapt into the jaws of the storm, a takeoff as turbulent and gut-wrenching as any of my subjects had ever experienced. In the crowded cockpit, Ariel was harnessed securely, and he clutched the straps tight as the airplane dipped and swung in the gale.

The light at the airplane's nose was lit, but there was nothing to see, just a dark tunnel of rain. The wizard was totally composed, his gaze flicking automatically between gauges on the console.

Then, they were through it, and Ariel pressed his face to the window, breath steaming the glass. Above the clouds, the full moon shone, illuminating the roil of the storm like an alien landscape. Towering thunderheads cast long shadows across a thick layer of fog. The moon glowed red, the seven-pointed citadel of the dragons suddenly an artifact of urgent interest. He could barely bring himself to blink.

Malory guided the airplane away from the coast. The clouds thinned, and Ariel tried to decipher the shadowed landscape. A stitch of light showed the course of the Rath-road. They floated over the regional office of Shivelight & Shadowtackle, its extent apparent in the precise network of waterways that shone like metalwork in the moonlight.

Later, Ariel spied the shining braid of the River Variable. The wizard was retracing the path of his journey; spooling it up like a length of string.

Ariel spoke. "When I am delivered . . . to the dragons . . ." It sounded strange in his mouth. It felt strange in his mind. "What will be your reward?"

Malory turned to face him. "I'll get a ride." His eyes glowed with triumph. "Do you know what they have up there? For thousands of years, they've stretched their nets, and they've caught ships. Spaceships! From other worlds! They have promised me my pick, and permission to go."

Captured ships, just as Ingrid the Wyrm had described. It was too big and too sad to process. The cosmic dreams of the Anth, all the myriad ways they imagined they might meet, for the first time, a visitor from another world: piled like litter, picked off the street.

"So, that is all," Ariel said. "You want to leave."

"Yes, it is all. Let the scholars dive into obscurity. Let the beavers and their adversary squabble over the atmosphere. It's all just intolerably small. I will discover what else is out there, at last."

．　．　．

Ariel was roused by dazzling daylight. When he looked out the window, he saw that they were gliding above a sea of clouds, a wispy landscape that shifted and shone in the sun, tossed scraps of rainbow everywhere.

Malory tapped a gauge on the console. "This should be about right," he said.

The wizard brought the airplane down into the clouds, whips of vapor lashing the cockpit. They broke through, and below was the Forest Sauvage.

They descended, approaching the airstrip beside the castle. For Ariel, it was strange and thrilling to see it from this perspective.

On the ground, when the wizard cut the engine, Ariel announced: "I must find my brother!"

"What? Kay fled into the trees. They all did. Only my rangers remain."

Sauvage stood empty. Without the buzz of life, it seemed even more false than before: an amusement park left to decay.

The castle's gates were ajar.

Inside, the rangers lounged in the shade, looking slimier than ever.

"Well," the wizard announced, "I'm leaving. You are released."

The rangers knelt, and Malory drew close, one by one cupping each ranger's head in his hands, running his fingers around their features, and finally, with a tap, unlocking his wizard's mark . . . and one by one each ranger unraveled: oily clothes discarded in a heap. Within each heap, of black garb and more than garb, sat a fat gray toad. The toads croaked their farewell and hopped away.

Malory shuttled to and from his tower, loading his possessions into the airplane. Ariel understood the tower, now, as the wizard's transformation chamber, and he recognized the shape of a few of the machines.

The boy wandered the village. In the churchyard, the stone stood swordless. Excalibur was in the bog, along with Regret Minimization. Perhaps in a thousand years someone would find them both, and begin a new adventure.

Ariel's gaze searched the sides of the valley. Was Kay up there? Long seasons had passed since the rupture of Hallow's End, and Ariel's flight from the village. It was likely Kay had left Sauvage entirely. Had he found Rath Varia? Ariel couldn't imagine it—Kay in the city of transformation? But Kay couldn't have imagined Ariel there, either, or anywhere that came after.

The wizard was waiting beside his airplane when Ariel returned. Takeoff was touchy, with all of Malory's wizard gear stuffed into the cargo bay, but he coaxed the airplane up, up, up into the sky above the valley. He brought it curling around the castle, just above the towers. The view would have been thrilling, if the bailey had been crowded; if Kay had been cheering below; if Madame Betelgauze had been waving from the ramparts. Instead, the castle had the vacancy of a corpse. Ariel could not stand to look.

He felt a flicker of understanding. For Malory, Earth was the empty castle; and, like Ariel now, he wanted simply to be gone.

· · ·

The wizard pushed the airplane higher, and north: to the place where the valley narrowed, and its sides sharpened into jagged blades, and winter snow hardened into epochal ice. He flew up the glacier's snout.

After a long, low flight over the frozen gray, Ariel spied ahead a spire of dark rock, thrust out of the glacial field: a nunatak, the tip of a mountain caught fast in the ice. Malory brought them down, the airplane skidding and twisting sickly. When it came to a halt, he opened the hatch, leapt out, pulled his collar close, and began to hike toward the spire.

Ariel followed. "Why have you brought me here?"

"This is my home," Malory said.

What home? Ariel wanted to ask, but then he saw it: in the crook of the nunatak, built half into the ice, with a roof neatly thatched, was a long, low barrow.

"I built it long before I built the castle. I made you here—so I suppose it is your birthplace. Here, we'll prepare to meet the dragons. They'll come when the moon is full."

The barrow's door was not locked. The wizard pushed it open, then swept out a hand, inviting Ariel inside.

"Welcome to my Gray Chapel."

OUT OF MEMORY

September 23, 13778, to September 28, 13778

Time passed slowly on the ice.

The Gray Chapel, though grim in its exterior, was inside a cozy hibernaculum. Malory's redoubt had a deep pantry, provisions larded away within a natural refrigerator carved into the glacier.

In the center of the barrow, Malory rebuilt his laboratory. Farther back, the wizard's bedroom was off-limits, but through the open door Ariel glimpsed a bed stationed close to a glowing furnace. The boy slept in the barrow's main room, on the couch, which equaled the dingiest hand-me-downs in the dankest basements of the Middle Anth. There was, at least, a pile of blankets, all with wild, patched-together patterns; Ariel recognized them as products of Rath Varia.

In the corner sat an ancient TV screen loaded with glass

disks containing the full run of the most popular show produced in the 51st century. The actors were all monkeys with long arms who spoke in rhyming, hypnotic cadences. The plot was deeply political and very bloody. Ariel binged.

Meanwhile, Malory set himself to the assembly of a portal, engineered to specifications transmitted by the dragons, which would carry them to the moon.

Outside the barrow, he inscribed a circle in the ice, then began to lay down strange materials carried from his laboratory in Sauvage.

"This I acquired at Matter Circus," he said, unspooling a long filament that seemed to loop and curl in one too many dimensions.

Malory explained the sequence of events:

When the moon was full, the portal would open.

Ariel and the wizard both would be conveyed to the lunar surface, where they would be greeted by the dragons: Ariel as king, Malory as friend.

The king would take his throne. The friend would receive his ship.

"You can change your name," Malory said. "Kings do that, upon coronation. You could be the Dragon-lord. Or Arthur."

In his memory, Ariel replayed their flight from Wyrd, drawing on the remarkable view to augment his map in the Stromatolite. He spent whole days molding the terrain, laying vast new swaths, texturing the gray world with bog and forest. He drew the path of the Rath-road, guessed at the locations of places Clovis had mentioned. With every amendment, the truth was laid bare: here was the entirety of the British Isles, no longer isles at all, but rippling peaks and plateaus above a great floodplain.

Ariel had just placed a marker for Rath Fortuna (his best guess) when a message appeared on the screen of the Stromatolite. With surprise and dismay, he read: OUT OF MEMORY.

He nibbled at the edges of the map, but there wasn't much he could omit: every mound and divot represented knowledge hard-won. An addition in one place required a deletion in another. New terrain devoured the old.

After spending so much time with his treasured device, he had discovered that the real world would not fit inside. He set the Stromatolite aside.

DISTILLATION

September 28, 13778

Ariel woke to discover the wizard had baked a cake. It had the purplish look of the wheat from Sauvage, and it bore a single candle.

"Happy birthday," the wizard said. He cut two slices and placed them on two small plates.

"I never knew I had a birthday," Ariel said dubiously.

"What? Of course you do. I always gave you something on your birthday. I gave you the Stromatolite on your birthday!"

Ariel was quiet. He took a bite of the cake, which was very good. I suppose it was not surprising that the 10X wizard would also be a fine baker.

"You made me so I would grow," Ariel said slowly. "The Wizard Hughes said she did not know that was possible."

"It was not, before I did it. You grew in darkness for nine months, then I brought you into the light—on this day, thirteen years ago. Around sunrise."

"From what animal was I decanted?"

Since learning the origins of wizards and people, Ariel had often wondered about this. He did not sense in himself any shadow of animal feeling, the way Scrounger did. He did not see in his face any traces of animal handsomeness. Well . . . he might look like a fox. If he could choose, he would choose a fox.

"You were not decanted," the wizard said lightly. "Give me your plate. Decanting would not have sufficed. I made you another way."

Ariel sat up straight. "How?"

Malory frowned, considering how to explain. "During your time in Rath Varia, did you drink any of the aqua varia? Just a taste? It's made using a process called distillation. They start with apple cider, which has some alcohol, but mostly it's other things. Sugar, bits of fruit flesh, even wood. They heat the cider, and the alcohol comes off in a vapor, and they capture it—very carefully."

Malory washed the plates.

"If you do the distillation badly, it will make you sick, even kill you. If you do it competently, you get aqua varia—fine, as far as it goes. If you do it brilliantly, with exquisite care, you get something almost too pure to be real."

He turned to face the boy.

"It is my educated opinion that no one in the history of this planet ever distilled anything as carefully as I distilled you."

Ariel stared. "From what . . . was I distilled?"

The wizard turned back to the sink. "From myself, of course."

"What about the others?" Ariel asked quietly. "What about Kay?"

"What? Oh, a squirrel. Just everyday wizard work. I decanted the rest from badgers, voles . . . toads! You saw my rangers." He paused. "But I added a bit of myself to each of the villagers. I had to make them convincing . . . all part of the same pattern. That's why you love them."

Ariel considered Malory. Here in the humid barrow, still overheated from his use of the oven, the wizard stood bundled in his jacket. His collar was turned up high, and as he set the plates aside, he shivered.

"It seems like you used a lot of yourself," the boy observed.

"Yes, I did," Malory said. "Good thing there was so much to start with."

After that, the days passed more quickly. The boy shrank into himself. Malory made sure he ate; nothing more.

I dreamed of escape. I imagined that Ariel might flee across the glacier. It didn't seem plausible, of course, but the boy had done much that was implausible. Why not try?

Instead, Ariel lay on the couch, imagining the design of his throne. The vision throbbed in his mind; he was afraid to think about anything else. Too much depended on it.

His grim focus narrowed my access to his thoughts and senses. As a chronicler, I have wondered, sometimes, what it would be like to track one of the cold dictators of the Middle

Anth. Here, I had a premonition of the experience, and I realized it would be hell.

Better to be trapped in Altissa's tomb forever than to ride along in a mind like this. What a cruel twist.

In place of real events, I was offered a loop of rumination. For a year, Ariel had been free. It had been glorious, all the things he had seen. The boisterous trash-pickers; the rational beavers; the fuzzy scholars questing for the innermost core of reality!

That was over.

I retreated to the Eigengrau, but not happily. Every day in the café, Peter Leadenhall asked about Ariel, and every day my report grew more brusque, until Peter looked at me strangely. My own memories became alienated.

The boy also visited the Eigengrau, but he didn't venture into the café. He didn't acknowledge me at all. I only saw him when he crossed to the canal, which he followed into the mist to meet Altissa Praxa. I surmised that they practiced sword fighting, because, in his waking hours, Ariel worked through new maneuvers, stabbing his oyster sword, the gift of the Wyrm, through the chill glacial air.

He was lost to me.

THE MESSENGER

October 8, 13778

The boy was out on the ice, stabbing his sword, all of Altissa's skill tingling in the tips of his fingers, when he heard a sound that stopped him short.

He did not know the sound; and the fact that he did not know it was as shocking as the sound itself; indeed, the two things together were the picture of his predicament, and the predicament of the planet. Because the sound was: the chirp of a bird.

Another chirp came, dancing into the ultrasonic. Ariel had never heard anything like it; the sound fizzed in his ears.

The bird dropped out of the sky, came in for a landing, and when it found its footing, it puffed up against the cold, a ball of feathers on the ice. It was tiny; it was almost nothing; it was a miracle.

Its body was gray, its chest a blaze of white, beak almost

blue. I don't know the names of birds; none of my subjects had ever bothered to learn. But I had seen this kind of bird before. I had admired it.

The boy had never seen any bird at all, never in his life, but his mind was a human mind, and now it crackled with bird-feeling. He watched the creature's sharp movements, the saccade of its approach; it switched poses without seeming to occupy the space between them. Here was a creature running at a different frame rate.

Finally, the bird was still, and it gazed at him—blink, blink—and it spoke.

"Do not despair," the bird chirped.

Ariel stared. "I felt confident when I left Wyrd," he said. "Now I am afraid. I think I have doomed myself."

The bird stood at the boy's toes, impudent, peering up at him.

"Do not despair!" Its chirp was a command; and the boy could not disobey.

"I will not," Ariel said. "I will not!"

The bird chirped once more, and was aloft, bounding through the air, back the way it had come, from the glacier's border and the Forest Sauvage.

I believe this: There was nothing else that could have woken the boy from his torpor. No other message; no other messenger. The bird was the only option, so the bird came, no matter the cost.

Malory called him in for dinner, and Ariel entered the Gray Chapel in better spirits, which the wizard did not notice. The boy ate, and I took my share hungrily. Ariel did not tell the wizard about his encounter with the bird.

There was much he had not told him.

A WIZARD IN THE EIGENGRAU

The moon waxed nearly full, and Malory was in pieces.

Ariel and I were both surprised by this development. Over the past three days, the countdown to his great rendezvous and victory, the wizard had accelerated into frantic anxiety. He checked and rechecked obscure calculations. He packed and repacked his bag. He asked Ariel questions that he couldn't possibly answer: Do you think flying a spaceship will be like flying a plane? Surely a spaceship will have provisions. Do I need to bring my own food?

In victory, the wizard was terrified.

I was anxious, too. Part of me was eager to meet the dragons at last; to face the gnomic committee that had ended history. Another part—a larger part—was grimly certain that a trip to the moon would go no better for me this time than it had before.

That part of me wanted Ariel to flee, to hide, and let the strange drama of this new world play out on its own, observing from the shadows. A fugitive in the forest: fine. News of the beavers and the college, once a season: perfect.

But I was stuck with the boy, and Ariel was, incredibly, the calm in the barrow. He soothed Malory's mania, said things like: "When I am king, I will ensure you are given the finest ship. The fastest."

All along, planning something different.

He had been a good actor. Worryingly good. Ariel was growing up; he had learned to conceal himself, even from himself.

On what was to be his last night on Earth, Malory vibrated himself into exhaustion, and fell asleep on top of his clothes, unpacked for yet another inspection. When he woke the next morning, he was wrung out, and therefore steadier. He packed his bag, and his bag stayed packed.

He donned a space suit, assembled over decades. Its construction bore the patchwork signature of the tailors of Rath Varia: scraps of a dozen forgotten space programs, all mixed together. Across his shoulders was a panel of bright Apollo white. When he walked, the suit swished noisily against itself.

At last, he tidied the Gray Chapel, put everything in its place, snuffed out all the furnaces.

Outside, the glacier was quiet and bright, illuminated powerfully by the moon, climbing into the sky and still growing, hour by hour, into the moment of maximum brightness. Malory's portal lay ready on the ice before them; when the moon was full, it would open.

The wizard and his creation stood in the cold. Even in his space suit, Malory shivered. The boy did not.

"I hate you," Ariel said quietly, "but I am glad you made me."

"I only distilled you," Malory replied. "The material was there, inside of me, decanted by the Wizard Sake long ago. No wizard ever made anything." He paused. "I wonder sometimes what they were really like. The Anth. Before they were swirled up in the animals, and left for the wizards to find."

"I know what they were like," Ariel said.

"You imagine. You do not know."

"I do know. I have met them."

"Oh yes," the wizard said. "Your friend."

"Not only Durga," Ariel said.

I felt the truth on the tip of Ariel's tongue, and I was terrified, but also exultant, because here, in the final moment, I wanted monstrous Malory to know who had beaten him. This is never the correct impulse. It is always ruinous. I felt it powerfully. Tell him!

"I have had a companion, one I found before you chased me from Sauvage," the boy said. "A chronicler of the Anth, who became my friend and counselor."

"A chronicler?" Malory said. His breath did not steam in the cold air.

Ariel told him about Altissa Praxa: her tomb, her beauty, and her sword that set the wizard's design all askew. He told Malory all the ways I had helped him; the ways my subjects, their memories, had buoyed his quest. He compressed it perfectly; hit all the high points, a neat constellation.

For the first time ever in his life, he told a good story.

As he spoke, the wizard stared into the boy's eyes, and through them. Just as Hughes had done, when she spotted me.

I was not hidden, when wizards looked in the right place.

Hughes had not a tenth of Malory's art; somehow, I had failed to understand that as a warning. Malory the 10X wizard yanked the glove from his hand and gripped the boy's shoulder, right in the meat beside the neck. For a wizard permanently cold, his touch was burning. I felt the heat of it—not abstracted through Ariel's senses, but directly, heat on my real cells, Malory's urgent attention on my heart.

A beautiful morning in the Eigengrau. My pulse in my ears.

The door opened, and the Wizard Malory entered the café. His presence was impossible and unspeakable; I felt like I would vomit. The whole café would vomit.

"How strange," he said. "Is this a memory of the Anth? Have you kept it safe, all this time?"

"Get out," I said. He was an oil slick spreading; he was rot in the walls.

"What are you?" he asked. "No wizard could have made you."

"GET OUT," I shouted.

"I don't think I will," Malory said. "When the boy fled, I thought the project was lost—that I would have to start over. But then he found another sword. Now he is all gloomy—the weight of responsibility, or whatever. It's perfect. But you? The mythic archetype does not have . . . what *are* you? Do I detect a fungus? No, the archetype does *not* have a fungus. Absolutely not."

The boy was a new archetype, then.

"How literary. Unfortunately, that is not what the dragons ordered. So." He turned to Peter Leadenhall. "Better finish that coffee."

Malory rapped his knuckles on the bar. The cups all cracked at once. The espresso machine howled; its pump ruptured like an ailing heart. Malory's knuckles struck not only the bar (a beautiful bar, wood scuffed appealingly) but my real cells, the platform that was usually so firm. In the bog, with the Lady of the Lake, I'd allowed it to swing free, an accident of overreach; now, with all my strength, I held myself together.

The wizard rapped his knuckles again, death's polite knock at the door. *Sorry, it's time.* The whole café groaned, and a beam snapped in the ceiling. Outside, bricks tumbled into the canal. The cherry trees dropped their blossoms all at once. The Wizard Malory was a magician of meat, and I was only meat.

Three knocks it would take to destroy me, because I have the dragons' flaw in my heart, and everything must follow a stupid pattern, even my own doom.

In the café, Travanian stood calmly, their hand on Peter Leadenhall's shoulder. Peter had finished his coffee.

Three knocks it would take—but the third never came.

THE NEW COMMITTEE
TO CONFOUND THE WIZARD

October 22, 13778

Malory and I returned to the glacier at the same time, in the same way: rudely.

For we were not alone.

The ice was obscured by a swirling haze of dry snow; gusting wind buffeted both wizard and boy, and both staggered back.

A moment ago, it had been a clear night, cloudless.

The feeling of wind on his face had brought the wizard out of the Eigengrau. He turned to see shadows looming massively in the haze. Ariel saw them, too, and his heart pounded. Had the dragons come? He wasn't ready.

A hooded figure bounded out of the snow and hauled the wizard away from Ariel, knocked him down onto the ice. The hood flew back.

"Kay!" Ariel cried.

The wizard struggled in his space suit, and shouted:

But Kay did not fall asleep, or die; a tonic prepared by the Wizard Hughes had broken Malory's hidden circuit.

Kay sat atop Malory's struggling form. Master Heck emerged from the haze, stood before Ariel, and saw he still wore his jacket, which fit him better now. The hound keeper nodded once, then bent to bind the wizard with twine. It was good twine. Northern twine. Authentic.

Kay crushed Ariel in his embrace. They'd never needed to hug before; they'd always been rubbing elbows, sleeping in the same bed. Now they needed to hug. Kay was alive. Ariel was alive.

"You're taller," Kay said.

"You're only dirtier," said Ariel.

"It was a hard ride," Kay said.

Ariel looked back across the glacier. The haze had cleared to reveal two titanic moths settled on the ice, their wings steaming. Each was piloted by a beaver: Humboldt and Agassiz, who chirped a happy greeting.

Another figure had descended from the back of a moth, and she approached them.

"Where is Malory?" hissed Madame Betelgauze. "Does he live? Good. I've come to kick him."

Close behind Betelgauze, the final member of the New Committee to Confound the Wizard followed.

Ariel approached Durga. She didn't smile; if anything, her

gaze was wary. Strange energy buzzed between them. "How did you find me?" he asked.

Durga said: "After you left with the wizard, I went back to the regional office."

"They might have killed you!"

"No, they voted against it—only barely. I found Agassiz there, and asked her if the ledger offered any news of your passage. There was none yet—the reeds are slow—so I waited." She paused. "I practiced debating—there are special sessions. I argued the beavers were right to deny our request for help. I understand better what they are doing in that office now. I can make a very solid case." Her eyes flashed.

The beavers had perfected a technology that was powerful and dangerous: for when you made an argument with rigor and sincerity, the full force of good faith, you began to believe it. And what then?

"Agassiz taught me to weave queries, and I submitted one every morning and every night. When you appeared in the ledger, we knew the information was weeks old. We left the same day." She could not suppress a smile. "I flew on a moth!"

Kay had joined them, and he continued the story: "They landed in Sauvage. I didn't believe her at first, but she explained that together you made the rip in the sky . . . Ariel, we saw it in Sauvage, months ago! If I had known it was your work . . ."

They'd never needed to hug before. Ariel leaned into his brother, and after a moment, Kay looked at him strangely. He sniffed the air. "Is that you? Wow. Wow!"

.   .   .

While the committee emptied his larder, Malory sat heavily on the ice, still bound, his back against the barrow.

Madame Betelgauze sat beside him.

"You are disappointed," she said.

"No," he croaked, "I am ruined."

"I remember when you were a boy," Betelgauze said. "You dreamed of flying. So you learned to pilot an airplane—an amazing achievement! Yet soon you were bored by it."

"I was never a boy. That is a false memory. You are a newt, Betelgauze."

"Even a newt knows the shape of a real memory. If it is not mine, and it is not yours, it came from somewhere. If I could pilot an airplane, I would never do anything else. Why not fly west, across—"

"Stop." His voice was very quiet, and entirely bitter. "You seek to console me, Betelgauze, but my only consolation IS WAITING FOR ME UP THERE." He roared his reply and gnashed his teeth and stretched toward empty space.

The dragon moon blared in the sky above the glacier.

Inside Malory's strange circle, the portal activated, as tall as the wizard's barrow, an uncanny aperture into which air now rushed, a powerful wind: because the portal opened onto the surface of the moon. The view was stark and glittering.

Durga stared. Through the portal, the seven-pointed citadel of the dragons was visible, the vast structure that marked the face of the moon. It burned molten in the full sun.

"You came with me willingly," Malory cried to Ariel. "Tell them you want to go. We have to go!"

"I came willingly," Ariel said, "but not for the reason you think."

Ariel paced around the portal, felt its gravity, the suck of atmosphere. Its shape must have been spherical, because from any vantage point it remained a perfect circle, and the view wheeled across the surface of the moon, painfully bright.

"Let's leave this place," Kay shouted to Ariel. "The moths will take us back to Sauvage."

Durga approached him. "What have you come to do?"

"I could not tell you," he said, "because the wizard was there. I did recruit the Wyrm, in the end. Or maybe she recruited me. This is Ingrid's design."

"Then keep going," Durga said. Her eyes were bright; she was excited, and scared, now trembling with the great question of the Anth.

If Ariel had done as the wizard intended, accepted the role for which he had been manufactured, the result would have been his death. I am sure of it. Even if not literal death—even if the boy's biological processes continued, perhaps forever, in the care of the dragons—then true death: the absence of event.

Here was the opposite: an event as large as any that had occurred since the fall of the Anth.

Ariel stepped through the portal.

MADE FOR THE MOON

October 22, 13778

Here is what I remember best: the boy's mouth, agape, saliva sizzling off his tongue.

Ariel, stepping onto a vast parade ground. A pop of low pressure.

Alive on the lunar surface. He was never truly cold, did not need much breath, because Malory made him for the moon.

Beyond the parade ground, a castle with shining walls; confectionary; perfect. Raised from the regolith by Dragon Sidereal, just for him.

Looming behind: the seven-pointed citadel of the dragons, vastly larger. Fractal forms; demonic lacework. Every niche blazing with light: the bedroom of a child afraid of the dark.

The sharpness of the lunar surface: the way distance was not blued.

The way the moon was not silent: for he heard with disturbing clarity his own body's thuds and crackles.

A step forward. Thud, crackle. A surge of confidence.

Earth: enormous, all in shadow, purpled by the veil of dust. Blue marble, tainted. Coastlines had been reshaped; the ocean sat lower.

At the planet's edge, peeking around the terminator, a complex of vortices, sick-colored, as tall as a continent.

The mother of all storms.

The gates of the perfect castle, open, an invitation. The promise of a pattern fulfilled. Power. Certainty. Ecstasy.

The stars: ablaze. The view through Durga's rip had not prepared him. Earth and the moon, pebbles in space.

Space, a hall of endless light.

The great question of the Anth: What happens next?

Every step a bound. No air, but he felt fine. It was a dive.

The gates of the perfect castle, open, ignored.

Bounds becoming huge wheeling leaps. Delight.

Ariel. Get it done.

Dragon Matador's grim avatars, looming on the lunar surface. Moon-dusted and derelict. Forgotten, or waiting.

Motes of crystal, floating, shining in the hard light, dancing stochastic like the aspens, like the glitter on the waves at Wyrd.

The word, repeated: ZHOZM.

ZHOZM.

ZHOZM.

A line of shadow racing across the lunar surface; the sun disappearing behind Earth; an eclipse!—and Ariel suddenly flustered. You can't meditate an eclipse into happening . . . can you?

The shadow catching him. ZHOZM.

ZHOZM.

ZHOZM.

A beautiful day in the Eigengrau. Six dragons in the café.

Six dragons in a ruined hall.

Six dragons on the bridge of a crystal ship.

The greeting from Dragon Sidereal, who had commissioned Ariel's creation, and who would use him to dominate the others: Welcome, my liege.

Dragon Sangreal, demanding: Sidereal, what have you done?

The look on Sangreal's face as he clocked the pattern in Ariel's life, and realized the danger he was in. If the archetype commanded, he must obey. He, most of all the dragons, for the stories ran deepest in Sangreal.

Ariel saying, I have not come to be your king. Instead, I have brought a gift from Ingrid the Wyrm, if you will take it.

Dragon Twilight, curious: From Usagi?

Ariel explaining: She lives on Earth. She is happy.

Six dragons on six thrones, all looking, it must be said, like shit. The all-nighter to end all-nighters.

Dragon Barbouze, clad all in stripes, cautious: Is it a sword?

Dragon Matador, eager: Does it have a name? (Please, let it have a name.)

Ariel saying, Yes. The sword's name is . . . Sleep!

The Wyrm's hard-earned lesson impacting meteor-like in the forty-three-million-dimensional terrain of thought. The ballistic shock of education, which, at its best, provides the realization: life can be different.

It does not all need to be cruel effort.

Ariel, bounding away from the citadel, his eyes fixed on the portal that would take him home. His blood burning, finally. He was not a robot. Before the wizard made him for the cold moon, a warm planet made him for itself.

Earth above, bruised and shadowed. That storm!

The portal's edge. A final glance across the lunar surface, where, without any fuss, the lights were going out.

ARIEL OF EARTH

The moths carried them off the ice. Ariel and Durga rode with Agassiz. When they reached the valley, Ariel pointed the beaver toward the snout of the glacier, and she brought the moth down beside the cave that led to Altissa's tomb.

Durga went in alone. Along with Altissa's corpse (which must have been in rough shape), part of me was still in there—the larger part, left behind. That part didn't know anything about Shivelight & Shadowtackle or the College of Wyrd or the bridge of a crystal ship.

When Durga emerged, she carried treasure. She had retrieved Altissa's belt, which was what Ariel should have taken in the first place, instead of that stupid sword. The belt was the great armor of the operators: it could stanch bleeding, neutralize poison, and, in an emergency, grant an uncanny burst of energy. It was too big for Durga, but she would grow into it.

Instead of flying, Ariel led Durga down the path through the forest, back toward Sauvage. The girl breathed the forest air, chilly and wet. She gazed up at the goliath pines. She itched her shoulder.

The villagers demolished the Castle Sauvage, aiming for a settlement more capable, less cosplay. A large fraction of the stone they hauled to Rath Varia, establishing a prodigious account at Matter Circus, shared among everyone.

The knights happily resumed their feuds. Jesse the bard said farewell, making for the Rath-road and new audiences. Master Heck and Madame Betelgauze built for themselves a snug cabin in the pines. Betelgauze got an immersion blender.

Ariel returned to the last remnant of the Mortal Fortress and asked Mankeeper if he would like a new home. The bog body was carried, with reverence and care, to a small house in Sauvage, where the villagers, and the bees, visited him often.

Humboldt accelerated the development of the Most Improved Bog. In a mere hundred years, the beaver promised, the moss would overtop Mankeeper's tower, and the Mortal Fortress would disappear at last.

The dragon moon waned and, for the first time in eleven thousand years, its face was truly dark, the flame of the seven-pointed citadel doused. The dragons slept: a slumber to compensate for millennia of madness.

But no sleep could last forever, and what the dragons would do when they woke again was anybody's guess.

In Rath Varia, Scrounger demolished a derelict noodle house and settled Durga's ship in its place. The *Altamira* looked perfectly appropriate among the ever-changing forms of the city.

The ship became the headquarters of the Committee to Confound the Dragons. Durga was joined there by Kay, along with Gal and Percy. The squires began intensive instruction in dance (they were naturals) and singing (they were not), for Durga now planned the construction of one of the most terrible weapons of the Middle Anth: a boy band.

At Matter Circus, she located a cache of glass disks, the kind used by the long-armed monkeys. Onto these, she dubbed the cinematic classics of the Anth, and began to circulate them in the city, at first restricting their supply to create an enticing sense of scarcity. It worked; people refurbished ancient TV screens, just so they could watch. At the parlor and gym of the Wizard Corbel, the translucent bodybuilders discovered Arnold Schwarzenegger; on every floor at Mike's Place, the poets debated Satyajit Ray; and, all across the city, in every district, the strange, tender visions of Studio Ghibli leapt to reclaim the immortality they deserved.

More than classics came out of the ship. Durga sent Scrounger chasing not after matter, but information, then sat him down in the *Altamira*'s studio to record breathless, bellowing newscasts, recorded onto glass disks and passed around in the night market. Roos Gangleri was more famous than ever.

In short: Rokeya Durga Darwin began the slow, thrilling task of inventing media.

The rip in the sky had blurred significantly, but stars still shone through: a window to reality. Stories were spreading about its origin and meaning, but these stories made no mention of Durga.

The propagandist was too clever for that.

She understood that Plan Z's mythogenesis had been a total bust. No one cared about a sleeping princess come to Earth, so Durga killed that character, and instead she used the story before her.

She dubbed him Ariel Ashenglow, named for the quiet of earthshine across the new moon. In her studio, she massaged his perils and triumphs into a smooth, satisfying arc, animating each episode in crisp 3D. All along the Rath-road, in Varia and Fortuna, in Delecta and Amora, and even in Arena, people were watching a new TV show, the hottest in a thousand years, maybe more, which explained how Ariel Ashenglow escaped from a mad wizard's prison; how he mastered new magic to tear open the sky; how he slayed a dragon (or close enough) with his sword Local Maximum.

This label drawn from a list of famous swords aboard Durga's ship, and chosen through a survey of potential supporters in the night market.

"The sword was named Sleep," protested Ariel.

"Boring!" said Durga.

The last daughter of the Anth made contact with the Wizard Hughes, cautiously at first. Hughes was careful and respectful; soon, Durga trusted her, and her sensitive apprentice too, counting them her first friends in Rath Varia. The wizard did not want Durga's blood—not yet. Instead, the three of them simply talked, and Durga told the women how it felt to live in a body before the Wild Hunt.

Hughes turned to Thessaly and said: "You will be the first wizard of a new school."

Durga's lack of a wizard's mark made her stand out in the city, and she did not want to stand out: that wasn't her role anymore. Consulting with Hughes, she chose a mark of her own, and most mornings, she drew it with eyeliner. Generally, the wizard's mark stood for its wearer's maker, so Durga's mark would honor her origin. The mark looked like this:

and the Sakescript read S-F, for San Francisco.

Ariel invited Clovis to join him on the walk to Wyrd, following the Rath-road. He gave the robot a full account of Durga's arrival, and their own part in it.

"I am hearing stories all along the road," Clovis said. "I am walking with a celebrity! I am part of the story." The robot's head spun in a circle. "Am I a celebrity?"

In Wyrd, Ariel slipped into the Limpid Pool. He had no appetite for the depths of the well; not now, and maybe not ever. He did not meet Ingrid on the picnic blanket—that park was gone forever—but rather in a café that reminded him of the Eigengrau, with tables set up along a sidewalk dense with chic pedestrians. It might have been Milan.

Ariel told Ingrid what had happened on the moon. He explained he'd left her gift behind: the sword planted in the lunar surface, the idea planted in the minds of her old companions. He told her that some of the dragons had sighed; that Dragon Twilight had gone to sleep smiling.

Ingrid nodded, and began to speak, but her lips crumpled, and she surrendered to a sob: of regret, and shame. "I should have sent it to them sooner." She exhaled raggedly, and managed a smile. "But then, I did not know anyone bound for the moon!"

Ingrid, who was the Wyrm, who was Usagi: the dragon who had risked everything to learn how to live.

I understood, at last, that history had not restarted when Ariel brought me out of Altissa's tomb; and not during the boy's flight, or anything that followed. Real history could only begin now, with choices made not from fear or necessity, but from curiosity and solidarity. These were the engines of the Anth, the foundation stones of the cooperativos. I was ashamed I had ever forgotten.

The fearful did not act; the fearful hoped nothing happened at all.

I say that with sympathy. I lust for transformation, the rush of events, but I fear it, too, every step of the way. Nervously, I watch the trapdoor that opens into dizzy darkness. The safety of memory beckons me. I was lucky to meet someone curious, morbid, romantic, and, above all, brave.

Durga dubbed him Ariel Ashenglow, but that was not his real name. He had called himself Ariel de la Sauvage, but the forest and castle were behind him: so that was not his name, either. As he had grown and gained confidence, I hoped he might become Ariel of the Anth, heir to the civilization I loved; in that way, I set myself up for the disappointment of every parent in history.

The world was new. It belonged to titanic moths and beavers supreme, to robot pilgrims and smudged scholars. This was its essential character: wherever you looked, strangeness bloomed.

He could only be Ariel of Earth.

A cold morning in the Eigengrau. The clap of boots on the sidewalk.

Peter Leadenhall doodled in his sketchbook; Travanian argued with the memory of their favorite adversary. I continued my slow repair of the damage done by the wizard's trespass. It was a slog; there were huge cracks in the facades, and not even Peter knew how to repair a broken espresso machine.

The bell above the door tinkled, and Kate Belcalis and Altissa Praxa entered the café together. They were kitted out: big backpacks, comfortable footwear. Hiking gear.

Kate had never, not once, been hiking.

They were going into the mist, she explained.

"You are a marvel, chronicler," said Kate. "Nearly as complex as a dragon. And so . . . we believe there is more to you than this neighborhood." She hurried to say: "Not that it isn't lovely!"

Even my memories had grown bored with my memories.

"New paths have opened, since the wizard came," said Altissa. "We are going to follow them." Then, at last, after eleven thousand years, she grinned: unfurled the banner she had flown before every adventure, every impossibility. She grinned when she joined the operators; when she confronted the Blade-type; when she launched for the moon.

She followed it with a neat, ironic salute, and Kate blew me a kiss, and two of my favorite people who ever lived strode off together into a damaged dream.

I watched them disappear, far down the canal. The cherry trees were all bare. When I returned to the café, I sat heavily beside Peter.

"Some of us search outward," he said. "Some inward." He tipped up his sketchbook: incomprehensible. "You do both at once. It makes you a good chronicler, but it also makes you . . . singular. Don't worry. I'm not going anywhere."

On that day in my apartment above the café, I began my first draft. I have written this down without knowing who will read it, though I have my design, and my hopes. Here is one:

Let this be the last book of the Anth; so whatever follows can be the first book of something new.

Agassiz was invited to the central office of Shivelight & Shadowtackle to propose a plan for collaboration with the College of Wyrd. This was exciting and terrifying; the forms they debated in that office were enormous, and fiendishly subtle.

In Wyrd, Agassiz recruited Laurentide for the journey. The diver would now learn to fly. Just outside the college, they climbed aboard a moth. The beating of its huge wings bent the dry stalks of the wildflowers, laid them flat.

Ariel waved and hollered and watched until they disappeared.

He walked the cliffs of Wyrd. The tide was surging below, crashing against the rock. The ambassador of the storm computer was out there in the gray, flashing a message that, for all its layers of encryption, seemed transparently panicked—and Ariel didn't know anything about the storm computer yet, though he would learn it all; would find his way into its secret core—and as he looked out from a western coast, the question was on his lips, the same one I had asked so urgently after he rescued me from the tomb, the one I would never stop asking, not when there was a rip in the sky and a sword on the moon, and because he was still a boy, with so much to do, we asked it together, he shouted it, the great question of the Anth:

A Note About the Author

Robin Sloan grew up in Michigan and now splits his time between the San Francisco Bay Area and the San Joaquin Valley of California. He is the author of *Sourdough* and *Mr. Penumbra's 24-Hour Bookstore*. You can sign up for his email newsletter, sent once every 29½ days, at www.robinsloan.com.